Nowhere to Run

Cassie Lee cried, this time not from pain but joy. Freedom had gifted her again. Finally, she made love with a man she desired, of her own free will. At this pure, defining moment, Cassie Lee knew that if she never loved a man again, that she once loved . . . . He fed her hungry heart, quenched her thirsty soul, and purged and cleansed her soiled body, rendering any previous violations nonexistent.

"Congratulations, Ms. Gunn, for introducing a new standard of excellence into the mainstream romance novel."

—Romantic Times Magazine

Nowhere to Run

by Gay G. Gunn

Genesis Press, Inc.
Columbus, Mississippi

INDIGO LOVE STORIES are published by
Genesis Press, Inc.
406A 3rd Avenue North
Columbus, MS 39701-0101

ISBN: 1-885478-13-5

Manufactured in the United States of America

First Edition

To those who gave me historical place and perspective.
To those on whose shoulders I stand, especially...

Doc Davis, 1842–1929
Normal Percy Gunn, 1904–1965
Ruth Dorothea Petway Ross, 1907–1949
Iva Ambrose Ross Jr., 1931–1996

and

To those who have loved and lost too soon.

Visit our Web page for latest
releases and other information.

http://www.colom.com/genesis

Genesis Press, Inc.
406A 3rd Avenue North
Columbus, MS 39701-0101

Indigo Love Stories

Nowhere to Run

Prologue

The Sierra Nevada Mountains
California, 1849

He slid the gold across the table, and his partner eyed the shining yellow metal coins before scooping them up and dropping them into his dusty leather pouch.

"You 'bout the onliest one I'd trust with my money and the mission," Exum said, watching his friend pull the string of the pouch closed with his teeth, blazing white in the darkness of his skin.

"You the onliest one I knowed who could stand being all by hisself four months down and four months back," Exum continued, until his gaze was stolen by a pair of roughnecks fighting over the last whore.

He chugged his last bit of whiskey and pointed to the empty glass so his boy could fill it again.

"We come a long way from McArdle's," Exum went on. "But I'm sick to death of stringy-haired white women or slant-eyed Chinks. I want a woman pert near my Ma. Least as much as I can remember of her. Never thought once we ran I'd ever want to see or be a nigger again, and here I am sending back South for a gal."

He downed his drink and watched the boy pour in more without

1

being asked. "You jus' might work out after all," Exum said to the grinning China-boy.

Everyone came to Exum for work, supplies, and recreation. It was his town. He began it, named it, owned it, and ran it. It was simple supply and demand. Of course, towns in gold rush territory sprang up overnight, and folded just as fast. A gold rush town was a euphemism for a hotel, saloon, supply house, and grub tent, all dotting a mud-filled street with planks running every which way. But folks weren't here for the aesthetics. They were here to strike it rich and high tail it south to San Francisco.

"Yep, yep," Exum said, rearing back in his chair, the rot-gut starting to take effect. "I want someone that looks like me. Not you, you too black. I want her to have skin the color of the syrup that used to set on ole massa's table. And long hair that got some density and curl to it. Not that hanging, limp-ass red and yellow mess, and I don't want that dead-straight black yarn that's been slapping me upside my face when I get a poke. I want her hair to have some kink, some waves. She got to have some tits, a butt, and some hips, for chrissakes. We always had the same taste in women, though you never got them first 'cause I am jus' too good lookin'."

He laughed as his friend just chuckled.

"I figure of the two evils," Exum said, "goin' or stayin', you'd rather go than stay here and watch these cutthroats try to cheat me outta what's duly mine. Broady'll fix you up with supplies . . . and here." Exum pushed Hawk a piece of paper. "You going south. You need a pass that says you can buy a slave for Ole Massa Exum Taylor." They laughed at the absurdity of it all. "Woo Lawd, if they could see us now!"

Exum took another swig of liquor and eyed a man at the next table cheating at cards. Under the owner's gaze, the man threw in his hand and left, knowing it was better to lose money than his life. Most times, Exum Taylor preferred shooting folk than looking at them, and few could ever gauge his mood.

"We did have some high times back there in Missassip and Georgia," Exum said, letting his tongue and the amber liquid carry them back. "You remember Esther? Lawd have mercy, she almost got me to stay. Yeah, get somebody that look like Esther, before she had that baby. I want this girl young, spry, and ready to gimmie what I want, when I want it, no questions asked."

Hawk covered his empty glass so the boy couldn't add more liquor.

"You the closest thing I have to a brother," Exum said, fixing his light brown eyes on his friend. "But we ain't nothing alike. I talk, you don't. I gots to have action and people, you live up in those Sierras happy as you please—alone with that horse, nature, and shit. Even took that last name Hawk, after a damn free-flying bird."

He chuckled while Hawk made small circles with his empty glass on the rough texture of the wooden table.

"Maybe that's why we get on, huh, Solomon?" he whispered his given name before continuing, "Although we both likes the womens, I jus' had more is all." Solomon only half-smiled this time; using his given name meant Exum's good sense and solemn promise was being over-ridden by liquor. "So when you fixin' to leave?"

"First light," Solomon said, bringing his glass to a stop.

"I really 'preciates you doin' this for me. I know you'll pick me a good one. If you don't—you gotta keep her. Hey!" Exum yelled, knock-ing his chair over as he jumped up to break up a fight. "You know that don't go in my establishment!"

Solomon watched his friend come between the two beefy white men. A black man breaking up a fight and tossing them out on their ears with no reprisal. Things were sure different here in this part of the country. Here, Exum had the opportunity to make his visions come true, to make and name a town after himself. Exum wasn't much of a town, but now with the Chinks there was even a laundry, and Broady's supply house was turning into a general store. His friend Exum ruled it all with an iron fist, which is what you needed when these miners came down from the hills to drink, gamble, and cavort with females. Exum supplied it all. He was the only game in the territory. Made so much money he had to sleep with one eye open until he established his reputation.

Now, no one crossed him—drunk or sober. He was a mean son-of-a-gun, despite his good looks and easy smile. Surrounding gorges were filled with those who'd found that out the hard way. Money and profit were his only true friends. Solomon didn't doubt the affection Exum had for him any more than he doubted that Exum would shoot him dead over "business."

3

Exum was kicking a miner in the tail when Solomon rose to leave. Seeing him, Exum did a quick wave before grabbing the breast of a passing play pretty.

"Somebody better than this table scrap!" Exum shouted as Solomon exited the saloon, one of only a few two-story wooden buildings in this town.

Solomon looked up at the blue, cloudless spring sky and pondered on how friendship was taking him away from the cherished solitude of his mountain cabin to seek a mate for Exum.

The earth here was just beginning to thaw despite the lateness of the season. He should be laying his traps, doing some ice fishing, and waking up just like the grizzly. His life was simple, predictable, and his—unlike the plantation where he had worked from sunup to sundown and had no free thought or time to himself. Here, in the pristine quiet of the mountains, the only time set was done by nature, and he was in full concert with her.

Solomon would only go South again for one man—the man who had forced him to run. The man who had guts enough to stand up for him in all those towns as they forged their way here. The man who had the vision and the gumption to set out in this god-forsaken land and mold his dreams on the backs of others' greed. The man who could stand up to any man: black, white, or red . . . and win or die trying. The man who had given him his freedom and his new life, and never asked for anything in return—until now. How could he refuse?

Chapter I

Solomon Hawk knew it would only take him two months' traveling time to everyone else's four to six, but he lingered in his territory where tall pine trees pierced the sky—where the air was crisp and clean and inhaling it too quickly could render you dizzy. The clear water ran in rapids, curling and hugging the shorelines as it tripped and fell over the low banks. The fish were so plentiful that they jumped into a man's hands as he stood at the water's edge. And quiet. Stark naked quiet, where no man's voice carried on the wind; only nature's echo clouded a man's vision or hearing. It was great country, and he tried to postpone the inevitable for as long as possible.

Into the clear, April sunrise, Solomon guided his beautiful, black stallion due east, heading for St. Joseph. When he crossed the Missouri River, Solomon Hawk immediately tensed up. In St. Joe, Solomon bought supplies and packed his horse as he watched the Saratoga wagons fill themselves with white settlers, hell-bent on making Indian land their own and threatening his peace in the mountains. From St. Joe, he descended into the bowels of the South. When he crossed the Big Muddy, he sped up as he entered the foreign country of his enslavement, and prayed that nothing would make him remain here longer than necessary. He intended to visit a couple of plantations in Tennessee on his way to Georgia, pick the best of the litter, pay for her, and get to tracking back home.

The terrain shifted again and offered a land that looked pretty to the naked eye, but gave off the stench of something not quite right, not quite human, but quite the South. You could smell the hopelessness, the oppression, and the bondage before you saw it. And when he first came upon it, it made him retch.

He had been long gone from it, and he thought he'd put it behind him—but seeing it, like opening an old wound, made him mad-angry. He had to buy her and get out. He had to keep his distance from this crazy vileness labeled slavery. Not think on it, for to do so would jeopardize his ability to leave. He was going to conduct business and vamoose.

* * * * * * * * * * * * *

Solomon Hawk cut an imposing figure. Well over six feet tall, he exuded confidence. He had a sway to his walk that left folks believing they'd have better odds tangling with a scalded grizzly. Black as tar with a nose sharp enough to open a can of beans, he was a study in contradictions. A broad-brimmed hat covered woolly shoulder-length hair, and a wiry beard, brushed smooth to his face by contemplative stroking, covered an angular jaw and camouflaged high cheekbones. Strapped low on his hips were matching, slightly worn, pearl-handled sidearms—turned outward, signifying speed and accuracy. Across his horse was a skin coat, fur turned inward, and near-empty saddlebags, testimony to a man who could use his rifle and live light and easy off the land as he traveled. The swagger in his walk and the gold in his leather pouch guaranteed that he never had to whip out the papers from "Ole Massa" Exum Taylor.

News of the black man who'd come from Oregon territory to buy his master a slave whipped though the Georgia countryside. No one tangled with this dog-eared drifter; instead, he was courted and invited to visit the larger plantations to see and test the wares of various slave women. All owners wanted to part this man from the gold he was carrying, the only way they could . . . on his say so.

Unlike white buyers who were offered a guest room, Hawk, as he was known, was shown the barn, but perplexed everyone even more when he preferred to be out under the wide open spaces, with the sky as his ceiling. They said he never slept, but he did—upright, with his rifle over his lap. He could hear a twig break from a mile away, and tell you whether it was man or beast who did the breaking. He was poised and ready to shoot when two men foolishly thought they could take his gold without swapping a slave girl for it. Only one of them, with a forever-maimed shooting arm, lived to tell the tale.

Solomon had focused his beady dark eyes on many a slave woman over the past two weeks and, as far as he was concerned, he was behind schedule. There were some of every describable color, shape, and face. Many were Exum's type; some were outwardly repelled by him; others were scared by the prospect of traveling all that way to be delivered to a man they didn't know. Still others, not wanting to leave slave life, were terrified of the unknown, of trading one hell for another—pretending that they had a choice in the matter. If Solomon picked one, she was his for the buying, and that was his dilemma.

As the whites shoved slave women at him for a price, Hawk could see the fear in their eyes. He alone had the power to tear them away from here, to take them there. All of this dredged up the gut-wrenching scenes that populated his childhood memories. He remembered his own sister being dragged away, his mother's primal wailing, and the ever-present dementia that followed all her living days. He refused to do that to another black woman. So when Atticus Whedoe gathered his female stock for Solomon to look over, he tried a new tactic.

"Any of you women willing to go with me to the Sierra Nevadas to pair up with a man who owns a town?" His eyes searched the crowd as they searched him back. "It's a few months' ride of here. It gets plenty cold, but it could be a good life."

As the silence rode on the Georgia heat, his gaze settled on the wide, front veranda where white women were being served cool refreshments while their pale flesh was fanned free of unwanted insects by slave men and women. They watched this sale as if it were entertainment orchestrated solely for their enjoyment, and Solomon longed to tell the black women before him that going with him would beat the hell out of slavery. He wanted to tell them that Exum was black, but that would be suicide to him here.

"Now looka here, boy," Whedoe spoke, and Solomon cut his beady dark eyes on him. "I mean, son," he corrected before continuing, "You

7

jus' pick one and give me the gold. They is my property, they got no choice."

"Yes, they do," Solomon decreed. His deep, powerful voice thundered through him and rumbled toward the shocked man. "Suh," he mocked and turned to leave.

"Would you be free?" a woman asked, and Solomon pivoted his body to the sound of her voice.

She was a godsend. Honey-brown skin with coal-black hair that rippled next to her scalp before twisting itself into a big knot at the nape of her neck. Her eyebrows were thick. Her cheekbones plunged into hollows before being rescued by full lips. Although tall and thin, she appeared sturdy enough to make the trip—or was it the determination in her eyes that made her appear strong?

Doe-eyes is what she had, Solomon thought, large and luminous with possibility, like she had just heard the opportunity of a lifetime. Big, black pools of color with hardly any white surrounding them, all set in a fawn-brown face.

"Yeah, I guess so." He hadn't thought on that, and at this point he'd say almost anything to get her and get going. "The territory is free, no slaves there, and you'd be pairin' up with Mr. Taylor—"

"So I wouldn't be his slave. I be his wife," her soft voice, which sounded as if it had been dipped into a vat of sweet molasses, clarified.

Solomon half-chuckled at the thought of Exum taking a wife, and said, "I spose anything is possible."

"Where dis cold place?" the girl asked.

"Northwest of here," Solomon answered.

"In California."

"Hush up, gal, you ain't doing the buyin', you being bought," Whedoe piped up.

North, Cassie Lee thought, as she rolled the word over in her mind and quickly searched it for options. She'd heard about the North where folks run to and, if they're not brought back, you never hear from them again. North—the uncertain word sent shivers through her, like an adventure hers for the taking, but not the same kind of shivers the young massa gave her every time he slipped into her bed at night. He'd been eyeing her up for years, and had finally come to her for a little more than a month

8

before her visit to Tante Fatima, and he'd been back steady ever since. She had fought. The small scar he wore had not healed as easily as her sore jaw and black eye. She figured one of them was going to die, and it likely wasn't going be him. If she stayed in this hateful place, her destiny was either a grave or to be sold down river—further from the North. Even if she stayed and young massa took up with some other gal soon, the best she could hope for was to stay a house slave, and they had it worst than the field hands. They were with them Whedoes morning, noon, and night. Alberta said she had to "sit with ole massa's father and feed him, wipe spit from his chin and shit from his ass like he a baby. Them spoilt children of theirs, them mean women, the cleaning—"

"I'll go!" Cassie Lee stepped forward and volunteered before anyone else could.

"No, not you, Cassie Lee," young Charles Whedoe said to her, as his wife dropped her teacup and its contents splattered across the clean-swept veranda. Then to Solomon, he said, "She ain't for sale."

"Why not?" Cassie Lee challenged, and a collective gasp rose from both the slaves and the Whedoes at her brazenness.

"I'll give you $500 for her," Solomon interrupted and bartered for his ticket back home.

"She's worth more than a mere—"

"Let her go, Charles," Mrs. Whedoe advised her husband through tight, pinched lips.

"Yes." Cassie Lee turned toward him, her hands on her hips, and drawled, "Let me go, Charles."

"Now see here, gal—" Atticus Whedoe began.

"$1,000," Solomon said.

"$1,000?" Charles Whedoe repeated with choked amazement, his eyes four times their size, while the slaves muttered among themselves.

"Sold!" Atticus Whedoe decreed.

* * * * * * * * * * * * *

"You a fool to go," Nubby said, dogging behind Cassie Lee as she made her way to the cabin.

"I be a fool to stay," Cassie Lee said, opening the paper-thin door.

9

"What 'bout Jonah?" Nubby asked.

"What 'bout him?" Cassie looked straight into her friend's eyes. "It wuz over 'fore it started." She shoved a razor into her satchel. "When I became Massa Charles' whore, he turned his back on me. Like I had a choice."

"But he do love you, Cassie Lee, if'n you stay maybe he—"

"He what? I jus' spose to wait on him to forgive me somethin' I didn't want nohow?" she drawled, thrusting a few threadbare belongings in next to the razor. "De way folk look at me—like I'ma cow turd crusted around some ole worn-out hoe." Tears welled up in her eyes and she sniffed them back. "I never gon be no man's whore again. Never! I die first, Nubby. I swear I will."

"But to go off with dis man. He not right. He look touched. Dat long har and beard and clothes—"

"I think he be alright. He seem a kind man."

"You talkin' crazy. You can tell from one look at dem little beady black devil-eyes of his."

"I got more chance wit him out dere than I got here. Tell me I'ma wrong, Nubby?" Her eyes challenged her friend's. "Dat's what I thought."

"You crazy, dat's what you is. He say it cold and a long way. How you gon go all de way to any place wit him? What you think you gon find in Californe?"

Cassie Lee shot her friend a knowing glance.

"Oh, no, Cassie Lee. Girl, yo' head ain't still full up wit all dem crazy dreams? Afore, it wuz harmless, somethin' to help ease de pain, but now, it dangerous. Slaves shouldn't oughta have no dreams."

"Dreams is all slaves got, Nubby."

"You ain't gon find nothin' our dere dat you ain't got here, Cassie Lee."

"Freedom. I'ma be free, Nubby. Free."

"Ain't nothin' but a word."

"Free." She let the word set on her tongue, and she tasted its sweetness. "I thought me a lot of things. Folks here in de quarter thought on me as a lot of things. Now dey can think on me as free."

"You jus' can't go, Cassie Lee. I got a bad feelin'."

"Dat be fate, Nubby. Dat dis man come here for *me*. He gon take me to my husband."

10

"Oh, Cassie Lee, he ain't said nothin' about no—"

"Don't use dat pity-tone wit me. I'ma be a sight better off out dere den here. I can't stay here and be massa whore. And when I'ma all wore out like Geneva and Bethesda, he gon throw me over fo' de next darkie's bed, leavin' me to care afta his clothes and leavings, and join his wife and all his other beat-down slave gals to watch him chasin' more black meat." She stuffed her satchel closed. "De wife got de best of dat deal. She ain't got to be bothered wit his white ass." They chuckled. "I'ma be a wife with troubles of my own. I'ma be married, Nubby. I can't be dat here."

"Oh, Cassie Lee." Nubby shook her head in despair and said, "You think dis is 'bout dat man you been conjurin' up since we wuz chilren? Dat Fo'ever Man who gon take you away from here? Ain't no sucha a man, Cassie Lee. You thought it wuz Jonah."

"And I wuz wrong."

"And you still wrong. Yo' Fo'ever Man ain't here, and he sure as hell ain't out dere."

"How you know? Dere be a whole new life out over dese plantation fences."

"You ain't never been off dis plantation."

"I'ma goin' off it today!"

"Mark my words, you ain't never gon find him," Nubby said, crossing her arms over her chest resolutely.

"You ain't never gon have Ben neither."

"You leave Ben outta dis. I got Ben when I want."

"You got a piece of Ben when he say so and his wife look de other way; most of him belong to Taffy." She saw tears brim Nubby's eyes.

"I don't wanna fuss, Nubby. Dis may be de last time we lay eyes on each other." With that bit of news, Nubby began crying.

"I got to go, Nubby," Cassie Lee said softly. "It be my only chance to get outta here legal-like. Dere won't be no slavers chasin' me, no dogs sniffin' me out or chewin' up my legs if'n I be found. I won't be dragged back and strung up to be no spectacle. God is givin' me dis one chance, and if'n I don't take it, I'ma not gon get no more." Wet washed her eyes, then stood at attention without falling.

"You should least ask Tante Fatima."

"I don't need no root-woman to tell me what I already be knowin'. I

11

can hear God say, 'Cassie Lee, either you *go now* or you gon die a Whedoe slave.'"

"Spose you die out dere?"

"Then I die away from de stench of dis place."

"Spose he rape you?"

"I get raped three times a week regular now."

"He ain't out dere, Cassie Lee—yo' Fo'ever Man," Nubby said, quietly.

"So be it. But I'ma be out dere. Free." Cassie Lee clutched her bag to her chest. " 'Member dis satchel?"

She and Nubby both recalled when a ten-year-old Cassie Lee found the discarded luggage outside the big house. Cassie Lee was attracted to the colorful, faded elegance of the tapestry cloth. She grabbed it and took it home. Nubby said it was bad luck to have a traveling piece, and predicted that Cassie Lee would use it when they sold her down river.

Now, Nubby shook her head as Cassie Lee hugged her and said, "I'ma usin' it, Nubby, to go north to California." She released her friend, headed for the door and looked at the bleak, dirt-floored cabin for the last time. " 'Sides, it be a done deal."

"What I'ma gon do without you, Cassie Lee? Who I gon bear my soul to?" Nubby began to cry again as she walked to the cabin door. "I'ma never see you again."

"Maybe not, but you always be here." Cassie Lee touched her heart before she held her friend. They shared private tears and silent memories from long ago.

"Take dis," Nubby said, breaking the embrace and untying the cowrie cross from around her neck.

"I can't—"

"Take it," Nubby mandated, sniffing back her tears, signifying she was done crying over something she couldn't change. "My mama gave it to me, and I never see her again either."

"One of dese days things are gon be different for *all* of us."

"Not dat we ever live to see," Nubby said, tying the cross around Cassie Lee's neck and embracing her again. "Now go. Go on away from dis Whedoe plantation and get married and be a wife."

Chapter II

"My name is Cassie Lee," she said.

"Hawk," Solomon said without looking at her as he saddled up his horse.

"Jus' Hawk?" she drawled.

"Jus' Hawk." Only Exum and his mama knew him to be Solomon. No man or woman got any closer to him than that.

"Seems none of us got last names," she said, her voice drifting·off when he seemed disinterested in anything she had to say.

Solomon outfitted Cassie Lee with denim pants, cotton shirt, vest, boots, socks, hat, and a duster. He bought her a horse and saddle and packed its accompanying bags with food. He was in a hurry to make it back before the snows came and closed off the pass. If he missed that window of opportunity to get into the Sierras, they might have to wait it out until the next spring thaw, and he wanted to deposit his charge and beat it back to the solitude of his mountain cabin.

So this unlikely pair set out north, his freedom papers next to her bill of sale. Having never ridden before, she was unmercifully slow. Sore most of the time, although she never whined or complained, just struggled in silence. By day's end, her voice, that southern drawl, grated on his nerves like the sound of the massa's lash against his brother's tender skin.

Maybe that was it, he thought—not so much the sound of her voice, but what it reminded him of.

Other things irritated him about her, mostly because she was human and he was responsible for her. No matter how late the hour or how tired she professed to be, she would take a brush from her satchel, uncoil her hair, and run it through her raven locks seemingly a hundred times. If they ever happened on a body of water, she felt obliged to submerse herself in it. Sometimes Hawk allowed it, and other times he kept moving. In the morning she would use precious water from her canteen to rinse out her mouth before applying some salve she rubbed across her teeth. Other times, she'd splash the precious liquid over her face. Plantation ways, he thought.

On the fifth night out, they camped on the Tennessee border. As they sat by the fire, Cassie Lee chatting incessantly, Hawk suddenly put his finger to his lips and jumped to his feet. He thought he heard a branch break. Cassie Lee was just about to ask him why he was shushing her when three scruffy-looking white men walked toward them from the woods.

Cassie Lee gasped. "Oh, Lawd have mercy," she whispered under her breath.

* * * * * * * * * * * * *

Hawk stood motionless and watched the men keenly as they approached them. They didn't look like bounty hunters. Country boys more than likely, he thought, huntin' and lookin' for fun. This made matters worse. Bounty hunters were looking for a reward, and with them he and Cassie Lee had a chance of being returned to the plantation. But with these men, there was no telling what was on their minds and how it would all pan out.

"Well, lookey what we got here. What you niggas doin' out here, you runnin'?" one of the men, who appeared to be the oldest, questioned.

Hawk didn't answer.

"Hey Sam, dat's a right hansom' li'l nigra there," the youngest one said, a lascivious grin spreading across his mottled face. "I think I'd like to ride dat li'l black heifer."

The third man stood glaring, his arm wrapped around his rifle.

Cassie Lee, fastened to the earth, swallowed hard. She vividly

14

recalled the time Cletas and Hattie had sneaked off the Whedoe plantation in the middle of the night, seeking freedom. Three days later, Hattie had staggered back to the quarters naked, bleeding, and talking out of her head. "Gal's insides looked like dey be eaten up by a pack of wild dogs," Nubby, who had tended her, had repeated often since that night. Cletas' charred body was found tied to a tree, and Hattie screamed for a solid week before she died.

Cassie Lee had heard stories of how marauders accosted slaves on the trail to freedom—women brutally raped, men tortured and hung, their scant belongings stolen. This man Hawk had taken her away from the only home she had ever known. Now her life was in jeopardy and in his hands. Could he protect her?

Slowly, Cassie Lee moved and stood behind him. She sensed the tension in his body, observing the tightness of his hairy jaw and the cold glare from his eyes. Even though the air was thick and warm and he wore heavy clothing, there was no perspiration on his brow. She was immediately comforted. In her heart she knew he would not succumb to this scum. They would not harm her unless they killed him first.

Hawk was all too familiar with this scenario. He had been both victim of and witness to the vicious attacks cowards like these inflict on innocent people. With all the talk about ending slavery and the government's opposition to it, these assaults had become more savage. He could show them his papers and her bill of sale, but that wouldn't stop po' white trash like these. They probably couldn't even read. He'd come up against their kind often enough in every no-horse and one-horse town as he made his way to his peaceful mountain. His frame was a lightning rod for unwanted attention from every wish-he-was-but-never-will-be master. They saw big and black, and expected dumb to be a part of the package. He was never bothered one on one, but put two or more of these white boys together, and they thought it was their racial duty to show who was superior. Hawk knew he could hold his own with any man in a fair fight; maybe even two. But was he a match for three with weapons?

"Wait a minute, Luke," the one called Sam said. "I ast this nigga a question. You hear me, boy?"

But Luke was anxious to get started. He stepped around the fire,

15

moving closer to Hawk and Cassie Lee. "Yeah, you hear 'im, boy?" he mimicked, spitting a viscous glob that landed on the toe of Hawk's boot.

Hawk glanced quickly at his boot, then locked eyes with the assailant called Sam.

To Cassie Lee's surprise, Hawk relaxed his shoulders, moved away from her, and walked toward the fire, leaving her exposed.

"You c'n have de woman," he said calmly, as he stooped to stoke the fire, "and den let us go. We don't want no trouble, suh."

Damn dat Hawk, Cassie Lee thought. She sure had him figured wrong. Well, she would fight as long as she had breath in her body. She yelled out and fought as Luke grabbed her.

"Look like you gon hafta rope dat heifer 'fore you ride her," Sam said, as the attention of the two men was stolen by the scuffle between Cassie Lee and Luke.

A split second was all Hawk needed. With lightning speed, he scooped up a handful of hot ashes while pulling his pistol from beneath his coat. A shot rang out at the same time he flung the ashes. With amazing accuracy, both objects struck their targets.

"You shot my brother, you crazy nigga," Luke screamed, as he unhanded Cassie Lee and ran to assist his brother, now sprawled face down in the dirt. The third man writhed on the ground, wailing and holding his burnt eyes.

Cassie Lee covered her ears and stood frozen for a second, paralyzed by the chaos. *Run!*—the thought screamed in her mind. The same voice asked, *Where?* Seeing the opportunity to escape, she dashed into the woods. *Nowhere!!* the hostile darkness shouted back and enveloped her. She trembled and crouched behind a tree. Over her pounding heart, she could hear screams and movement from her hiding place, then all was quiet. After what seemed like hours, but was only minutes, she heard Hawk's beckoning voice.

"You can come out now. They gon."

She didn't move.

"Come on now," he called again. "I said they gon."

Emerging slowly from the woods, she saw him gathering up their belongings.

"Hurry up, woman," he yelled. "And keep yo' hair up under that hat. What you think I gave it to you for?" He glared at her; the strain of the ordeal had made him jittery. He couldn't wait to get back to the solitude of his mountain cabin.

"Come on, we movin' out," he said in a softer tone. "Once they get back with that boy's body, they'll be sending folks after us. Trash always hangs together—all they got is each other and a good fight. We can lose them easy with a head start."

As he doused the fire with coffee, Cassie Lee noticed a strange but pleasant feeling, both in her heart and in her groin, whenever she neared Hawk; a feeling totally unfamiliar to her. Once she was almost tempted to touch his arm. She smiled to herself. This man was sure something.

As they mounted their horses and stole into the dark wilderness, Cassie Lee was still smiling. No man had ever fought for her before.

They rode five hard miles after the encounter, and Hawk decided that they could camp at least until first light. Cassie Lee tried to make the two saddle blankets a bed and settled down before she said, "Thank you, Hawk. I ain't never had no man protect me like dat."

"It's my job to get you to Exum." He rolled over on his side away from her. His gun was poised by his head.

"And you always do your job." She hid the hurt in her voice.

"That's all a man got is his word, and I gave it to Exum that I'd bring him a woman. That's what I aim to do, or die trying."

"My Exum . . . he white?"

"No, black."

She smiled, her faith restored. "Why come you ain't never said so?"

"Not too smart for me to tell slave owners that I'm buying for a rich black man, now is it?" God she was dumb, he thought, and she talked too damn much.

"Tell me 'bout him."

"Not now. Night."

"Good night." Exum being black was enough to fuel her sweet dreams.

* * * * * * * * * * * *

17

"Cassie Leee!!" her name rang through the slave quarters, slicing the night quiet as it careened through slave alley like flood water consuming everything in its wake. Her name bled through the thin wooden slats and soaked into the dirt floors. "Cassie Leee!!" the plaintive cry shattered, ricocheted, then echoed in the ears of every slave who grunted and turned over to snatch sleep back. There was no cause for concern. It was just Charles trying to turn another girl into Cassie Lee at his moment of climax. For almost two weeks it had been their nocturnal lullaby. Instead of getting better, it was getting worse.

Atticus Whedoe took his morning breakfast in his study. He couldn't bear the sight of his son. His son Charles had been a disappointment to him for as long as he could remember, long before he had been drummed out of West Point for undisciplined behavior, which meant he had taken up with the local low-lifes in the area. Once back home, Charles had added embarrassment to his credits when he continued drinking and ruthlessly chasing after slave gals. From day one, Atticus could never deny that boy anything. He couldn't deny his mother either, which is why that boy was spoiled, rotten to the core. His only boy among six daughters, Atticus should have taken more time with Charles instead of leaving the rearing up to his wife, Emily. When he did step in, it was only to correct or punish the boy, and Emily would reverse it when he went away on business. Back then, Atticus was afraid Charles would be a pansy. Instead, Charles became a lothario—the natural order of things when a mother smothers you with everything you ever hope for before you can wish it. Charles turned out to expect and get that treatment from every woman he met. He spread himself all across Georgia, cattin', consortin', and carousin' with every sort of female so that when it came time to marry, no decent woman would have him. They had to get him a wife from Virginia. Her family had the aristocratic name, but had lost their tobacco fortune to worms. The only reason Louisa stayed with Charles was because she didn't want to go back home. Maybe he should send Charles and his family to Virginia for a visit with the in-laws. He'd give his son another week or so to get this slave gal out of his system, or at least stop screaming her name at the top of his lungs every night.

* * * * * * * * * * * *

Cassie Lee was awakened by the smell of coffee and the clang of the cup on the pot. The sun was rising and she soaked in her surroundings, marveling at being free to just look up and absorb God's work. Her surveying gaze fell on Hawk and startled her.

"Good mornin'," she said.

"Mornin'," said he, as he watched her rise and go through all her rituals. Luckily, there was no body of water so she'd just waste what was in the canteen, Solomon thought.

They ate in silence.

"C'mon, we got dust to eat," he said as he stomped out the fire, anxious to put more miles between them and the Tennessee boys.

When they were mounting their horses, Cassie Lee asked, "What's your horse's name?"

"Black."

"Oh," she said when she realized he wasn't going to say anymore on it. "He certainly is dat."

They had traveled a mile with Cassie Lee talking incessantly, and since the silent treatment wasn't working on her, Solomon asked her point blank, "Do you always jabber on so?"

"Sorry." The horse rolled and pitched a few more steps. "It's jus' dat—" She saw him visibly cringe, and she stopped talking altogether.

She knew he didn't like her, but she didn't care. She was on an adventure, and she was free, once they got into free territory. Hawk seldom looked at her, and cared for her like she was a horse—seeing that she was fed, watered, and bunked down for the night; that was the extent of any interaction. She thought she saw him smile when she had plunged into the big river and he had to fish her out. One strong arm had grabbed her by the shoulder and raised her up. She was a drenched pup. He was only wet to his knees as he stood her on the banks near the thigh-deep water.

"Least I got a bath," she had smiled. Had he? Or was it the sun in his eyes that made them squint even smaller? She had to change clothes behind a bush, and when she came out he was already saddled and ready to continue. She wanted to stay and look at the water a while

19

longer. She had never seen so much water all together in one place before. She wished Nubby could have seen it. But they had to move on. Hawk said so.

* * * * * * * * * * * *

Having put considerable distance between them and the Tennessee border, they progressed in welcome silence. Solomon looked ahead so he could pretend he was alone, except for the sound of her horse on the trail. Besides her constant chattering, which he knew was only momentarily stopped, she was doing pretty good for someone who never sat a horse before this trek. He could tell from the way she walked that she was getting over the soreness, although she still did not sit down to eat at the campfire. He could imagine the trip being much more unpleasant had he picked another slave girl who might be scared and crying by now. But this one, Cassie Lee, just plugged on, waiting for whatever lay around the next bend. He didn't quite have the heart to tell her that Exum wasn't the marryin' kind, but his job was transporting, not warning. He only had second thoughts once, after she fell into the river. She was a little skinnier than he recalled, and he wondered if her tits were big enough for Exum.

That had been a sight. Her falling in that river. He chuckled anew. That night she had shivered by the fire in spite of herself. He hadn't planned fur for her. Since they had crossed the river the temperature had dropped severely, and while he had his bear coat and hat, he could stand the chill for at least the next couple of days. She obviously could not. He threw her his coat, which she wrapped in up to her blue lips. He lay on his bear blanket and could still hear her teeth chattering on the other side of the fire.

"C'mon over here," he sighed as she sprinted to his side and lay on his bearskin roll. His body blocked the cold from the north side. In no time flat, he could hear the change in her breathing.

She smelled . . . sweet, if he could recall how that smelled. It must be those sticks she's always chewing on, or that powder she dusts on that makes me and my horse sneeze, he thought. Even though his back was to her, she had cuddled right up under him, and the warmth of her sleeping body aroused him in a way he hadn't expected. He thought of the three

20

times a year he traveled to Exum to trade his furs and spend alternate nights with Elsie or Ming. Elsie was a lively redhead whose enthusiasm made up for her lack of skill, while Ming, the China girl, could deploy his release with exquisite technique, compensating for the fact that the root of his sex was too large to accommodate her slim build. Ming worked her wonders with physical agility and a talented tongue. Still, after four days of being with the two of them, he headed back to his solitude.

Now he wished for either one of them, just to momentarily meet his needs, then vanish. He wondered if Exum would mind his taking a poke this night with Cassie Lee. Probably not. Exum would expect it, but it wasn't right, and he had miles to go with this girl. If he had sex with her, there would be no shutting her up, and she might read more into it than a man just answering a call from nature. He tried to shake off the feeling and go to sleep, but it eluded him for most of the night. When it finally came, it did so fitfully.

* * * * * * * * * * * *

Atticus had made the necessary introductions of General Warren to Charles as they stood near the front steps of the wide veranda stretching out before them.

"You tangle with a pole cat?" Charles asked one of the general's two escorts as his father chatted with his guest.

"You could say that," he said. The burns around his eyes had healed into a bright pink, but his arm lay limp by his side.

"Got his shoulder shot up over a piece of nigra ass," said Luke.

"Shut up, Luke. I wouldn't be laughing if my brother'd been kilt."

Luke stiffened from the statement and said, "Only reason we doing this chicken-shit escort stuff is 'cause that big black buck shot up his shoulder and ruined his shooting arm. Jus' one big, black man—"

"This darkie gal," Charles asked, "She good lookin'?" Atticus cringed when he overheard his son's question. All four men stared at Charles, stunned.

"This man, what did he look like?" Charles was too excited to notice the embarrassment that straightened his father's stance as disgust blazed on his red face.

21

"Big, tree-top standing nigga—" Luke began.

"With a big hat, duster to the ground?" the young massa continued excitedly. Atticus's searing glare was wasted on Charles as the elder Whedoe ushered the general into the house.

"Long woolly hair and a beard," Luke added.

"That's them! How far back?" Charles asked.

"A coupla weeks, give or take—"

"You want to make some money? Go fetch that gal and bring her back?"

"Hell no!" The man with the shattered shoulder piped up.

"How much?" Luke ignored his partner, Gus.

"$1,000," Charles said. The craggy men eyed one another as if Charles were daft. "That big buck stole my property. I want her back—you can kill him for all I care."

"Told you that was his woman," Luke said to Gus. "They probably be easy to catch. They didn't look to be in no particular hurry, and you know she givin' it to him ev'ry night on the trail, so that's slowing them down some."

With that comment Charles became infuriated. "Bring him back dead, there's an extra $1,000."

"I don't care if he gives me this house to boot, I ain't goin' after that nigga—"

"Excuse us," Luke said as he dragged Gus out of Whedoe's earshot for a powwow.

Charles paced with nervous anticipation as he glared at the shady saddle tramps. It was possible he would never see his money or Cassie Lee again, but they had a bead on them. They had seen her. If they worked out, he could cancel the other two bounty hunters he had hired from down Texas way. They were expensive, but they guaranteed results. But if these two caught up with them first, he'd have Cassie Lee back before hog-killing time.

"We'll do it," Luke spoke up as Gus fell behind. "We know jus' where she's at."

"I'll give you $500 now and $1,500 when you bring her in."

"Hey, you said—"

"That'd be fine," Luke interrupted Gus.

From his study, Atticus saw Charles rush in and take the carpeted steps by twos. He glanced outside and saw the escorts still there as he listened to his son's frantic footsteps overhead run from room to room before Charles flew back down the stairs and out the door toward the two men. Atticus squinted his eyes outside toward the three curious men before the general called him to attention.

Atticus offered the general a cigar, helped him light it as he ordered Bethesda to pour brandy for the two of them. When Atticus looked outside, he was relieved to see the two men riding away.

* * * * * * * * * * * * *

God answers prayers, Solomon remembered his mama saying, and there it was. Fur for this gal to get to Exum in one good piece. The gigantic, red-brown grizzly bear roared as it stood on two legs towering over him. The bear's thunderous growl didn't deter Solomon as he swung his knife again and again.

Cassie Lee was immobilized by the sheer size and ferocity of this animal. Seconds ticked like hours as the petrified Cassie Lee watched the beast make sport of her escort. The bear savagely approached Hawk and effortlessly knocked the gleaming steel from his hand, sending the metal and then the man tumbling across the jagged earth. Hawk scrambled for the knife as the bear pounced toward him, missing him by inches and infuriating the grizzly. The sound was deafening as the mammoth beast assaulted Hawk. The bear swiped at him. He dodged and rolled over just as the grizzly caught him across his face. The bear flung Hawk again, then picked him up and, locking his furry tentacles around the man, began squeezing the life from him. Hawk coughed and spat as air was being expelled from his lungs. Fear propelled Cassie Lee to snatch Hawk's rifle from Black. She cocked and aimed.

Bang!!

A piercing sound rang out and bounced over the rocks.

The bear froze in mid-roar then fell, releasing Solomon, who spun across the ground like a ball of yarn. He looked up to see a dazed Cassie Lee still poised in the stance that rendered the bear dead. The smoke

23

from the rifle evaporated in the chill of the afternoon. Finally, she dropped the heavy gun to her side.

"I never shot no gun before," she said almost reverently.

"Damn good shootin'." Solomon climbed to his feet. He took the rifle from her hands and slung it back over his saddle, pausing to rest himself.

"You cut!" Cassie Lee noticed.

"Jus' a scratch." He puffed. "'Sides," he picked up his knife, "we got to get started on your new coat."

He rolled the bear over and, in one swoop, split the bear open from crotch to neck. When the fleshy belly gushed blood and intestines, Cassie Lee fainted. By the time she came to, Solomon had hollowed out the innards, scraped the hide clean, and salvaged a few steaks for the road.

"Oh God, the stench," Cassie Lee said, covering her nose and beginning to retch.

"You care 'bout warmth or smell?" He rolled up the huge skin, wrapped twine around it, and packed it on her horse. "Come on," he ordered. "With that stink we're likely to have some unwanted visitors soon."

They outran the smell in a couple of miles, but the jostling from the ride opened his wound again.

"Come on, Hawk, lemme tend that wound. Least I could do for a man who jus' bought me my first fur coat." She smiled and he reluctantly relented.

He sat perched on a rock by the creek as she wiped the wound clean, then whipped out her razor.

"What you meanin' to do with that?"

"I got to cut dis hair off your face away from de wound or it'll get infected."

"Where'd that come from?"

"My dorey."

"Dowry?" he corrected, and she proceeded to scrape away his beard.

Cassie Lee noticed how his speech slipped into the way she talked when they were attacked by those white boys. He said "the, they, and that," to her "de, dey, and dat." She was going to start working on her talking. She wondered if Exum talked as good as Hawk.

"You can read, huh?"

"Some. My wife taught me and my son at the same time." Cassie Lee's razor hesitated in mid-air, only a split second.

"How she feel 'bout you comin' all this way to pick a wife for Exum?" She noticed the smooth, even, dark chocolate complexion his beard hid. "Leavin' her and him all alone in dem . . . them hills."

"I never leave her. She's always with me. They always with me." His eyes narrowed as she applied some bacon lard to prevent more bleeding.

"There!" She smiled brightly, but he just got up and walked away.

Deep in thought, she figured, probably missing his family. She wanted to love somebody the way he did. She wanted somebody to love her the way he loved his family.

After about an hour alone, he came back to move on. He threw the blanket on his horse and cinched the saddle on Cassie Lee's horse before going to do the same with his. As she approached her horse she let out a bloodcurdling scream, and Solomon immediately drew his gun.

"A spider, a spider!" Cassie Lee shouted, and fanned her hands toward the top of her saddle as the hairy arachnid crawled lazily across the oiled leather. "Shoot it! Shoot it!" she yelled.

Solomon went over, looked at it, looked at her cowering by a nearby rock, and squashed it with his hand. She felt stupid as he swaggered back to his horse and continued to saddle up.

Through her embarrassment Cassie Lee heard another unfamiliar sound. A rumble, something else coming to spook her, she thought. She looked up and down the mountain gorges, wanting to identify it before she called him to her aid again. Then she saw Hawk's massive back moving. The sound was coming from him. He was laughing. She was stunned and pleased at the same time. She laughed too at the absurdity that she could kill a bear, but was petrified of a little spider. He reared his head back and his voice filled the canyon, echoing and ricocheting off the rock, and Cassie Lee laughed tears. It wasn't that funny, she thought, but maybe he hadn't laughed in such a long time, he had it all bottled up inside of him and it had to get out. The sunlight hit his eyes, and she stopped and stared at him. His eyes weren't beady-black at all.

"Your eyes," she drawled, "they light brown." She was sorry the moment she'd said it. He stiffened, squelching his laughter like he had just swallowed a bug.

25

"Let's get a couple more miles in before sunset," he said, swinging his large frame into his saddle, and commenced on. Two things he coveted—not letting people close enough to know that his given name was Solomon, or that he had brown eyes. It was just one more thing for simple-minded people to latch onto and make fun of—a black man with light brown eyes. He hid the lightness. That's why he wore the broad-brimmed hat low on his forehead, plunging his features into constant darkness. Over the years he had perfected his perpetual, tight-eyed squint to keep the color in and others out. As a result, he had a keen focus on life, on just the things that mattered. He could see out, and no one could see in—to his heart or soul.

* * * * * * * * * * * *

Atticus had ridden his horse with such fury from town that it frothed wet with foam. As slaves grabbed the spent horse, Massa Whedoe staggered up the steps. Unleashed rage fueled the shouting of his son's name and carried him into the dining room where the family sat for supper. Atticus raised his riding crop against his son's forearm.

"Is there no end to the dishonor you gon cause this family?" he shouted as he whipped his son again and again. His wife screamed, and the pandemonium rang through the house and out into the nearby fields like wildfire over dry timber. "I gotta go to town to find out you hired more men to go fetch that nigga gal?"

With that tidbit of information, Louisa gathered her three children and ushered them out from the sight of their grandfather whipping their father over a colored girl.

"She and that root-woman done put a hex on you, boy, and if'n I thought I could beat it out of you, I would!" Atticus thundered as a tearful Emily tried to stop him. He pushed his wife into Bethesda and Silas. As if she couldn't bear the sight of two more black faces mocking her, Emily fled the room.

"You disgraced the Whedoe name for the last time. I will not be the laughingstock of—"

Atticus grabbed his chest and stumbled to his study. He managed to pour himself a whiskey and settle into his carved desk chair. He sought solace in the genteel furnishings of his room—the paneled walls, the imported marble fireplace, the smell of fine cigars, and even better liquor—everything he had built up that his son seemed hell-bent on tearing down, beginning with their good name.

He had worked so hard for it all—the four thousand acres of prime Georgia land, three plantation houses, the three hundred slaves, and a son he couldn't stomach looking at. Was this who he was supposed to pass it all on to? And if he got his hands on it, would he spend every dime chasing after this Cassie Lee?

Charles stood in the doorway, bloody and unapologetic.

"I'ma going into town to meet them men tomorrow, Daddy." Atticus, weary and tired of his son and the situation, made no sound. "I'ma going with them."

"You thowing good money after bad," he said quietly. "You paid them other country boys whose only intention was to part you from your money."

"That's why I'ma going with them this time. They guarantee me they can find her. It's a bounty hunter and a Indian scout."

"Ah, for chrissakes! Boy, you actin' like po' white trash, consortin' with niggas and Injuns." Atticus stopped the burgeoning tirade and sighed. He just wanted it over and the boy out of his sight. Maybe if he went and didn't find her it would all be over. He had tried everything else, and nothing was working.

"Then what?" Atticus asked his son point blank. "You bring her back here—then what?" He held his son's gaze and saw the torture that lived there.

"I don't know, Daddy."

Atticus stayed in his study until the house went to bed, then took the almost empty bottle to the porch and sat in the rocker, absorbing the peacefulness of his sleeping land. He got up and walked past the slumbering slave quarters, until the winding dirt road gave way to marsh and trees with tendrils of hanging moss. Haunting nocturnal sounds accompanied him: the coo of an owl, nearby fluttering of wings, the unidentifiable hissing of some night animal announcing an intruder in their midst. In the short distance he saw it. The tiny cabin backlit by an eerie twilight, like stars had fallen from the heavens and smoldered there, sending up a strange daylight patina.

At the door he hesitated before knocking. It had been years since he had been back here. The door swung open and the old, bent, black woman fixed her eyes on him.

"I been expectin' you, Atticus." She stepped back and let him in.

After a few hours, the door whined open again, and Tante Fatima watched his light suit fade then become consumed in darkness as he retreated further and further away.

Nubby had been to see her every third night, and now Atticus had come. It was probably the first time black and white wanted the same thing—that Cassie Lee make it safe to California.

The next morning Charles rose early before the rest of the house. By noon, he, Taggert, and the Indian had set out to track down Cassie Lee. By the fifth day, Taggert had had enough of Charles Whedoe who wanted to ride day and night, and bought three extra horses solely for that purpose. They had covered phenomenal ground in a short time, but all the money in the world wasn't going to make more hours in a day or change the terrain. None of it was good enough for Charles Whedoe, who began making unrealistic demands like sending the Indian to scout days ahead of them. As they closed in on the hunted pair, the driven son of the southern planter became maniacal, and no one would be happier when this was over than Taggert and the Indian.

*　*　*　*　*　*　*　*　*　*　*　*

Solomon and Cassie Lee had left the July heat of Georgia more than a month ago, and had finally settled in to each other's ways. Solomon was now content that Cassie Lee's constant chattering had given way to soft singing. He supposed that somebody like her, used to being around people, had to adjust to somebody like him who wasn't and who liked it that way. He took to her singing because it was not overly intrusive on his quiet, and it required no response from him. In fact, Solomon found it kind of soothing.

As Cassie Lee left the Whedoe plantation and the South further behind, her excitement relaxed and anticipation took over. She followed behind Hawk and let her singing be the backdrop to planning her life once she reached Exum the town and Exum the man. She pondered on her husband, their house, a hot bath, and good food. She thought she'd miss nothing but Nubby, but what she wouldn't give for anything but beans, bacon, coffee, hard tack, and jerky. Hawk often added rabbit, squirrel, and venison to the mix, but Cassie Lee craved some greens, potatoes, and chicken. She never thought she'd want chicken again, but she did. She supposed if they were to see one, Hawk would kill it for her. He was a good guide and provider. One night she watched him poke holes into her bear hide before he tightly strung twine through most of it. When he was finished, she had a big coat with sleeves that almost dragged to the ground. He cut off some of the bottom and made her a hat. She was as warm as fresh biscuits in the winter.

Hawk even got used to her bathing every morning, sometimes suggesting they go a different way because it had a creek or stream. He started washing his face in the morning. He never stank, perspired, or got cold either. When water poured from her to the point she had to remove her coat, hat, and open her shirt some, she'd looked over at Hawk, and there he rode, cool as you please, with his hat cocked over his eyes and his body hidden under that duster. With all that hair on his neck and face, he never sweated.

As she followed him in their companionable silence, she noticed that he seemed satisfied just sitting on his horse and chewing those thin, dark brown cigars. The sweet smoke wafted back to Cassie Lee, gently mingling with the smell of the earth, the pines, and her thoughts.

* * * * * * * * * * * *

"Hold it right there," Solomon's voice halted the two men in their tracks. "You all been doggin' me for three days now. Why?"

Taggert and the Indian looked straight into the barrel of his shotgun.

"Mister, I was hired to do a job is all," Taggert spoke. "Seems you have some property that belongs to the Whedoe family and we come to claim it."

"Shoot him! Just shoot him!!" Charles shouted, riding up from the rear, stunning both Solomon and Taggert.

"What you doin' here?" Cassie Lee became visible for the first time.

"Kill him, I said!" Charles ordered Taggert.

29

"If he hands over the girl, there don't need to be no killing," Taggert told Charles, who became enraged.

"I hired you to—"

"Locate your property. There she is, we'll escort you both back."

"I'ma not his property. Hawk bought me free and clear for $1,000!" Cassie Lee spoke up while Solomon held his gun poised for firing whichever man moved first. "I got papers!" Cassie Lee shouted and massaged her cowrie cross and looked frantically from one man to the next. "I ain't gon back, I ain't gon back—"

"Be still!" Solomon commanded her. She was becoming hysterical, and he couldn't watch her and these men.

Cassie Lee couldn't calm herself down. There was no way she was going back to slavery with them. She had tasted freedom, and she'd kill herself first.

"Do you have a bill of sale?" Taggert asked Solomon, knowing he did not.

"I'll get it," Cassie Lee volunteered and headed for Hawk's saddlebag.

"Now, wait just a damned minute!" Charles protested. "I am paying you good money—"

"Shut up, Whedoe!" Taggert snapped as he took the paper from the girl and read the bill of sale. He eyed Charles Whedoe with disdain, not believing that he and his Indian companion had been duped by this southern gentleman. "What did you expect, Whedoe? That we'd kill this man so you could get the girl back?"

"She is mine!"

"Not according to this legal paper. I guess you better take this up with your daddy. Sorry," he said, as he handed the paper back to Cassie Lee, who snatched it from his white hands triumphantly and clutched the treasured document to her breast.

"You can't jus' let them ride off!" Charles spat.

"You got bigger problems," Taggert came in between Solomon's gun barrel and Charles. "You owe us some money."

"You didn't do your job," said Charles.

"And you lied. C'mon, we going back to Georgia to get the rest of our money." Taggert took the reins of Whedoe's horse as if taking him prisoner.

Unable to accept the defeat—to return home without Cassie Lee and still owe these men money, to see his father's disappointed and accusatory eyes—Charles began to weep. For the first time, he realized what a colossal fool he had become. A buffoon for chasing this gal across country. He looked back at Cassie Lee and saw her walking further away from him on the other side of that big nigga. The idea that another night would pass and that black buck would be dipping his big, black wick into his well ignited a rage that blazed through his body.

In almost slow motion, Cassie Lee turned from Charles to get on her horse as Solomon uncocked his rifle and backed away before swiveling around to mount Black. Taggert and the Indian were facing south.

"Cassie Leee!!" Charles yelled her name, pulled out his revolver, and fired two wild shots.

Solomon pushed her out of the way, drew his pistol, and fired one shot. Charles Whedoe clutched his heart and fell to the ground with a hollow thud. Solomon was ready to shoot again, but there were no takers.

"Damn!" was all Taggert could say.

As Solomon straightened and placed his smoking gun back into its holster, Cassie Lee went over to her ole massa's body and looked down at his surprised and contorted expression, not unlike the face he made all those nights he forced himself on her. Looking down on him, she felt nothing—not happy, not sad. A faint, wicked smile tickled the end of her lips as she identified her emotion. Cassie Lee felt relief. It was truly over. Charles Whedoe would never take another innocent slave girl because he felt it his right and duty to do so. He would never dirty a clean black body with his twisted desires.

"You takin' his body back?" Cassie Lee asked the still-mounted Taggert.

"I reckon it's the only way we'll get any money. I guess his family would want his body to bury."

She knew Miss Emily would want her precious Charles back, although ole massa would rather he be fed to the wolves.

"You gon tell them what happened?" Cassie Lee asked, fixing her black eyes on his cold blues.

"I'm going to tell them the truth. Their son drew on this man and got off two shots to his one that killed him."

"Have a safe trip," Cassie Lee said without a backward glance as she swung her body up into the saddle of her horse, looking west. She didn't need to worry about Massa Charles or any of them Whedoes no more. She decided not to think on him ever again.

* * * * * * * * * * * * *

Within the next few days, Hawk and Cassie Lee stopped at a little trading post on another big river to replenish their supplies. Cassie Lee crunched into an apple as she looked at the water rushing by. When Hawk finished packing the saddlebags with goods, he told her to mount up. They rode next to the river until he picked a site to safely negotiate the water to the other side. Once they successfully crossed over, she followed him to a high bluff, and when he dismounted so did she. She walked over to where he was standing and hopped up on a rock. Hawk seemed to be staring and inhaling the air in a way Cassie Lee had never seen him do before. She shielded her hands over her eyes, trying to see what had captivated him so. It looked like more of the same to her.

"Well, Cassie Lee," he said with a sigh.

It was the first time he had called her by name.

"This is Indian Territory. Everything you see is free—including you."

Cassie Lee gasped with delight. A strange brew of hopes and dreams percolated in her body as she drank in the far-as-your-eye-could-see land. It was wild, untouched, with trees and mountains and birds and life—all free. Her heart pounded with a fierceness she had never known. Her breath shortened and her body trembled as the word "free" screamed through every pore. All emotion finally accumulated in her eyes before cascading down her face and dripping off her chin onto her shirt.

"*Free*. I'ma free." Something she had dreamed of, but never thought she'd be until she died. "Free," she cried, and grabbed the cowrie cross around her neck, rubbing it like a constant ache, soothed. Nubby, I'ma free, she thought.

Solomon watched her in silence. The way those innocent doe-eyes absorbed the terrain before her. And when she closed those thick, heavy eyelashes on them once, a waterfall of tears rinsed her face. He knew what an intoxicatingly powerful feeling freedom could be. He wished it for every Negro on this earth, but he was happy to have been a part of bringing it to just one.

"I sing because I'm happy," Cassie Lee began, wiping her joyful tears from her face. "I sing because I'm free. Free!!"

With that declaration she jumped from the rock into Hawk's arms and said, "Thank you, Hawk."

When he set his brown eyes on her like she was crazy, her euphoric mood evaporated, and she slid down from his body in embarrassment.

"Sorry," she said, swooping a restless tendril back behind her ear and stroking her cowrie cross. She thought of Hawk's wife, and supposed she wouldn't want any woman hugging on Exum either.

"Umph." He cleared his throat. "I guess freedom is somethin' to get excited over. Let's get going," he said without looking at her.

Cassie Lee turned back to her freedom vista again, wiped her face, gathered her horse's reins, and followed her escort.

For the next few miles they rode amid the towering trees in silence.

"We almost there, ain't we?"

"Closer than we have been."

"Tell me about Exum."

"How old are you, gal?"

"Don't call me 'gal.' Gal is what white folks calls us what's already got a name, but not important enough for them to remember. They call you 'gal' when they don't want to even bother to know your name." She was almost talking to herself. "You called me Cassie Lee back there," she said to him, but when he didn't respond, she added, "I reckon I'ma eighteen, nineteen, give or take."

She didn't know her exact age, but she knew it was about two years ago when Massa Charles dropped Poppy and took after her like a jack rabbit heading for his hutch. Poppy tried to slash Cassie Lee's throat, like she wanted massa Whedoe. He had Poppy sold down river and moved Cassie Lee into the big house kitchen. Neither slave nor white folk bothered her after that. That's when she found out what lonely was. House slaves tolerated her, field slaves—including Jonah—despised her. Neither of them understood that she didn't want this no more than they did.

Massa used to come to her room almost every night except when she was on the rag. She fought at first, but then he'd punch her and have his way. He spilled into her, never noticing the silent tears running down her face. In order to stand it, she turned hard, and took her mind to a place that he couldn't go. He had her body, possessed it, owned it, trashed it . . . but he couldn't touch her heart, her soul, or her mind. She was saving them for somebody special—her Forever Man.

She went to Tante Fatima in the swamp beyond the quarter and had her scrape away his seed and begged her to fix it so none would ever root there as long as she drew breath. Tante Fatima obliged and kept Massa Whedoe from her for almost two months. When the Massa got her back, Cassie Lee got a perverse pleasure in knowing that he could never give her anything that lasted. She would never stare into the Massa's eyes set in a brown face, or see those eyes sold away from her in the back of an open wagon. He had only her body, her meat, but he had no real hold over her.

When she made love with her husband, it would be for the first time. She longed to give her heart, mind, soul, and body to one man before she left this earth. She longed to accept him in love and give herself in kind. So it didn't matter about Massa Whedoe, not then and not now. Only Exum Taylor mattered, and she hoped he would stir up the same feelings that Hawk did—in her heart and groin.

"Tell me about Exum Taylor, Hawk," she said quietly.

"Exum," Solomon sighed, then smiled. "Exum is what you call an original man. There ain't nobody like him. He got ideas and vision and money. He's a handsome cuss. 'Bout your color, maybe a tad darker, got light eyes, wavy hair, and pretty white teeth despite all the liquor he drinks." Solomon laughed, missing his friend.

"He a drinkin' man?" Cassie Lee was not impressed.

"Some." Solomon figured she'd find out about him soon enough, reminding himself that his favor was for transporting, not for filling in the blanks. "Men respect him. Women love him."

"Well, them womens better step aside for when Mrs. Cassie Lee Taylor comes to the big house."

"Nobody said nothin' about a big house. You get the galdarnest ideas from nothin'—"

"You said he owned the town and had plenty money—"

"But that don't mean he got a house like them Whedoes—"

"Jus' so the house has love. It don't need doodads and frilly pretties. There was no love in that house, that house was for show is all. My house can be a shack like I left, jus' so we free and we have love . . . and somethin' to eat." She laughed, and he smiled . . . for the first time.

Chapter III

Cassie Lee's head tunneled from beneath her bear coat to face the waiting sunrise. Every morning she woke up to a new, spectacular happening. This morning the wide-open, golden plains were covered with moving black dots.

"What is that?" she asked in wonderment, and Solomon again noted her big doe-eyes free of surrounding white.

She had asked him the same question when she first saw Indians. "We don't bother them none, they won't bother us. We not white in a wagon coming to take what's theirs."

"Why they spyin' on us?"

"You'd watch too if somebody was passing through your front parlor."

She aimed those big doe-eyes to the mountain tops where they looked down on the harmless pair.

Now, as they lay on their bellies at the edge of a butte, looking down at one of nature's creatures graze, he answered her, "Buffalo."

"Wow, you can walk across their backs from horizon to horizon," she noted absently, totally hypnotized by these animals, not seeing Solomon looking at her.

"What is it?" Cassie Lee shouted as the white flakes whipped around her face, almost rendering Hawk and his horse invisible.

"Snow," he yelled back at her over the swirling wind that accompanied the surprise September storm.

Solomon and Cassie Lee climbed the side of a jagged-edged mountain to seek refuge in a carved-out cave. As Solomon checked the cave for other inhabitants and removed the saddles from the horses, Cassie Lee stood at the mouth of the cave, watching the heavens belch the puffs of cold cotton.

"Where does it come from?" she ran back to ask as Hawk started a fire.

"From the sky. It's frozen rain, is all," he said in irritation, not at her but at the early and unpredictable weather.

Once the fire ignited, he watched her go and let the snow fall in her hands and melt. She'd lick it, ball it up, and throw it, then run back to the warmth of the fire and wrap herself up in her bear fur coat and hat.

The blizzard had cost them two days, and provisions were low. On one gray day Solomon left their cave home to hunt for game that could stretch their supplies. Cassie Lee stood at the mouth of the cave and watched the morning snow fill in his footsteps. That afternoon she returned to her former perch and let her eyes search for the sight of him—the movement of a black man against the white snow amid the towering trees.

At early evening she repeated the same exercise. From where she stood she was tree-top level with the pines, and as her eyes scanned down there was no movement, neither man nor beast, and she absently said, "The Lord is my light and my salvation, whom do I fear—"

Before the words left her mouth, Cassie Lee realized that there was no one to fear. She hadn't seen another human being since the four people at the trading post more than a month ago. Though a handsome people, she didn't think the Indians would come to her aid if she needed them. She didn't know where she had come from, where she was, or where she was going. She had nowhere to go. She was a woman completely and utterly alone in this wilderness. The thought sent a shiver through her body.

This cave could become my coffin if Hawk doesn't return, she thought. A woman with a bear coat and hat, a canteen of water, a horse, saddle, bedroll, and a little flour left. She'd hold on and hold out, like her people always did.

Twilight came, and there was still no sight of him. She had no way of knowing whether he was dead or injured or needed help.

Cassie Lee prodded a stick against a log, and long flames shot up, finally adjusting into an even yellow. She sang spirituals *sotto voce,* alternating her gaze between the fire's dancing shadows on the dark walls and the mouth of the cave. She tried hard to ignore the gnawing hunger that rivaled her fear as she rocked back and forth.

She'd grown used to this territory over the past month—the quiet nonexpectancy of it, where things grew and flourished unencumbered. The rush of the wind through the pines carrying a smell so fresh and clean. The coyote's distant lullaby, the hush of the land gone to sleep. Hawk's gentle snore. This country gave her a spiritual experience unlike any she'd ever felt in a slave church deep in the Georgia woods.

Here you were not called to account by other folks ruling your life. Here you were not jarred to duty by the slam of your door against the wall as the massa entered your room uninvited and entitled to take what he wanted. No constant demand to fetch, tend, clean, work, "do for me." Here no one called you lazy for resting, or stupid for dreaming, or heathen for praying, or sneaky for trying to decipher words in a speller, or sums on a piece of paper. Here nature accepted you for what you were. "No-good, no-count darkie" had never been uttered here. Cassie Lee had been seduced by this strange and new land. For the very first time, Cassie Lee felt *truly* free. Free to do and to be.

"The Lord didn't bring me this far jus' to leave me," she said aloud, and thought, I'll just go on. Like all the black folks who run north—I'll make a way out of no way. I'll get on that horse and ride until I come upon folk or die.

With freedom came responsibility and choice. She could choose what to do. And if she died, she would die free.

Her thoughts were interrupted by the sound of muffled footsteps scraping along the edge of the cave. Man or beast? Her heart leapt to her throat. Her eyes fixed to the bend near the opening. When Hawk came into full view, Cassie Lee sprang to him and jumped into his arms, almost knocking him over.

"Oh, God, I thought you was dead!" She hung around his neck, and again he didn't react. She unfastened herself from his tall frame. "Sorry. I was worried."

"Fish!" he said, ignoring her outburst and holding out the six of them twined in a row.

"Oh, goody. I got somethin' special too." She whipped back the skillet cover. "Biscuits. I saved the flour for this special meal. Since we'll be in Exum in two nights." She hunched her shoulders.

"Good." He eased his pack from his back. "You know how long it's been since I had fish?"

"You like fish?" She scriggled up her nose. "I didn't like it much on the planta—back there."

"Well, Cassie Lee, you in for a treat. Fresh trout." He split, gutted, and spliced the fish over the hardwood fire. "I heard you singin' when I came in."

"Yeah, songs from my 'other life.'"

As they cooked and after they ate, Hawk joined in and sang those spirituals he remembered until only the lateness of the hour and the crackle of the fire lay between them.

"I guess you think I'ma bit cold for not feeling nothin' for that dead man," Cassie Lee said, unable to speak the name of Charles Whedoe, dead and unmourned by her.

"I speck you got your reasons. He weren't nothin' to me."

"How'd you know he was gon try something?"

"Instinct." He gulped coffee before continuing, "A man don't hire two men to track you cross country to ask how your trip is goin'."

"You saved my life—again."

"Jus' doin' my job is all." He accepted the stream of hot, brown liquid she poured into his nearly empty cup.

She settled in beside him, facing the fire. Through the silence, again, she hoped Exum was like Hawk. She felt an easy comfortableness with him, even if he didn't talk much. He wasn't like any man she had ever met before, and maybe if he didn't have a wife and son, and she wasn't going to get married, things would be different. Even though he didn't say, she knew they shared some things.

"You used to be a slave," Cassie Lee said quietly.

"Long time ago." He stared into the flames. "Seems like a lifetime ago. I'd forget it all together if it weren't for my mother. She was a good woman. Tall, proud, half Indian—Cherokee. Didn't know my father,

40

some pitch-black buck most likely. They worked my mama so hard one winter she took sick, died in the spring. She was never quite right after they sold off my brother and sister anyways. With a bunk free, they dumped Exum in the cabin with the rest of us. Seems he got a little closer to his massa-father than his nonslave children and the wife could cotton to. So she had him sold while his father was on a gambling binge in town. He and his dad used to frequent those halls. They had a close relationship, according to Exum. I think a lot of his wild ways is him tryin' to be like his old man—his way of stayin' close to him. Exum don't say so, but he was hurt his father didn't come after him. But it didn't matter no how 'cause he was happy-go-lucky all the time. Had no reason, he was a slave too. Least his body was, but not his mind." He stopped himself. "He'll tell you all the details."

"You tell me, Hawk."

"Solomon." Her eyes knitted together in a question. "My given name is Solomon." He didn't know why he told her.

"Like the king—strong, proud." She watched the golden flames lap at his chiseled features. "Where did Hawk come from?"

"When I got out here I saw this bird flying high and free. I thought it was a hawk. So I took that name. Kept it even when I found out it was a eagle."

"Solomon. I like that."

"No one calls me that," he snapped, regretting and feeling oddly strange sharing this bit of history with her. "My mother, then Exum is all." For once, he felt that he was talking too much instead of her. They fell into a brief silence.

"So Exum's like me, my body was a slave but not my spirit. After making this trip, I know I can handle anything."

"Keep that in mind when you meet Exum." An unfamiliar feeling set in on him, one he had never felt before and couldn't identify.

On the one hand, it was like leading this lamb to slaughter, but he picked her because she could handle herself and apparently she was no virgin. Even Whedoe's wife knew about them. But getting to know her over these past few months, he knew her to be young and inexperienced in the ways of the world, and not at all what she appeared.

On the other hand, Exum must be good and tired of those seven

41

whores by now. Maybe when he saw her, he'd realize that he had a chance at something decent. A chance to make the type of home that neither of them had. In Cassie Lee, he'd have a partner who would love and be true to only him, and wanted to build a home with curtains, and children, and biscuits, and church on Sundays. Exum and Cassie Lee were as rough as a core blasted from the mountains, but with a little cultivation, together they could make a real go of it.

*   *   *   *   *   *   *   *   *   *   *   *

The day was bright and crisp as the reverend's words pirouetted above the white mourners inside the cemetery fence. The slaves were positioned beyond the iron gates. It was a solemn occasion as the body of Charles Whedoe was lowered into the freshly turned earth. Emily's tears were accompanied by fits of fainting and fighting anyone who tried to keep her from the coffin of her beloved son, while the wife of the deceased hid her grief discreetly behind the black veil that covered her entire face.

Atticus Whedoe stood stoically by his wife, embarrassment replaced with a compilation of emotions—grief, remorse, guilt. He had prayed that this slave girl would get out of reach to California. He should have prayed that his son would come to his senses. He couldn't even recall if he had ever known who she was, but she had grabbed Charles' attention and loyalty the way he, his own father, never could. It was all over. Atticus and this slave girl had more in common than they realized. They shared the same sentiment about Charles Whedoe—relief.

Two weeks later, Atticus Whedoe escorted his wife into the sheriff's office.

"I want to swear out a warrant for a man named Hawk, for the murder of Charles Whedoe," Emily recited rigidly as the two men exchanged weary glances, knowing that Taggert had reported the shooting had been self-defense.

"He may be in California or Oregon, he mentioned Oregon when he bought—that—girl. He's big, black, got long hair, a beard. Do you hear me, sheriff?"

"Yes, ma'am," the sheriff said, looking at an exasperated Atticus who had turned to look out the window, detaching himself from his wife's obsession. She and her son were more alike than he remembered.

The sheriff pulled out a piece of paper, deciding to indulge Emily Whedoe. He knew that west of the Mississippi River was still uncharted territory. He knew few bounty hunters who'd risk getting scalped by Indians, and none who had either the money to travel by ship or the patience to hook up with a wagon train going west to find some nigger. He knew there would be many who would kill a nigger and try to pass him off as this Hawk, and Mrs. Emily Whedoe alone would be responsible for the identifying. But maybe in a perverse way that was her plan—to slowly and systematically rid the South of as many black men as she could. Her own private quest was to kill these darkies and honor the memory of her fair son.

"How much is the reward?" the sheriff asked.

Emily Whedoe narrowed her gaze and said, "$5,000, dead or alive."

* * * * * * * * * * * * *

It was a dreary, overcast day when the bedraggled pair meandered down the mud-filled streets. They had generated a crowd that followed them to the front of a saloon. Solomon only glanced at Cassie Lee who seemed oddly excited, probably thinking that these were her husband-to-be's friends welcoming her, although they were more uncouth than she imagined.

In her excitement she looked over at Solomon, but he wouldn't return her gaze. He had been aloof on that last night, more like he'd been when they first started out and were strangers. He was quiet, probably anxious to see his wife and son.

"Oh, my God!" Exum had been summoned out by the shouting crowd. He stuffed his shirt into his pants and smoothed back his curly black hair. "Ain't she pretty?" he asked of the crowd as he held out his hand to her. "My own little tar baby."

Cassie Lee's smile froze, and Solomon groaned and looked skyward.

"You done good, Hawk," Exum said. "She's worth the wait."

"Come here," Solomon said to Exum as some of the girls led a reluctant Cassie Lee into the bar. "She's a nice girl, Exum. Try to act like you got some sense."

"Hawk, you come for dinner some night?" Cassie Lee managed before the ladies dragged her inside.

"Dinner?" Exum roared with laughter. "Yeah, we gonna be eatin' alright."

"Exum. You listenin'? She's decent—"

"Man, I didn't ask for no 'decent' girl. I asked for ass, tits, and color. Ah, I get it!" A sly smile claimed his face. "Did you get a little some on the trail? How is she?"

"Goodbye, Exum." Solomon walked off in disgust.

"Come on. Least have a drink!" Exum called after his friend.

"I'm getting supplies and goin' home," Solomon yelled over his shoulder without looking back. If he had, he would have seen a bewildered Cassie Lee standing in the window.

"C'mon honey," said the lady with blazing red hair as she led Cassie Lee away from the window. "My name is Elsie," answering Cassie Lee's quizzical gaze. "Let's get you some decent clothes."

"Bring my new meat over here!" Exum shouted, patting the seat beside him as he resumed his poker game. "Where you takin' my woman?"

"Keep your shirt on, Exum," Elsie said as she led the perplexed girl up the steps.

"I wanna see her without a shirt," Exum laughed and slapped his knee to the joy of his audience.

"He's more bark than bite, honey," Elsie whispered, as she entered her second floor room and closed the door. "My Lord, those clothes are a sight. Lemme see what I can rustle you up to wear."

As Elsie began pulling clothes out of her wardrobe, Cassie Lee went over to the window and saw Solomon's horse standing outside the general store. In her mind, she'd been calling him Solomon once he shared himself with her.

"Look!" Elsie proudly displayed her finest clothes on the bed. "Any color you want. Pick one."

"Oooh." Cassie Lee eyed the garish, gaudy dresses with the baubles and feathers hanging off of them.

44

"The other girls'll come in to meet you when they get up. It's early yet." Cassie Lee's eyes didn't leave the sight of the devil's painted clothes.

"Where's the tops?"

Elsie howled with laughter, causing Cassie Lee to jump. "Girl, you are a card. Lemme help you." She moved toward Cassie Lee, who backed away.

"I jus' need regular clothes, nothin' fancy. You can catch your death of cold in these."

"You ain't in them long if you lucky," Elsie said, laughing drool that she wiped away with the back of her hand. "Exum likes his women dolled up."

Cassie Lee took offense at the woman and her statement. "I'ma jus' leave these until we go home."

"Home?" Elsie laughed uproariously. "This is home, honey."

"No." Cassie Lee looked around her. "I mean a house with two floors and windows and curtains where we can have Hawk and his family for dinner."

Elsie momentarily stopped, eyed the girl and began chuckling. "What the hell kinda lies did he tell you on the trail? There ain't no house with floors and curtains, and Hawk ain't got no family."

"But he said he had—"

"Had. Yeah. He had a wife and a son, died some years back of the fever or froze or somethin'. He put her up on stilts and lit her afire, 'cause she was Indian and that's the way they do it. Exum says you can still see the four stakes left in the ground on account of the snow kept them from burning all the way. Hawk comes to town 'bout three times a year if the snow ain't too bad, and let's me and China-girl comfort him." She winked, before continuing, "But he don't talk about his family. Hell, he don't talk at all much. But he's a real gentleman when it comes to lovin', you know?"

"No, I don't." Cassie Lee didn't want to hear this.

"Well, maybe you'll get lucky." She laughed loudly and continued, "Usually big men like Hawk got them li'l peckers, but Hawk got the biggest one I ever seen—and I seen aplenty, honey." She hunched over the stunned girl. "Hawk musta been standing first in line when God was passing out—"

"Elsie!!" Exum yelled up the stairs. "Where's my woman?"

A flushed and mortified Cassie Lee went to the window to escape the woman's testimony on Hawk's private parts and Exum's screaming up the stairs. Was she in Sodom? But I'ma free, she kept reminding herself. She looked down at the general store, and Solomon packing her horse with supplies. She watched him scrape mud from his boots, remembering how much he hated that. He glanced toward the direction of the saloon, then hopped up onto Black. He guided his pack horse down the street and never looked back, leaving her to figure out Exum—the man and the town—and why he had lied about his family.

Chapter IV

"I'ma cut you like a pig what's ready for roastin'!" Cassie Lee shouted, wielding her razor in the air, and stopping Exum in his tracks. The crowd in the doorway egged him on.

"Now come on, honey. It's been two weeks, and it's time for me to get what's rightfully mine."

"Keep away from me." She jumped up onto the cot in her little room so she could go for his jugular. "I was a man's whore one time and had no say. It ain't never gon happen to me again. I'ma kill you first, so help me God."

Her eyes blazed crazily, but Exum took a chance to save face. He lunged at her, and Cassie Lee swiped him with the razor. Red spewed from his cheek.

"Shit! This crazy bitch cut me!" Exum grabbed his face, not believing that any woman would deny him. He had looks, money, and power. "Solomon picked me a crazy whore!"

Exum's eyes locked with Cassie Lee's, and he could see she meant to finish him off.

"Go head, rape me like the massa raped your mama!"

Her head split and her body went flying, then crashed against the wall. The razor flung from her hand. Although dazed from the blow, she scrambled to recover her weapon. He could have stepped on her wrist, but he let her retrieve the steel blade and watched her inch her body up against the rough boards of the room. She held it precariously as her head continued to spin and she slid down the wall.

"Ain't no piece of ass worth tarnishing my pretty face," Exum spat at the crumpled girl slumped on the floor.

"Lemme see, baby," Elsie said to Cassie Lee, a towel in her hand to tend her bruised face and busted lip.

"Get that crazy bitch outta here!" Exum shouted.

"Exum, you can't mean that," Elsie said. "It's the dead of winter. She'll die."

"Better winter kill her than me. Those are her choices." He yanked the towel from Elsie's hands. "And death to anybody who helps her." Exum glared at Elsie.

"I want you to get the hell outta here in fifteen minutes," he ordered down to Cassie Lee.

Cassie Lee tried to focus, but passed out.

* * * * * * * * * * * *

The coldness from the wet snow had awakened her. She looked at the whiteness streaked with red. Blood eked from her mouth. She looked into the brightness of the sun and wondered how long she had been lying there. Her bear coat and the contents of her slave satchel were strewn about the street. She eased her aching body against the side of the alley where she'd been discarded. She didn't know what time it was, but from the shine of the sun and the lack of activity, it must have been seven or eight o'clock in the morning, which was early for the town of Exum.

She was alone, stranded in an unforgiving land with nowhere to go. She had volunteered to come, trading a plantation-hell for a free-hell. Abandoned in a place with no reality, no morals, no values—Sodom and Gomorrah. She looked to the right and then the left, and had no idea which way was out, or to Solomon. According to Elsie, only Exum knew where Hawk lived, and he had only been there once.

Cassie Lee was mad, hurt, hungry, tired, and wanted to cry. She gathered a handful of snow to suck. Even it was dirty. "Oh, God, deliver me from evil," she said, asking for God's mercy but getting nothing back but the devil's laugh.

A figure blocked out the sunlight, handed her a piece of cooked meat, and ran, but not before Cassie Lee realized who it was. It was the little girl she had helped the week before when some men were picking on her in the middle of the street. They called her "chink" and "yellow boy," taunting her, making sport of the laundry she carried. Cassie Lee had intercepted the clothes and returned them with a hug to the little girl before she fixed her wrath on the grown white men. When she turned back to face the little girl, she had run, just as she had today.

"Cast your bread upon the water and it comes back to you," Cassie Lee said, chuckling wryly before painfully devouring the savory meat.

*   *   *   *   *   *   *   *   *   *   *   *

Cassie Lee fashioned boxes behind the general store and lived there at night. She tried to find work, but Exum's threat rang in everyone's ears. She resorted to eating discarded food, and often stared out over the mountains wondering if that was the right direction to the next town. No one would tell her. No one would take her. No one would talk to her. She could steal a horse, but she would be shot dead the next day when they tracked her in the deep snow.

Now, besides drinking and whoring, Exum Taylor added watching Cassie Lee's dismal fate to his list of pleasures. Expecting her to come crawling back to him, begging him to take her back any time now. Exum didn't know his opposition.

She walked around town and asked for work, never begged. She took the broom from just inside the door and began sweeping out the general store for free. Broady would shoo her away for fear that Exum would see her, buying her off with goods if she stayed away. She moved her makeshift house down near the stable so she could keep getting goods from Broady, and hopefully hear about the next towns beyond Exum and how to get there when the spring thaw came. All she heard about was San Francisco, with hills, hotels and opportunities abounding, but it all seemed way beyond Cassie Lee's immediate reach.

One day after she finished washing out her other shirt and pants at the stable pump, the little China girl stopped instead of just leaving the food.

"Hello," Cassie Lee said to the little girl, who did not respond, but just watched. "Thank you for leavin' me the fruit and meats. It's real good." No response. "Can you understand me?" Cassie Lee asked with a smile, and the little girl summoned Cassie Lee to follow her.

The little girl moved quickly behind buildings down to the outskirts of town to a section that Cassie Lee didn't even know existed. There were about four houses circling an outer area filled with Chinese people. The strange chattering assaulted Cassie Lee's ears, but the smell of delicious grilled meats and vegetables filled her nose, and the smell of clean . . . soap and boiling water.

The little girl pushed open the door to one of the cabins onto family sitting in the round. Cassie Lee felt immediately huge and self-conscious.

"My family," the little girl finally spoke, giving the names of people Cassie Lee knew she would never remember. "My name is Kwan," the little girl said to her. Cassie Lee smiled. "I am a boy." They all laughed. "For your kindness to me, we want you for dinner."

Cassie Lee, not knowing much about the Chinese, hoped they weren't the ones who ate people. Her fears were allayed once a sumptuous meal was served and consumed with delicious hot tea.

She didn't understand a word, but was struck by the warmth of these people and the fact that they were all together living with grandparents when Cassie Lee didn't even know who her mother and father were. She would never have children, and therefore, never be a grandparent. Was happiness always to elude her? She began to cry, alarming her hosts.

"I'ma sorry. I feel like a fool," she said, to which Kwan had no translation for his family. "I'ma go." She stood. "Much obliged." She bowed and spoke too loudly, trying to compensate for not speaking their language.

"You must stay," Kwan said.

"Oh, no—"

"You can stay there." Kwan pointed to a cot against the wall near the window, and the big kettles of boiling water.

"No. You been very kind—"

"You stay here, and you work here." He smiled a toothless grin.

"Work?" It was music to her ears.

"We give you money. Not much money, but money so you can go back to your family."

Cassie Lee bit back tears. Not because she had no family, but because she had a chance. A chance to make money, buy a horse, and follow somebody to the next town. This was her way out.

"The Lord do provide," she said, wet standing in her eyes as she twirled her cowrie cross.

"You stay? We need you too," Kwan said as the others nodded in agreement.

* * * * * * * * * * * *

Cassie Lee stirred the boiling clothes in the huge cauldrons by day and ate with the family in the evenings, excusing herself when they began their prayers and rituals at night. She had tried the pungent smoke they inhaled from the funny-looking pipe, but it made her dizzy and sick to her stomach—probably because she wasn't Chinese.

One day when she was lifting a sheet from the boiling kettle, Chang, Kwan's older brother, came to help her as usual. He seldom said anything, just gave a smile followed by a deep, intense gaze that always made Cassie Lee chuckle.

Despite the month she'd been with the family, their language totally eluded her. When Kwan was not around to interpret for her, Mama and Papa-san and the rest just gestured. Cassie Lee knew her routine now, so talking was unnecessary. She didn't plan to be here long enough to learn the language, and didn't expect to ever use it beyond Exum. She didn't need to speak the dialect to know that Mai Ling of the fourth house liked Chang, and that the hateful looks she shot Cassie Lee were all wasted effort. Of the men Cassie Lee would ever consider pairing up with, none would ever be white or Chinese.

With her first wages, Cassie Lee bought three chickens from Kung Shu of the second house and began delivering the eggs early in the morning to the Chow House and private homes before she started her laundry work. After supper, when she left the Wongs to their family ways, she tended the small plot of garden they'd given her in the hot house behind the room they slept in.

"Slaves ain't spose to dream," Nubby's words rang in her ears as Cassie Lee cultivated her plants. Of all the things she overheard at the stable and around town as she went quietly about her duties, the one about boarding houses springing up all around San Francisco struck a cord with her. If the white folks were staying in those places instead of hotels, then surely black folks would need them too. Not just a place to stay for one night, but to stay for weeks at a time. Not just to sleep in, but to eat in too. It was perfect. She could get a house with an upstairs, with three bedrooms, and she would grow her vegetables, cook them, and earn money for doing the things she enjoyed doing anyway. It would be like having your own family, she thought. She'd make the place so clean and the food so good that they would never want to leave.

So as she tended her crops for sale, Cassie Lee pretended that she was going to use them to make meals for her own guests who were waiting for her in her boarding house. It would be a pretty house, yellow like sunshine, and she would fill it with respectable black people who would make a fuss over her efforts and pay her well. These thoughts kept Cassie Lee company after she had delivered eggs early in the morning, sweated in the laundry at mid-morning, delivered clean-smelling sheets in the afternoon, fed her chickens, and swallowed some supper in the evening before going out back and coaxing her plants into bearing wonderful vegetables.

Her imagination was hungry for any morsel of information she could use as fodder for her new dream; anything to catapult her from the reality of where she was, to someplace else. At spring thaw, San Francisco, the city by the water, was her destination where she could get away from Exum—the town and the man—and start her new life. Finally, Cassie Lee had someplace to run to, nothing to hide, and something to be—an owner of her own boarding house.

These dreams were the only companions she needed, comforting her as she ended each day of her multiple tasks. She would not glance at the back of the laundry, where the entire family lived in one big room with no privacy. It reminded her of the slave quarters, except at least the Chinese were all related. She was the only one with a cot at the front of the laundry near the steaming kettles that made deliciously thick condensation on the windows at night. Sometimes after she had dressed for bed and uncoiled her hair so one long braid fell down her back, she wrote her name in the window and it shimmered against the moonlight. She smiled at her name in the lunar spotlight, then stopped—she didn't know how to spell Solomon.

* * * * * * * * * * * * *

It was during one of her early morning egg deliveries that Cassie Lee ran into Exum for the first time since he'd kicked her out.

"Black China girl," Exum said, as she walked up the steps to the general store. "With your little black pajama set on." He eyed her mandarin-collared top with the slant frock closures.

"What you want, Exum?" she said, turning her full body to him, looking him dead in the eye. The scar she'd left on his face was still raised, red, and ugly.

"You coulda had it all." He smiled expansively. "I set Zora up in her own house. She got her own girls, runs it all—"

"I'ma sure you get your piece of the pie." She rolled her eyes and turned to go.

" 'Course I do. I'ma business man, and you didn't take advantage of the situation. No. Instead you want to labor in a laundry, peddle eggs and vegetables."

"It's honest work," she drawled. "I'ma not askin' you for nothin'."

"Yeah, you owe me the $1,000 dollars I spent on your—"

"You best be forgettin' that, Exum. That money spent and gon." She pushed past a smiling Broady who was standing in the doorway enjoying her sassy exchange.

"What you grinnin' at?" Exum snapped at Broady. "I'ma well rid of that crazy hellion." He kicked his horse and galloped off toward the edge of town to make his opium connection for the Chinese miners.

That Cassie Lee was a ponder to him. Exum had never hit a woman before. Never had to. He loved women of all sizes and shapes, and they loved him. In all his years, he never paid for loving—young, old, married or not, they all responded to his good looks, easy charm, and recklessness. Whether banker's daughters or preacher's wives, he never had to force himself on any female. Since he was a boy, he remembered lying awake and listening to the muffled sounds and animal-like grunts of

53

men pleasuring women. Long after Solomon had turned his back to go to sleep, he delighted in watching the copulating couples get the only pleasure out of slavery they could. If he was lucky, a stream of light would allow him to see the face of the woman the moment her man set her free beyond the crowded cabin. He was about twelve when he put that expression on fourteen-year-old Lottie's face. She had lured him into the barn, telling him how she had been watching him and how he was big for his age as she shimmied out of her second-hand dress and exposed her breasts while watching Exum's nature rise. "You got de devil in dem pants," she had said. As he stroked, kissed, and devoured her taut velvet body, he slid his fingers into her throbbing, moist forest and said, "Now, I'ma gon put de devil in you." He got his first taste of power as he witnessed that gleeful expression cover Lottie's face, transporting her from slave gal to the Queen of Sheba. Exum was hooked on power and pleasure, and took to giving it as freely as his time would allow. By the time he was fifteen, he had had all the McArdle slave women except for the old and infirm, including two white girls who tasted and taught him things he would have never imagined in all his born days.

It was the story of his life. Exum Taylor was always sought out and never refused, so when Cassie Lee rejected his advances, it shocked him. When she jumped at him with a knife, it startled, then angered him beyond redemption. As a reflex, he slapped her. Cassie Lee continued to puzzle him something powerful. As he watched her over the past month, the confusion turned into a begrudging respect, like a man would have for another man who bested him. Whether it was bravery or stupidity, this slave gal had more regard for herself than any woman he had ever known—the rich or the common. He didn't like her, he told himself because he couldn't get a bead on her. She disarmed him, and made him feel like a young pup starting out, instead of the seasoned womanizer he prided himself in being. Like her or not, he had to admit, Cassie Lee was a hell of a woman.

He noticed that the townspeople of Exum took their cues from him. They knew him to be both treacherously moody and volatile—heating up and cooling down, depending on the situation. None were willing to jeopardize their life and limb for this girl, but when they saw that Exum took to tolerating her until she came to her senses and went back to him, they were civil toward her. They accepted her laundry deliveries. Bought her eggs and the most beautiful vegetables this territory had ever seen. But it was all business, not friendship they gave her—nothing more.

* * * * * * * * * * * *

Cassie Lee swirled another sheet in the sweltering pot, while the overattentive Chang smiled and buzzed around her. As she wiped her brow, she thought she saw a familiar image in the distance.

"Solomon?" she said, almost to herself.

She didn't trust her eyes through the steam as the imposing figure just stood in front of the window, waiting to be seen. With his duster almost grazing the ground, his hat cocked over his eyes, he looked left, then right, then straight ahead as his presence in the Oriental community caused quite a commotion.

"Solomon." Cassie Lee slammed open the door and ran out to him. When he made no outward movement of recognition, she slowed to a walk. "Hello."

"Heard what happened. You alright?" said he.

"Yeah. I'ma black China girl." She smiled, fingering Nubby's cross nervously, and slooping her hair behind her ear.

"Was that your China boy?"

"Who? Chang?" She almost told him the truth exposing him for the nuisance he was, but she didn't appreciate Solomon's tone, and decided that she would play with him. She didn't know why she wanted too. "He's no worse than Exum, I spose."

"Might as well get your things," he said, as he turned and began walking away.

"For what?" She let the cross rest around her neck.

"Guess I got to figure out what to do with you."

"What to do with me? Like I'ma a dog that needs caring for?" She folded her arms across her chest. "I'ma not no concern of yours."

When he didn't stop walking, she ran around in front of him, halting him in his tracks, and said, "'Sides, I remember what happened the last time I followed you somewhere. I'ma doin' fine on my own. I got a job and a way out of here come spring thaw." She folded her arms again.

55

"Suit yourself." He glanced at her as he rotated his thin, brown cigar between his lips.

"Why is it you can't never look at me? You didn't look at me hardly at all on the trail—" She stopped herself. She hated whiners, and the Whedoe plantation was full of them. "You can tell me one thing." When he didn't comment, she asked, "Which is the way outta here?"

He pointed. "Prince River is about one hundred miles, but it's no better than here. River Bend is about two hundred miles due south."

"Much obliged."

"Need anything? Money?"

"I'ma makin' my own."

"Suit yourself." He started to walk off again.

"You make sure you come see me in San Francisco. I'ma have me a boarding house called Cassie Lee's. It's gon be yella with white trim."

"If'n I'ma ever down that way, maybe I'll drop in." He touched his hat with polite finality.

"You do that." She began walking away from him, then stopped and spun around. "Which way do you live, Solomon?"

He stopped and turned slowly into the sound of her calling his given name. "Due north." They stood facing each other for only a moment. "Good luck to you, Cassie Lee." He turned and walked out of her life— again.

* * * * * * * * * * * *

Cassie Lee worked so hard during the day that she nearly passed out at night from exhaustion, with hardly enough time to think on her boarding house. On this night she felt a presence over her bed, and in the limbo between asleep and awake she saw a male figure standing over her bed.

"Solomon?" she said softly. The man lunged at her and put his hand over her mouth, shocking her fully awake. She struggled before the moon caught his features.

"Chang, what you doin'?" She scrambled loose and backed herself against the wall.

"Me, my turn," he said as he began to remove his clothes.

Cassie Lee threw soap shavings in his face and screamed, waking the entire house and the other three houses as she fought him. His breath was thick with that sickening odor from the pipe.

The Wongs came in from the other room, pulled Chang from her, and began to smack and hit her instead of their beloved son. They were yelling in high pitches with angry looks and snarled expressions as they threw Cassie Lee, her coat, and her satchel out into the courtyard. Through her dazed shock, Cassie Lee saw Mai Ling smile smugly before running to comfort Chang.

Some of the women began to chase her as she scuffled for her belongings—confused, bleeding, and wondering what she did to deserve such treatment. As she backed away she caught a glimpse of Kwan in the doorway as he quietly watched the melee.

Cassie Lee shrouded her bear coat around herself as she limped up the main street of Exum, past the few respectable residents fast asleep in comfort. She hobbled past the closed general store dressed for Christmas with striped peppermint sticks, small blackboards, bolts of colorful material, and a ten-dollar red sled with a big white bow decorating the window. She continued past the Chow House where she delivered vegetables and eggs, past Madame Zora's with its red lantern hanging by the door, past Exum's boisterous saloon. She dodged a man who was thrown out onto the street, where he landed in the dirty, muddy snow. She looked into the saloon's window and saw the ladies in their garish outfits with feathers and flounces sitting on men's laps, kissing them while allowing them to run their rough hands up stockinged thighs to disappear unseen.

The smell of smoke and stale liquor disturbed her senses, and Cassie Lee forged on. It would be so easy to just go in and let Exum take care of her. But she couldn't. She wouldn't give Exum the satisfaction of knowing she failed, and that the Chinese had thrown her out—for what?

Since Solomon's visit two weeks ago, they had begun treating her differently. Subtle things. Chang no longer smiled, but ogled her the way the ole massa had. Mai Ling watched them both, and whispered things to him as he leered at Cassie Lee. The family fell silent when she entered the back room for meals. She began eating alone on her cot, and when Kwan would join her, he was called away. She did most of the delivering and washing by herself, and chalked up the change in the Wong family to their increase in smoking that dried plant and burning the incense that gave her a headache. She supposed she would never know why Chang attacked her.

These thoughts, the pain of a busted lip—again, and a spinning head kept her company as she walked out of town. Again with nowhere to go and no place to hide, not even for the night, she trudged and trudged through thigh-high snow into the enveloping gray darkness. Her feet grew frozen and brittle, and finally she collapsed from exhaustion.

She awakened when the frigid sunlight kissed her face. Her eyes blinked open, and the sight of tall pines both comforted and frightened her. She was stiff with cold but rolled over on her stomach, crawling before she struggled up. The arctic air stung her nostrils, setting fire to her lungs, and her eyes leaked moisture involuntarily. She clutched her satchel and stroked her cross as she listened to the eerie, smothering quiet. The night's snowfall had covered her tracks. She was lost and alone in this blinding wilderness.

"Solomon!" she cried and heard her own voice bounce back and mock her. "Solomon!! Solomon!!"

She knew they would be the last words she ever spoke—her last prayer.

Chapter V

His snowshoes left crisscrossed marks across the white snow as he finished checking his traps and hoisted the beavers over his shoulder. It was then that he saw it. Something slumped down at the bottom of the gorge, a dead animal. As he continued on, he hoped it had frozen to death; otherwise it meant that some intruder had invaded his world. He hadn't heard a shot, he realized. He stopped in his tracks. Maybe he should check it out. He didn't want any surprise visitors in his mountains.

Solomon negotiated the steep incline, dropped his beavers, and poised his gun as he approached the animal—bear fur with no head. He kicked the lump with his foot—no movement. No trail of blood. And then he saw the satchel. He dropped to his knees and rolled her over.

"Cassie Lee?" She was blue with cold.

* * * * * * * * * * * *

Her eyes fluttered open and adjusted to the darkness set off by the glow of a blazing fire. The room was swathed in a golden patina with a warm, cushioned quiet, buffered by hewed timbers and animals skins. Earthy smells mingled with coffee, tobacco, simmering soup, and— apples. Cassie Lee couldn't move for the heavy furs heaped on her.

Flames flickered at the foot of the bed and could be seen in broken images on the other side of the table and chairs as they licked up the sides of the stone fireplace. She saw no one, but she felt safe and comfortable. Maybe she was in heaven, she thought, as she drifted off to sleep again.

A cool hand across her forehead awakened her. She jumped and started to scream at the sight of a man towering over her.

"It's me, Cassie Lee."

"Solomon?"

"Yes."

"Am I dead?" she asked quietly.

"No."

"What happened?"

"You tell me." He wrung out the cloth and placed it on her forehead again. "I found you frozen in the snow. You hungry? I got some broth." She shook her head in answer.

He smiled at her. He looked so handsome, with the reflected embers dancing in his face and his shirt sleeves rolled up to his elbows. She had always done the tending to. Never been cared for by anybody. It felt nice.

The next day, weak but fully conscious, Cassie Lee sat up in bed on a hill of fur as she received spoonfuls of the warm broth Solomon had prepared. The cabin came into full view, one big room with the front door opposite the huge stone fireplace. The centerpiece was a table with chairs—just two. Behind the door was the big bed cornered against the wall; directly across from it, a cast iron stove, then a long, narrow table and open shelves housing pots, pans, and dishes. To the right, well-worn books were raised on planks of wood. To the left was a small area before the trap door to the root cellar. Next to the door, the only window of the cabin—shuttered from both inside and out—rendered a permanent darkness. All manner of things and tools hung from the ceiling rafters. It was sparse, functional, comfortable, straightforward—it sang of Solomon.

Upon returning to his cabin the following day, he smelled something deliciously unfamiliar in the air. He checked on Black before opening his cabin door to find Cassie Lee setting the table.

"What you doin' up?" he asked

"I'ma fine. I can't lay there forever. 'Sides, I need the practice cooking for my boarding house." He set his pelts down by the root cellar door. "C'mon and eat while it's hot." She spooned the thick, viscous stew topped with dumplings onto his plate.

He removed his coat, but not his eyes from the mouth-watering meal at his table, as Cassie Lee added, "You can wash your hands over there in the bucket."

Solomon looked at his hands and saw nothing wrong with them, but did as she suggested. He sat, endured her short prayer of thanks, and then devoured the tasty meal, wondering how she made it with the same ingredients he had.

Over the next few days, they began to settle in. Solomon slept on the floor in front of the fireplace while she slept on the bed. He still went out every day to check on Black, whose barn was next to the cabin, and his traps. And he still looked forward to coming into a range where he could smell the food coming from his cabin and ponder what magic Cassie Lee had set to the meat and vegetables he provided.

These niceties had their price. He began washing his hands before meals and even his face in the mornings without being reminded. He balked when Cassie Lee asked that he clean his pelts outside instead of in the cabin where they slept and ate. Solomon didn't like it, but he did it. He even came home one day to find the door wide open.

"You gon be sick again in no time," he admonished her.

"Don't be silly. Fresh air kills germs," she said as she swept the dirt floor clean with the branch from a nearby pine tree.

Plantation ways, he thought, as he reluctantly chopped more wood for the fire because Cassie Lee had let all the accumulated heat escape while "airing-out" during the day.

To his list of usual supplies to get at Broady's in Exum, she added more flour, sugar, potatoes, turnips, carrots, a needle and thread, and soap.

"Black ain't no pack horse, Cassie Lee," he gruffed as he guided his horse down the familiar trail to Exum.

Broady made a comment about the increased supplies. Solomon answered with a stony stare and quiet lips.

Still, Solomon was getting used to having someone with him at his cabin. He was getting used to seeing the puff of smoke from his chimney in the distance and anticipating something good to eat; getting used to his shirts being washed and ironed. And at night, after supper, as he would oil his traps, sharpen his tools, clean his gun, roll his thin, brown cigars, or pour gunpowder into shells, he was getting used to her absent-minded humming as she would painstakingly mend his socks or sew a button on his shirt.

"You don't have to do that," he said.

"I know that," she beamed. "I want to practice for my boarding house."

"Suit yourself."

"What day you figure it is, Solomon?"

"Don't know."

"I figure it's Sunday. *Come . . . mm, mm . . . the river,*" she sang quietly. She remembered one of his favorite hymns from the trail. He stopped polishing his gun and stared into the fire, singing with her until they finished.

"How about another piece of apple pie?" she asked.

"All right." He ate amid her mild chatter.

"Solomon," she broached quietly. "Teach me to read."

"I don't rightly know if'n I can teach. My wife—"

"How did she learn, being Indian and all?"

"Missionary school at Fort Wilson. She taught me as I was learning her tongue."

"I can do my name some, but can you learn me all my letters? If'n I'ma have my own boarding house, I need to learn to read."

"I speck so."

Cassie Lee watched Solomon kneel in front of the planks by the fireplace to pick a book, not sure whether she was excited by him or the fact that she was finally going to learn to read. Being near him all the time like this evoked the same feelings she had for him on the trail. But now it wasn't just her heart and groin he warmed—it was her whole body.

* * * * * * * * * * * * *

"I'ma gonna turn in now," Cassie Lee said after closing the cover of the blue back speller, signaling the end of her lesson.

In all these weeks, Solomon never made any advances. He slept on the other side of the table on the floor directly in front of the fireplace.

62

"Goodnight. Damn!" He shook his finger. "Cut my finger!"

"Lemme see." She looked at it and wiped away the blood. "Not that bad." She plunged it into cold water to stop the bleeding and then applied pressure by holding his hand. "What you gon do without me?" She looked up into his eyes and asked, "What you gon to do with me, Solomon?"

Her eyes held his as she watched his light brown eyes travel from confusion to want. He reached up and caressed her cheek with the back of his fingers. She moved in closer to him, and he lifted her chin to kiss her lips—then hesitated. She kissed him, quick and tentative, and it seemed to shock him. Through the mutual awkwardness and fear she smiled, her doe-eyes vibrating with the fireplace's reflected light, and she kissed him again. This time he kissed her back—short kisses at first. Then more inclusive, more intensive as their bodies meshed, filling in any gaps between them.

She felt his strong shoulders. And the same hands that saved her life, fought for her, and cared for her, now explored her. Across her back, down her spine, cupping her behind, then up her spine again, squeezing her as fiercely as that grizzly did him on the trail. She couldn't kiss him hard enough, long enough . . . enough. She moaned with pleasure at the taste of him. She had kissed Jonah before, but he never made her feel like this. The soft firmness of Solomon's full lips, his tongue darting and probing, as his hands coveted her entire body. He was taking her to a place she had never been.

I could kiss him all day long, she thought.

In one swoop, he picked her up and carried her to his bed—to her bed—to their bed and laid her on the soft, yielding fur. Every fiber of her body tingled for him, and his hot hands seared her flesh. He peeled the clothes from her fawn-colored body, and she watched the delight in his eyes at the sight of her supple breasts. The heat from his intense gaze made her dark nipples quiver with anticipation. He tore his eyes from them and let them drift down her slender abdomen, resting finally at her curly triangle.

He shed his clothes, his massive ebony body silhouetted against the golden blaze of the fire. Then she saw the legendary muscle Elsie had told her about, the chocolate projectile she now only wanted for herself. When he lay beside her, she felt his swollen passion pulsating against her thigh.

63

She wasn't daunted. She craved him and desired him to massage the throbbing ache in her moist center. She stroked his back and felt the raised whelps forever etched into his flesh by an overseer's whip. He flinched.

"It's all right, Solomon," she drawled quietly, and the purr of her accent comforted him.

He kissed a trail down her neck and she giggled with delight, ceasing immediately as his tongue inhaled her ripe nipple. She gasped. It was the single, most exquisite feeling she had ever known. She thought she'd pass out from the sheer pleasure of it, as he exchanged one for the other. She wanted to watch his luscious lips devour, then flick the taunt tip. No, she wanted to close her eyes and savor the deliciousness of it. Torn between the two desires, his expert manipulation finally forced her eyes closed, to see only stars on their back lids. And when he wiped his fingers down her body, exploring the juicy readiness of her hairy canyon, she thought—I've touched the rim of heaven. Cassie Lee had *never* felt this way before, and was sure she would never feel this way again. She had never desired a man before—never craved him before. It was wonderfully strange.

In her inner frenzy, Cassie Lee sought his outward projection of passion and delighted in the feel of him in her hands. He moaned huskily as she intuitively stroked him as he did her.

"I don't want to hurt you, Cassie Lee," he breathed into her ear.

With those words, Cassie Lee recognized her Forever Man in the flesh. All of her childhood hopes and dreams collided and manufactured a Forever Man she could now touch, taste, tease, feel—and love.

"You won't, Solomon," she said, and the mere tenderness of his concern relaxed and opened her to the most magnificent of possibilities.

Unable to bear the undulating rhythm they had established, Solomon took himself from Cassie Lee's tender-tight grasp and slid himself, slowly, into her pulsating orifice. Cassie Lee reached her hand behind her to grasp the bar of the headboard so she could move against him. The rhythm intensified, and they exploded together in cascading spasms.

"Oh, Solomon, Solomon, Solomon, . . ." she whimpered in ecstasy, as he raised himself and delighted in watching his explosions echo through her. She lay beneath him as an empty pitcher, and he filled her with his being. What was him, what was them, became her, and she knew that from this day forward, Solomon Hawk would always be a part of her.

Cassie Lee cried, this time not from pain but joy. Freedom had gifted her again. Finally, she made love with a man she desired, of her own free will. At this pure, defining moment, Cassie Lee knew that if she never loved a man again, she had once loved and made love to a man named Solomon. He fed her hungry heart, quenched her thirsty soul, and purged and cleansed her soiled body, rendering any previous violations nonexistent. She had been a spiritual virgin until Solomon entered her walls of innocence and filled her with liquid rapture.

As she wrapped her legs around his waist, she thought, This is how it's supposed to be. If she couldn't have it this way every time—she would do without. The memory of this time, with this man, could never be duplicated or replaced.

"I didn't hurt you, did I?" he asked.

"No, Solomon." He moved and Cassie Lee held fast to him. "Don't leave me jus' yet." She squeezed him tightly with every love-starved pore of her body, enjoying the splendor of this miracle. A smiled tickled her lips. For the first time since she had known him, Solomon was sweating.

In her lifetime, Cassie Lee never thought she'd be free. She never thought she'd find her Forever Man. In this cabin in the Sierra mountains, she found him—truly found him.

From that night on, they shared the bed. Their days were full of activities and their nights full of passion. Cassie Lee loved the nearness of him, the scent of him, the power of him. She loved riding the crest of indescribable joy, weightless, floating on a cloud. By depositing a wealth of kisses along her lithe, nude body, Solomon launched her through the heavens. She touched down to earth only long enough to reciprocate his kiss, caress his back, and stroke the outward manifestation of his passion. He countered by inhaling her triangle and, thereby, launching her again, this time to the moon, then out of this world, where finally she exploded into a million pieces and became the sparkling stars that graced the velvet sky.

As she lay in his arms, she thought of how Solomon defined what she had been looking for all her life. As he filled her with the ebb and flow of his love, he created in her an omnipresent need for him as long as she breathed. They were like some ancient, immortal souls from a long-ago past life that had made a mystical connection and found their mates again. They had been together before, in some other time and place, and belonged together now. I wonder what Tante Fatima would say about that?, was her last thought as she drifted asleep in Solomon's protective arms.

* * * * * * * * * * * *

From bed Solomon watched Cassie Lee complete her morning ritual, cleansing her body with the snow she left in a bucket to thaw overnight. When she used the reflection from the glass of the window pane to twist her hair into a ball at the nape of her neck he said, "This is all I have for you, Cassie Lee." He offered her a huge, shiny green apple.

"What for?" She left the side of the fireplace and sat on the side of the bed.

"It's Christmas. Merry Christmas, Cassie Lee." She took the apple and caressed it. "Oh, Solomon, I don't got nothin' for you!"

"You give to me every day, Cassie Lee."

I love you is on the tip of his tongue, she thought, but said, "It's my pleasure. This is my first Christmas free."

"We gon to have to do something real special."

"Being with you is special enough."

"Nope." He hopped out of bed. "Get your coat on."

They went out into the crisp, bright sunshine and frolicked in the snow. They balled up the white and threw it at one another, made a snowman and snowwoman, and walked by the frozen river. Solomon cracked the ice with a branch he shot off with his gun, and pulled out two huge fish. Cassie Lee salvaged the branch, deciding that it would be their Christmas tree. They collapsed and rolled laughingly down a ravine and made love under her bear coat beneath the low, sweeping branches of a mammoth pine before they trudged home.

As Cassie Lee approached the cabin hugged by the base of the mountain on three sides, she understood why it was so well insulated and had only one window. She took the fish while Solomon went around to check on Black. As she entered the house she saw the remnants of the four charred wooden posts used to burn his wife and son long ago. They stood black and singed like a memorial in the pristine snow. She hoped his first wife approved of the way she was loving him now, she thought, as she removed her coat, then stoked and revived the dying fire. She commenced to gut the fish and prepare dinner, delighting in the feeling of this place.

This is what having roots was like, of belonging somewhere, of not needing to go anywhere because you were already where you wanted to be. Where you were supposed to be. Where your heart, soul, and body could rest and feel safe. She turned from her task.

"Ahhh!" a bloodcurdling scream bolted from Cassie Lee's body, summoning Solomon who crashed through the door, gun drawn, and saw an Indian facing her.

The Indian stood between her and Solomon, so she couldn't run to his side. She stood fastened to the dirt floor and then heard Solomon laugh instead of shoot. The Indian turned to Solomon, they embraced and exchanged foreign word greetings before the Indian pointed to Cassie Lee.

"It's all right, he's an old friend," Solomon said to Cassie Lee. Solomon lifted up his hands and pulled another chair from the rafters. The three of them sat at the table, enjoying a jovial visit and sumptuous meal. *

Since Cassie Lee was obliged to wait for Solomon to translate their conversation to her, she used the time to look at this man. It was the first time she had seen an Indian up close. He was a handsome cuss with smooth skin that had never seen a razor and long, flowing black hair made shiny by living alone, she suspected. His eyes were hauntingly beautiful, and his cheekbones as majestic as these mountains. He turned abruptly and said something directly to her, which made her flinch.

"He called you Black Deer Woman," Solomon said.

"Is that spose to be somethin' good?"

"It's high praise when Running Bear takes time to call you anythin'."

Running Bear lay in front of the blazing fire, and Cassie Lee in the arms of Solomon on their bed.

"Who is he, Solomon?" she whispered.

"My wife's brother." His lips brushed her forehead as he spoke. "We go huntin' four times a year. It's time for our winter hunt."

"When you leavin'?"

"Told him I'd catch him in the spring." He tightened his grip, and kissed her forehead goodnight.

Those words said I love you to Cassie Lee more than the words themselves and made her heart sprout wings. Solomon had tapped into a part of her she never knew existed—a capacity to love and be loved. In discovering him, she was discovering herself as well. Like walking around all your life using just one arm until someone comes along and shows you you've got another one, that's what Solomon did for her—and she would forever love him for the treasures he gave her. She melted into his muscled body and fell asleep with a smile gracing her full, wide lips.

* * * * * * * * * * * *

Solomon's second trip to Exum for supplies was far different from the first. Broady teased him about some of the items and the frequency, since he had just been there last month.

"Sheets? Like at Madame Zora's?" Broady tried to loosen up his customer to no avail.

Next to the gunpowder and tobacco Solomon added three shirts so Cassie Lee wouldn't have to wash so often, then placed on the counter a pretty, round looking-glass surrounded by a gold starburst frame.

"Now you talkin' money," Broady said to Solomon's silence. "You must got company of the female persuasion."

Solomon picked out a comb, brush, and soap and said, "Tally it up." He fixed his beady eyes on Broady and chewed nimbly on the stub of his thin, brown cigar, making Broady so uncomfortable that he had to add up the total three times.

He negotiated Black and his supplies back to his mountain sanctuary, anticipating the joy his gifts would bring Cassie Lee. "Oh, Solomon! It's beautiful!" Cassie Lee exclaimed, looking at her reflection in the mirror. "It's so fancy! Where we gon put it?" She flitted around the small cabin in a tither of excitement.

"Here." He took it from her, and hung it on a nail over by her clean-corner where she did her morning body washing.

"Perfect." She admired it and her image in it. "Can I take this with me to my boarding house?" she teased.

"It's yours, I give it to you, and this." He handed her the comb and brush set.

"Solomon! Is it my birthday or somethin', or you jus' tired of seeing me rake my hair with my fingers? All I really wanted was some green apples." She coyly sashayed up to him, but when she got close all the sass vanished. "Thank you, Solomon."

"You welcome." He cleared his throat nervously and asked, "What's for supper?"

"Solomon stew," Cassie Lee said with a grin. "Whatever Solomon kills for me to cook."

"Guess I better get busy." He grabbed his gun and Cassie Lee walked him to the door. The sunlight hit her face.

"I got bread risin'," she said.

"What's that rash on the side of your face?"

"It's the combination of our lovin' and your beard."

"Umm. I be back after while."

It took him no time to bag a rabbit, so he thought of Cassie Lee on the way back. She was sure excited about those little gifts, and that's what he liked about her. She was so giving and never expected anything in return. He had been partly chased to the mountains by other women's wants, needs, and expectations, especially after they claimed to love you. Cassie Lee wasn't like that. He trusted her—her caress, her words, her actions. He had never completely trusted a woman before—well, only once before, and never a black woman—but Cassie Lee was a woman worth knowing—worth her weight in gold.

"You gon call it Solomon stew at your boarding house?" he asked as she set the plate of piping hot, fragrant smelling food in front of him.

"Sure am." She smiled as she cut the still-warm bread. "Got to feed them somethin' else besides gravy. You gon come see me now." She loved playing with him.

She had just finished cleaning up the dishes when he came to her with a razor and lathered soap.

"Why don't you cut this beard offa me?"

"Really, Solomon?"

He sat down in the chair in front of the fire in answer.

She could not keep her eyes from his emerging, pitch-black face. "You a handsome man, Solomon Hawk."

That night, Solomon knelt beside her as she lay on the new sheets

69

and anointed her nude body with tiny, searing kisses. Her entire being quivered and quaked at his touch. As she writhed in anticipated consummation, he fluidly slid beneath her, jarring her from her celestial perch, a movement that placed her over him. She exploded almost immediately, looking down at his handsome, clean-shaven face. She collapsed to rest atop him.

"No rash this time?" he asked, his smiling lips nibbling her ear.

"No," she said breathlessly.

* * * * * * * * * * * *

Reading had taken a back seat to other activities. What had started as a simple shave evolved into her cutting his hair and trimming his fingernails, although she told him, "You on your own with them toenails."

He helped her soap up and wash her hair, cutting the final rinse with vinegar. She sat in front of the fire, towel-drying her black locks. Then Solomon brushed her hair before she braided it for the night.

Cassie Lee loved going out with him some days. As he checked his traps, she collected juniper berries for cooking and chewing, and pine cones for scenting the cabin. But it was the walks and being with him, often in companionable silence, that she relished. In his quiet company, she conjured up all sorts of plans for cleaning the cabin in the spring, probably while he went hunting with Running Bear. She would sweep the dirt floors clean, wash all the pelts, scrub down the timber walls, the stove, the hearth and fireplace, make curtains for the one window, and adorn the cabin with wildflowers—whatever they turned out to be.

One morning they had awakened after a fierce-sounding blizzard. Cassie Lee rolled over the mountain that·was Solomon's body to throw more wood on the fire, clean her teeth, and start the coffee. She absently opened the shutter, then the window for light. When she couldn't push the outside shutter any further, she opened the door onto a block of white.

"Oh my God, Solomon, look!" She shouted like an excited child as she ran her hands across the floor to ceiling cold. "We snowed in!"

"No, jus' got to dig out."

Solomon dug a tunnel up to the cabin's roof to make sure the chimney and stove pipe were clear. When he disappeared from view, Cassie Lee called up to him. He reached down and offered his hands, which she took, and he lifted her up onto the roof with him.

"Oh, my," Cassie Lee said as she witnessed the peaceful, insulated hush that only the aftermath of a snowy blizzard can produce. The ravines had been smoothed out, making everything the same depth. Tree trunks were buried, and no animals scampered for food.

Solomon came up next to her, and she reached for him. It was beautiful—her life was beautiful. A tear stood in one eye at the simple abundance of living with him on this mountain. She was rich beyond her wildest imaginings. With him, she had been born again, had found a safe haven in this world. She was happier than she had a right to be. She was content and . . . home.

February was paradise for Cassie Lee. The snow kept them cabinbound and kept Solomon close. Besides checking on Black, they were together morning, noon, and night. She made meals, bread, cakes, cookies, and love.

"Your boarders are gon be fat," Solomon said.

"I aim to please," she teased as she rolled from him and snuggled beneath his hairless chin.

He cleaned and sharpened his tools, traps, and gun. He taught her to play checkers, and when they tried to resume the reading lessons, they always ended up making love instead, since it required the same visual intensity and concentration.

One morning she rose to the sound of water rushing into the wash tub. Solomon was filling it with hot water from the stove before sprinkling in green apple peels. These baths became a once-a-week tradition, and Cassie Lee wished the tub were big enough for the both of them.

* * * * * * * * * * * * *

"I love you, Solomon. You my Forever Man. I jus' wanted you to know," Cassie Lee said as she served him his favorite meal of fried rabbit, potatoes, and gravy.

Her revelation stopped Solomon in mid-chew. She was behind him now, at the stove continuing on with some inane conversation about adding a second floor onto the cabin, leaving him to ingest her words. He stared at the fire and the bed beyond the rim of her chair. Absently, he took another bite, tearing the moist meat from the bone and wiping the end of a biscuit across the deep brown gravy.

It was a proud and profane moment. Solomon was proud that a decent woman like Cassie Lee could feel that way about him, but he cursed what this confession would mean to their union. He could tell how she felt about him without her labeling it. Surely she knew how he cared about her, but now that the plain words were spoken out, the expectations would come. He was content living just as they were, where the essence of love was sufficient without the declaration of it. Now he had a responsibility and an obligation to her once she had put her thoughts in the wind. Would his contented world become discontented?

* * * * * * * * * * * *

The predictable yet unseasonal February thaw had occurred, and Solomon was out checking his traps and hunting game. The cocooning of the past month had depleted their supplies. Cassie Lee hummed as she worked, feeling complete, respected, and loved, even if he didn't say so. She was content to share the unspoken love his eyes screamed, even if his luscious lips never uttered a word. For him, perhaps love was an inexpressible state, but his actions made up for the lack of verbal commitment.

Sometimes after they made love, she smoothed her finger across the notorious pair of lips that had just ravished every inch of her body. He would kiss her fingertip gently before she nuzzled between his neck and shoulders, fastening herself to him for the night. Still, sometimes you just want to hear it said out loud, she thought. She didn't know if this was the way of man; if the woman was supposed to openly express feelings, and the man only show his. She was so unschooled in matters of the heart. She really could not measure her love for Solomon, because she had nothing to compare it to. But she did know that she could never feel so loved yet so free with any other man, ever. She could stay in his arms forever.

Chapter VI

Hearing the sound of muffled hoofs, Cassie Lee stopped kneading the bread, wiped her hands free of flour, and went to open the door for Solomon.

"Back so soon?" she said as she swung the wooden planks that separated them out of the way.

"Howdy to you too!"

"What you want? Solomon's in town."

"I know that," said Exum. "I know jus' where he is, who he's with, and what he doin'." He stood up straight since Cassie Lee blocked the doorway. "I figure since he's in town visiting my girls, I'd pay his a visit."

Cassie Lee eyed the scar she'd given him. It was beginning to flatten out, she thought to herself, so she wouldn't ask Exum where Solomon was. She folded her arms.

"Mind if I come in? It's a long ride from town."

"Yes it is, so you best be gettin' on back."

She was trying hard not to sound bothered, but she wanted to yell out loud, Why is Solomon visiting another woman?

"Coffee sure smells good. You'd let a dog in there for coffee, why not me?"

"I trust a dog," she said, as he stepped inside without an invitation.

She slammed a cup down on the table and took down the huge skinning knife, setting it in plain view and within easy reach.

"Cassie Lee," Exum said, shaking his head in mock wonderment as she poured the hot liquid into the cup, "I mean you no harm. It pains me you have so little trust."

"Then why you come out here when you know my man ain't home?"

"I always liked you—really." His charming smile was wasted on Cassie Lee's rolling eyes. "That's why I hate to see you being played a fool."

"The only fool here is you if'n you don't drink up and get."

"I mean, you up here cooking and cleaning for a man who's in town lovin' on Elsie and Ming."

"You's a lie," she said calmly. She wanted to jump up and scream but being a slave had taught her how to hide her true feelings.

"Wish I was, but I saw it with my own eyes." He took a gulp of coffee. "They was headin' up the back stairs, he and Ming. See, we had a little fire in Exum town. Most all the buildings burned down, but I saved my saloon. Of course, it's no good if folk who buy my wares leave. A lot of folk are leavin', so maybe this was just a farewell poke between old friends." Cassie Lee gritted her teeth to keep from speaking. "Old Solomon knew both them gals long before you came along. He's used to at least two women. Going from two to one, well, that's a big adjustment. Maybe he's thinking about changing partners. Maybe they do somethin' you don't—"

"Get out!" Cassie Lee stood, yanked the cup from his hand, and opened the door all in one motion.

Exum sauntered to the door, with a crooked smile, and said, "I'ma be movin' on most likely. So I pretty much come by to say goodbye—"

"Bye," Cassie Lee spat.

"Hey, as them Romans say, 'Don't kill the messenger.'" He stepped down onto the snow and into the bright sunlight. "Oh, and don't mind Solomon if'n he's a little late. He's got goodbyes of his own." He managed a grin and wink before Cassie Lee slammed the door in his face.

Cassie Lee paced and breathed, trying to calm herself and make sense out of what Exum had said. She walked rings around the table as she fumed. Solomon had no reason or right to go to another woman. She wasn't going to be nobody's side-woman like Nubby.

"You can't have no pride in yourself if'n you content with a piece of a man," she said aloud. "You can't respect yourself, and the man can't respect you either. I ain't gon be no side-woman or tolerate knowin' about none neither."

Cassie Lee absently grabbed the knife and smacked it flatly against her clothed thigh as she proceeded her inner search for why. I give him no call to go noplace else, she thought.

Maybe men are born with some unnatural need to bed a tribe of women. Men on the plantation, black and white, had that disease. From the overseer to the Whedoe men—and even their friends who visited with their own wives made it a point to bed a slave girl before they left.

"Naw," Cassie Lee said aloud, because Heath and Obadiah were true blue to their mates. Their bonds so strong that they even prayed together after their children were sold off.

Solomon was like Heath, or so she thought. It was all a puzzle. She didn't have any experience with men. Did all men have this sickness? If Solomon had it, she wasn't willing to nurse him back to health. She wished she could talk to Tante Fatima. Cassie Lee stabbed the table with the knife, and the blade sank deep into the assaulted wood. What would the old woman say?

"Is Exum lyin'?" her wise old voice traveled the distance to ask Cassie Lee.

"Of course," Cassie Lee said with a grin. "Exum is lyin'!" She laughed aloud with giddy relief. "That lyin' dog."

She went on with her cooking and when Solomon was a little later than usual, she refused to be the receptacle for Exum's poison again.

Through the panes of the window, Cassie Lee then spotted Solomon and the reason he was late. The man done bought me a horse, she thought, as Solomon, atop Black, guided the new addition up the hill. So we can ride together this spring and summer. So I can go with him wherever he goes, because he loves me and wants me by his side.

"So what'd you bring me from town this time?" she teased as he dismounted. "That don't hardly look like all we need," she said as he loosened the two canvas bags of supplies from the second horse.

"I be in in a minute," he said, handing her the groceries and taking the two horses around to Black's barn.

Must be tired, she thought, as she closed the door and began unpacking the goods.

Solomon opened the door onto the sight of sheets draped and drying over the table and chairs, washed clean of the pungent remnants of their lovemaking last night.

"So how is old Exum?" she probed as she put the salt away.

"There is no more Exum. It burned to the ground."

"A fire?" Exum hadn't lied about that.

"Happened a few days ago. Don't take much, those clapboard buildings so close together. One goes, they all go."

He sat down at the table and Cassie Lee began folding the sheets. "Some folks are staying to rebuild. Some are going on," he continued. Then, he looked up at her. "This would be a good time for you to hitch a ride down San Francisco way."

His words hung between them as limp as the muslin in Cassie Lee's hands. The air was suddenly thick and in short supply. As her eyes searched his, Solomon looked away. Cassie Lee felt a powerful, sharp pain in her stomach like she had just been kicked by a mule. Had she heard him right? Had Exum been right?

"I got you a horse and saddle to make it easy on you," he said, still not looking at her. "Anything else you might need, jus' let me know."

Hurt, shocked, mad, she didn't know how to respond. She wanted to double over in pain; she wanted to punch him, kick him, fight him. She wanted to cry, but didn't.

"I spose it would be the perfect time to move on out," she heard herself say. She put the clean sheets on the shelf and set his plate in front of him.

"You got your dreams—"

"What are your dreams, Solomon? Certainly you want more than this mountain." If she could get him away from here.

"I'ma simple man. I like it here, and it likes me."

"You musta wanted more sometime. You good with horses, didn't you ever want no ranch?"

His head jerked at her so abruptly she jumped. His eyes, full of fury, held hers, then rolled away. "I told you I was happy with my life here. I got no cause to change my ways."

"I guess you don't," she spat. She took off her apron and folded it over the chair. "I guess you be hunting with Running Bear come spring." She left "and sleeping with Ming at night" unsaid.

"Speck I will."

"I speck life will jus' go on."

"It always do, less'n you die."

She yanked her coat from the rack and slammed the door behind her before the first teardrop fell. He would not see her cry. He was dismissing her. Soon it would be warm and his life would pick up where it had left off before he had his little winter bed warmer named Cassie Lee. Now she was being replaced for a spring and summer thing with Ming. Cassie Lee laughed an ironic tear from her eye.

She had been in a bad situation before—it was called slavery. I ain't never gon be no man's slave again, she thought. If she couldn't get as good as she gave, she would get out. She was free now—she could do that.

Cassie Lee stomped the same trail they had used so often as conflicting emotions battled one another. How could she have been so wrong? As certain as the sun rose in the east, she *knew* he loved her. But if he did, why was he letting her go? She was mad at herself for being so stupid—for letting this man do her wrong even if she loved him.

As she paused by the river, she could see the rushing water beneath the frozen veneer. She loved him, but he didn't love her. That's why he never said it, because he never felt it. He cared for her the way he cared about Black, or any other living creature who needed tending to. Like that water rushing just beneath the surface, Cassie Lee was going on too. She would never stay where she was not wanted—never.

There were two things she promised herself by that river. She would never beg for anything. She would never be any man's whore again— Exum Taylor could bear witness to that. What else were you but a man's whore if you stayed when he wanted you to go? You getting all used up, until you get fed up and leave on your own account because there's nothing else left for you to do. She didn't want any man who didn't want her. Cassie Lee was going to save herself the extra time and humiliation. He wanted her gone. And gone she was going. She was free to leave.

At nightfall Cassie Lee eased back into the cabin. Solomon sat at the table. She looked at him cleaning his gun. He wouldn't go and she couldn't stay—not that he asked her to. All the time she thought him the brave, fearless one, but it was she who took the chances and sought what was on the other side of the mountain.

"I'ma pack and head on back to Exum tomorrow morning." Please at least ask me to stay, she pleaded silently. I won't, but at least ask me. So I'll know you at least loved me some. She stopped searching for answers to questions unborn and prepared for bed.

Their relationship had come full circle. That night she lay in the bed, and he on the floor in front of the hearth. Neither slept. In the morning, Cassie Lee readied for the trail. Once again she packed her tapestry satchel for moving on. It was the third time in less than a year—this last time, she thought she had found a home. She was still in search of a place where she could unpack for good. Next place she went, she would keep it ready to go. She was sure learning the lessons of life the hard way.

She took a bar of soap, her comb, and brush, but left his shirts she had used as sleeping gowns.

"That looking-glass belongs to you," he said.

"I don't want seven year's bad luck," she said bravely and thought, I don't think I can stand much more. "Bring it to me when you come visit my boarding house." She tossed him a saucy half-smile.

"How you gon set up this boarding house?"

"Work. I worked for free afore. I can work jus' as hard for my own self."

"I been to San Francisco. Women alone can only earn money one way—"

"I think you know me better than that. I got some money and a respectable means to get more."

She watched him disappear into the root cellar. "Here." He slid her a leather pouch, and she opened it to see its gleaming gold contents. "That's $1,000 in gold coins."

"Where you get this kind of money?" She couldn't believe her eyes.

"Look around, Cassie Lee. I'ma simple man with simple needs. I only need gunpowder, tobacco, flour, bacon, beans, and salt. I trap because I like to. I make plenty of money."

"I can't take—"

"Think on it as a business investment." She started to protest again when he said, "Foolish pride is gon to be the death of you one day."

"Sometimes pride is all you got," she said, taking the pouch. Solomon stood by the horse he had packed for her as she gathered her things. Before she walked to Solomon and the horse, she looked around the cabin for the last time and tried not to think of how happy she had been there.

"You got supplies enough to carry you for more than a week or so," Solomon said.

"C'mon, Moses," she decreed to the horse. "You gon lead me to the promise land." She mounted the horse and looked down at Solomon, the man she loved and hated all at the same time.

"Things ain't always what they seem, Cassie Lee."

"I ain't never had no daddy, and I sure as hell don't be needin' one now. You take care, Solomon Hawk." She swung her horse's head around so that Solomon had to duck to get out of the way.

"Jus' follow the trail!" were his last words to her.

A big lump stuck in her throat. The end of a dream is hard to swallow. Warm tears washed her face clean of any cold, and she wouldn't wipe at them—she wouldn't give him the satisfaction that he had made her cry. She didn't even look back. If she had, she would have seen tears standing in his eyes.

* * * * * * * * * * * *

Cassie Lee returned to Exum to find only two buildings standing, and only a few folks considering rebuilding. She rented a room with a cot from the Broady's at an exorbitant price while she readied for her trip southwest.

"You keep looking to those hills, gal," said Exum, who'd lost most of his property but still had plenty of gold. "He ain't coming down."

"You think he knows it's not jus' the fire but the mines went bust and now the whole town is pulling up stakes?"

"Why you care?" He looked at her and she looked away. "Sure, he was in last night buying up all the supplies. Enough to last him for years. He don't want to go all the way to River Bend to get gunpowder."

79

Cassie Lee wasn't listening to Exum. She continued looking to the hills, not believing that he was here and didn't come to see her. His message was clear. Maybe he came to pick up more than just supplies—maybe Ming was with him.

"Give it up, Cassie Lee. The woman hasn't been made yet that can get to ole Solomon's heart."

"Shut up, Exum."

In just two days, everybody had prepared to render Exum another gold rush ghost town. Cassie Lee mounted Moses, putting off the inevitable for as long as possible. She led a pack horse behind her as she stared back at the mountains again for a sign, any sign—maybe just one last glimpse of him. A wave, something that had mattered to him a little. He had hidden his heart from her while she had laid hers open—it was his for the taking. But only the tall pines and snowy ground met her gaze. Cassie Lee fell in behind the last of the people pulling out.

Exum pulled up his loaded wagon next to Cassie Lee's horse, looked back at her, and said, "I told you he ain't coming down."

"Why don't you travel up there with Zora, Elsie, and the rest of your whores?" Cassie Lee snapped. "By the way," she tried sounding casual before continuing, "I didn't see Ming."

"Me neither. Haven't seen her since last night." He eyed Cassie Lee with a sly smile. "I didn't know yo'all was such good friends. I guess you all share the same taste in men, huh?"

Cassie Lee calmed Moses as the other wagons made their way past the pair.

"Solomon's lucky in a way," Exum said, looking back at the mountains again. This would be the first time they were separated for good since running together. "He already found what makes him happy. We the fools. We still searchin'." Cassie Lee looked ahead at the others. "It weren't easy for him. Being big and black, he was a target for peckerwoods and ne'er-be-massas everywhere we went. They expected him to be strong as a bull and dumb as an ox. And you expect too much from him, Cassie Lee," Exum said, scratching his arm before continuing. "He gave you all he had to give. He didn't have no more." He inhaled the last of the fresh mountain air and spoke, "We ain't no spring chickens like you, Cassie Lee. We got pert-near ten years on you. Hell, Solomon done lost his mama, brother, and sister when you was jus' being spit into the world. We lived a lifetime afore comin' here."

"You startin' over again."

"Yeah, but I ain't found the peace Solomon has. I might never will." He steered clear of the approaching Broady wagon. "I know we had our differences, but you the only woman I ever respected. The one that got away." He smiled.

"You never said truer words."

"If you ever need anything, you jus' ask. No strings attached."

"When fish fly."

Cassie Lee pulled up the reins to Moses, stopping him at the swell where the mountain dropped off and the town that was would disappear from her sight. All the others negotiated the hill, but Cassie Lee had one eye on her future and one on what might have been. She stopped and turned all the way around on her saddle for one last look. She stared at the forest, memorizing every tall tree and high cloud just above their tops. She waved and, feeling foolish, went for her cowrie cross, remembering that it no longer hung around her neck. She faced her future route again and clicked her horse down the swell.

Solomon ducked back when she waved, as if she could possibly see him in the camouflage greenery. He squinted his brown eyes back into their beady slits, setting them against the bouncing whiteness of the deflecting sunlight and the world. He watched the spot she had just left, half expecting, half wanting her to come riding back—but then what? Could she be happy trading her dreams for him? He blew his hot breath into his cold hands, adjusted his hat low over his eyes, and slung his rifle over his shoulder as he began laying his footprints behind the deer he was tracking.

During the trip to River Bend, Cassie Lee was outwardly quiet and remote. Inwardly, she tried to harness a mental riot of emotions that pulsated through her with every breath. She loved and hated Solomon Hawk. She was thankful that he showed her what love was or could be. Then, she wished she had never laid eyes on him.

On the second night she started second guessing her feelings for him—his feelings for her. What had he and Running Bear really talked about in that foreign tongue? She bet they had had a good laugh on her. She wondered if Ming was warming his furry bed now.

She cursed herself for spending too much time on something long gone. It was time for her to set her sights on beginning her new life—again. But whenever her mind wasn't consciously focused on something, like negotiating Moses over a difficult crossing or thinking about her boarding house, it unconsciously drifted back to the source of its aborted pleasure for more than three months. She found that trying to control her thoughts was like trying to harness the wind.

She then realized that all she wanted was more time with him, even if it had to eventually end. Time for them to get wary or tired of one another. Time for his habits to grate on her. If she had just known the last time they were going to make love, or she would sleep in the shadow of his warm body, she could have savored it. Apparently Solomon didn't even know. He returned from Exum with his mind made up that it was time for her to go. He was ready to resume his solitary life, and she just wasn't part of it—time just wasn't on her side. Or maybe God figured she and Solomon loved so hard and so deep that they had used up all the time they were allowed in those few short months. Maybe that was all the time and worldly happiness ex-slaves were entitled to.

The further away from Solomon she got, the more Cassie Lee thought on him. Her mind just got used to going back to thinking on the old familiar thoughts. Her brain was in the habit of rehashing it over and over, looking for reasons and answers. The thousands of things she could have said—she should have said—what was left unsaid.

Things ain't always what they seem rang in her ears, and she was consumed with wondering. *Seemed* she loved him. *Seemed* he loved her. *Seemed* they could have lived in peace and happiness on that mountain forever. If what he had shown her wasn't love, then what was it?

The last night before entering River Bend, Cassie Lee decided she was tired of thinking about it. Her past be damned—all of it. She set her sights on her future and moved toward it like she always did—alone.

"To hell with you, Solomon Hawk," her lips said and her mind joyously seconded. But her heart wept, and her body cringed.

Chapter VII

The rag-tag group of ex-Exumers straggled into River Bend in the early morning hours. As together as they were for the five-day trip down, they dispersed, each gravitating toward their survival predispositions.

"C'mon and join me for a drink, Cassie Lee," Exum said, as he headed for the White Horse saloon. "You look like a man in them pants anyways."

Cassie Lee ignored him as she let her eyes fall over the town, marveling in its wonder and deciding where she would fit in before moving on. She could tell from the buildings and permanency of River Bend that it had been a town before the nearby strikes of gold, although it no doubt profited from the yellow metal all the same. Over the last few days, she silently figured on how to proceed with her plans. Some of the gold Solomon had given her was sewn into her pant cuffs, and the rest was in the saddlebag on which she lay as she thought on the best way to get what she wanted in life—her San Francisco boarding house. She decided that, depending on the kind of town River Bend turned out to be, she would stay and work awhile to earn more money. She wanted to arrive in San Francisco with the $1,000 intact so, she had to work to earn the funds to get there. From folks' conversations, she learned that she could ride

Moses to Sacramento, but from there she would have to catch a stage-coach or wagon train to San Francisco.

She hitched her horse to the post and squinted her eyes against the piercing morning sun. Her boots thudded as she stepped up onto the dusty sidewalk planks. The smell of freshly brewed coffee drew her to a small cafe, but the looks she garnered when she stood in the doorway told her she was not welcome. She turned from the doorway, trying to feel free despite these folks wanting to enslave her again, putting her back in her place with their eyes.

She passed a laundry, immediately recognizing the smell of soap and clean, and paused at a shop with ready-made dresses. It was then that Cassie Lee realized she had never seen a real town before. She only knew the plantation and the trading post on the trail to Exum. Here, people seemed to live over or behind the stores. There was a hotel beside the saloon, and a livery across the street. With all these newfangled and wondrous things, there still seemed to be no place for her to make some traveling money. She just couldn't spend her boarding house money on getting to San Francisco. Solomon said there wasn't anything for a woman alone to do but one thing, and Cassie Lee sure as hell wasn't going to do that.

She then saw baskets of things in the walkway shaded by a canopy. She meandered to the writing on the glass pane and could not sound out General Mercantile, but walked into the inviting coolness. Cassie Lee was hypnotized by what she discovered. There were all manner of goods from bolts of material to mining tools, cans of beans, sacks of flour, sugar, and blankets. Everything from kerosene and coal oil to nails and chicken wire. Candles, soap, guns, barrels of crackers—and apples. She smiled.

"Can I help you?" the man gruffed, startling her.

"Do you have any green apples?"

"Jus' what you see." He went back to pouching loose tobacco as Cassie Lee's eyes fell upon the crystal-clear jar of black strips on the counter. She knew rock candy and taffy, but these other things were a puzzle to her.

"I'ma looking for a job," Cassie Lee said in her loudest voice. "I can figure real good—"

"No job here," he interrupted her, staring at her like she was dirt from the bottom of his shoe.

"I'ma take these crackers and some of this jerky." Cassie Lee decided to make him wait on her.

"That's licorice sticks," he identified for her questioning eyes as he snatched the crackers to wrap. "Jerky is over there."

"I'ma take four of them sticks and get some jerky too." She turned on her heels, picked up the jerky, an orange, and two red apples.

"Anything else?"

"Since you ain't got no job for me—no."

"Eight cents."

Cassie Lee fiddled in her pocket, counted out the coins, then grabbed her lunch and supper for the day. Her eyes fell on the guns displayed in the glass case on top of the counter. There were so many of them—all sizes, shapes, and prices, she imagined.

"You want a gun too?" The sarcastic edge to his voice insinuated that she could not possibly afford to buy one.

"Not today," Cassie Lee said as she pivoted her body away from the sneering man, passing another customer as she left.

Once outside she absently drew a cracker to her lips, and the salty crunch was so satisfying. She hadn't figured a gun into her plans, but she knew that it was essential for a woman traveling alone. Cassie Lee got Moses and sat inconspicuously so she could study the town and where she could get a job to earn enough money to move on.

Boisterous voices violating her peaceful sleep awakened her at night-fall. The crisp, juicy apple snapped between her teeth as she led Moses to the outskirts of town where she had seen the only other black person. A resident, Cassie Lee surmised, since the lady had only a purse and some packages and was on foot. Cassie Lee settled in, hidden by a nearby bush a few comfortable feet from the house she had seen the lady disappear into that afternoon.

The house was all lit up like Christmas, and there was a for-sure party going on inside. Cassie Lee didn't smell any food, but there was a lot of loud music, silhouettes of dancing folks, and a lot of movement—men mostly, coming and going. She couldn't tell whether the people giving the party were black or white; those who kept entering and leaving were both. Maybe the lady she saw earlier was just a slave—or rather, a servant, as they said in these parts. She couldn't move any closer without being discovered, so she watched this curious scene before falling to sleep for the night.

She woke with the sun high in the sky. She must have been more exhausted than she thought from her trip to River Bend. She brushed herself off, doused her face with water from her canteen, and rinsed out her mouth, bypassing the licorice for a sassafras stick.

As she chewed the sweetness from its bark and twisted her hair into a bun at the nape of her neck, the door of the house swung wide open and a lone white man walked out.

"Here goes," Cassie Lee said to Moses as she sashayed around to the back steps and knocked on the door. First timidly, and then louder.

"Yes?" An irritated black woman with a husky, man-like voice swung the door open.

"Ma'am—" Cassie Lee stuttered as she watched the woman's red feather plume, flying freely from her headband, blow in the breeze. "I'ma," she stammered on while soaking in the woman's heavily smeared makeup and the red satin dress that showcased more breasts than Cassie Lee ever hoped to have. "I'ma lookin' for a job."

And then the truth of it snapped like a mighty tree struck by lightning. This is a bawdy house, and these women are like Elsie and Ming!

"Well, you a pretty young thing, but I'm all full up—"

"No!" Cassie Lee shouted, then quieted down. "I don't want to be a—you know—um—"

"A whore?"

"Oh, ma'am—um, I was thinkin' more of a cook or—"

"Sugar, you don't look like much of a cook. Folks I know can cook, look it. You don't weigh more than a shadow on the wall."

"Oh, no, ma'am, I can cook real good, and I can figure some."

"Ummm," the woman said, eyeing Cassie Lee and rubbing her jaw as if summing up the worth of this girl. When she spat tobacco juice to the side of the steps, Cassie Lee jumped. "I'll give you a try. C'mon in." She opened the door. "Haven't had a decent cook for a spell now. Maybe with some good food in 'em, my girls will have more staying power."

She talked as she went through the small screen porch to the kitchen door and around the table, then proclaimed, "This here is the kitchen. It's all yours. You gimme some idea of what you need and I'll give you the money, or you can put it on account at the general store." She stopped short. "I settle up first of each month. Mr. Schmidt just loves that—cash on the barrelhead."

She was on the move again before halting and sticking out her hand. "My name is Bohemia Jones, and this here is my place." She smiled proudly.

"Nice."

"Your name, Sugar?"

"Cassie Lee."

"Uh, how—ordinary."

Bohemia was in motion again as she led her new employee through three expansive, flowing rooms to the center hall. "I got six girls and seven rooms up there." She pointed up the polished mahogany staircase. "I got a girl who comes in to do the house cleaning and such, and another girl who comes in for the hygiene stuff during our peak times—you know."

Bohemia winked at Cassie Lee who obviously didn't have a clue, and the madam knew it.

"Ummm—," Bohemia led Cassie Lee back from the center hall to the kitchen. "It's too early for the girls. They rouse about noon or so—so I guess they'll have breakfast at regular folks' lunchtime. Then dinner a little before they start serving." She laughed, and Cassie Lee didn't get it. "They probably want to eat a little something 'bout two, three o'clock in the morning after their customers leave. But you can make that something light."

"One thing, ma'am—"

"Bohemia," she corrected. "I got neither chick nor child, and I'm nobody's mama or ma'am."

"Yes, ma'am—Miss Bohemia." By her raised left eyebrow, Cassie Lee could see she was vexed.

"Go on, chile," an exasperated Bohemia said, cutting her eyes.

"I only want to do the cookin'. I don't want to be a—" Her hands were whipping up a stir in the wind, but nothing was coming out of her mouth.

"A whore?" She watched Cassie Lee shudder. "I'm hiring you to cook is all. Relax. Your room is right back here, away from all the action. You can bolt that kitchen door during our busy hours so no one mistakes you for a whore. But, Sugar, you gonna have to wear a dress or at least a skirt. The only pants I take to in my establishment are those with a man in them."

"All right," Cassie Lee drawled.

"You can use today to settle in, but I expect my first meal tomorrow at one o'clock."

"Ma'am—uh, Miss, uh, Bohemia," Cassie Lee stammered to a halt. "How much I'ma gon make?"

"Well," Bohemia said as she aimed her big body directly at her new cook, "you not as dumb as you look." She watched Cassie Lee flinch at the reference to her intelligence. "One thing, Sugar. I don't watch my mouth. I don't have that kind of time, so if you thin-skinned—"

"How much, Bohemia?"

"Let's see." She rubbed her chin again, then let Cassie Lee in on the calculations. "I paid the last girl a dollar a day." She witnessed Cassie Lee's eyebrows knit together. "But if you can really cook—"

"I can."

"Two dollars a day for two meals. That's twelve dollars a week for six days. That's forty-eight dollars a month plus room and board."

"Sounds fair."

Cassie Lee had no idea what fair was. She had been a slave, and never earned any money on her own except at the laundry, where she worked like a horse, got two bits a day, and was almost raped.

"Fair!!" Bohemia bellowed. "That's damned good money, Sugar. The likes you ain't never seen afore."

Cassie Lee countered her new boss with a semi-embarrassed smile.

"You know, Sugar, I got a feeling 'bout you." Bohemia's face straightened up and she let her eyes drop down on Cassie Lee in a playful sneer. "Might be something to you after all, Miss Cassie Lee."

Cassie Lee smiled. She had never been called *Miss* before.

"I guess you got some plans?"

"Yes, I do."

"Just so they don't interfere with my money or my meals. If things work out, I may tip you two dollars so you can make $50 a month. How's that sound?"

"That sound right nice, Miss—Bohemia." Cassie Lee's face split into a wide grin, and Bohemia joined her.

"Well, go on and get settled." She walked past her kitchen window. "That horse yours?"

"Yes, ma'am."

"Well, I ain't got no barn, just a hitching post out front for customers. So you gonna have to sell him or board him at the livery. I suppose that depends on how long you plannin' to stay."

"Yes'm."

"If you decide to board him, you can put it on my account; I got one there too. Me and my girls like to take Sunday rides in the surrey and have a picnic. That's our church. I suppose you go to church?"

"Not lately."

"To each his own." She headed for the polished door. "Just tell Ezra to take good care of your horse. Shoddy treatment there will mean shoddy treatment here."

Bohemia laughed uproariously at her own joke as her dark hand shoved open the door and she left the room. Her laughter bounced off the walls and headed up the stairway with its source.

Cassie Lee carted her few things from her horse, including the saddle, and rode bareback to the livery. After she set Ezra straight about her role at Bohemia's, she walked back. She eyed her new home as she approached the house. It was almost as big and beautiful as the main house on the Whedoe plantation. Bohemia's was better kept. The windows were sparkling clean, the paint not a year old. The porch was newly swept and Cassie Lee was sure when spring really rolled around there would be beautiful flowers in the planters that flanked the gleaming wooden double doors.

Cassie Lee ambled around back pushing back the screen door on the little porch, then the door to the kitchen. Finer than the one at the plantation, this room had a cook stove and a treasure trove of fine pots. She supposed it was because Bohemia was concerned about quality, whereas the Massa didn't care anything about quality, or the comfort of his slaves while they toiled for him.

Cassie Lee inspected the cupboards and found dainty china plates, silverware in the drawers, pretty bowls, and matching cups, saucers, and glasses. She went into the pantry, noting what was there and what was not. She found a pad and paper, sat down at the round table that occupied the middle of the room, and began to draw pictures of what she was going to get at the store.

When she was ready, she went out into the hallway and was awed anew by the splendor of the house—the rugs, the wallpaper, and the light fixtures where new candles stood ready to be lit for the night's festivities. The drapes were as fine as any she had ever seen. The couches, chairs, and the mirror over the two fireplaces put the Whedoe house to shame.

Her foot was poised on the carpeted bottom step and, although she could hear some muted talking upstairs, she hesitated and decided not to go up. She would just put the supplies she purchased "on account." After she took one last look around, she decided on the long way back. She tiptoed through the one big room through a set of pocket doors into another room that led back to the hall and the kitchen. She never knew any black people to live like this. Her boarding house in San Francisco wasn't going to be this grand, but it was going to be hers like this was Bohemia's.

Instead of leaving by the kitchen door, Cassie Lee walked back down the hallway and eased out the front door and down the steps. She felt as grand as the house she had just left. She looked back at the house with the slanted roof crowned by a tower. When her eyes fell on the second floor window, the curtains dropped over a figure beyond the glass, and Cassie Lee abruptly stopped her surveying and walked toward the store.

With her list balled up in her hand, she tried to imagine what kind of life Bohemia had lived. She talked kinda proper, better than them Whedoes ever could wish, Cassie Lee thought. She had this magnificent house, paid the girls, and had "accounts" all over River Bend, plus money enough to pay her $50 a month. Bohemia was just a puzzle to her. She wished she could tell Nubby about her. Nubby wouldn't believe a word of it. She wouldn't believe a black woman could have her own nice clothes, much less her own house.

Cassie Lee entered the store where the man had shunned her the day before. Unlike her previous visit full of fear and apprehension, her eyes fell and lingered on all types of things she could buy with Bohemia's money. She was so excited she didn't need to refer to her list. This store was better than Christmas. Everything was so abundant and within her reach, not like the rations of beans, salt pork, and corn meal the Whedoe slaves got from the massa on Fridays and tried to stretch out the week. It was never enough. Folks ran out by Wednesday and took to picking greens around the cabin waiting on next Friday to come. But here, in this store of plenty, it was here for the reaching.

"You again, huh?" Mr. Schmidt greeted, reminding him and her who they both were.

"Yes. I need some supplies," she said, wiping the smile from her face.

Mr. Schmidt eyed her curiously. "I'ma filling an order for Miss Jones."

"Bohemia?"

"Yes, I'ma her new cook."

"Well." The grin Cassie Lee had forsaken found a new home on the lips of Mr. Schmidt. "Just lemme know what you need."

Cassie Lee bought salt, flour, coffee, sugar, rice, oats, hominy, potatoes, onions, kerosene, and soap. She hesitated in front of the big barrel of white beans. Lord, she'd eaten enough of them in her Georgia life and on the trail, but she got two pounds of them anyway. She turned from that barrel to a basket full of green apples.

"Solomon," she must have said aloud.

"What's that?" Mr. Schmidt asked.

Cassie Lee took the large green ball and held it in the palm of her hand. She lifted it to her nose to inhale the sweet-tart bouquet before rubbing it to her cheek. She was lost in remembering when Mr. Schmidt snapped her out of it.

"You want some of them apples too?"

"Yes, 'bout twelve."

"Gonna make a apple pie, huh?"

"Umm," Cassie Lee answered, thinking that his friendliness was irritatingly false, and he too had a certain penchant for the color green. "You got any eggs?"

"No, most people raise their own or eat at Marge's."

"You have any chickens ready to cook?"

"Gotta go to Chinatown for them." He noticed when Cassie Lee bristled. "You got somethin' agin the Chinese?"

"How 'bout butter?"

"Folks churn their own or eat at Marge's."

"You got bacon?"

"That I got." He disappeared and came back with a healthy slab of salted pork. "You best get in with some of the farmers around here that raise cattle and pigs. You'll need big sides and hams to feed them girls at Bohemia's."

"I won't be stayin' here that long," Cassie Lee said, as she added a few peppermint sticks and licorice whips from the glass jars. "Oh, I need cloves, cinnamon, and vanilla."

"Two outta three ain't bad. I'm gonna have to order the vanilla from San Francisco. It come up from Mexico. It'll take about two weeks. This it?" He smiled like the owner of the goose who laid the gold.

"Yes." She looked around and remembered, "Oh, I need a skirt."

"Folks around here either make their own or order them from San Francisco. Got material over there." He'd never hear the end of it if he sent her to Lavinia's.

Cassie Lee sauntered over to the bolts of cloth, refusing to miss the conveniences of the plantation that always had butter, eggs, vanilla, and ready-made clothes, even if they were hand-me-downs they only got twice a year from the big house. She selected a blue and white pattern.

"Gimme three yards of this, some blue thread, and one of them aprons." She pointed to the off-white canvas material.

"They's for miners."

"It'll have to do. And the smallest shirt you got over there."

As Mr. Schmidt tallied the goods, her eyes fell on the glass case that held guns, reminding her again of the additional expense.

"Here." Mr. Schmidt laid the pencil and paper in front of her and asked, "You got a wagon outside?"

"No." Her eyes were riveted to the pencil and paper.

"OK. I'll send them to you by this afternoon," he said, watching her pick up the pencil and make a shaky C and L on the bill. He gave her one copy, which she folded and stuffed in her pants pocket.

92

"I need these things early afternoon," Cassie Lee said, trying to recoup some authority. "I'ma jus' takes these now." She grabbed the green apples and the candy.

Cassie Lee felt intoxicatingly important as she stepped onto the wooden plank walkway. Wouldn't Nubby just love this? she thought, as her eyes surveyed the town that was coming alive in the early morning mist. As she started off to the livery to visit Moses, a little boy with a basket of eggs ran past her.

"Hey, you—" She stopped short because she had vowed she would never call another little black male child "boy" ever again.

"Yes'm?" he said as he retraced his steps back to her.

"You deliver eggs?"

"Yes'm. The best in River Bend!" His white teeth blazed against his coffee-and-cream skin.

"Well, I'd like you to bring some to me tomorrow morning—early."

"Yes'm. How many?"

Cassie Lee smiled at the businesslike demeanor in one so young. "A dozen." He smiled even wider.

"Yes'm. Where to?"

"The large gold house at the end of the street."

"Miss Bohemia's?" He liked to burst.

"Yes. I'ma the cook."

"Oh. OK."

"Tomorrow morning—early. If you do good I'ma want a dozen every day. And butter, you got any butter?"

"Butter, ma'am?" He scrunched up his nose and scratched his head with his free hand.

"Well, if you can scare me up some I'd be much obliged. So I'll see you tomorrow."

"I'll be there. Early. Bye, ma'am."

* * * * * * * * * * * *

After visiting Moses, Cassie Lee returned home and set about cleaning the kitchen until her groceries arrived. The dirt was more from lack of use than anything else. The pantry with the glass doors had the

93

beautiful plates, serving dishes, platters, candlestick holders, and trays. The other one without glass doors held the preserves, vinegar, and other food materials. She swept the pantry and toted out the potatoes with eyes and sprouting onions onto the screened back porch.

If'n I was going to be here next year I would plant them, she thought. She peered out over the expanse of the yard. The outhouse was a few yards from the back door and looked unused, as it tilted a little to one side. In the distance was another small shed, and beyond that mountains.

Cassie Lee shook her head and hopefully any thoughts of Solomon. Like a stubborn bronco rider, the more she tried to shake him, the more he clung to her mind. She brushed the round table with her hand as she turned into her room. Last night had been the first bed she had slept in since being with Solomon.

"Damn." She hated this, and hated herself for being so weak-minded about him. She'd slept soundly last night because she was so whipped. The trick was to work hard and stay beat-down and bone-tired so he wouldn't creep into her dreams at night.

"I like this room," she said aloud so her mind would have to pay attention to the spoken words and break the fix Solomon had on it.

It was a long room with the bed against the only full wall, which it shared with the kitchen. On the other side, floorboard went halfway up the wall, then screen took over from there to the ceiling. At one end was a dresser on which she had hoisted her saddle. She put her bear coat and saddlebags in front of it on the floor. At the other end, where the opening to the kitchen was, there was a potbelly stove with its pipe snaked up and into the ceiling. There was plenty of wood for kindling on the screened porch where she put the potatoes. She liked the view.

Cassie Lee eyed the vista, the outhouse, the shed, and the lilac bushes, thinking she had to find a place to stash her money once she cut it out of her britches and started to wear that skirt. Somewhere near that shed. Somewhere she could see it just by looking. Somewhere she could get to easy when she was ready to move on—be it San Francisco or back to the Sierras. A knock on the back door from the delivery man rescued her from that last wistful, hopelessly stupid thought.

Cassie Lee spent the remainder of the day putting things away and readying herself for tomorrow's first meal. She let the feather bed cradle and soothe her as she nestled her tired body in it. She didn't hear the men and women of Bohemia's house do what comes natural as she drifted to sleep.

Chapter VIII

Cassie Lee's head seemingly had rested only a few minutes before a knock at the back door roused her awake.

"Wha?" She sat straight up in bed before identifying the intrusive sound as a knock. With her eyes still heavy with sleep, she shrouded a blanket around her and stumbled to the back door.

"Mornin', ma'am!" The little boy's smile was as bright as his voice.

"What time is it?" Cassie Lee asked as carefully as possible, realizing she hadn't had time to wash her teeth with salt.

"It's 'bout six thirty. I been up since dawn. Farmers get up early. Here your eggs. A dozen, like you said."

"OK," Cassie Lee said, just because she didn't know what else to do. "Have you ate breakfast, uh?"

"Samuel. Samuel Davenport."

"What?" Cassie Lee then realized that the boy was giving her his name. "Have you ate yet, Samuel?"

"I had coffee and a biscuit with my Pa."

"Well, that's hardly a breakfast for a workin' man. Tell you what, Samuel Davenport." She looked up and out at the yellow-orange sunrise kissing the horizon. "You come back in about two hours, and I'll have your money and a breakfast fit for a growing boy. OK?"

"Yes, ma'am!"

By the time Samuel returned, Cassie Lee had washed and refreshed herself and donned the apron that hid her pants. She had Samuel wash himself up at the kitchen pump, then sat him down to a plate full of eggs, bacon, fried potatoes and onions, and biscuits.

"Thanks for the butter," Cassie Lee said as he slathered a blanket of the thick yellow paste on his biscuit.

"You welcome." He smiled up at her and she rubbed his head. "There's some jelly here," Cassie Lee offered.

"No thanks, hides the flavor of the biscuit."

When she turned around, Samuel had inhaled the meal, and she offered him seconds, which he gladly accepted.

"My goodness, you got some appetite."

"That's what my Pa says." He wiped his lips with his napkin. "I got to finish my runs now. But thank you, ma'am."

"You think you could call me Cassie Lee? Ma'am just makes me sound so old." He grinned widely.

"Yes ma'am—uh, Cassie Lee. I like the sound of that."

"Good." She walked him to the back door. "During your runs you think you could scare me up a plump chicken?"

"Sure. I can do that."

"Here's your money for the eggs today, and money for the bird. If'n you need more, jus' come on and get it."

"OK. I'll see you later with the chicken, and tomorrow with the eggs and butter."

"Good."

As the ladies of the house drifted in, circled, and finally sat at the round table, Cassie Lee knew this audience was going to be harder to impress then an eleven-year-old manchild. They eyed the table setting with the napkins, and sat in silence until Bohemia bounded in.

"Well, something sure smells good!" The lady of the house came in and sat, flapping, then flaring her napkin on her ample lap, as Cassie Lee poured the aromatic black coffee. "These are my girls: Gypsy, Scarlet, Candy, Pearl, and Diamond. Girls, this is Cassie Lee."

"How do," Cassie Lee mumbled, as she poured the piping hot brown liquid into each waiting cup. "Dig in," she instructed and Bohemia went straight for the potatoes and onions as the others all grabbed for something different.

They chit-chatted among themselves while Cassie Lee tried not to stare at Pearl, the only white girl, wondering what she was doing being a whore. A white girl could do or be anything she wanted to. She could be some rich man's wife, but she was a whore at Bohemia's. Cassie Lee didn't cotton to Pearl at all, because she didn't take advantage of what God gave her. Only a stupid person wouldn't use what the good Lord gave her. Being white meant you were halfway to success. All your lazy butt had to do was go the rest of it, she thought. Cassie Lee could not understand or respect a white whore.

Cassie Lee began to relax by the meal's end and accepted over-the-shoulder compliments as she cleaned up from this lunch and began preparing for tonight's dinner.

"What we havin' this evenin'?" Gypsy, the most vocal after Bohemia, asked.

"Chicken and dumplings."

"Oh, my God!" Bohemia threw her hands up in thanks. "I love chicken and dumplings."

"We all gonna be fat inside a week," Scarlet said.

"You better not go gettin' fat on me," Gypsy snapped playfully.

"Can you make rice pudding?" Pearl asked.

"Yes—"

"Don't go ordering the girl," Bohemia interrupted. "Let her do what she does best. We know we gonna eat it." They all laughed, Bohemia louder than everyone.

"You done real good," Candy said as she was leaving.

"Keep up the good work," Scarlet said.

"Thank you, Nettie Jean," Cassie Lee said to her.

"Who the hell told you you could call her Nettie Jean?" Gypsy assaulted.

"I just heard you—"

"Only I call her Nettie Jean. You hear me?" Gypsy was within inches of Cassie Lee's face.

"I didn't mean nothin' by it."

"She's Scarlet to you and everybody else, you hear me?"

"Sure."

Cassie Lee noticed that everyone, including Bohemia, seemed to be preoccupied by something on the floor. Gypsy's wrath was not challenged as she ripped herself from the kitchen with Scarlet in tow. The others followed; only Bohemia stayed behind.

"I was only tryin' to be friendly and show that I remember her real name—"

Bohemia silenced Cassie Lee with her hand. "Don't worry about it, Sugar. Gypsy's just a little high-strung when it comes to Scarlet. You did real good today, Cassie Lee. I can't wait for my chicken and dumplings," Bohemia said, smiling as she left the kitchen.

While the chicken softened in the boiling water, Cassie Lee fed Samuel some of the raw carrots she'd sliced for the stew and joined him on the steps. She ran a threaded needle through the calico material at the waist, whip-stitched a seam, and then the hem.

"You know I can take you to get some already sewed clothes from Millie's?"

"Yeah?" Cassie Lee said, and tore the thread between her teeth. "She sell to colored?"

"Yeah, my mother used to get some of her dresses there on special occasions."

"Good, I can plug up a hole but I ain't no sewer, and I think I'ma need some better-looking skirts than this." She held up her long, lopsided skirt.

"It don't look half bad, Miss Lee."

"No. It look all bad," she laughed, "but I wasn't hired to be no sewer. And Samuel, please call me Cassie Lee."

"How old are you?"

"What? Didn't your folks ever tell you not to ask nobody their age?"

"I got to know if it's all right to call you by your first name."

"Such a gentleman. It's OK. I say so. 'Sides, an important man like you, who knows where to get eggs, butter, chicken, and store-bought clothes—we should be on first name calling." She smiled at him as she went down the five steps and lifted the wet chicken from its hot bath.

"You old enough to be my mama?"

100

"Not less'n I started at ten or so." She sat on a stool and commenced to plucking the feathers from the meat of the bird.

"So you about twenty?"

"Get that shovel over there and start turning over that dirt there," Cassie Lee directed.

"You don't wanna tell me, do you?" Samuel said, obeying her and looking dejected.

"Oh, handsome and smart," Cassie Lee said with a smile, and he joined in.

Cassie Lee didn't know how old she was. She didn't know who her parents were, either—whether they were sold from her, or she was sold from them. She was just a child of the plantation, lost in the shuffle until she was old enough to be of some use. Her earliest memories were of toting and fetching water when she was about three or four, and being hit square across her mouth for spilling some on the porch on her way to the kitchen. She remembered splinters from carrying firewood, and being smacked again when she sassed Julie, the massa's precious daughter. She didn't find out about caring until Ruth, Nubby's mother, took her in. When Ruth died, she and Nubby were left alone together. They were as different as night and day—in looks and temperament—but they stuck together through hell and high water. Each other was all they had.

"This shovel ain't no good," the boy said.

"You right 'bout that," Cassie Lee said, looking up, "You done real good with it, but it's fixin' to get dark, so you better head on home now."

She held up the naked bird, and flinched when excrement flew out the side upstairs window. "What the—?"

"Emptying the slop jars," Samuel said, beaming at his knowledge.

"I think you know too much for your own good. Go on home now so your folks don't worry."

"I'll finish up tomorrow," he said, placing the shovel by the base of the steps as Cassie Lee climbed them. "What you want tomorrow?"

"A dozen eggs, butter. Can you get some more milk? I wanna do some bread. And meat. Can you lay your hand on a ham or roast?"

"Sure can, my name is Sam Davenport." A wide smile split his handsome face. "See you tomorrow, Cassie Lee."

"Watch going around the side of the house," she warned, looking up at the window from which the human waste had been flung. "And not so early!" she yelled behind the running figure as it cleared the lilac bushes into the street. "No wonder them flowers do so well."

At dinner the accolades were just as high, but Cassie Lee remained silent except when Bohemia eyed her trousers beneath the apron.

"I'ma working on it," Cassie Lee said as Bohemia raised her left eyebrow in minor irritation. Cassie Lee didn't feel she'd get fired today for wearing pants. Tomorrow was another story.

"Bohemia," Cassie Lee said as she was leaving her kitchen to prepare for work. "Do you got another shovel?"

"A shovel? What you want with a shovel?"

"I'ma gon plant some of them potatoes on the porch what got eyes."

"You can check the shed out back, we got some tools in there."

Cassie Lee cleaned as the girls finished eating so her dishes were all washed and put away. There were no leftovers, but she put the butter in the cool box on the pantry.

She could hear the house start to come alive. The doors opening and shutting. Loud voices, even louder piano playing, creaking floorboards, tinkling glasses, and smoke. Under the cover of twilight, Cassie Lee made it down to the shed, allowing her eyes to adjust to the dim light before she pushed the shed door open as far as it would go. The little building was crammed with junk, old furniture, fixtures, and farm implements. Cobwebs clung to her face in the eerie darkness.

"Enough of this," she said aloud. As she backed away, her hand fell on an object. A shovel. "The Lord is with me sometimes," she thanked aloud, and eased the implement from the wall.

She stood outside the shed absorbing the sounds of the night—the music of crickets, the distant sound of a breaking branch under some marauding animal's weight. The air was so fresh and clean, still crisp from the retreating winter. She looked back at the house, which was lit up from top to bottom. The sounds were muted, but silhouettes passed from the downstairs parlors to the upstairs bedrooms. The very top window was dark. That must be the room Bohemia had offered her if she didn't want the porch-room off the kitchen. It would be ideal if Cassie Lee was staying through the winter, Bohemia had said. But Cassie Lee could not fathom being cooped up so high, and away from nature and free-circulating air.

She turned her attention to the task at hand, burying the money stashed in the cuffs of her pants. A crusted log lay across the land a few feet from the shed, its neighbors, woodland debris and rocks. Cassie Lee attempted to push back the largest granite formation. It didn't budge, but the one next to it gave way after she jiggled, twisted, then forced it away. She dug a hole, ripped the thread of her cuffs, and carefully removed the gold coins from their denim home. She counted them again before returning them to the leather pouch and dropping them into the dirt cavity.

Returning the dirt, then the rock, Cassie Lee sat atop it for awhile, looking up at that big, gorgeous moon—and wondering. Wondering what Solomon was doing at this exact moment. Was he asleep? Was he stalking some night prey? Was he wide awake, tortured by thoughts of her? Was he on top of Ming? She had to stop this insanity. It did her no good. It was clear that he wasn't thinking of her, and it was clear she was exhausted.

Cassie Lee raised her weary body and pointed it in the direction of the house. She walked slowly back toward the raucous laughter and high times. She climbed the stairs and went through the back door, through the porch into the kitchen, and straight to her bedroom. As she shed her clothes, she realized that this would be a nice home for a few months. It had a potbelly stove and a feather mattress which she never had before, certainly not at the Whedoes where she and Nubby shared a mix of cotton and moss, and not at Solomon's. She eyed the shed through the screens of her porch-room before lying down and letting the feathers cushion her body. She liked that the place where she had buried her money was in full view and, with an easy eye, she could keep tabs on it. She also liked the privacy she had when she wasn't in bed, and the screen, which began a foot above the bed, allowed her to see the sky, the stars, and the moon.

Cassie Lee pulled her bear coat over her, curled her body into a ball, and fell into an immediate deep sleep, not realizing that the name "Solomon" slipped from her lips.

* * * * * * * * * * * * *

"Cassie Lee, Bohemia say bring her a cup of coffee," said Candy, sticking her head through the swinging kitchen door before disappearing.

The smell of the fragrant coffee must have roused Bohemia's taste buds prematurely, Cassie Lee thought, as the breakfast was ready. The flapjack batter was ready for the griddle, the bacon was drained and warm, and the bread for that evening's meal was rising on the cutting board.

Cassie Lee went into the "pretty pantry," the one with all the fancy dishes and trays. She pulled down one of the polished silver trays and took down one cup, one saucer, a sugar and a cream holder, and a bud vase. She pumped water into the bud vase, darted and ducked to the lilac tree, snapped off a fragrant bloom, and ran back. She poured the strong, black liquid into the elegant cup, put out a linen napkin, and pushed her shoulder into the kitchen door while balancing the tray. Again, she just marveled at the magnificence of the house as she negotiated the first three steps to the landing. The walls stopped her. On them was a fabric with raised, fuzzy flowers. It was beautiful!

"It's called wallpaper, country," Gypsy spat as she and Scarlet passed, plastering Cassie Lee awkwardly against the wall.

She stared at their full, shining skirts flouncing about their stockinged legs, their feet perched in high-heeled shoes, their hair piled up high on their heads in big curls and crowned with small hats cocked to one side. They were gorgeous and smelled so good as they opened the door, laughed gaily and ventured outside.

Cassie Lee continued climbing the stairs and stopped as she caught sight of the second floor through the varnished mahogany banisters. The carpet continued into the hall, and there were four rooms to be seen immediately. She proceeded past two of the open doors and, even with the messed-up beds, the rooms were breathtakingly furnished. As she approached the large room on the front where Bohemia sat at a desk, Cassie Lee managed a glance to the right at a short hallway that must have had about three doors leading from and entering into it and a window.

"Come on in, Sugar," Bohemia coaxed her further down the hall without looking up from her paper. Hearing the voices of her girls out front, Bohemia looked up through her drapes in time to catch a glimpse of Gypsy and Scarlet rounding the corner.

"Advertising, I speck. Oh!" She looked at Cassie Lee and her tray, bearing coffee. "How fancy. Sit it over here, Sugar."

Cassie Lee slid the tray onto the glass tabletop, not removing her eyes from the immensity of the room. It took up the whole front of the house, and was full of elegant doodads the likes of which she had never seen. The bed with four glossy posts headed for the ceiling seemed miles away. The mattress was so high that climbing on it required a stool. Cassie Lee tore her gaze away from the mounds of pillows with the lacy cases, right into the sight of jewelry and feathers and glistening baubles, all rounding out the cacophony of the scene. Hordes of clothes spilled from massive wardrobes, and colored jars filled with amber liquids had aromas that put the scent of the lilacs to shame.

"This is good, Cassie Lee," Bohemia said, sipping her coffee. She let the young girl's eyes absorb and dance over her belongings. "I was reading something that may interest you."

Only then did Cassie Lee notice that Bohemia sat in the midst of papers. She watched her boss put on glasses. She had never seen a colored person with glasses before.

"River Bend tends to get its news a little late, but they passed this Fugitive Slave Law. You heard about it?"

Bohemia looked up so fast that Cassie Lee flinched. "No, ma'am."

"Seems that its passing means they can drag your black ass back to slavery if they want to."

"I'ma not a slave," Cassie Lee stammered. "I be free."

"Wrong!" Bohemia thundered, and jumped from her seat. "You say it like that, and you'll be hog-tied and on a boat back to Mississip in a heartbeat. I am **NOT** a slave!" she shouted. "Don't explain nothing unless you got free papers to back you up. Knowing them white devils, they'd tear them up and take you back anyways. They wouldn't try none of that mess with me cause I got something for them. Foolproof. I ain't never been a slave, and I'm too old to learn. But you—you'd fetch a pretty price. So you practice. I am **NOT** a slave! Say it with conviction— that will be the difference between them believing you and letting you alone, or conking you over the head and dragging your dusky black butt to slavery."

"I ain't never been no slave either," Cassie Lee lied.

"Sugar, I don't care, but if you expect that lie to work on somebody else, you better learn how to stop mumbling when you talk to folks with authority. Learn to look them dead in the eye—not the chin, not the throat—and stop fidgeting and swooping your hair behind your ear when you're intimidated."

Cassie Lee had never heard that word before, but figured it meant afeared.

"You better stop acting like a slave, and start acting like somebody with a future."

"Yes'm—" Cassie Lee stopped short, looked up at Bohemia in time to catch her disapproving, raised eyebrow.

"Look me in the eye," Bohemia commanded, and Cassie Lee complied.

Bohemia held the young girl's eyes in hers, supporting her weakening gaze, but not letting her fall.

Cassie Lee did not blink, and felt the power of this woman, the strength of her, but was relieved when Bohemia finally looked away.

"Let me say this, Miss Cassie Lee. You got gumption, you got the inside to be anything you want on the outside. If you think you can, you will as long as you don't go and do something stupid. But I guess we all been stupid some time or another." She smiled at Cassie Lee.

"Thank you, Bohemia." It came out so easy.

"I'm looking forward to breakfast," Bohemia smiled again, as she flipped open another paper. "And tomorrow when you bring me coffee, put one of them biscuits or bread or something on the side. That'd be right nice." She was back to poring over her old papers for more news.

As Cassie Lee backtracked her steps on the carpet runner down the stairs back to the kitchen, her head was full of this Fugitive Slave Law thing. She wasn't a slave, she was free—or did she still really belong to Exum? The thought sent shivers down her spine. I could ask Exum for free papers, she thought, but if what Bohemia says is right, they wouldn't do no good, no how. She wasn't going back there—not now—not ever. She'd die first, and asking Exum for anything, free papers included, would just about kill her. She didn't even know where he was, or care, until now. She'd just have to practice sounding convincing.

"I am not a slave. I am **NOT** a slave!"

Chapter IX

After dinner Cassie Lee sat by the shed making letters in the dirt with a stick, practicing her name; but she still got the big and the little letters mixed up sometimes. She just *had* to learn how to read.

"Another great meal," Candy said, as she walked up to join her. "Didn't mean to scare you. Mind if I sit?"

"No." Cassie Lee erased her letters, tossed out the stick, wrapped her arms around her legs, and stared out at the mountains.

"Pretty, ain't it?"

"Yeah," Cassie Lee said.

"Where's your little boyfriend?"

"I don't got no boyfriend!" Cassie Lee spat.

"I meant Samuel," Candy said, getting the message.

"Oh, he jus' lookin' for a big sister is all," Cassie Lee softened.

"Not the way he looks at you. I think he got a crush on you." Candy smiled. "All of us around here aren't bad, you know. Don't judge us all by Gypsy."

"Jus' what was that all about?" Cassie Lee's curiosity gave her voice.

"Everybody got preferences. I got a preference for a man who don't know I'm alive because I'm too dark for him. Samuel got a preference for you, and Gypsy and Scarlet got preferences for each other."

"I guess everybody needs a friend to ease the pain of living," Cassie Lee said, thinking of Nubby. "Scarlet seem nice."

"Well, they don't want nobody to be their friends except the two of them."

"You tellin' me. I was jus' tryin' to be friendly is all. Remembering her given name, and Gypsy jumped clear down my throat."

"That's cause you was messing with her woman."

"Her woman?" Cassie Lee looked over at her for the first time, her questioning eyebrow speaking loudly.

"Cassie Lee, to be so smart, you sure is slow sometime." Candy slid down to where her companion sat. "You ever been with a man?" she asked, and Cassie Lee bristled at her nerve. "That's how Gypsy and Scarlet are."

A slow recognition claimed her features. "No!" Cassie Lee's face was awash with skepticism. "How? She got a—"

"No. They—" Candy stopped and thought, and then said, "I don't know how they do, but they do it—all the time."

"I never—"

"Me neither, and I ain't gonna start. One time Gypsy grabbed me by my tits in the hall, and I told her to back offa me!"

"How she go with men *and* Scarlet?"

"She do it easy. The men love her. She a wild gal. She used to jump up on the top of that round red couch in the front parlor, and do the hoochie goochie to the music. Then, she start stripping off her clothes till she was naked! Then, she'd jump down in front of a man and just start grinding her body into his."

Cassie Lee's mouth was wide open.

"Bohemia put a stop to it. She says ain't nothing free in this house. You want Gypsy or any other of my girls that'll be twenty-five a poke. One hundred for all night."

"Dollars?" Cassie Lee gasped, and when her wind returned she continued, "You get $100 a night?"

"We don't. Bohemia does. These mining men got plenty money. It ain't always been this much, but you gotta milk the cow while you can. They want cheaper, they can just mosey on down to the saloon."

Cassie Lee made a mental note to talk to Bohemia about more

108

money for doing the cooking. She worked hard preparing those meals. Her mind was ablaze with questions that she threw at the willing Candy.

"What about Libby?"

"I don't know what she makes. I wouldn't do that job for nothing," Candy concluded. "Whatever she makes ain't enough."

Cassie Lee kept the fact that she'd do Libby's cleaning job before she'd do Candy's to herself, and said, "Maybe that's why she so evil."

"She evil cause Bohemia told her she was too ugly to be one of her girls. Bohemia says she got ugly ways, but told her if she wanted to clean up and downstairs, which included changing the sheets and emptying the slop jars, then she got a job."

"She throw that stuff right out the upstairs window by the kitchen. It stink as bad as that asafetida they put around your neck when you sick."

"Asa—what?"

"Never mind. It be old medicine." Cassie Lee didn't mean to reveal the old slave remedy, and continued, "Bohemia was talking about the Fugitive Slave Law and said she ain't worried cause she got something *foolproof* for anybody who try to make her a slave. What she mean?"

"Must be Boofus. Her gun," Candy said.

"Bohemia got a gun?

"Yep. You notice she ain't got no men to help her guard her house or her money, like the others. She take her own money to the bank, in broad daylight. Know why?"

Cassie Lee shook her head.

"One day when she was going to make a deposit, a man tried to rob her," Candy related. "Bohemia told him to get outta her face. He tried to grab her purse, and Bohemia pulled out Boofus and shot the man dead. She stepped right over him and went on to the bank. She say Boofus is a businesswoman's best friend. Now she makes her deposits at high noon, and nobody bothers her. You know how she sets up her desk and chair on the landing at night? She keeping track of the men, the girls, the gold, and the guns. She got the only gun in the house. She makes the men check theirs at the vestibule, and says she is not responsible for them if they disappear. 'Don't want your guns stolen,' she says, 'leave'em home or go somewhere else for a poke.' Bohemia is some kinda woman."

"She sure is."

"Candy!!" Bohemia yelled down to them from the back porch.

"Gotta go to work?" Cassie Lee hated herself the moment it left her lips.

"Naw, I'ma on the rag—the best week I have all month," Candy said, and laughed. "I guess she wants me to sit with Cherry."

"Who's Cherry?"

"See ya, Cassie Lee."

Cherry must be the sixth girl who never comes down, Cassie Lee thought. She must have one of those rooms down that little hallway near the one where Candy said that for an extra twenty-five dollars a man can take a bath before or after his poke.

* * * * * * * * * * * * *

Cassie Lee slipped the hardened-off potato pieces into the rich, brown dirt. The color made her think of Solomon, and her thoughts unwantedly returned to him. She felt childish thinking about a man who never gave her a second thought, but in the barren landscape of her life, those few precious months had been like no other. They were rich and fertile with promise and hope and happiness that she had never known before and was sure she would never know again. She would be forced to compare every other pleasurable experience with that treasured winter. Solomon would always be what she was looking for, and deep in her heart, a flame would always burn just for him—but it was over. At least she had had him in her lifetime. Some, like Nubby, would never even get that much. How could the same one who brought you such pleasure bring you such pain?

As Cassie Lee mounded the dirt around each set, she thought how all these feelings were brand new to her. She had never experienced love before. She had never felt so connected, yet so free, as she had with Solomon. She had endured the physical pain of being beaten, hit, touched, and raped, but she had never felt this invisible pain that left no outward scar.

People can see a lame or a blind person with outer afflictions, and know that's why they are the way they are. But when your pain is deep

110

down inside, so deep it can't get out—no one knows or sees that. No one understands . . . but it sure do hurt. It hurts real bad. Worse than any outside scar.

Cassie Lee mounded more dirt over the potato sets as she proceeded down the row, wiping her brow and nose.

"Hi, Cassie Lee. See what I brought you!" Samuel held up a mess of fresh fish.

"Hi, Samuel." Cassie Lee stood up, and as she faced him his face fell.

"You been crying?"

Cassie Lee sniffed, not even realizing that she had been.

"No, got something in my eye is all." Her voice was raspy, so she cleared her throat and said, "Well, that's right nice of you. They'll fry up real good. You put 'em in the kitchen for me. I left you some fried chicken and a piece of pie on the table."

"Thanks!" He disappeared, and Cassie Lee shook her head free of thoughts of Solomon.

She aimed her closed eyes toward the sun, and it sure felt good on her face. This earth was warming up slower than it did in Georgia. Hell, in April the slaves were already working from sunup to sundown, she thought. Knowing ole massa, he probably had them clearing cypress and oak trees to plant rice since March. He was always trying to use up the land as fast as he could, cotton for some, rice for others. They had to widen that creek to water the rice plants while she was still there. Then at harvest time, they all had to go out there to cut the rice stalks; swinging those sickles and scythes meant someone always got cut bad. When she was just a child, she had to drive the oxen that pulled the carts on which the grain was loaded. Then they put her on cotton for awhile, and she hated the way it used to slice up her tender hands and break her back, but at least you were through with that white horror before that rice crop.

During the winter, they had to pound the grain in wooden bowls to separate the rice from the husks. But neither cotton nor rice compared to that hellish indigo. The slaves had to plant it real careful like, cut it while the blue juice was still full, and then carry it to vats for curing. Then they had to beat the mixture to get that rich dark blue color the massa liked, after which the water was drained, strained, and placed in linen bags.

After the material was cut and dried in log houses, the slaves had to turn the square pieces three, four times a day and fan the flies away. Slaves weren't finished with that hateful indigo until they packed it into barrels for shipping to England.

Like the rice, old massa got that idea from his relatives who lived in Charleston, and—unfortunately for the slaves—it worked just as well in Georgia. Indigo slaves were forever branded by the blue color from their hands right up to their elbows. If the house slaves were supposed to have it the best, then the indigo slaves had it the worst with their lifelong blue markings. Cassie Lee had been both—field and house slave. Truth was, no slave had it good. A slave was a slave.

* * * * * * * * * * * *

"That sure was good, Cassie Lee," Samuel said, coming through the screen door licking his lips.

"Wipe your mouth." Cassie Lee straightened up and walked toward him and they sat on the top step. She was reflective and stared out over the hilly land. "We'd be lining up for that white, awful-tasting mess. A spoonful a year in the summer, and then again in the winter. One big old gulp per—" She caught the word "slave" in her throat, and the curious look in Samuel's eye.

"You in a mood, Cassie Lee?" He looked up at her. "You miss the folks back home?"

"No, Samuel. My home is wherever I am at the time."

"My pa says home is where your heart is."

"Yeah, well, I guess he be right. My heart is here with me. No one else seems to want it," she finished quietly. "Got somethin' else for you." She disappeared into the kitchen and came back with two cups of green liquid. "Drink," she commanded.

"What is it?" He scrunched up his nose.

"Pot liquor. It's good for you." She watched him take a sip and retch. "Make you big and strong."

"Ugh, my pa says—"

"Don't your ma ever say nothing?" Cassie Lee finished off her cup and smiled.

"No." He twirled the cup in his hand without looking up. "My ma's dead."

"Oh, Samuel. I'ma so sorry." She hugged him around the shoulders.

"She used to say a whole lot, but now it's just me and my pa."

"You lucky to have him, and he's lucky to have you."

"She took sick one day and died, my sister too. It was the cholera."

Cassie Lee regretted her thoughtless remark. This was just a funny kind of day. Tante Fatima would say it had to do with the full moon and the stars.

"I'ma go now," Samuel said and stood, gulping down the green liquid and handing the cup to her. "I'll see you tomorrow."

"Hiram say my vanilla is in. You want anything from the store?"

"No, thank you. But maybe next time I go fishing you can come along."

"Not too early?" She teased.

"No." He smiled.

"Would you take Moses back to the livery for me? I gotta start on dinner."

"Sure." He gladly loosened the rein and hopped on the horse's back. "See ya, Cassie Lee."

He was back to normal by the time he left. Such a brave little man who had the same kind of invisible scars that she did. No one knew about his either, until they asked. And even then, it mattered whether a person wanted to share their scars, wanted to open them again by talking about them.

Samuel was some special little boy. He'd taken her to Millie's, where she bought four skirts and four blouses and some female underthings. Samuel supplied her with meats and other produce, which allowed her to make those scrumptious meals that were the rave in the house and the envy of the town. But what made him most valuable to her was that Samuel accepted her unconditionally, no questions asked.

She stood to go into the house and finish up dinner. She looked out over the view toward the mountains and back to the beginning of her vegetable garden. Seems if he could lose his mother and sister and get over it, she should be able to shake the likes of Solomon Hawk.

* * * * * * * * * * * *

With her kitchen cleaned and the girls preparing for their callers, Cassie Lee wandered down to her usual spot on the big log by the shed where she practiced the letters Samuel had been teaching her. She sat etching her name in the dark soil, pondering on what a funny kind of day it had been, as she waited for the house to heat up and then settle down so she could go to bed.

"Howdy."

Cassie Lee jumped at the sound of the male voice.

"Didn't mean to scare you none," he said.

"Mister," Cassie Lee began as she erased her name, but kept the stick and stood. "I think what you want is in the house."

"I just came down for a little conversation," he said.

Cassie Lee tapped the stick in her hand.

"My name's Elijah Cobb." He removed his hat and extended his hand in one swift motion. She didn't accept it.

"Mr. Cobb, like I say, what you want is in the house."

"I just came to talk to you is all, Miss Lee." Surprise registered on Cassie Lee's face. "It is *Miss* Lee, isn't it?"

Cassie Lee considered her options. Her direct path to the house was blocked by the frame of this man. She could probably poke him in the eye with the stick, and then run like hell to where . . . ? Folks in the house would laugh at her for resisting. The sheriff or any of the other citizens of River Bend wouldn't think anything of a woman in a whorehouse objecting to the advances of a man.

"Miss Lee you have no reason to be afraid. I know you the cook and not—" he stumbled, "a workin' girl."

"You don't think cookin' is work, Mr. Cobb?"

"Elijah," he corrected before continuing, "I just hear tell that you have a drawl as deep as mine, and I thought we'd have some things in common is all. I know you may find it hard to believe, but sometime a man just don't want a poke."

When she didn't respond, he ventured on, "I'm up from Texas. Not much to do down there since they joined the Union except keep the Mexicans on their side of the Rio Grande. I'm a ranger. You heard of them?" Cassie Lee shook her head no.

"Texas sounds a ways away, Mr. Cobb."

"I got the wanderlust, and a hankering for these parts. It be pretty hot, dry, and dusty down there."

"Ummm," Cassie Lee said, and thought on how one man got the stay puts, and this one got the wanderlust.

She looked at him standing there, tall with hat in hand, and tried to decipher him. His skin shone bright in the moonlight, brighter than hers. And his features were neither quite like hers, nor like those she left back home on the people she loved, like Nubby and Tante Fatima. Most vexing was his hair. The rays of the moon caught and strayed through his light-colored curls. She couldn't tell whether Elijah Cobb was black or white, or maybe he was Indian or Mexican. Being here had opened up more possibilities than the South ever had.

"You ever been to Texas?" he asked.

"No sir, I haven't." Cassie Lee began walking toward the house. "I'ma turn in now."

"I'll walk a ways with you. Nice night. You like it here?"

"It be all right 'till I can do better."

"Probably got your sight on Sacramento or San Francisco." Cassie Lee almost stopped walking. "No big secret, everybody is on their way to one or the other."

"I expect it take big money to get there and stay there good."

"One hundred and fifty dollars for the boat from Sacramento to San Francisco."

"One hundred and fifty dollars?" Cassie Lee's voice broke.

"Yep. There's cheaper ways to travel, but not all that safe for a woman as handsome as you. You'd want to go direct."

They'd reached the bottom of the steps, and only his unabashed grin yanked her back from the sum of one hundred and fifty dollars.

"Well, goodnight, Mr. Cobb."

"Elijah." He stood and smiled.

"Have a pleasant night," Cassie Lee said with a finality that didn't seem to matter to Mr. Cobb, so she turned and walked up the five steps to the back porch screen door.

Without looking back, she walked through the open kitchen door and closed it tightly behind her. She prayed his footsteps would not follow her, as she cut the kitchen lamp and went to her back room in darkness. She eased herself next to the potbelly stove and saw Elijah Cobb's silhouette still at the bottom of the steps. She moved quietly into the kitchen and got the butcher knife. She tiptoed back to the slit of screen between the stove and the porch wall, and looked for him again. He was gone.

Her heart beat faster, and frayed nerves forced sweat to her skin's surface. Had he come up on the porch and she hadn't seen him? She clutched the knife close to her chest as she dared to look at the kitchen door through the screen opening in her room. He was not there. He had gone. She sighed relief and thanked the Lord. She set the knife on the rim of the stove only while she struggled to coax the seldom-used pocket door, which separated her room and the kitchen, shut. After several attempts she nudged it to within six inches of its complete closing.

She sat on the bed with knife in hand, fully clothed, and stared out at the bucolic view. The wind whispering through the pine trees sent refreshing air to cool her sweat. The shimmering moonlight danced on the distant mountains, and the piano playing jostled the rafters and jarred her to the more immediate circumstances.

As the weariness of the day grasped her, she fell over and lay on the soft feather bed. Her last thought was, "I got to get me a gun."

Chapter X

Bohemia was still Cassie Lee's source for news when she carried her coffee and toast up to her in the morning. That's how she knew about the white folks in Oregon not really owning their land because it still belonged to the British, and about some Indians who were being forced to work the gold mines for white folks.

"Slavery comes in all colors," Bohemia said, as she sat her paper aside.

"But the massa is always white," Cassie Lee said as she left, not seeing Bohemia's smile of approval.

After breakfast with her girls, Bohemia came into the kitchen for her usual cup of hot water for tea. She placed it on the tray herself and took it back upstairs. Despite the heat, Bohemia always came down several times a day for a cup of hot water and left. Never saying anything. Cassie Lee pondered this as she made her way to the general store to get her vanilla.

"I know what you come for!" Hiram Schmidt said.

"Been a long wait. Oh, look at these." She picked up the spiny fruits.

"Pineapples. They too green now. Got to let them set out awhile, and when they turn yella, cut this all off, core it, and cut the slices."

"I'ma make a pineapple upside-down cake." Cassie Lee had never seen a whole pineapple. When she worked in the big house kitchen, Bethesda must have already cored it up.

Cassie Lee loved coming to the store and seeing what they had new. As the earth awakened in these parts, she sent up various new fruits and vegetables, and Cassie Lee delighted in experimenting with them. All practice for my boarding house meals, she thought.

"Hiram, put this gun on the bill too."

"That's mighty expensive. It's a Colt Walker Revolver six shooter."

"Shoots six times straight? How much?"

"Twenty-five dollars. Sam Colt started making them in '47, replaces the Colt Patterson five shot. The men work down Texas way say the .44 caliber six shot is as accurate as you can get."

"Put it on the bill and gimme some of them shells, gunpowder, and pistol balls. How much?"

"Seventy-five cents."

"Well, that's more like it. I'ma pay for them."

* * * * * * * * * * * *

Cassie Lee stashed the gun under her mattress until she could carve out time to practice shooting. She had the gun. All she needed now, she thought as she climbed the steps to get Bohemia's morning tray, was to learn to read and save her one hundred and fifty dollars passage from Sacramento to San Francisco.

The house was sure quiet when they was all out, Cassie Lee thought. Only Libby using the upstairs pump and swishing her broom across the carpet and stairs could be heard. There was just a thin seam of time after Libby left and before everyone came back from their outings. On Sunday they weren't welcomed in church, so they held services of their own on the outskirts of town with a picnic lunch. Cassie Lee liked exploring the finery they left behind in silence.

She tiptoed down the short hall in search of the room Candy had described. As she pushed the door back, the smell of sweetness and sweat commingled in a delightful aroma, and a grand grin washed over Cassie Lee's face. There it was before her, just like Candy said—a gigantic brass tub surrounded by fluffy clean towels, fragrant soaps, and unlit candles.

The room, clad with drapes, was dark even in the daylight and had a smoldering, smoky feel. Cassie Lee laughed aloud and opened the door so she could see inside. Just like Candy said, the tub was big enough for two people. It was big enough for her and Solomon.

Involuntarily, Cassie Lee's heart took off for the high Sierras as she recalled how Solomon had brought her a tub from Exum. It was after they had established their once-a-week baths. And she didn't know how he managed to get it to the cabin. But she remembered coming back to the cabin after gathering juniper berries to find it full of hot water Solomon had boiled on the stove.

* * * * * * * * * * * *

"Solomon! What's this?" she had asked, as she set her basket down, and removed her hat.

"I thought you'd like to take a hot bath in a bigger tub for a change." He poured more water into the tub, and the smoky mist rose up from the liquid. He was peeling a green apple and letting the fragrant skin float on top.

"Oh, Solomon." She had run to him and melted into his arms. He was hot and shirtless. She was cold and fully dressed.

Slowly, he had removed her bear coat, and it fell to the floor. He reached and undid her bun, and her black hair fell in ripples down her back. He kissed her, and the heat from his tongue relaxed and ignited her at the same time. She could feel his maleness against her thigh, and she leaned into him as his massive hands encircled her body protectively like the wings of an archangel.

The glow from the fire lapped at his handsome face as he reared back to look at her. He kissed her neck and slid her blouse from her shoulders, exposing her taut, ripe nipples that resembled the luscious, dark berries she had just plucked. Cassie Lee stepped from her pants and savored the reflection of her body in Solomon's eyes. He stepped back to remove his pants, and his gaze boldly crawled all over her body, lingering at her breasts before traveling down her slim abdomen to her curly dark triangle. He made her feel deliciously female just by looking at her, and her juices began to flow.

119

When he could no longer bear to look at her without touching her, he stepped up to her and eased his hands around her waist, bringing her to him. His hungry kisses seared her face and neck, and her body quaked. He bent down to devour her breast, and she quivered beneath his touch. He knelt to pay homage, depositing a wealth of kisses before swooping her up and carrying her to his bed. As she kissed him, her hands held his handsome face before cascading down the length of his body, cupping and rubbing his masculine fruits before he took them from her, steered, and then released his male energy into her.

"Cassie Lee, Cassie Lee, Cassie Lee," he had whispered into her ear at every rhythmic wave.

Cassie Lee jumped as she stood in the doorway looking at the tub, missing Solomon even more. She felt weak and spent just thinking about him. She massaged her heart, as if that would make the pain of what used to be go away. She smoothed the hair around her ear, and her hand rested under her chin as she sighed out loud.

An answering moan came from somewhere. It startled her. She was alone in the house. Libby had left. The moan came again—from the room across the hall. Another moan was followed by a sigh, and Cassie Lee tiptoed toward the noises.

She pushed open the door to find another darkened room. As her eyes adjusted from the bright hallway to the dim light, she saw a figure lying on a bed. She turned to leave.

"No, come in please," a weak voice urged.

"I don't think I'ma spose to be—"

"When did that ever stop you, Cassie Lee?" The woman rolled over on her stomach so she was now facing her visitor at the door.

"How you know my name?"

"Bo talks about you all the time." The woman tried to sit up, but was too weak, and collapsed on the rim of the mattress. She was draped so precariously on the bed, Cassie Lee feared she would fall off, so she went over and caught the woman before the floor did.

"Thank you," she said in a drawl as thick as Cassie Lee's.

Cassie Lee noted that the woman was as light as a bird, frail, and so pale you could see blue veins through her skin even in the dimness.

"My name is Cherry. Cherry Pie," she laughed hoarsely at her own joke. "You so serious. Bo said you were. We're dear old friends. Just like sisters, even though she's black and I'm white."

Cassie Lee swallowed hard. She knew she wasn't supposed to be here with this woman, and she wasn't supposed to be hearing this. Oh, I have messed up, she thought. I'ma gon lose this job and not get that extra money to get to San Francisco.

"Relax," Cherry said in a hoarse whisper. "I won't tell her you was here."

Yeah, I'ma gonna trust an old, drunk, white whore with my future, Cassie Lee thought. I ain't never gon put my life in nobody's hands ever again—black or white. She stood to go.

"Where you going?" Cherry managed. "I know you want to hear this, Bo says you got a real curious nature." She winced from pain somewhere in her puny body. "And I could use the company."

"I was jus' gon open the curtains some and let fresh air in here."

"Death sure do stink, don't it?"

"You dyin'?"

"Yeah, I got the sex sickness. It's taking too damn long. Painful too. Thanks to Bo, I don't feel much of nothing, but I'm tired of living. Tired of breathing in and out. Some say this ain't living at all. I told Bo to cut the morphine and give me mercury, but she's hard-headed."

Having opened the windows, Cassie Lee stood awkwardly in the middle of the room's faded elegance.

"Tell you what," she said just above a sigh. "I promise not to tell you was here, if you promise not to tell Bo what I'm gonna tell you." Cassie Lee swooped her hair behind her ear and rocked from one foot to the other. "C'mon, sit down here while I tell you about my sister Grace Cogswell." Cassie Lee drew up a stool from the vanity.

"That's how I first met her in St. Louie. We was both gonna be teachers. She was from Philadelphia, I think. I was from Virginia. My daddy was Irish, and my mother was French. They was high-natured folks, so I grew up with high-natured ideas about marriage and the like. My family was rich beyond imagining. So I was paired up and married to a handsome rich planter from South Carolina and went back home with him, but that's another story. Suffice it to say that there's a lot of white folks that got a lot of black in them—some know, some don't." She fanned her weak wrist in mid-air and stared off as if trying to determine the pattern to her wallpaper. "I met Bohemia while her family still lived in St. Louis, I think, but she had struck out on her own. She was everything I wasn't never gonna be. She was big, dark, and strong."

She chuckled before continuing, "We was up for the same teaching position and I told them, who was doing the hiring, that me and Miss Cogswell was a package deal. I mean, we had been looking for a job for months, and she had studied Greek and Latin and such, and our money was running out to pay that rooming house. The school members passed us both up. Two for one deal, they didn't care. You know what Bohemia say to me? She say after we left, 'That was a stupid thing to do.'"

Cherry laughed as loudly as her frail body would allow. "Bo said if they had offered her the job she wouldn't have thought twice about me. She was right. Bohemia has always been a tough cookie. She takes care of me now though. She takes real good care of me." Her voice trailed off.

"Bohemia said if I had taken the job at least I could feed her. But I wasn't thinking. Nobody think quite like Grace 'Bohemia Jones' Cogswell do. When the rooming house kicked us out, I got a job working in a saloon, and Bohemia was a washer woman."

Surprise registered on Cassie Lee's face.

"Yeah, can you believe that? Not for long. She say washing other people's dirty draws ain't for her. So we pooled our money and went to St. Joe where the wagon trains was leaving from. No better there. I took a job at a saloon. I liked it. I was pretty then, and I got lots of attention and money. I forgot all about teaching. So Bohemia got the notion to offer them men more than they was getting. She was the one who steered the men to me, and we split the profits. Before long, we had two rooms—one to sleep in and one to work in. Then other girls saw Bohemia's action, the way she made sure you ate and were protected from the men—cause it is hard for a woman out there alone. These other women wanted in, so then we rented a house with four bedrooms. To this day, I have never seen Bohemia turn a trick. I know she never been in love. Bohemia may be the oldest virgin in America." She chuckled, then laughed.

Cherry's breathing became thin and sporadic, and Cassie Lee grew fearful. "It's all right," Cherry said as she inhaled deeply, trying to get more air into her lungs. "It won't be long now." Cherry's sunken eyes fluttered closed, and the circles around them looked like ink.

Cassie Lee put the sheet around her feeble body and closed the windows, as Cherry seemed cold to the touch. She drew the curtains as she had found them, closed Cherry's door, and headed into Bohemia's room for the breakfast tray.

As she made her way back downstairs, Cassie Lee thought she had seen the most gruesome way to die. There are certainly quicker ways. She wondered about this disease that was killing Cherry so slowly. She knew that Tante Fatima had a cure for what ailed her, but she also knew Tante Fatima would never lift a finger to help Cherry Pie.

* * * * * * * * * * * *

Cassie Lee stood with the bright sunshine to her back. She raised the six-shooter to eye level and aimed at the tin cans. With each shot her body jerked, and missed its mark.

"Your aim seems pretty good."

Cassie Lee jumped.

"You always seem to be scarin' me, Mr. Cobb."

"Not my intent," he said, tipping his hat with a smile. He looked more white today then he had the other night. "If I may?" He came up beside her and shot all six cans up into the air.

Cassie Lee was visibly impressed.

"Just takes practice," he said.

"And a hat like that, I speck," Cassie Lee said with a smile.

"Well, here." He removed his hat to reveal a shock of light brown curls and placed it squarely on her head. She laughed. "That's better," he said, returning her smile. "Now, if I could give you a lesson."

Cassie Lee watched him walk to place the tin cans back on the platform. He was tall, and not bad to look at. She wanted to reserve any further compliments until she found out whether he was black or white. The way he swaggered and stood and the run of his physique said black, but his hair, eyes, and skin said white.

"Now," he said, walking toward her.

123

Cassie Lee grew nervous as he circled her and ended up standing behind her. He lightly touched her waist with one hand and raised her arm with the other.

"Close your left eye, and let your right eye run the barrel of the gun. See?"

Feel is more like it, Cassie Lee thought, as his body heat leapt from his to hers. His cheek was inches from hers and she felt a chilly surge, as if she were sticking her hands into snow. The gun fired. She hadn't meant for it to discharge.

"Whoa. Not bad. This time just look at where you want to shoot and squeeze the trigger. Gently, just squeeze."

Cassie Lee couldn't *squeeze* air from her lungs. Why did she feel like this?

"Ha! Bull's eye," he said once she sent the can flying. "All you got to do is practice. Finish out the barrel." She did, hitting three of the five cans left.

"I think I got the hang of it. Thank you, Elijah—" It got tangled on her tongue.

"Well, finally calling me by my name, just when I'm fixin' to leave."

"Going back to Texas?"

"Yep." He accepted the hat she handed back to him. "Got to make an honest livin'."

"Dangerous work being a Texas ranger?"

"Living these days is dangerous work, Cassie Lee. I was wondering," he said, twirling his hat around his hand, "If, when I get back this way, I might call on you?"

"Oh." Her hand flew to her neck to fiddle with Nubby's missing cross. Remembering she'd left it in the mountains, she let her hand rest on her collarbone. "If'n I'm here. I don't plan on being here long, but if'n I'm here, I guess that'd be fine."

"Well then, take care, Cassie Lee and take care of that gun. It's a beaut. You need to clean the oil out of the barrel on a new gun. I got two like that—you take care of it, and it'll return the favor. In case I miss you next time, I wish you luck."

"Bye. You too," Cassie Lee said, and went back to loading and shooting her Colt.

Cassie Lee tossed and turned in her sleep that night. Being that near and touched by a man not Solomon conjured up all sorts of wild representations of them both. It was like Solomon the man couldn't care less about her, but his jealous memory wouldn't stand for no such foolishness. In the end, it was Solomon that reigned over her thoughts and finally sent her into a peaceful sleep near dawn.

Chapter XI

You could hear it in the distance. Six steady shots. Time for a reload. Six more shots. Reload. Shots. For the town of River Bend, it meant it was about two o'clock in the heat of the day, and Cassie Lee was practicing her shooting. It meant she must have something good simmering on the stove or bread rising or chicken soaking in hot water almost ready for the plucking, which meant she didn't have the time to mount Moses and ride out of town to her favorite spot near the water for target practice. It meant she made do with the time she had, to do something she intended to do that day.

"Cassie Lee," he said, strolling up to her like a long lost, invited friend. "No matter where you go, girl, you do make your mark."

"Exum." His name fell from her lips like venom. "I thought you were long gone from here."

"It pains me you don't keep track of my comings and goings." He idly scratched the scar she had gifted him. "Miss me?" He swung his leg up and over a nearby stump.

Cassie Lee cut her eyes and went back to firing six shots, hitting her mark each time.

"Them cans got my face on 'em?"

"I wouldn't waste the lead," she said, reloading and firing another volley of six sure-fire shots.

"Well, I came back up here to get my money and carry it back to Gold Canyon." He continued because she didn't ask, "That's a wild little town. You should come by on your way down to San Francisco."

"You in it? Then I don't want no parts of it." Cassie Lee kept shooting and reloading.

"San Francisco ain't nothing but a sleepy Mexican village that's been woke up by the gold rush. It's beginning to come alive. Got people moving in on it all the time." Which was why he was on his last opium run to the Chinese miners. He was too old and this work was too dangerous, especially with the Tongs from San Francisco wanting to control the religious habits of their own people. Besides, he could make money hand over fist by staying put in a place like Gold Canyon, providing his goods and services.

"Umm humm." Cassie Lee continued to reload and shoot, not the least bit interested in Exum's assessment of any place.

"You was always one of my favorite people, Cassie Lee."

"Then you in a hurt for people, Exum."

"Can't I do nothing for you? I'm on my way to making my second fortune in that town. It's just starting out, but it's gonna make me rich. Got all the ingredients: gold, bankers, card sharks, miners, and whores." He laughed. Cassie Lee didn't as she continued her task. "So I can afford to give you anything you want or need."

"I don't need or want anything you got to give, Exum."

As she closed one eye, aimed, and squeezed the trigger, she thought of the Fugitive Slave Law and freedom papers, but by the time she finished the sixth shot, she decided she couldn't be beholden to Exum Taylor for anything. She didn't no more "belong" to Exum than the man in the moon. She was free. Period. Besides, the price of his "help" was too high.

"He'd of been here by now if he was comin', Cassie Lee."

"What?" She hadn't even realized that she had stopped firing and was staring at the mountains. "I don't need you to tell me that!" she spat, reloading her gun as she walked toward the house.

"He sure left a big old hole in your heart." Exum followed her, watching her hips sway invitingly beneath the gingham skirt.

"I just 'sume you don't tell nobody about my past life," she said, stopping abruptly looking at him while wondering if the word was sume or assume. She was still factoring on some of Bohemia's words.

"Done." They had resumed walking. "I feel responsible some for you, Cassie Lee—"

"Don't worry none 'bout me. I be jus' fine."

"Yes, you certainly are that." The appreciation in his voice caused Cassie Lee to look back and roll her eyes at him and his innuendo. She sucked her teeth in disgust and proceeded to walk faster.

"Oh, I know you be all right. Once you get your mind fixed on somethin' you like a snap turtle that won't let go. You got a whim of iron."

"You still tellin' me stuff I already know."

"And you still the prettiest filly around these parts even if you sweat on your nose. Sweatin' on your nose means you mean."

Cassie Lee just looked at him with that Tante Fatima thinking and said, "Goodbye, Exum."

"How 'bout I tell you something you don't know?" Cassie Lee clearly wasn't interested. "It's about Solomon." She stopped in her tracks.

"You seen him?"

"Not since you has, but I got to tell you somethin'."

"Well, spit it out, Exum."

"I got to 'pologize, it's been kinda eatin' at me for awhile now." He shifted his weight from one foot to another as he clearly read Cassie Lee's impatience. "I get the devil in me sometimes. Seems I can't stand to see nobody happy, even my best partner Solomon—and you did make him happy, Cassie Lee."

She gritted her teeth and looked away a second before firing her ebony eyes right at him. "What you got to tell me, Exum?"

He sighed heavily, then reluctantly began, "Solomon was the only family I had. We been together since we was pups. He let me live my life the way I saw fit and I obliged him the same, but we always knew we'd be there if one needed the other. Then he brought you here. Forget that I paid $1,000 for you; forget you showed out on me in front of folk." He stopped and looked toward the distant mountains before continuing, "You came between me and Solomon like a piece of gristle between perfectly happy teeth. Sure, we had plenty women before. Solomon even had a wife and kid, but she was no threat, she let him do whatever he wanted and I was right partial to that kid myself. But you . . ." He scratched his chin and looked away. "He came down from that mountain more often, but not to come by and see old Exum, no. He got his supplies and high-tailed it back home—back to you. It was hard for me to take. For the first time, I knew in my gut that if the chips were down, he'd most probably choose you over me. That didn't feel none too good. I wanted things back the way they was. I couldn't do nothing to you 'cause that'd just push Solomon further away from me. I have to admit I thought about it." A sly grin claimed his face. "So I had to make you go away." Cassie Lee looked at him hard. "He and I had words over you. Seems he took issue with the way I treated you once you refused me and left."

Cassie Lee glared at him and couldn't resist, "Is that how you remember it?"

"All water down the sluice, now," Exum waved off her remark and continued, "We said some pretty harsh things to one another, the kind of stuff only those closest to you know will hurt you the most. The worse anybody can do to Solomon is question his principles. I know that better than anybody, but that's exactly what I did. I don't know how or why, but Solomon got some high principles. When you attack the only thing a man got—he gets his back up."

Exum rolled the gist of the argument over in his mind.

"I told you she was decent," Solomon had said.

"I didn't ask you for no 'decent' gal," Exum had answered.

"Where is she?"

"Workin' at the Chinamen's laundry. I ain't bothered her none."

"You ain't helped her neither."

"What you gon do?"

"I dunno. Give her money to go where she wants."

"Ain't nobody going nowhere in twenty feet of snow. You gon keep her with you?"

"Not less'n there's nowhere else for her to go."

"Wait a minute," Exum smacked his head, recognizing the situation, and continued, "I got it now. The reason she didn't want to give me none is because she give it all to you on the trail. Boy, am I the fool? Did you take advantage of my good nature and my woman, Solomon?"

Silence met his question as Solomon fixed a cold stare against

Exum's verbal attack. He reduced his eyes into the narrow slits, funneling his anger, and said, "That was your woman, Exum."

"Well, hell, she ain't nobody's woman now except maybe them chinks," Exum had continued, trying to make a joke, but Exum had heard it—the irrevocable snap of the bonds of friendship.

Exum knew now as he knew then, he had crossed the line of loyalty: questioning Solomon's honor and stabbing him in the core of his being. He, above all, should understand how much character meant to his friend, and he called him on it—like a stranger. Exum saw it coming, and stepped in it anyway.

"I jus' get the devil in me sometime, Cassie Lee," he said, apologetically. "I knew I was wrong, I knew what would happen if I kept it up, I wasn't that drunk, but I did anyway. Later, I tried talking to him, but he had no use for me. It was clear I stomped on what was sacred to him." Exum grew quiet for a moment before pressing on, "Seems I may have misrepresented myself about seeing him and Ming going up to her room that afternoon." Cassie Lee stared at him without blinking. "Oh, he went up there alright, I sorta had Ming ask him up." He cleared his throat before continuing, "She was suppose to get him there any way she could, but it turns out he just helped her move some boxes and then left. So—" He grinned sheepishly and hunched his shoulders. "Nothin' happened, Cassie Lee. Solomon stayed true to you."

An exasperated puff of wind left her full lips as she shook her head in disbelief. "Damn you to hell for that," she said quietly, and commenced to walking again.

"Now you can go back up there to him!"

"And say what, Exum told me he lied so here I am?"

"Well, yeah, for starters. Blame it all on me."

"He never said he loved me, Exum." She didn't mean to tell him that, especially when he reared his head back and laughed at her.

"Hell, Solomon never told nobody he loved them. He never said it to that Indian wife or nobody else."

"It's more to it. It's jus' too late." She walked faster, half comforted that Solomon didn't seek the wiles of another woman, but perplexed that he still didn't want the one who waited at his cabin either. Ming or not, Cassie Lee wasn't going to tell Exum that Solomon wanted her to go.

When he came back from town with a horse and supplies, that told her to leave.

Propelled by her thinking, Cassie Lee was out-stepping Exum, leaving him in her dust. What was she supposed to do, travel six days by herself, beating a path to his door to find out he was either bedded down with another woman or wasn't glad to see her anyhow? He would invite her in, offer her his bed while he slept on the floor that night, then show her the way down the mountain in the morning. She'd feel like a bigger fool than she already did, because she knew better. She would know she should have never gone up there in the first place.

"It's jus' too little to go on, Exum. We both too late," she concluded aloud. "We both lost him to those mountains. He knows where I am if'n he wants me. Apparently, he don't."

Exum ran to keep pace with her and fished a paper from his pocket. "There's something else, Cassie Lee."

"What?" she snapped and whirled around toward him as she reached the bottom step. He handed her the folded-up paper. She didn't need to read all that good to decipher the words and picture on the sheet of paper.

There was a face, not Solomon's, with words WANTED over his hat and HAWK underneath his chin. She figured the long word said MURDER, and $5,000 was broad and clear.

"It says on the bottom it's from the sheriff at West County, Georgia," said Exum. She just stared at the paper as he continued, "I got it off a man who owed me money. It was all tucked back in his saddlebag."

"This don't look nothin' like Solomon."

"Yeah, 'specially that nose spread all over his face like that. You know we all look alike to them white folks." His chuckle fell on deaf ears.

"But you got to go tell him anyway!" Cassie Lee's eyes searched Exum's.

"Well, that's why I was hopin' you were going that way—but he'll make it."

"You not going to warn him?"

"For what? If'n they're out here, they'll all fall into gambling and gold hunting, and won't be thinkin' about going after 'Hawk.'"

"What kind of friend are you?"

"Warning Solomon is like warning a grizzly bear that people are in the vicinity. Solomon thinks those hills belong to him anyway. He'd shoot me first and ask questions later. I ain't worried at all about him. You better worry if'n anybody's fool enough to go up in them mountains after him. They the ones who need the pity." Cassie Lee sighed again, and walked up the steps. "It don't even look like him!" added Exum.

She let the screen door punctuate the end of the visit. "Hell, if'n anybody ever caught up to him, ole Solomon could pay them triple that money in gold jus' to be left alone!" he yelled, then added *sotto voce,* "If'n he didn't shoot him first." Exum eyed the closed screen, then spoke up again. "Somethin' sure smells good in there. Can't an old friend get some grub?"

"Ask Bohemia," Cassie Lee said in a tone that dared him to take one step toward the back porch.

"She a hard case like you," he yelled at her through the closed screen door. "See you 'round, Cassie Lee!"

"Not if'n I see you first," she said, stirring a pot of fragrant greens simmering with fat back.

Cassie Lee thought about Solomon's predicament as she sank a cup into the green liquid and set it aside to cool. Exum was wrong most of the time, but he was right about one thing—Solomon could take care of himself. What was she worried about him for? He wasn't worried about her.

Cassie Lee let the spicy liquid slide down her throat. She couldn't help but think of Samuel whenever she drank pot liquor. He was helping her learn to read words. Now, with mail coming more regular to Sacramento, Bohemia started throwing out some of her papers to make way for new ones, so Cassie Lee and Samuel started reading things that were happening all over the country.

It was so exciting. She didn't have to depend on Bohemia for all her news now, although she was still trying to imitate her boss's speech. Cassie Lee knew she would never lose all of her southern drawl, but she had wiped the word "ain't" from her vocabulary. Her "I'ma's" had turned into "I am's," her "gots" to "have." She was working on putting "ing's" at the end of her words and replacing the "no's" with "any;" I don't have "any" more dishes to wash. She was becoming a regular lady. By the time she got to San Francisco she was going to speak proper, and add reading to the way she figured sums—which was a gift, Bohemia told her.

* * * * * * * * * * * *

"You ready, Cassie Lee?" Samuel peeked into the kitchen.

"Sure am." She got her fishing pole and a lunch for them.

"Got something for you," Samuel said, as they walked down the steps toward Moses. "Surprise!" He sprang a newspaper on her. "It's a current one."

"Currant? Like raisins?" Cassie Lee asked, as she swung up on Moses and extended her hand to hoist Samuel up.

"No. You so funny. Like in recent or up to date."

"I knew that," Cassie Lee said, as Samuel situated their snack and led Moses out onto the road by his reins.

The three of them loved to ride outside the town a ways and stop where the river bent and ran up on the shore. The ritual dictated that they tie Moses to a nearby tree where he could feast and drink whenever he pleased, while Samuel readied and stuck fishing poles in the water as Cassie Lee spread a blanket and lay out the snack. Samuel would return from his task and dive for a fried chicken leg as Cassie Lee commandeered the paper. Fishing was just a ruse for their hidden agenda: eating and reading.

"OK, this one's from St. Joe," Cassie Lee identified as she scanned the fine print.

"Pretty soon, San Francisco will have its own paper," Samuel said, and began gnawing on a new chicken leg.

"You better slow down that eating, or you gonna finish up what I brung."

"Brought," Samuel corrected with a smile.

"What I brought," Cassie Lee repeated to get the sound of it right. "They got anything in here on black folks or San Francisco?" She handed him the paper.

"Here." Samuel pointed to an article.

"Got some big words in it," Cassie Lee noted as her eyes perused the article.

"All we got to do is sound them out. We can get most of them and the meat of what they saying."

They read about Iowa passing an act that prohibited the immigration of free blacks to the state. Every free black was given three days to leave once notified by a public official. Those who refused were taken to court and, if convicted, ordered to pay two dollars for each day they stayed in the state. Then they were put in jail until they paid a fine or left. Virginia had a new law that freed slaves had to leave the state within one year or be enslaved again.

"Gal-dang," Cassie Lee said in amazement. "Glad I ain't going to Iowa or Virginia."

"Or Illinois and Indiana either," Samuel read on. "It says in Oregon they punish not only the blacks who enter, but those that bring them."

"You got a bite!" Cassie Lee exclaimed, and Samuel threw down the paper and ran for his line.

"It's a beaut!" Samuel yelled and held up the big fish.

"Some good eating there," Cassie Lee said, as she rolled up her pants above her knee and guided her pretty brown legs down to where the river curved and created a pool of tranquility. "But we need quantity. Lemme show you how to fish."

Samuel watched her wade into the still pool of water and stand there patiently, then stab fish after fish with a sharp stick.

"Good God almighty!" he exclaimed.

"You not taking the Lord's name in vain, are you?" she said, as she threw her catch up from the hollow and made her way back up the rocky incline.

"Naw, I'm thanking Him! You got to have some Indian in you!"

"Could be." Cassie Lee preferred Indians over white or some other less handsome group of people for that in her which was not black. "That water's a might chilly." She rubbed her cold feet in the blanket.

"Comes down from the mountains."

Cassie Lee looked up toward the Sierras, thinking it was good something comes down from the mountains. Solomon sure wasn't.

She liked this spot. The air was fresh with a nip to it as it rode on the scent of pine, and the sound of rushing water tripping and falling over rocks as it made its way to who knows where. It was like a soothing

135

lullaby. She looked back, and Samuel had fallen asleep, the sun gracing one side of his face with a gentle caress. He flicked an insect from his nose and rolled off to the side. He was going to grow into a handsome man one day, Cassie Lee thought. Hopefully he'd make some lucky woman a great husband. He'd want to marry proper and all. His parents had—so would he.

Husband. The word hung in the mid-air of her mind. Would she ever have one? Mate. A lifetime mate would suffice. Slaves seldom had either, and when they did, it was subject to the whim and feelings of the master. She'd met her lifetime mate even if they would never be together again. Even if Cassie Lee was not good at figuring, it didn't take a genius to know that it was only a five-day ride to River Bend. Probably only two, three tops, for Solomon. If he had wanted to come, he could have been there and back a thousand times by now.

Cassie Lee snatched up some grass near her and threw it—snatched and threw . . . as she watched the rush of the river and remembered the pleasurable rush of Solomon exploding inside her. The way he rocked, then filled every cavity of her being. The way he was inside her, knowing just where and what needed attention— stroking, kissing, caressing, touching, nibbling—before she did. A need would arise in her, and before she could get a fix on it, he was there massaging the need away.

She closed her eyes, and she could feel his breathe on her cheek— the warm, moist, scented sweetness of it. She could taste the salty nectar of his body on her lips. She ached for him. Her breast tightened. Her center expanded and she felt the film of wet all over her body.

"Cassie Lee, you OK?" Samuel asked, as he sat up rubbing his eyes.

"Oh." He'd brought her back from the mountains. "I'm fine," she said hoarsely, clearing her throat. "It's just a little warm is all."

"You looked a million miles away. You missing back home?"

"Didn't your pa and I agree that home is where the heart is?" Then my home would always be in the mountains with Solomon, she thought. "Tell you what I do miss," she said, flashing a smile at him, and he relaxed.

"What?"

"Picking choke cherries by the water. Roasted sweet potatoes, muscadine and mulberry wine, boiled goobers and pawpaws."

"Pawpaws?" he laughed.

"You eat 'em, and they smell so good, they perfume up the whole house."

"Really? We have them?"

"No, you ain't got the climate for them." She hooded her eyes as she looked towards the sky and said, "From the slant of that sun we best be getting back." She got the blanket while he gathered the fish and threw them into the now-empty picnic basket.

"Cassie Lee, spell this!" Samuel touched an object.

"T-r-e-e."

"And this."

"G-r-a-s-s!"

"And this!" When her eyebrows knitted together he said, "sound it out."

"W-a," she hesitated, "t-e-r!"

"Great! And this!"

"R-o-k!" she said and Samuel looked dejected. "Rock."

"R-o-C-k!" he corrected.

"That don't make a lick of sense." She swung her arm around his neck playfully. "We gonna change that, you and me." He smiled up at her. "You can ride Moses in the front this time."

"Sing that song for me, Cassie Lee."

"*. . . I sing because I'm happy. I sing because I'm free. For His eye is on the sparrow, and I know He watches me.*"

* * * * * * * * * * * *

Candy was waiting for them when they rounded the back on Moses.

"For folk who go fishin' all the time, you don't never catch nothing," she teased.

"Oh yeah?" Samuel jumped down and showed off their catch.

"I stand corrected," she said before turning to Cassie Lee. "You want to learn how to make these tortillas or not?"

The three of them sat on the steps of the back porch drinking pot liquor and watching the sun dance its diminishing rays of light on Cassie Lee's garden.

"You know what else I miss?" Cassie Lee asked the pair. "Okra!"

"Okra," Samuel repeated. "What's that?"

"A slimy little pod of nasty white peas," Candy chided.

"It's good eating, and thickens soup and such. Came over from Africa." The word hung between the silent trio. "Of course, there's a plenty to keep me busy here."

Cassie Lee reflected on the abundance of fruits and vegetables to which she had been exposed. There were plants and foods she would miss and probably never see again: sugar cane, cacao, cassia, maguey, cochineal, indigo. There were the same plants with different uses and names, like maize for corn that Candy was teaching her about—and all kinds of beans with stripes and spots, and one was even all black. There were those long, skinny noodles, and ginger, coriander, and all kinds of green leafy vegetables from Chinatown. There was cumin and all sorts of fiery peppers from the Mexicans. The Indians used the same beans, squash, and pumpkin as blacks did in Georgia, but they added yucca and prickly pear cactus. There was food that sometimes came up from deep Mexico and Panama—colorful, exotic stuff like the coconut that she and Samuel had bounced all over the ground trying to break, until finally they took a hammer to it. They raised the regular stuff like chickens, and hunted deer, squirrel, and rabbit. But they didn't have bear, antelope, or buffalo back in Georgia. With this bounty of food, Nubby would never have to eat clay or pick polk salad behind the cabin or worry about rations from Friday lasting the week.

"I sing because I'm happy," Cassie Lee began, and Candy and Samuel looked at her and smiled. *"I sing because I'm free. His eye is on the sparrow, and I know He watches me."* They all laughed at her exuberant burst of joy.

"Candy," Bohemia's husky voice interrupted. "There's someone here to see ya." The three fell silent as Candy stood and left.

"I despise it when she talks like that. She knows better," Cassie Lee seethed about Bohemia. "I heard her speaking in a foreign tongue the other day, and I asked what it was. It was French. She speak French, Spanish, and English real good; she don't have to talk like that. She sound ignorant." She hated to see her teacher cow-tow to anybody. Especially customers.

"Sometimes you got to do what you got to do," Samuel said, as he hunched his shoulders and stood.

"Guess you better be getting on home. Take Moses."

"All the way home? Really?"

"Then you won't be late, and your pa won't be mad."

"Thanks, Cassie Lee." He ran and hopped on the horse before she could change her mind.

"In fact, why not just keep him. If you promise not to brush a hole in him when you pat him down."

"I'll take real good care of him, Cassie Lee. I promise! Thanks!"

Cassie Lee witnessed the sun plummet into the horizon, sending up the moon and stars in a splash to take its place. She stretched out her long legs as she heard the Professor start up on the piano, which meant Henry was pouring drinks at the small bar. The house was coming alive. She swatted away a buzzing mosquito as the moon washed her garden, outhouse, and shed in a silver patina. The sun had taken the heat of the day with it and all that remained was a welcomed coolness, the kind that ensured a deep, peaceful sleep.

* * * * * * * * * * * *

She had had her Solomon thought for today. She had finally stopped fighting thoughts of him and just rationed in her mind that she was entitled to one per day. It was easier to embrace him, then let him go, than to fight him. He was up to his old tricks, taking a ribbon of her consciousness and wrapping himself in a pretty package her mind could not resist opening again and again. Not that he didn't sometimes arrest her dreams and hold her hostage until daybreak. Even then, she wasn't sure it was him who gave her such a demon night until her body, upon waking, told her he had been there—if only in her dreams.

Cassie Lee stood and brushed off her pants, despite the fact that she swept these steps clean each and every day. It felt good to be in pants again. When she left for San Francisco she was going to buy a few more pairs of those tough denim work pants that Levi Strauss made for miners. She'd be running her own place, and she could wear pants if she wanted. But that wouldn't fit into Cassie Lee's boarding house decor, she thought, as she readied for bed. She climbed in beneath the sheets and concluded, I'll think on that tomorrow.

It was just too hot to cook all day long. But Cassie Lee prepared

Bohemia's morning tray amidst the smell and splatter of fried hominy, bacon, and sausage for breakfast and the beginnings of dinner as well.

There was a powerful rattling at the door. "Samuel! Why you keeping up such noise this morning?" Cassie Lee asked, as she unhooked the screen door. She looked into the swollen red eyes of the little boy. "Samuel," she bent to him. "What happened?"

"I can't keep Moses!" he blurted out uncontrollably. "My Pa says I can't keep him, and I can't see you or come here any more!"

"But why?" She wiped his fresh tears with the hem of her apron. "You'd be doing me and Moses a favor."

"Because—" he stopped, as if it pained him to say it. "Because— because I shouldn't be hanging around this house with people like you all. My Pa says he thought I was running errands all this time, and if he knew where I was all this time, he would have come and got me from here," he tumbled to an end.

"Well," Cassie Lee said as she stood. "Did you tell him that I was just the cook?"

"He don't believe that, Cassie Lee." He tried to swallow his tears. "He said if you work here, there's no telling what you do. He said I should only be around decent folk, like he is and my mother was, and my sister was growing up to be."

Cassie Lee's back stiffened and her lips hardened. "C'mon, I got a few words of my own for yo' daddy."

She started to undo her apron when the water from the potatoes boiled over, sending up white steam and threatening to douse the stove's fire. When she ran over to tend to it, Samuel followed.

"You going over to see my daddy?" he asked with a mixture of panic and confusion.

"I sure would if'n I didn't have all this going on the stove." She turned to him. "Listen, you tell yo' daddy that he shouldn't judge a book by the cover. You tell him that he doesn't decide who is *decent* and who isn't. You tell him if he got something to say about me—a 'decent' person would come say it to my face."

She switched the pots on the stove and continued, "You tell him that 'decent' folks don't spread lies. You tell him if he think I'ma whore, come and call me one to my face. You tell him that!"

"I'm sorry, Cassie Lee." He began crying more. "I'm sorry."

"Ah." She stopped fiddling with the pots. "It's not your fault you got a ignorant daddy, Samuel." She comforted him as he looked up at her, and then hugged her waist.

She read a double dose of pain in his eyes. The two people he probably cared for most right now had harsh words to say about one another. One had the power to keep him from the other.

"I'm sorry too, Samuel."

Wiping his eyes again with her tear-soaked apron, she said, "It's gonna be all right." Her ebony eyes held his. "Would you take Moses to the livery on your way back home?" she asked quietly, smiling at him.

"But I'll never see you again!"

"Oh, Samuel. I'll talk to your Pa and we'll have it—" she stopped and corrected, "work it out. It might be that you'll be right."

Her words caused such distress in his young eyes.

"He *is* your pa, and what he says goes, Samuel. He is right, you are quality—a special, decent little man, and you should only hang around special, decent people—"

"That's you, Cassie Lee!" He started up crying again, and she joined him, though she didn't mean too.

"Why, thank you for that." She stood up holding the tears in her eyes. "Now you take Moses to the livery and run on home. Go on, here." She threw him a big, green apple. He smiled through the tears. "Everything'll work out like it suppose to. Go on, now."

Samuel paused at the threshold before waving and jumping down the steps.

"Damn dirt farmer," she spat, as she heard the horse's hooves trot away. "The gall of—Oow!" She burned herself on the cast iron handle.

Chapter XII

Cassie Lee was quiet as she served breakfast, finally realizing that, at least, Samuel had someone to watch over him. As she simmered down, she recognized that she would be leaving soon, and she had no right to come between father and son. She didn't like it, but she decided to stay out of it. Samuel was such a good boy, he would obey his father—and maybe that was the last time she would see her friend.

As Cassie Lee dried the breakfast dishes and finished up preparation for the dinner meal, her quiet was assaulted by sounds from the piano. Music she had never in her life heard the Professor play. "Oh Susanna!" it wasn't. It was a high-toned melody unlike anything ever played from a voice or instrument.

The captivating sounds drew her from the kitchen like a snake charmer. The glass she was drying with the towel was an unwilling hostage as she pushed her shoulder to the second parlor door. There, perched on a stool with a glass of amber-colored liquid within arm's reach, sat Bohemia. The feather in her hair shook with the powerfulness of the music as her dark brown fingers danced up and down the black and white keys. Cassie Lee stood transfixed.

"Close your mouth around a glass of something, Sugar," Bohemia offered, as she took a gulp of the amber liquid. "Go on over to the bar and pour yourself a shot of wine or something."

She licked her lips and positioned her hands over the keys to play another piece. "It ain't muscadine, dandelion, or mulberry, but I think you'll like it."

Bohemia began tinkering with the keys. She played another song with such passion that it mesmerized Cassie Lee. At this song's end, Bohemia opened her eyes and held her finger on the last vibrating note.

"Some piano, huh?" she asked, as her fingertips glided over the ornate carving. "Took me three tries to get one. The other two left out on the trail or in some Indian's tepee—so they tell me. This one's all the way from St. Louie!"

"I ain't never heard no music like that."

"Mozart," Bohemia said, as her eyes took a trip back where Cassie Lee couldn't go. "I do Beethoven, Chopin, Bach—"

"Who are they?" Cassie Lee asked, and Bohemia let out her roof-rattling laughter. "Better still," Cassie Lee ventured on, "Who are you, Bohemia Jones?"

The old woman choked on her swallowed laughter and looked at Cassie Lee like she had just slapped her. Bohemia closed the lid over the keys as if shielding them from what was about to be said. Her full, rubied lips drained her glass of liquid, and she set it back up on the ledge and swung her stool around to face Cassie Lee. A rumbling began in her chest, then exploded through her big white teeth, and the laughter filled the room. Then, she stopped abruptly.

"My daddy wouldn't like that. My daddy liked proper-acting folks. He'd die all over again if he knew I was talkin' like this. My daddy, the Reverend Archibald Cogswell."

Cassie Lee watched Bohemia rise from the stool, go over to the bar, and pour herself another healthy glassful of liquor before returning to her small round seat.

"My daddy was a slave who escaped to Boston. He married my pretty mama, who was born free like her parents before her. It was a mixed marriage." Bohemia winked. "You know, an ex-slave marrying a free woman." She took a sip from her glass. "My mama loved that black man. My mama had nothing to prove. She was everything any man would want. Pretty, cultured, had money. My daddy had a lot to prove. Or a lot to overcome."

She shrugged her shoulders and continued, "So we moved to Philadelphia, out from under my mother's father's shadow. We had a fabulous house. We had servants, not slaves—servants. Anything me and my sisters wanted was ours for the asking. We went to Europe three times."

She looked sideways at Cassie Lee, who didn't know enough to be impressed.

"Then when I was about eleven, we moved again to St. Louis, where my daddy decided to become a soul-saving preacher. Somethin' to prove," she said softly. "I liked it there. Too much maybe, or my daddy thought so. He found me one night with a boy in the barn. Humph, you would have thought we were doing something else besides kissing." She stopped and stared off.

"My daddy never looked at me the same again. Like his baby girl was horse mess to be avoided in the street. My older sisters had all married well and were living respectable lives with husbands and children. But what to do about Grace? Poor little Grace Elizabeth Cogswell. Hadn't he given her everything? Hadn't she studied Greek, Latin, French, math, and surveying? Hadn't she read *Beowulf,* Chaucer, and Shakespeare? And couldn't she play the piano beautifully?"

Her tongue grew silent again as her eyes took off on another private journey.

"Well, the second time, I got caught down on the seedy side of town. I was just young and curious, and fascinated by what went on down there on Front Street. But it seems my inquisitiveness wasn't appreciated, and I brought disgrace upon the Cogswell name. Cogswells were into saving souls, not becoming ones in need of it. So."

She swung around to face Cassie Lee, reared back forcing her ample bosom forward, and placed both elbows back on the piano lid.

"When I was sixteen years old, I left before he could throw me out. My older sister told me that was the plan, along with the fact that none of them could take me in once our father threw me out. So I took my little luggage and some money and moved out, tried to make it on my own before buying a ticket to St. Joe where I was going to be a teacher. Even with my background, it seems I had something to prove to my father, the ex-slave."

Bohemia stopped and placed her hands in her lap, rubbing and inspecting them.

"Things didn't quite work out the way I planned. There was little call for an educated Negro woman to teach anybody, anything. I shoulda gone on home," she said, quietly looking off into that same distance. "But I was young, determined, and no failure, which I would have surely been called once I returned home to the Cogswell domain. As bad as it has been all these years—it was never as bad as going home and seeing my father's cold, righteous 'I-told-you-so' eyes boring a hole through me like I was scum you ladle off boiling stew."

She sat there twirling one of the many rings on her fingers for so long that Cassie Lee began to leave.

"So!" She snapped out of it. "I did what I had to do *not* to go home again." She slapped her generous thighs disguised beneath the thin silk. "A little of this, a little of that, and the rest, as the Greeks say, is history." She stood.

"Maybe why I have a hankering for high yella men 'cause my daddy was as black as the ace of spades. My own color is the only reminder of him I need, but when I lay up next to a man I want a contrast." She laughed and poured another drink.

"Umph, umph, umph." Bohemia's eyes danced, her lips split into a wide grin. "A mellow, yellow fellow. Nothing like 'em. Their skin so fresh and smooth and clean-looking, and when they got the hair and eyes to match? Lord have mercy!"

"To each his own," Cassie Lee said, thinking she was probably promoting Elijah Cobb.

"And I don't mean no Elijah Cobb," she said, as her eyes narrowed, and she saw Cassie Lee's surprise.

Lord, the woman can read minds, Cassie Lee thought.

"He's pert near white," said Bohemia. "Go that far might as well cross the bridge." She eyed the unresponsive girl. "Not your cup of tea, huh? I guess you like 'em raisin black? Black-coffee black?"

"I don't have time for such foolishness," Cassie Lee said to stop this line of conversation. "I got plans."

146

"Who don't at your age. Been stung, huh?"

"What?"

"You're pining over somebody, Sugar. Black or yella, he ain't here with you where he's suppose to be, so just forget him. Put him right out of your mind."

She can read minds! Cassie Lee thought.

Bohemia paused to soak in Cassie Lee's open-mouthed expression. "You got it bad, Sugar. You take the time to mourn and grieve before you move on. Before you bury your love, make sure it's dead or when you least expect it, it'll come back and bite you in the butt. He gave you that bear coat, didn't he?"

"I shot that bear myself," Cassie Lee said, proudly looking directly into Bohemia's eyes. The woman smiled at her progress.

"You skin and cure it too?" Cassie Lee dropped her eyes and swooped the hair behind her ear. "You best piss those demons outta you or they'll eat you alive, Sugar."

"Ummm," Cassie Lee said, as she pushed the door back out of the parlor to the hall and into her kitchen. Some folks judging other folks unfairly, and other folks getting all liquored-up—human nature was all a puzzle to her.

She became totally absorbed in finishing up her preparations for dinner. She drained the noodles and folded them into a big black pan. Having cracked and beat the eggs, she stirred in the milk and began to grate the hard cheese when there was a knock at the back door. She rose from her chair and saw the figure of a man darkening the doorway. Her heart skidded three beats, and her pulse quickened ever so slightly as she went through the kitchen door across the short porch filled with kindling to the screen door.

"Yes?" The man had to move down one step so she could push the door open. She looked into hard brown eyes that turned soft at the sight of her.

"Miss Lee?" The man with vaguely familiar features etched across his copper-brown face inquired.

"That's right." She smiled as he removed his hat.

"I'm Lucas Davenport. Samuel's father." They said the last two words together, and it was Cassie Lee's turn to change her eyes from warmth to ice. "I came to—"

"Apologize," Cassie Lee offered.

"Well, yes. I suppose so."

"Oh, you didn't mind calling me a whore when I wasn't none?"

"No, ma'am. I think my son took some liberties with the interpretation of my words."

Lord, this man could talk pretty for a dirt farmer, Cassie Lee thought.

"It is true that I do not want him hanging around a place where he could be in danger or get hurt."

"Not much chance of that happening here. Samuel's long gone before the *dangerous* men come around." She thought she saw him smile. "Still, I do understand, Mr. Davenport. If I had a son as fine as Samuel, I speck I wouldn't want him hanging around a place like this either." She hunched her shoulders. "Tell him I will always think on him as a real special little boy, and I'm sure he'll grow into a fine young man. Thanks for coming by."

She closed the screen and turned just as Lucas put his hat back on and started down the steps.

"Miss Lee?" He had ascended the steps again and spoke through the screen door. "It's Samuel's birthday on Saturday. He'll be twelve. I'm having a celebration for him on Sunday." He stopped—he hadn't had feelings like this for three years, since his wife had passed. "I think Samuel would like it if you came by for dinner. Nothing fancy—"

"That'd be right nice, Mr. Davenport. About 4:00?"

"That'd be fine."

"Can I bring anything?"

"No. Your presence will be enough."

My 'presence' will be enough, Cassie Lee repeated in her head.

"I know a few things he's partial to, I'll bring that," she said, and smiled. "Let's keep my coming a surprise. If you think—"

"No, that's a good idea." He turned the brim of his hat in his hands. "So. I'll see you on Sunday, then."

"Fine. Thank you for the invite, Mr. Davenport."

"C'mon, girl." Candy came bursting into the kitchen with her mother's cast iron griddle in hand. "Oh, I didn't know you had company," she said, as she watched Lucas Davenport walk around the side of the house. "I tell you, you got all kinds of gentleman callers: Elijah Cobb, Exum Taylor, Samuel, and now his daddy."

"Just been invited to a birthday celebration is all," Cassie Lee said, swinging the round griddle up on the stove. "You gonna teach me how to make tortillas or not?"

"Lesson number three coming up," Candy said. "Now, that Elijah Cobb can put his boots under my bed any night."

"He has."

"Oh, Cassie Lee, that's mean."

"Is he black or white?"

"Black. I suppose he's white when necessary. You can tell by the half-moons down in his fingernails. If they're there, that's a black person."

"Tsk, that sounds like something Tante Fatima would say."

"Who's that?"

"Somebody I used to know." Cassie Lee helped Candy scrape the corn from the cob and changed the subject. "So your mother gave you this griddle?"

"I took it when I left, as a remembrance of her."

"She didn't mind?"

"No, she was dead. Had been dead for almost four years. I stayed with my daddy for as long as I could, but he seemed to blame me for her dying, or at least took it out on me because she did. So, I walked off one day, me, my satchel, and this comal."

"He didn't come after you?"

"Too drunk to stand, most likely. All he'd want is the comal."

"So what's your real name?"

Cassie Lee watched Candy bite her bottom lip, and look at the door before whispering, "Mary."

"Mary," Cassie Lee repeated.

"Plain, ordinary old Mary." She ground the corn. "I always wanted me a fancy name. I like the name Juanita." She let it roll from her tongue like music.

"That sounds right pretty. Juanita. Well, one day when you leave here you can be Juanita."

"Ha!" Candy laughed, and Cassie Lee wondered if she was laughing at taking the name Juanita, or at the notion of ever leaving here.

"You don't intend to stay here all your life, do you?"

"It's not a bad place. You get food, clothes, a roof over your head, and a doctor when you get sick."

"The doc ain't helping Cherry much," Cassie Lee said to Candy's silence. "But you're young yet. You got things you want to do."

"Like what?"

"Like—" Cassie Lee was lost for words. She had fashioned her own dream, but didn't think of any for anybody else. "Like sell Mexican food."

"There ain't a lot of us black Mexicans around who'd want it. Bohemia says I can stay here as long as I want."

"So you can end up like Cherry?"

"Sometime, Cassie Lee, you can be so mean." She slammed the roller down on the round corn mixture.

"No, I'm serious. You really intend to stay here until you're a fifty-year-old whore dying of the sex sickness? Not much of a future."

"Everybody ain't like you, Cassie Lee. You on your way to some-place. Some of us is already here."

"Your choice."

"No, it ain't!" She jumped up. "I can't do nothing, and ain't nobody ever gonna marry me. I'm stuck."

"If you think you are—then you are." Cassie Lee stared into Candy's tearing eyes.

"Candy!" Bohemia yelled from the hall. "You got company!"

The two women held each other's gaze before Candy broke the silence.

"Everybody's not like you, Cassie Lee," she spat and left.

"No, some of us had mothers and fathers. And some of us were slaves."

* * * * * * * * * * * *

The next morning Cassie Lee used the eggs Samuel was still leaving her, then went to the General Mercantile to look for his present. She wanted to give him something special. She looked over everything that seemed too grownup or useless for a twelve-year-old boy. She looked at the books but could not read most of the titles, and since she didn't know what he already had, she bypassed them. She wanted it to be something he could always keep and remember her by once she left.

Her eyes fell on the watches.

"Howdy, Cassie Lee. Haven't heard your gunshots all week," Hiram Schmidt said.

"I'm so good I don't need to practice no more. Lemme see that pocket watch there."

"You got some expensive taste."

"Expensive 'cause I just took a liking to it. How much?"

"Twenty dollars."

"For a timepiece? Are you funnin' me, Hiram?"

"All right, for you, fifteen."

"Twelve."

"Cassie Lee, this here is pure gold. In New York it would cost—"

"We ain't in New York, Hiram. I don't see no other buyers around here. Do you want the twelve dollars or not?"

"You drive a hard bargain." He accepted the beautiful watch back from her.

"You got a box? And let me see that little Bible there."

Cassie Lee opened it, and the fresh pages came alive when touched by air. It fit perfectly in her hand. Knowing the Davenports they probably already had a big family Bible, like the one Hiram was trying to push on her. But this little one would be ideal for Samuel to travel with. For some reason she didn't see him staying on the farm with Pa once he got some age on him.

"I'll take this too."

On the way back Cassie Lee caught a glimpse of Samuel, who had, unbeknownst to her, apparently been watching her. She smiled boldly, and he answered with a sad little wave before turning to walk in the opposite direction.

He'll be so surprised, she thought.

Back at the kitchen table, Cassie Lee sat erect as she started the inscription on the first page of the Bible. Her tongue lodged into the corner of her mouth, helped her concentrate on her letters.

To Samuel Davenport on the occasion of his 12th birthday.
August 4, 1851

Love, Cassie Lee

She sat there admiring her penmanship when there was a rap on the door. She carefully blotted, then closed the Bible on her fine lettering before placing it in her apron pocket and answering the door.

"Yes?" She looked into scared round eyes set in pitch skin of a little girl no more than ten or so.

"I'ma looking for a job, ma'am."

Cassie Lee heard the thick drawl, saw her threadbare, shabby clothing that she held at the neckline to keep closed, and smelled the odor of despair and desperation. It was all heartbreakingly familiar. She could just imagine what this young girl had gone through to get this far.

"Come in," Cassie Lee invited. "I'll go see about a job for you, but you wash up there and sit down here while I fix you something to eat."

Cassie Lee was so overwhelmed by the neediness of this little woman-girl that she thought of clothes she had for her while she piled fried chicken, potatoes, greens, corn, and cornbread on a plate.

"Thank you, ma'am." The girl smiled before lowering her head into the food like it was manna from heaven.

Cassie Lee poured a healthy glass of milk and set it before her. "How old are you?"

"Twelve," she managed through a mouthful of potatoes.

"Slow down, you gonna choke to death," Cassie Lee said as she smoothed her hands over the girl's unkempt hair, thinking that poor nourishment made her look much smaller than twelve. Cassie Lee would wash her hair good, grease, and plait it for her once she settled in.

"Where your folks?"

"Got none."

"Oh." Cassie Lee went over and got a shirt and a pair of pants for her. "Here, you can change into these once you get a bath."

"'Bout dat job, ma'am?"

"Sure." Cassie Lee wiped her hands on the apron as she backed out of the kitchen. She didn't relish disturbing Bohemia or asking her for a job she knew her boss didn't have.

As Cassie Lee climbed the steps she knew there was none here, but maybe she could get her on at the store or the livery or Millie's or somewhere.

"Yes, Cassie Lee," Bohemia invited her into her bedroom.

"Excuse me, Bohemia, but there's a little girl downstairs looking for a job—"

"You talking about that little shabby pickaninny?" Bohemia interrupted.

Cassie Lee was shocked.

"Close your mouth, Cassie Lee, and open your eyes," Bohemia said, as she left her desk and poured brandy into a glass. "I already told her that I didn't have a job for her. So she sneaks around back and asks you."

"I don't think she was sneaking—"

"You see big old eyes surrounded by black skin and you go all to pieces. You can be so naive, Cassie Lee."

There was that word again, and Cassie Lee surmised it wasn't a compliment.

"She's hungry and she's scared and she's alone—"

"I ain't running no home for waifs here, Cassie Lee. Word gets around town that Bohemia's taking in strays, putting out for the down and out, and where does that leave me?"

"She's just a little girl—"

"They're like cats, feed them and you'll never be rid of them." She eyed Cassie Lee. "Don't look so hurt. It's survival of the fittest, pure and simple." Bohemia stood facing her, her snifter of brandy poised elegantly in hand.

"You think I got where I am by giving everything I got—I *earned*—away? I worked hard, Cassie Lee, damned hard to get it, and to keep it. No one knows the sacrifice I made or the expense of keeping it up. You think running this house is easy? You think that furniture or those rugs and draperies are free? You think that piano was a gift? Painting every spring to keep this house looking fresh and inviting. Paying for these costumes for the girls, to have the Chinaman do the laundry, to have a doctor come in to check on my girls so they won't get sick? To pay Libby, you . . . have I ever asked you to cut back on your food buying? Have you ever bothered to look and see how much you spend at the mercantile? The Colt notwithstanding?" She raised her eyebrow for effect. Of her many attributes, being a good judge of character was one of Bohemia's prized assets. Unlike the other folks she dealt with, she was never threatened by Cassie Lee's having a gun. Cassie Lee had a big heart—perhaps too big.

"No, of course you haven't. I am not a young woman, I'm not a whore with a heart of gold. This gold rush stuff isn't gonna last forever. So you let that waif and all the other slackers do what I did, and let them get while the getting's good." She looked dead at Cassie Lee.

"Because when all this goes bust, you won't find me going door-to-door asking for handouts. If I gave something to everybody who knocks on my door, there would be nothing left. Then it'd be nine of us, you and Libby included, with our hands out. Feed her and put her on her way," Bohemia concluded with a fan of her hand.

"Can I at least—"

"Feed her and put her on her way," Bohemia repeated distinctly with a raised left eyebrow.

As Cassie Lee descended the stairs, she wondered what the girl would do. Where she would go or what would become of her? She was willing to work, and Cassie Lee was willing to help her find a job. Cassie Lee promised herself that if she ever became as rich as Bohemia she would at least make sure that little black children would have food and a chance to work. As she rounded the landing and took the last three steps, Cassie Lee thought of the egg money she kept in the jar on the stove.

She pushed open the kitchen door. The plate was empty and the girl was gone. Cassie Lee dumped the contents of the jar into her hand and ran down the back porch steps, looking out toward the shed.

"Little girl!" she called out. Only silence answered.

She ran down into the yard, then around one side of the house to the other near the kitchen, and out onto the street. She looked up and down the bustling wooden planks and into the dusty roads. She saw no children. As she wondered how much the girl had heard, an open buckboard wagon came toward her. A grizzled old white man slapped the reins on the back of his old horse. Next to him sat the girl.

"Wait a minute!" Cassie Lee screamed. "You don't have to do this! I have money!" She held out the paper dollars in her hand. "See."

Cassie Lee smiled at her. The girl did not return the gesture, but asked, "What I gon do fo' tomorra and de day afta dat?"

"She jus' where she spose to be," the white man said, grinning a tobacco-stained smile. "She gon be my bed warmer for as long as I see fit." He slapped the reins again, as his worn-out horse trotted off, leaving Cassie Lee haunted by the vacant, helpless look in the girl's eyes.

Cassie Lee stood in the middle of the street, watching the wagon until it was out of sight. She felt powerless and hopeless as she watched yet another girl-woman with nowhere to run.

Slowly, she removed herself from the street and walked back to the house. In the front yard she looked up to Bohemia's room in time to see the net curtains fall over her dark brown full figure.

"I will share my wealth," she vowed aloud. "When I have, so will others."

Chapter XIII

The sun illuminated the pattern of her gingham shirt as she tied Moses to the back of the wagon. She checked the security of her presents and hoisted herself up into the driver's seat for the trek to the Davenport place.

"You be careful now, Cassie Lee," Ezra warned.

"You more concerned about me, or your rented wagon?" Cassie Lee clicked and the horse took off. "Besides, I can handle anything, don't you know that by now?"

"I just bet you can," Ezra said, and waved her off.

Cassie Lee listened to the sound of the wooden wheels as they turned over the rutted path. Once again she was in the company of this beautiful country—the tall pines that stayed green all year long and the sweet fresh air that stung your nose in the early morning before it was warmed by the sun's glow. And the land—your eyes could feast on miles and miles of green and rocks and valleys before being stopped by the majestic mountains in the distance. She was sure going to miss this peaceful place.

This land was forever. It existed before her, and it would after she was gone. Forever, like the love she felt for Solomon. It had no limit of time and space—it would always be. It was before she even met him, like she had loved him in another life—and had it not been for her distraction of getting to Exum in this mortal life, she would have recognized him for the love they had shared in another realm. He had stirred her on the trail west, but her sane mind had ignored her heart's yearning and disregarded him for the potential marriage to the stranger, Exum. Even while there, in that god-forsaken town, Solomon had moved in and out of her consciousness. But once they made love, she *knew* him to be her Forever Man—the man she had conjured up in her young mind to combat the atrocities she was forced to endure. In this life his name was Solomon—not knowing what he was called in her last life, nor what he would be called in the next but here, in this time and place, his name was Solomon, and he would always be a part of her.

Now, as a bird cawed from overhead, Cassie Lee knew with a soberness of mind and sure realization that her Forever Man was now even beyond her in this life. She now knew that the blissful few months they shared in the cabin was all she was to have of him here on this earth. Now she could only hope to find him in her next life; to discover him sooner and have him longer. What she had with him could not be replicated, and for the remainder of her life on this earth she would look for second best when the time was right.

Cassie Lee would study her options with her mind and body, but not her heart and soul. She now recognized that she would have an eternal yearning for Solomon, like a thirst that couldn't be quenched. She knew that Solomon would be what her heart and soul longed for, but would never have again. She would choose another man when the time came. Someone who had acquired as much as she had. Someone who respected her, who she could talk to, and who made her laugh. Someone she could grow to love and who didn't mind that she could not have children. Someone to keep her company until she died and rose again in another life to search for Solomon. But now, in this life, he was not coming—and she must move on.

The sight of the small homestead warmed Cassie Lee as she rounded the bend and it came into full view. She liked that Samuel came from such a homey place. The house was tucked beneath three big trees, while the barn and the corral shared both partial shade and sun. The well was near the kitchen door and the porch, with two rockers poised for action, had been swept clean. Cassie Lee wondered how long it had been since anyone had time to sit a spell in those rockers. When she stopped the wagon, Lucas Davenport came out to greet her.

"Good afternoon. Right on time," he said.

"Four o'clock." She gathered her skirt and accepted his hand as she climbed down. "Really a nice place you have here."

"Thank you."

"Where's Samuel?"

"He should be coming back in a few minutes. I sent him down by the river to pick berries for dessert."

"I know just where he is. We used to do that," Cassie Lee said.

"I know." He smiled at her and she smiled back.

"Well, I hope you don't mind, but I brought some of his favorites." She whipped back the sheet.

"Some?" he said with a chuckle at the sight of the dishes.

Lucas grabbed two parcels and led Cassie Lee through the front door. A stone fireplace dominated the spacious, well-lit room. The dappled sunlight painted pictures on the wood-paneled walls. To the right was a good working stove that showed little recent use, and a table set for three circled by four chairs. A Happy Birthday banner was hung from left to right, and Cassie Lee delighted both in its presence and the fact that she could read it.

The two unpacked the wagon and began to arrange the fried chicken, the fried hominy, biscuits, greens, pineapple upside-down cake, and apple pie around the table.

"A *few* of his favorites?" Lucas joked.

"Yes, you know he likes much more than this."

"It sure smells good," Lucas remarked, as the door swung open.

"Cassie Lee!!" Samuel screamed and ran to her, grabbing her around her waist.

"Happy Birthday, Samuel."

"Surprise!" Lucas added lamely.

"Thanks, Pa. This is the best birthday ever! Wow, look at all this food!" His eyes surveyed the laden table. "What, no pot liquor?" He and Cassie Lee laughed. "Or okra."

The threesome devoured what Lucas had cooked out of courtesy, and what Cassie Lee brought out of good old-fashioned gluttony. As they

159

talked, Cassie Lee noted the easy exchange between father and son. In all her life, she had never witnessed a conversation like this. They sang happy birthday over the cake and pie before Lucas presented Samuel with a brand-new rifle, a rite of passage.

"My father gave me one on my twelfth, and so the tradition continues."

Cassie Lee smiled at the genuine affection between father and son, neither of them realizing that they had already given each other the most precious of gifts. No material things could hold a candle to that.

"Wait, son," Lucas cautioned as Samuel began to run from the cabin in excitement. "We have a guest who also brought you something."

"Ah, let him go on. Mine will keep." Cassie Lee waved him on.

"Oh no, Cassie Lee," father and son spoke in unison, and chuckled as Samuel carefully put his rifle on the table. "Your being here *was* all the present I needed."

"Oh, my!" She blushed before presenting him with the first gift. "Nothing as fancy as that rifle."

"It's special because it came from you," Samuel said, as he tore off the wrapper. "Wow!" He held up the pocket watch so that its gold chain dangled between his slim, brown fingers.

"Where I come from, that's mighty fancy," Lucas said, as his son marveled at the timepiece.

"I figure it will help him keep better track of time," Cassie Lee said. "When to feed Moses and all."

Samuel stopped inspecting the watch. His eyes darted to his father.

"It's all right," Cassie Lee piped up. "Your Pa said you could keep him."

"Thanks, Pa." Samuel hugged his father briefly before letting go.

"I got you something else too," said Cassie Lee.

"More?" Samuel said, placing the watch in his pocket, and accepting the smaller package. He untied the string, and a tiny book tumbled into his hand. "A Bible?"

"I know you all probably already have a big family one, so this is so wherever you travel you'll have the Good Book close by."

Lucas watched the relationship between the two as his son opened up the front page, read the inscription, and told her, "You did real good, Cassie Lee."

She beamed like a schoolgirl. "I did it all by myself." She grinned wide before catching a vision of herself through Lucas' eyes, and swallowed her pride.

"See, Pa." He showed his father as he went and hugged Cassie Lee.

"That's real nice," said Lucas, as Cassie Lee smoothed her hands across her skirt when Samuel took back the Bible from his father's hand.

"Well, I guess we better see about cleaning some of this up before I head back," said Cassie Lee.

"No, you are a guest at the Davenport home. Why don't you and Samuel go out and sit on the porch. I'll start, and we'll both finish up later." Samuel just stared at his father in disbelief. Lucas Davenport had never volunteered to wash a dish before. "Go on. Not much to clean, we ate everything up. Go on."

Samuel led Cassie Lee into the burgeoning coolness the sun cast as it prepared to set. They both eyed the rockers and opted for the porch step under the banister. The words "Davenport home" still rang in her ears. She looked about for traces of the deceased mother and wife. Her feet dangled inches above what had surely been a flower bed when she was still alive. There were faded traces of femininity in the set table her husband had tried to copy, in the dusty doilies over the arm chairs, the unironed linen tablecloth, the choice of china pattern, and the dry, empty vase where no flowers now stood. It must have been some home, once. Now, Mrs. Davenport would still be proud that her husband and son were such perfect hosts to their guest.

"Cassie Lee, you married?" Samuel broke the silence.

"Where'd that come from?" She wiped her hands of imaginary dirt.

"I was just curious." He shifted his weight before asking, "Would you marry my Pa?"

"That's not for you to ask." She punched him in mock seriousness. "Whenever your Pa marries again, if he marries again, it'll be between him and the lady. You gonna grow up and maybe leave, but your Pa will stay on with his new wife." She watched Samuel roll her words over in his mind. "Of course, could be your Pa never marries up again."

"Why not?"

"Love doesn't die when the person does. Sometimes you stay to the person, whether they with you or not. Their body can't be seen by the naked eye, but the heart can see them as plain as day. And their spirit can be felt all around you. And the love you once had is still here." She touched her heart.

"You know this 'cause you been married before, Cassie Lee?"

"Yes I have," she lied without hesitation. "In every way that counted." Might as well have been, she thought. A man and woman could never be as connected as she and Solomon. They were married in every way that mattered.

She smiled as she thought of the man who saw beyond the slave she had been on the Whedoe plantation—saw through the outer hurt, the veneer she threw up for other folk. The man who saw into her heart and touched her soul. A man who healed her, who made her feel like she belonged someplace. Who made her feel special and protected and important. A man who wrapped his powerful arms around her, soothing her. The man who rocked her like a child and loved her like a woman.

"Yes, I have," she repeated wistfully.

"I'll marry you, Cassie Lee," Samuel blurted out.

"You determined to make me a Davenport, huh?" She tickled him, and he giggled. "I can't deprive some nice woman of the chance to have a wonderful man·like you."

Samuel stopped giggling, focused his big black eyes on her, and said, "I love you, Cassie Lee."

"Oh, that's sweet." She hugged him around his shoulders. "I love you too, Samuel." She rested her face against his head. "Like the son I'll never have," she whispered softly into his thick black hair.

"You never gonna love a man like you did him?"

"That's right. It ain't possible. No one can ever take his place. My Forever Man. Maybe I'll marry up again after I get my boarding house."

"You leaving soon?"

"Probably in September."

"That's next month."

Cassie Lee hadn't realized it until he said it. Would she be making her way down to San Francisco in a few short weeks? Her heart fluttered and her stomach churned at her unreadiness. She had the money and the resolve, and nothing here was holding her back.

"Well, I guess I better start on back." Cassie Lee stood and stretched.

162

"Awww," Samuel whined, and she looked at him as if he were daft. "Sorry," he said, and they laughed. "You'd never leave without saying goodbye, would you?" He squinted up at her although there was no sun.

"Course not." She rifled his head. "And comb that hair."

Cassie Lee waved at her hosts as she turned the wagon and headed back out the same road. She thought of how lucky they were to have one another. Then she thought of fathers: of Bohemia with a rigid one; of Candy with a hateful one; and of the waif with none, like herself. Samuel had a loving father who made protecting and providing for him his major priority. He was Samuel's bridge over troubled waters. Samuel, in turn, would learn from him, grow up, and repeat that positiveness . . . and make a good father himself. You can't give away what you never had, she thought.

The gigantic silver moon was momentarily covered by a cloud traveling toward the Sierras. Going to Solomon, she thought. Then she wondered, did he ever think of her? Did she ever cross his mind at least once or twice? Was he as haunted by her as she was by him? She had to stop that line of curiosity immediately, because if she ever thought there was any possibility that he regretted sending her away, she would be compelled to run to him and tell him that she could live with him forever on that mountain and be happy for life everlasting. She hated admitting that even to herself. This compromised her dreams, so she had to stop thinking on whether he thought on her.

The filmy cloud returned the clear moon, like wiping away tears, and Cassie Lee realized that she never cried over Solomon. She was angry, frustrated, and felt rejected, because her best wasn't good enough for him, but she never cried for Solomon. What was there to cry about? He had destroyed her dreary past, and contaminated the future some by creating a void so huge that no one could ever take his place, but she held fast to all he had given her, had shown her, had taught her. The love and the tenderness. Of it all, she prized his tenderness with her. That is what she would always look for—the love, happiness, and tenderness.

"I'm not thinkin' on you no more tonight, Solomon Hawk. That's the end of it," she announced aloud to the horse and her surroundings.

Cassie Lee was content to be here in this peaceful valley that shone silver in every fold of the landscape. A coyote howled its arrival—a lonely, haunting, primal sound. As the wagon continued to rock and pitch over the road, she thought of Samuel and his father and, once again, realized that she had no beginning and that her end was uncertain. She was her own marker in this world. She had no mother to set her place before she came, and she would have no children to set her place after she left. Her life was her life. All that would be of her was what she would do with the time she had on this earth. But it was hers to do or be what she wanted. Through her desolate thinking, she smiled and sang.

"I sing because I'm happy. I sing because I'm free. For His eye is on the sparrow, and I know He watches me . . . ."

* * * * * * * * * * * *

Candy tried not looking at Cassie Lee when they returned to the house. When her eyes darted up, she found Cassie Lee's warning eyes ready to greet her. The optical blaze was so hot that Candy jerked her brown eyes away and ran up the stairs.

"I fixed you all something to eat," Cassie Lee said, as the motley crew filed though the front door.

Bohemia headed for the bar. Gypsy flopped on the red velvet divan as Scarlet stepped up to the brass rail and let Bohemia pour her two drinks, one of which she took over to Gypsy. Diamond and Pearl grabbed drinks from the bar, and they all raised their glasses.

"To Cherry," Bohemia toasted. "May she rest in peace."

"Amen," the girls all said, and Cassie Lee made her way back to the kitchen.

Another life shot to hell, Cassie Lee thought as she wiped the stove of grease. They found Cherry's cold body one morning. No sooner had the undertaker come to cart the eighty pounds of flesh away, than Cassie Lee started dogging on Candy's heels when she fled onto the back porch to escape her.

"What you want from me?" Candy had turned on her like a caged animal.

"I want you to look and see what you headed for if'n you don't change your course," Cassie Lee had seethed through clinched teeth. "Your years leadin' up to being put in a cold box and planted six feet under should account for something." Cassie Lee cut her eyes. "And you free."

"That don't mean nothing," Candy said, folding her arms on themselves.

"Spoken like somebody who ain't never been no slave," she spat. "Don't you care no more about yourself than to be some man's whore? Don't you think you deserve more? Hell, you can read and write. I had to learn myself how to do that, and I still don't have it all right. You a whole few jumps ahead of me, and you lay up under some grunting man, let him spill into you, clean yourself up, and do it all over again, and you call that living?" She squinted her eyes at Candy.

"You gonna end up just like Cherry, a dying old whore full of regrets, hooked on pain and laudanum, drinking morphine, wishing for mercury, and dying from the inside out. Time slips up on you, Candy, and before you know it, you just an old, wore-out, broken-down whore."

As Cassie Lee finished wiping down the stove, she knew that when she got fired up her speaking skills went out the window—but she didn't care. She didn't have time for the likes of Candy or anybody else who didn't care enough about themselves to do better. She wasn't taking care of anybody but herself. If she pointed it out to you, and you decided not to do anything about it, then, Cassie Lee figured, her work was done. She was a pointer-outer, not a fixer.

"I can't wait to leave this place," Cassie Lee said aloud to no one in particular. The stove sparkled under her ire.

* * * * * * * * * * * *

The house was somber when it was just the girls, but once the men came, it was business as usual. The days were getting shorter, and the sun hid behind high gray clouds more frequently. Cassie Lee made out her list of things she needed to buy and do for her sojourn south to Sacramento and on to San Francisco. Based on the tales she'd heard about the wild and reckless place, she was filled with anticipation and anxiety, but she was physically and mentally ready for her next venture. She knew she could handle anything. The worse that could happen was that she'd die. But she would die free.

She snuggled under the bear coat she used as a blanket, and the familiar feel of cold and the scent of Solomon caused her to oversleep. Her eyes blinked awake at a white, artificial brightness.

"Ummmm," she said, as she rolled over and her cheeks sought the warmth of the fur. "Oh, no!" She bolted upright, watching her hot breath dance smoke on the still air. "Oh, no!!" Her bare feet hit the frigid planks of the porch as she ran to the screen and saw the blanket of whiteness. "How can this be?" She witnessed the puff of her words evaporate in the chill. "It's barely September!"

"Hell," Bohemia shot from behind, dressed in a gorgeous, thick, quilted bathrobe. "We have snow up here as early as August." She bent over and threw kindling into the kitchen stove. "Slept a little late, huh? Well, I guess I better get used to doing my own coffee anyways, since you fixing to leave and all."

"Where am I going in all this?"

"Good question. And it's the wet, heavy snow too. Maybe it'll let up in October or so."

It snowed thigh-deep through Thanksgiving, Christmas, and New Year's. In February, the fresh whiteness clung to the earth for dear life, and Cassie Lee's life waned because visits from Samuel or gentlemen callers were all affected by the weather. The girls slept, ate, drank, played cards and checkers, and waited—like everyone in River Bend—for the thaw.

* * * * * * * * * * * *

An ocean of snow engulfed the cabin in waves, requiring the inhabitant to stay close. Solomon stared out the window at the hushed richness of the icy Sierras as he waited for his hot coffee to cool. He hated being confined and preferred being busy with his trapping. But as he looked at his pelts piled high by the root cellar and thought of those in Black's barn, he wondered if there were any other critters left in these mountains for him to hunt. He worked hard during the days hoping that sleep would covet him at night, but it was often elusive and haunting when it finally came in jagged snatches.

He went over to the stove to stir his beans, and glanced to the right at Cassie Lee's cowrie cross draped over one point of her starburst mirror.

166

He had found it last week and, after trying to put it in several locations around the cabin, it had ended up hanging in her clean-corner. He had tried all the seats around the table to avoid the sight of it. He never sat with his back to any door, and sitting in front of the fire was too hot. Sitting with his back to the bed only made that memorial to her more visible, so he ended up where he always sat—but facing the fire, not the bed where they had shared so many nights of honest loving. Sometimes in the smoldering embers of the flames, her laughing doe-eyes smiled at him.

Solomon served himself a pile of beans and sat at the table. He wondered what the weather was like in San Francisco. It was almost a year since she had left, and he wondered what she was doing. Was she serving her Solomon stew to her guests and talking their ears off? He knew she was going to church, and probably singing in the choir. He wondered if she had everything she wanted and needed? He wondered if her dreams had all come true. She sure had a hankering for that boarding house of hers, he thought. That was all she talked about when she was here—the cooking, cleaning, mending, even the reading was "practice for her boarding house."

He'd done right by her by not putting his feelings into words. If he had, she would have felt honor bound to stay, and that wouldn't have been fair. He couldn't keep a young, newly freed woman up on a mountain, not with all those ideas she had. That would have been trading one form of bondage for another, especially when Exum-town went bust. If she stayed with him, not only would she have given up her dream, but she wouldn't have had any of the nice things she was used to like soap, green apples, and dress material. Who would she talk to besides him? And if they had children, who would help her with the birthing? His first wife had her people, who came and helped out with the delivery of his son, but with Cassie Lee it would be just her and him. He did the right thing, he reminded himself again as he shoveled beans into his mouth. They both got what they wanted. Cassie Lee got her boarding house, and he his solitude back.

With each passing season, it would be easier as time moved on. He never shared a spring or summer with her company, although she had a way of making winter feel like spring.

"Ahem," he coughed out loud to jar thoughts of her from his mind. This spring when he went hunting with Running Bear he'd go back to his lodge with him for a visit. He sipped coffee, trying not only to stop wondering about Cassie Lee and her boarding house, but to stop wondering if she had found someone else to love. Cassie Lee was so easy to love.

"Huntin' this spring ought to be pretty good," he said. He spooned in another mouthful of beans, and listened to the creak of tree limbs twisting in the unforgiving wind.

* * * * * * * * * * * * *

Almost a year to the day of her River Bend arrival, Cassie Lee was packed and ready to go. The roads were still slick and muddy, but those willing to get in and out of River Bend were ready to chance it.

"I'll never see you again," Samuel lamented without tears. After all, he was twelve and a half.

"Never say never," Cassie Lee warned. "When you come to San Francisco, you come on by my boarding house. No charge."

"Really?" He smiled.

"Give me a few years to get it all set up. I don't know what I'll have to do to get it going." Cassie Lee bit her bottom lip in doubt.

"You'll do just fine, Cassie Lee," Samuel said.

"Why thank you, Mr. Davenport." She smiled at him. "Look at how much you have grown in one year."

"Almost as tall as you."

"I got an awful lot to thank you for, Samuel. You were my best friend, you taught me to read—"

"You got to keep that up or you'll lose it."

"I know, I know. My boarding house is gonna get the paper every morning."

"Well, I'll come back and say goodbye to you tomorrow."

"Please don't," she said, tears welling up in her eyes. "I'm no good at goodbyes. Only hellos." She smiled and saw his eyes glistening with tears.

"Okay," he said softly. "I'll never forget you, Cassie Lee." He almost knocked her over with a big bear hug.

"You better not, Samuel Davenport. I love you." She kissed his cheek.

"I love you too. Sure you won't marry me?" He tried to lighten the mood.

"Go on now." She swatted him on the back. "You take care of Moses, and tell your Pa to take good care of you. You're a right special person."

Cassie Lee brought her trembling hand up to her chin so she wouldn't dissolve into tears at the sight of his leaving. When he got to the corner, Samuel gave one grand wave, which gave her tears permission to fall. She was forever leaving good men in these mountains. At least this time it was her idea.

She trodded down to her hiding place by the shed and, with her full weight and the use of a mount, the rock finally budged. It took two kettles of hot water to soften the ground so she could extract her pouch of money. As she walked her gold coins to her room, she was pleased with the arrangement she'd made with Mr. Nieldmen, Hiram's supplier, to hitch a ride with him to Sacramento. The man talked incessantly, but she would be one of five people traveling that way tomorrow morning.

Cassie Lee dumped the contents of the wet leather pouch on her bed as her eyes canvassed the belongings she'd be taking. Her five blouses and skirts and underthings would fill the tapestry satchel. She'd wear the denim pants and her bear coat. And she could carry her saddle after she sold the horse, right before catching the boat to San Francisco. She had bought a holster for her pistol, but hadn't decided whether to wear it or store it in a handy place.

Even the gold coins seemed to multiply like seeds in this lush soil, she thought, as she began counting them.

"Wait," she said aloud, and counted them again and again. After the fifth time, Cassie Lee decreed, "There's fifteen hundred dollars here!"

How can that be, she thought, as she quickly scooped them up and began distributing them into the various pockets she had sewn all over her pants so they would not jangle when she walked. Solomon had given her one thousand dollars. Where did the other five hundred come from? The money she earned from Bohemia was kept separately, and what she didn't spend for supplies was kept in a leather belt to be strapped around her waist.

That was a heap of money, she thought as she tidied up, pondering on who she even knew who could spare it. Bohemia? She wouldn't go that far into the yard, and certainly wouldn't dig. Bohemia Jones would also want credit for her generosity. Elijah Cobb? Hadn't seen him since he took off for Texas. Samuel or his father? Not likely. She sat there, staring out at the view that had been hers for a year. Exum Taylor? That crazy man might just do something like that.

"Cassie Lee," Candy said, sticking her head into her porch-room. "Bohemia wants to see you." The girl eyed Cassie Lee and then her belongings, ready to go, before turning to leave.

"Thanks," Cassie Lee said to the girl who hadn't spoken to her in months. Cassie Lee figured she was leaving tomorrow and could afford to be gracious.

"You wanted to see me?" Cassie Lee asked Bohemia once she reached her second floor room.

"So this is the day you been talking about since you arrived. Leaving River Bend."

"Yes, I am. I want to thank you for—"

"We ought to do the thanking." She reared back in her plush velvet chair. "You can sure cook. I'm going to miss that most, but I wanted to tell you that I think you will make it, Miss Cassie Lee. Life is ten percent what is, and ninety percent how you see it. You got vision and a mission. As I told you before, you got gumption and nerve and you're still a little naive, which means you'll get things done because you won't have enough sense to be afraid. You got a powerful burn to get this boarding house. And come hell or high water, you gonna have it." She chuckled. "Anyway, I wanted to give you a little parting gift."

"Oh, no," Cassie Lee declined, thinking it would be perfume or some other nonsense she couldn't use. "Really. You done quite enough. I know I'm not the same person I was when I got here. I've learned a lot. If it hadn't been for you, well, I just don't know what I would have done—"

"Hold on, hold out, and survive like you always do, Cassie Lee. For all your strengths and faults, there is one thing about you. You are a born survivor, Sugar. So whatever your parents gave or didn't give you, they gave you a will to live, and stubbornness. Lord, you are a hard-headed woman." She shook her head knowingly. "But that's two things you need to be in this world. Here." She threw a pouch at her, and Cassie Lee heard the familiar jingle jangle.

"I can't take—"

"Didn't I just compliment you? A survivor would take that for a rainy day. Now when you get to San Francisco, you put this money in a bank. I trusted a Mr. Micah Coffey when I was down there. Of course, he might think you were a whore too, so that's your call whether you want to use my name or not, but he's a good, fair banker—if there is such a thing."

"Thank you."

"There's something else I want you to take with you besides my good wishes."

"What's that?"

"Candy."

"What?"

"The girl will never make a good whore. Her heart ain't in it. The men like her because she's cute and has a good body, but that ain't gonna last forever, so she needs to start on another line of work."

"I can't take Candy with me." She watched Bohemia arch her left eyebrow. "She'll just slow me down. I ain't a caretaker. I don't look after nobody but me." Bohemia let her ramble on. "I got things to do. I have dreams to lay out and get to going on. I don't have time to be worrying about nobody else. Besides she's older than me, she can go wherever she wants—"

"Oh, I see. I should add hypocrite to my description of you."

"What?"

"You were Miss Bleedingheart over that little no-name waif, but when somebody you've lived with needs help, it's all right as long as they don't ask you."

"Did Candy put you up to this?"

"She did not. You think Candy knows anything about anything except maybe how to cook?"

"Bohemia," Cassie Lee began slowly. "My dreams were always just my own. I never figured anyone else in them but me."

"Well, maybe that's your problem. The world can be a lonely place, and somewhere, sometime, you gonna need a friend."

"When that time comes, I'll get one."

"They gonna like you for you, or you for what you can do for them?"

An exasperated Cassie Lee said, "So I guess you want your money back?"

"No, I gave that to you."

"So why not just give Candy some money and let her go?"

"Candy has no direction. She can go with you as far as Sacramento or San Francisco. Let her decide when she wants to go off on her own."

"You know it costs one hundred and fifty dollars to catch the boat from—"

"Yes, I have her traveling money too."

Cassie Lee eyed Bohemia, not sure just what her purpose was for throwing the two of them together. But if she wasn't responsible for Candy beyond Sacramento, then why not give the girl a chance? Cassie Lee silently vowed to herself that neither Candy nor anybody else was going to stop her from getting her boarding house.

"If she wants to go, she can travel as far as I do," Cassie Lee relented halfheartedly.

"Well, now we'll have to see if Candy wants to leave."

Chapter XIV

The next morning there were two women from Bohemia's house setting out with Mr. Nieldmen's troupe heading for Sacramento. Candy was outfitted in the bare necessities and fiddled with her horse, trying to mount it. As Cassie Lee tied her bear coat over the back of her horse, she caught a glimpse of Samuel on Moses in the distance. He waved, and she returned the gesture. She swung up, sat her saddle and guided her horse behind the Nieldmen wagon as the other five people followed suit.

"Mr. Nieldmen, I hope you don't mind one more?" Cassie Lee approached the wizened old man.

"Not at all," he answered in his sing-song voice. "The more the merrier. What's your name?" he asked Candy.

"Juanita," Cassie Lee spoke up before Candy could. "This is my friend, Juanita."

The two women's eyes locked, and a slow smile crawled across Cassie Lee's lips as she swung her horse around to the wagon's other side for one last look. Once again, she was leaving the high country and inching closer and closer to her dream.

* * * * * * * * * * * * *

The trip to Sacramento was uneventful, and any silence was sacrificed for Mr. Nieldmen's stories of the old country and his peddling goods up and down these gold trails. Sleep was their only peace.

Cassie Lee's apprehension grew as they boarded the boat for the ninety-mile journey to San Francisco. Neither had been on water before, and it wasn't at all what they expected. Despite the exorbitant fare, the conditions were crowded and the people were low class. It took only one night for a gambler to stop eyeing Cassie Lee and walk over and introduce himself. He was tall, his dark hair slicked back like soaked chicken feathers. A black moustache sat atop his lips, which were wrapped around a thick, stinking cigar.

"Hello, little lady," he said to the pair standing on the deck, hoping for fresh air to free them from the fetid smell on board.

"Hello," Cassie Lee said curtly, while noting that his clothes were quality cut, and his satin vest reflected the moonlight.

As he followed them around the deck, he spoke of New Orleans, high-stakes poker games, and money to burn. Neither of the women rose to the bait as he spoke to them from one side of his cigar while deftly blowing smoke from the other. Cassie Lee though unschooled in dealing with men figured he was adept at many things, but getting them to come to his cabin that night wasn't one of them.

"We have our own, thanks," Cassie Lee dismissed him, and they circumvented the deck once to lose him before ducking into their hired room for the duration of the trip.

"Two hundred dollars for this!" Cassie Lee looked around the tight cabin with bunk beds and the porthole that cost an extra fifty dollars. A questionable lock required them to carry anything of value with them on their person when they left. After sizing up their traveling companions, Cassie Lee changed back into her comfortable getup of pants, shirt, and hat, and they rarely ventured out until the pitch, roll, and creak of the ship finally stopped.

"San Francisco!" someone yelled outside their porthole, rousing the pair from a nap.

If her traveling companions were a surprise disappointment, then seeing San Francisco was a shock. Cassie Lee's anticipation died on her face and slipped into the quagmire of her soul as she saw the crowded port. There were a million ships of all sizes, shapes, and descriptions—some manned, some deserted, some left to sink or rot—all rampant with rodents and cats, which accounted for the smell. A thick blanket of stench was held just beneath the fallen cloud so dense it threatened to separate her and Candy.

As she descended the gangplank into the mass of marauding humanity, Cassie Lee thought she was descending into hell. People populated and crawled over the area like ants on a discarded cake crumb. People, like the ships of every size, shape, and color, smelled of stale liquor, unwashed flesh, and unclean teeth. Hardened tobacco juice dribbled down the sides of their mouths and onto their yellowed clothes while yesterday's food stuck to their beards.

The people smell commingled with the fish smell, and Cassie Lee thought she'd throw up if she had the time, but to turn her back, even momentarily, would invite folks to relieve her of her worldly goods. So, she swallowed hard, and told Candy to stay close as they cut a path through the tangled flesh, making their way, hopefully, to fresher air. More than just the sight and smell of people was the sound of languages and tongues Cassie Lee couldn't recognize. Neither English nor Spanish, it was all foreign to her untrained ears.

"That's a mighty nice saddle," a man spoke, and Cassie Lee recognized the words, the tone, and his intention of snatching it from her.

Cassie Lee tried to maneuver around him, but Candy was caught by him as the prized possession hung between the two women.

"I think I'll jus' be takin' it," he said simply.

"I think not," Cassie Lee said, as she raised her duster enough for him to get a clear look at her six-shooter.

He snort-laughed and advanced, and, in one motion, Cassie Lee cocked and whipped her gun to rest on that fleshy space between his eyes.

Candy froze, just like the man.

"Hey, hey, hey," the man placated. "I don't even got no horse. I was just funnin' some."

He held up his hands and tried a toothless grin as the women swung around him. Cassie Lee's eyes never left his. She backed away from him into the enveloping fog. She stopped and faced the mist to wait and see if he was coming after them. When he didn't, she proceeded with Candy up a hill in silence.

175

Candy was still stunned and impressed. Cassie Lee's knees still shook, and she remembered Bohemia's words. "Friends don't need no explanation. Enemies get none." She and Candy didn't speak of it, as they looked for a place to stay the night.

"Can I be of some service?" the New Orleans gambler removed his hat with flair, inclining them into his waiting carriage.

"You could tell us where to find a bed for the night," Cassie Lee said flatly.

"I'd be glad to share my accommodations with you."

"No thanks. Any other ideas?"

"Well," he said, replacing his hat, and hiding his anger. "You'd want the Bottoms."

"How do we find that?"

"Keep on walking up that road a piece. It'll find you. Ladies." He tipped his hat, climbed into his carriage, and instructed the driver to ride on.

They dredged past more curious-looking folks; neither black nor white nor Indian nor Spanish. Cassie Lee noted that they had skin the color of hers, eyes like the Chinese, hair black, long and straight like the Mexicans and Indians, but they were none of these. These curious folks gave way to skin color, hair texture, and features she and Candy happily recognized.

The pair was directed around the corner, and disappointment once again claimed Cassie Lee's hopeful face. Laid out before her was a field of shacks like those she had left in Georgia. She hoped it was the dim light. She hoped it was that she was bone-tired from the journey, spent from her encounter with the man who wanted her saddle, and hungry beyond imagining that made this area seem so desolate. This didn't look like a place where she could build her boarding house. These were not people who wanted or could afford to stay there.

"We are lookin' for a place for the night," she heard Candy ask.

A man pointed to a bend in the road where they were taken in by a half-blind woman who sat on the shabby porch of the one-room shack. She was pleasant enough—but when she offered the pair some food, Cassie Lee, staring down at the rancid gray mush, immediately lost her appetite. She just wanted to go to bed so that tomorrow would hurry up and come, so she could be gone.

176

They were directed to a pallet on the floor. Candy collapsed on it and fell asleep instantly while Cassie Lee fished for the last of her trail jerky. She chewed the dry, brown meat as she laid her head against the slats of the shanty. She watched the moon move snail-slow across the sky and wondered if she had been delivered into another form of evil. Sleep came unsolicited, in snatches between her peering out to see how far the moon had moved since her last watch.

A loud crash awakened Cassie Lee and Candy, as the smell of rot-gut whiskey assaulted their senses. A man had entered their shack. He cursed and fell on the pallet across the room, fast asleep before he hit the worn blanket. Cassie Lee and Candy eyed each other in the tattered moonlight. Before they could speak, a volley of profane language was surging up the hill like a surprise storm, growing louder and louder until the man and woman were right by their window to the moon. She punched him, he slapped her, knocking her to the ground where he commenced to kick her before rummaging through her purse and taking her money.

Cassie Lee moved to go and help her, but Candy took her arm and shook her head, no.

"Leave 'em be, Cassie Lee," was all Candy said.

Before they could argue about it, a pair of men appeared from the eerie mist, picked the woman up, and carted her away.

"Will this night ever end?" Cassie Lee whispered to Candy as she accepted the offered jerky.

"Every town has a place for people like these. And there is a place for people like us, too. We'll find it tomorrow."

"Or we'll just make our own," Cassie Lee said without a thought.

Candy chuckled, and said, "You are something, Miss Cassie Lee."

The next morning Cassie Lee pressed a ten dollar gold piece into the old blind woman's hand and thanked her before they left.

The new San Franciscans walked farther up the hill for seemingly miles, noting, now and again, some respectable black men and women in wagons or buggies. They sat awhile, as the thin air, the saddle, and bear coat taxed them momentarily.

"I want a bath, a bed, and a meal," Cassie Lee decreed on one of their rest breaks.

"You do look a sight."

"I know I smell a sight too." She stood up. "Let's go, Juanita."

Their smiles returned as they hit the black mecca of this city. They stood on the threshold of their new lives, and the sight before them was like entering the Promised Land.

"I left Moses with Samuel, but my feet will carry me fine!" Cassie Lee smiled.

The houses were modest, some with two stories, neat, clean, well-kept, not grandiose like Bohemia's; but Cassie Lee figured she wouldn't see any Negroes with houses like that in her lifetime, not respectable ones anyway.

"We going to church," Candy said, pointing to the A-frame building with a cross on top.

"If you don't mind, I'd like to eat and wash before I go to—"

"Trust me. If you new in town and want to know the whats and whys of a place, you go to church. C'mon," Candy instructed as they toted the saddle between them.

"May I help you?" an elderly man approached and asked as he scrutinized the motley pair, one of whom he wasn't sure was a boy or girl. "I'm Reverend Burris." When neither of them spoke he added, "You've come up from the Bottoms, haven't you?"

"Yes," Cassie Lee stepped forward and said, "and we aren't going back." When he seemed taken aback by her directness, she added, "Certainly a man of God can find a place for two decent women to stay?" she drawled as her eyes challenged his.

* * * * * * * * * * * *

Miss Anne Soujay showed them to their room. It was bright, cheery, clean, had two beds, two bureaus, curtains, wallpaper, and a sturdy door. Cassie Lee paid for two weeks in advance, and asked for a bath immediately.

"Supper is at six," Miss Soujay said, softened by Cassie Lee's cash payment. "I'll have a tub and water set up for you right away."

"Thank you," Cassie Lee said, and jumped for joy when Miss Anne closed the door behind her. "This is what I'ma talkin' 'bout."

When the two joined everyone for supper, Miss Anne and the other guests were astounded by the transformation. They had seen and received

178

a woman and the manchild they thought Cassie Lee to be. They were pleasantly surprised by these two very attractive women who had exquisite table manners—thanks to the charm school of Miss Bohemia Jones. The conversation was lively and guarded as they wanted to know about their new residents, who in turn wanted to know about this settlement.

Later, the Reverend Burris came to check on the new arrivals, but Cassie Lee surmised that he came to check on Miss Anne and make sure the notorious pair, especially the one with a gun, meant his neighbor no harm.

"Miss Anne tells me you are interested in opening a boarding house. Respectable, I'm sure?" he said, as he balanced a cup of coffee on his knee while sampling one of the offered shortbread cookies.

"Indeed," Cassie Lee said, picking up the word from Mrs. Powell, who was also staying here. "A place where respectable Negroes can stay while they visit the area or build homes of their own. I would take only referrals from other residents."

"Well, that's very fine, but you know prices here are exorbitant."

Cassie Lee hid her confusion over the word, but surmised it meant a lot of money. "I think I am prepared to at least start—"

"Well," Reverend Burris rose to a standing position. "If that is true, I'd be glad to take you to town tomorrow to look over what is offered and introduce you to a man who handles such things for us."

"That's very kind of you." Cassie Lee stood with the reverend and Miss Anne.

"About nine? Come to the church," he directed before saying, "thank you for your hospitality, Miss Anne. Good night. And to you, Miss Lee."

"Hospitality," Cassie Lee rolled the word over in her mouth that night as Candy drifted off to sleep. "Cassie Lee's Hospitality House."

"You gonna have to pay extra for all them words. Or get a bigger house," Candy advised.

* * * * * * * * * * * *

Cassie Lee climbed the four steps to the chill of the Community of Faith Baptist Church's vestibule and saw Reverend Burris arranging candles at the altar.

"Good morning, Reverend Burris," she said cheerily.

"Good morning," he said and turned. "You must be Cassie Lee. I am Reverend Nathan Burris. You spoke to my father last evening." He cleared the confused look from her face.

"My father isn't feeling up to the tour today, so if you don't mind, I'll be taking you around and making introductions."

"Fine. Thank you."

He walked her to the side entrance and the waiting wagon.

"Wouldn't two horses be easier?" she asked.

"Not for me," he chuckled, and helped her into her perch for the next few hours.

As he guided the wagon around town, Reverend Burris the younger chattered on amiably about the town Cassie Lee had selected as her new home. He told her about how this infamous town began as the Mexican town, Yerba Buena, which meant Good Herb, and became San Francisco in January of 1847 in honor of St. Francis of Assisi. He confided that this was a new town with growing pains, as was California, which had only become a state in 1850.

"Legend has it that when William Tecumseh Sherman visited in 1847 he recalled that 'there was neither a shod horse, nor tavern, nor hotel, nor wagon road.'" Cassie Lee interrupted.

"What are those people?" She had spotted four of them walking by their wagon.

"Hawaiians," the reverend identified. "From Hawaii, an island in the Pacific. There're all kinds of people here, mostly brought in by the discovery of gold. They come from all over the world, across the plains in covered wagons, sailing around Panama or around Cape Horn." He watched Cassie Lee absorb his information along with the sights.

"In 1844, Yerba Buena reported 25 to 30 whites, and in 1846, the school board counted 700 whites; half of them American, and 150 Indians, Negroes and Hawaiians. Two years later with the discovery of gold, 250,000 had come from all over the world, I'm afraid bringing their bad habits with them. They had to establish vigilance committees to restore some law and order. They struck gold in Australia last year, so some of the ne'er-do-wells went down there. It isn't perfect, but it's home. Then add all the Chinese, and it's quite a mix of people. That's why your real estate folks advertise that they 'transact business in English, Spanish, French, and Italian.'" He chuckled, but Cassie Lee was still mesmerized by all the action.

"So you want to buy a house?"

"Yes."

"I'll take you to a reputable banker and real estate man."

"Is he good and honest?"

"Yes. He handled all of the Leidesdorff properties."

"Who?"

"William Leidesdorff. He came up here from St. Croix in '41 after an unsuccessful love affair. He was wealthy when he arrived on his 160-ton schooner, the *Julia Ann*. His father was a Danish planter and his mother African. He had a 35,000 acre estate here called Rio Del Rancho Americana, and in '45 he was appointed a United States sub-consul to Mexican California. He was treasurer for the San Francisco City Council and helped set up the first public school. He built the first hotel, the City Hotel, introduced the first steamboat, and organized the first horse race."

"A black man?"

"Yes, and when the American troops arrived, he assisted in establishing the new government and hosted a fancy dress ball at his home."

"Now that's a man I should meet."

"He died in 1848 of brain fever shortly after gold was discovered."

"But the man who handled his affairs—"

"I'm taking you to him now. Mr. Micah Coffey."

Cassie Lee smiled. It was the same name Bohemia had given her for the man who could be trusted, and Cassie Lee didn't even have to use the old madam's referral. Instead, she was being introduced by a man of God.

After the pair was received by Mr. Coffey and he explained the basics of financing a house or business in this rough-and-tumble town, Cassie Lee asked. "Is there any way I can keep my gold in the vault and use paper money to get my house?"

"Nathan, you didn't tell me I was dealing with a shrewd business-woman," Mr. Coffey chuckled, as he exchanged a glance with the preacher.

Cassie Lee didn't know anything about what he was saying, she just wanted to keep the gold coins Solomon gave her and still get her house.

"You can take out a loan, borrowing against the gold coins," he finally said. "Then when your business starts making money, you can repay the loan with paper money from your profits."

"And I get to keep the *same* gold coins in the safe?"

"Yes."

"Well," Cassie Lee breathed and smiled in one motion. "I guess after I see how safe your vault is, I can give you my coins."

Cassie Lee never saw so much metal, heavy thick bars, paper money, and gold in her life. She relinquished her fifteen hundred dollars in solid gold, and the loan was set up at the bank.

Reverend Burris took her on the tour of the Negro sections of town again, giving her the pros and cons of building from the ground up or taking over a house that might need repair.

"This all sounds like more than I got in that loan," Cassie Lee said.

"Well, you can get some help from the Mutual Benefit and Relief Society," said he.

"What's that?"

"In December of '49, thirty-seven of us formed it to help people help themselves. We believe in standing on the shoulders of our black brothers and sisters to achieve positive goals—not on their backs, like people of the Bottoms."

"That's it. Stop!" Cassie Lee commanded.

"That house?"

"Yes," she smiled all over herself. "I saw it when we were going up the other side."

"Well, it's vacant. It'll take some work. You know it's not really in our section of town."

"That's what I like about it." Cassie Lee jumped from the wagon, and stood in front of it envisioning a white picket fence around it. "I like that it is near that main street, but I wouldn't hear the noise because it's tucked back under this big tree. I like the way the sun hits it now that the fog's burned off for the day."

She looked around without moving and continued, "There's a barn back there, and the livery is right across the main street which means my guests can board their horses there and I don't have to worry about it."

182

The reverend smiled at her assessment of the property. "That livery and feed place belongs to Travis Lee," he said. "He's black."

Cassie Lee grinned. "Reverend, that's a good sign."

"Call me Nathan."

"Well, Nathan, let's go see if the inside of the house is as good as the outside."

* * * * * * * * * * * * *

Candy joined Cassie Lee as she stood in the sunlight outside her new house.

"My, my, look at all those men. Swarming all over that house like bees in a beehive just to whip it into shape for you," Candy teased.

"Folks helping folks is all," Cassie Lee answered.

"Not a woman in sight."

"You ought to just hush."

"Who is that one building the chicken coop?" Candy eyed his muscular physique.

"That's Travis Lee, the blacksmith."

"Any relation?" Candy asked.

"Not yet," Cassie Lee said, and sauntered on off.

Chapter XV

Cassie Lee's first introduction to the Community of Faith Baptist Church came when she went to their annual spring painting party. From there she had received her volunteer militia of able-bodied men who had worked to get her house together in record time, including the porch, the chicken coop, the yard, the barn, the picket fence, and the window boxes. The fresh yellow paint and the white trim gave Cassie Lee a heartfelt pause.

"Dreams do come true, Nubby, if you don't give up."

Cassie Lee wasn't much for socializing with all there was to do inside the house, now with furnishings and such, but she always took time out on Sunday to thank and praise God. She not only enjoyed the service when preached by Reverend Burris the elder or younger, but she loved to come early and see the families enter, the husbands and wives and their children all dressed up and proud. The Ross, Keswick, Merchant, Chapman, Fauntleroy, Mayfield, and Shamwell families almost filled up a pew apiece with their five-plus children. If Cassie Lee was to envy anything, it would be to have a husband and children, but she mustn't be too greedy. She was blessed, and she knew it. She was so far from Georgia and even the Sierras in time and space. She wasn't the same naive ex-slave girl of two years back. Not including the way slavery steals childhood, Cassie Lee had

185

packed considerable living into her last twenty-four months. Her cumulative life experiences made her appear mature beyond her years—whatever age she might truly be.

As she played with the chubby dark hands of little Absalom, Cassie Lee knew that dealing with life had its consequences. That her life was the sum total of all her choices. That her past with Tante Fatima crossed her future and she would never have a child of her own. That she would never draw life from a man and give it back again. She had no regrets. Given the same life and options, she would have done the same thing over again.

When the choir stood and led the congregation in the final hymn, tears of joy streamed down her face as she joined in,

"I sing because I'm happy. I sing because I'm free. His eye is on the sparrow, and I know He watches me."

"I found the perfect rug for your parlor," Nathan told Cassie Lee as they filed out of church shaking the pastor's hands.

"Wonderful."

"I can bring it around today after supper."

"Why not *for* supper?"

"I was hoping you'd ask."

"My, my, my," Candy spoke once they were out of ear range. "He doesn't seem your type." They began walking home.

"Like you know what my type is."

"One thing I can say about you, you get some quality men interested in you."

"You attract what you reflect."

"You ever been in love, Cassie Lee?

She couldn't suppress a grin. "Once," she said and swallowed hard. "A long time ago."

"Tell me about him."

"Why? He's dead and gone. My Forever Man," she said reverently, and smiled.

"Oh, I forgot to get that pattern from Effie," Candy said. "I'll be right back."

"I'm going on because those heathens the Briscoes will want breakfast," Cassie Lee said of her dear, delightful guests except in their disbelief in God. "If there is a God, He don't care nothing about Negroes," they believed.

Cassie Lee was home putting the final touches on the meal when Candy slammed into the kitchen in an uproar.

"What ran over you?" Cassie Lee asked, as she continued to ice the cake."

"I went back to get the pattern from Effie, and I overheard that hateful Hannah Weams saying awful stuff about us," Candy fumed, and paced as Cassie Lee kept icing. "It don't matter about me, but she got no right to mean-mouth you. You ain't never been no whore, and they shouldn't be saying such a thing. They say that's how you got your money."

"You want to keep your voice down," Cassie Lee said quietly, as she continued at her task.

"Aren't you mad? Don't you want to go and punch that high-and-mighty sneer offa her coal-black face?"

"She got no coins in my coffer."

"Aw!" Candy was outdone at her friend's calmness.

"What happened to the one about me killing the master, the mistress, and all their children before I stole all their money and headed West? I was partial to that one."

Candy began to chuckle.

"You can't let every little thing somebody says rile you. That gives them the upper hand. Hand me those candles. She just a woman who ain't never been loved, is all."

"I wonder why?" Candy said sarcastically. "Make love to all them cats, most probably." She swiped a finger full of icing from the bowl, and Cassie Lee slapped her hand playfully.

"To feel the way you do, Cassie Lee, you must have had some powerful love wrapped around your heart." She eyed her friend. "Tell me about your Forever Man."

"Tsk," Cassie Lee sucked her teeth. "Don't make me sorry I told you that much." She wiped her hands on her apron and set the cake on the pedestal server.

As she cut the lemons in two and pressed them over the hard surface to extract the tart juice, Cassie Lee continued an internal conversation sparked by Candy's curiosity.

The Lord and Solomon decided that I should have this boarding house, and I'm just obliging them both, she thought. No use hankering over or waiting on something that ain't yours, and ain't never gonna be yours, like Nubby waiting on Taffy to die or be sold so she could have Ben all to herself. Nubby was too stupid to see Ben wasn't studyin' about her for permanent. He had Taffy and their children. He just wanted a side-woman to spice up his life some, and that itty bit of stolen time he threw at her every now and again was all Nubby could hope for. Everyone could see that even if Taffy was sold off or died, Ben still wouldn't want her for permanent. Every time he'd see Nubby, she'd be just a reminder of how bad he treated Taffy when she was there. Nubby didn't have sense enough to know she was in a bad situation, either way. But me, Cassie Lee, I know Solomon was married to those mountains, and me to my dream. It was paradise with him, but it is gone. When the time is right, I'll settle for a little bit of heaven.

"But he's dead and gone," Cassie Lee spoke aloud to Candy, who looked up from the stove at her friend.

"At least you had love once," Candy said.

"Yes, I did, and you will too if you lucky." She smiled wistfully and said, "A man who can walk on water and make you feel like you can sail a ship on dry land."

Cassie Lee realized that she could have shared her thoughts of Solomon with Candy, but she wanted to hold him close. Keep him all to herself—pure, solid, and strong. To talk about him would dilute him and invite unwanted comments. If she just held fast to his memory, then she would always have him when she needed him.

"How did you deal with his dying?"

"Still dealing," Cassie Lee said, as she pumped water into the pitcher of tart juice. "My mind knows he's dead, but my heart . . . still—"

"What about the body?" Candy lightened the mood.

"Tsk." Cassie Lee rolled her eyes in mock disgust as Candy laughed. "Hand me that sugar."

That's what Solomon had been to her: the sweetness of her life. He had given her enough love to last for the rest of her days, but his legacy was a double-edged sword. He'd also gifted her with a pain she hadn't expected. Physical pain she knew about first hand. The lash of a master's whip. The wails of a stomach feeding on itself due to an empty hunger. The bite of a snake and the twist of an ankle running from the master to Tante Fatima's deep in the swamp. But inside pain was harder to endure. It was all yours—no outside sympathy or understanding—just you and your hurt, dealing, mending, and doctoring your own wounds back to health. Even so, she had to admit, the ride was worth the fall.

Cassie Lee could have told Candy that Solomon came last night. Slipped past her mind in the darkness, caressed her heart, settled in her groin, and from there swirled upward throughout her body until it quivered in response to his coming—then he left. Even the essence of him always returned to the mountains. Cassie Lee had accepted these sporadic, nocturnal visits as matter-of-fact. Like acts of nature, nothing she could control or embrace. Like a twister that just happened and left— with want and destruction the only remnants of its coming.

* * * * * * * * * * * *

"I am so sorry about your father, Nathan. I didn't know him well and I didn't know your mother at all, but I do know that they raised a wonderful son," Cassie Lee said at the funeral. She hadn't visited with Nathan since.

In the two weeks that followed, she caught glimpses of him as he assumed the tasks at hand. All the responsibility fell to the young, energetic man who didn't want to disappoint his congregation or his father's memory. But Cassie Lee saw less of him, and she missed her friend.

Candy had blossomed into a respectable woman of the community despite the rancor of Miss Hannah Weams. Cassie Lee had waited for her old ways to resurface, but Candy had indeed become Juanita. She worked hard at the boarding house during the day, and on the days when she didn't go to choir practice, she taught Spanish to men, women, and children in the rectory hall. Juanita was earning and saving money. Bohemia would be proud of her. Cassie Lee was proud of her.

Cassie Lee walked her horse, Sierra, across the main street to the livery stable, taking extra care as he had picked up a stone during their morning ride.

"Good morning, Travis," Cassie Lee said, averting her eyes so as not to stare at his bulging biceps.

"Mornin', Cassie Lee." He placed the red-hot shoe in the bucket of water, and the sizz and steam it sent up seemed to mimic the feelings he generated in her.

She didn't know why she was attracted to him. Travis was more Bohemia or Juanita's type. His light skin seemed ever-so-kissed by the sun, and his hair was the color of both darkness and bright. His eyes were penetratingly light, and the rise of his cheekbones and in his nose hinted that what wasn't black was Indian. He was about five feet ten inches, she surmised, and powerfully built.

"Well, business is always booming in here," she said, looking anywhere but at him.

"I try to do a good job," he said with confident modesty.

"What a beautiful carriage," Cassie Lee said, as she fingered the fine tapestry fringe.

"Belongs to Mrs. Fairmont."

"The white lady?"

"I have a lot of white customers. Good is good, I suspect."

"Yes."

She knew why all of the single ladies and half of the married ones came to Travis Lee's Livery. It wasn't just the excellent work, the view wasn't bad either.

"If business keeps up like this, I'm going to have to expand. As it is, I don't have the time to do the things I'd like." He looked at her, and said, "like taking a pretty girl to dinner." His even-toothed smile made her blush.

The talk in their community verified that he often worked late at night on his harnesses and wheels. Some folks said he was rich beyond belief, but Cassie Lee often glanced over to the stable at night and saw his light on. Like her, he too was a man with a dream. He was linked to no one romantically, though many had tried but not endured. Those society girls didn't like taking a back seat to dreams.

"How's that milk cow?"

"Fine as ever, and the chicken coop is—" Oh, stupid, stupid, you're talking about the chicken coop he built you months ago? "Ah, Sierra has a stone. I tried to get it out myself."

"Let's take a look." As he bent over, Cassie Lee was about to take full advantage of the view when the door swung open.

"Hello, Mr. Lee," the familiar whine of Melody Bumbry, complete with parasol and gloves, glided in.

"Good mornin', Miss Bumbry."

"I told you to call me Melody," she sang to him before saying, "Hello, Cassie Lee."

"Melody."

"Let me get your saddle for you," Travis said to the heavily perfumed woman.

"I can come back later," Cassie Lee said.

"No, just let me get the saddle for Miss—Melody."

"Oh, I can wait," Melody offered.

"No, I know how anxious you are to go riding," Travis said.

He hoisted it down for her, accepted payment, and put it in her buggy as she feverishly twirled her parasol.

"Thank you for your business," he said with his patented smile as Melody huffed off.

"Seems she wanted to spend a little more time here," Cassie Lee said.

"She always does. Now, let's get that stone out." He bent down again, and his muscles rippled. "There."

Cassie Lee was disappointed at his skillful quickness. He plucked the stone away too fast, leaving her to feel as desperate as Melody.

"Why thank you. How much?"

"No charge."

"Well, thanks again. If you are serious about expanding, will you let me know?"

"Why?"

"Well, I think this would be a good investment."

"You've got the house, the vegetable stand on Market, and now you want in on the livery business too?"

"Egypt runs the vegetable stand for me, but why not?"

"Well, if it means I'll get to see more of you—" He walked up toward her and stole her breath away. "Ah, Mr. Wheeler," he greeted the man as he walked in.

"Hello Travis, my fireplace grate ready?"

"Thank you, Travis. I'm going to leave now," said Cassie Lee.

"Thanks for stopping by, Cassie Lee. Hope to see you again soon."

As Cassie Lee guided Sierra out of the livery, four more customers showed up, three of them women dressed more for the stage than to carry on blacksmithing business. Cassie Lee wondered when would be a good time to drop by again. With her schedule and his, there was little time for courting.

Courting? The thought tripped and fell through her brain. Was she thinking of courting? "I don't think so," she said aloud, while silently vowing to stay away from Travis Lee.

Cassie Lee tried not to think about courting but decided to build two rooms on to the side of her house, just in case. For privacy, she rationalized. Her new accommodations had its own entrance directly from the front porch, adjacent to the main parlor. Her bedroom was behind a small sitting room, while Juanita's new room was on the back. These two additional bedrooms were connected by a narrow hallway that led directly into the kitchen. Business was so good that all four guest bedrooms were always full, the draw being the cleanliness and attractiveness of the house, but the delicious meals kept the guests there.

"Well, we're home mighty early," Juanita noticed, as Cassie Lee came in from spending the afternoon with Nathan.

"Nighttime has expectations that the daytime don't," Cassie Lee said, removing her hat and smoothing back wild tendrils from her face. "Got enough tongues wagging around here that I don't need to add fuel to the fire."

Cassie Lee shimmied out of her skirt while Juanita flopped on her bed. When she fanned Juanita off her bed and into the chair, she continued, "Don't want no misunderstandings."

"Don't you like Nathan?"

"Yes, very much, like I like Samuel."

"Nothing more? No Forever Man?"

"He's one man too late for that. Why? You interested?"

"Tsk," Juanita sucked her teeth and left, throwing "Good night" over her shoulder.

* * * * * * * * * * * * *

"What are you doing?" Cassie Lee asked as she shrugged from Nathan's embrace, tearing her lips from his. "And why?"

"Because," a stunned Nathan answered. "Because I like you."

"Well, I like you too, but not like that!" She brushed her fingers across her lips as if removing any evidence of his indiscretions.

"Cassie Lee," he said simply, then laughed and laughed and laughed, "You are something else."

"So I've been told. I believe you are relieved."

"I just thought this way we could be friends forever. I romance and marry you, and then we'll always be friends."

"So you felt it was your duty to kiss me?"

"Well, not exactly. I guess I had to prove to myself that it wasn't anything more to us than just enjoying each other's company."

"So we won't be going through this again?" she drawled.

"Promise. Friends." He stuck out his hand.

"Friends." Cassie Lee shook it.

Although Cassie Lee and Nathan understood, their relationship was an unintelligible anomaly to onlookers. In a time when the measure of a woman was when and who she married and how many children she bore her husband, no one understood why their liaison seemed stalled. The Reverend Nathan Burris was a catch, and the fact that he and Cassie Lee were simpatico but not going anywhere was also a puzzle to the perplexed community.

* * * * * * * * * * * * *

The deep-throated howl shook the tranquil mountains as the steel trap clamped down on his forearm, tearing open his skin and crunching into the bone—that sound almost as foreign as the manic yell.

Solomon fought the trap as a high-flying bird cawed mockingly at a hunter caught in his own trap. His red blood sprayed the white snow as he tried to angle his massive body, contorting it and wrestling it to the ground so that his arm and trap finally rested flatly on the frigid surface. He anchored his foot on the side of the metal and pulled up with his other hand until the gripping teeth released its prey. As he looked at his dark, mangled flesh rendered a pulpy red-purple, his only thought was to get to his cabin's fire so he could seal the wound.

He tried climbing out of the white ravine, but the slanted sides would accept his attempts for awhile, then contemptuously spit him back down to the bottom again. As the snow bled red, Solomon, time and time again, hurled his muscled body against that mountain. Exhausted and weak from loss of blood, he lay at the bottom, trying to catch his breath from the tiny crystalline particles of cold that doubled as air. He had cheated death plenty of times in and around these mountains. He'd do it again.

Night began to fall, and he prayed that this would not be the way his life ended. Buried alive in the mountains that once offered him solace and comfort, but now seemed to consort with the devil and turn on him. If this was where he'd meet his Maker, then he had no regrets . . . except maybe one.

He saw her doe-eyes, wide, innocent, and accepting, smiling down at him. Was this the Lord's way of saying his time was up? He didn't go to her whole. He would not go to her mangled. He didn't want to die in these mountains alone to be discovered years from now as a skeleton at the bottom of this ditch. Not when his life could have been filled with sunshine, laughter, children, and Cassie Lee. What he wouldn't give to just hold her again.

Lying prone on the cold mountain floor, he finally admitted to himself and the Lord above that he loved her. He loved her like he had never loved anyone before—so easily, so completely. He had told himself he sent her away because of some unwritten, honor-bound duty. The reality of it was fear. Fear that he could not live up to her expectations of him. Fear that if she stayed with him, in time she'd want more then he could give, and she'd wonder about her boarding house. Fear that in the end, he could not hold onto her. So he had decided to give her up while it was easier on them both. You can't miss what you never had. But he had waited too long, for she had already vexed him, touched him tenderly with her healing hand, and resurrected long buried feelings of desire. And once they surfaced, he didn't rightly know what to do with them. Now he knew. But the knowing of all this was a far cry from the acting on it.

"Lord, you have a mighty funny way of gettin' your point across."

He lay there in the twenty-foot open coffin with nowhere to go, nowhere to be, and no one to care. He chuckled wryly before yelling, "Cassie Leeee!!"

* * * * * * * * * * * *

The milk pitcher slipped from her hand and crashed to the floor.

"You got the butter fingers?" Juanita asked as Cassie Lee stared off into the distance in a trance. "Cassie Lee?" Her friend called her back.

"Oh, Lord, look at this mess!" Cassie Lee said as she sprang into a cleaning frenzy while Juanita eyed her curiously before returning to her task.

"What are these?" Cassie Lee asked Juanita as she arranged the fruit bowl.

"What?" she asked as Cassie Lee pointed to the dark, purple-black round fruit. "Plums?"

"They're obscene!"

Juanita's smile radiated from her lips to encompass her entire face like a single raindrop in a pond of calm water. "Cassie Lee," she said, as she moved closer to her friend and whispered in her ear. "Just who was the whore at Bohemia's? Me or you?"

"Shush!" Cassie Lee declared, as her friend plopped the round balls into each of her hands.

"They are real sweet, firm and soft at the same time," she teased, and watched Cassie Lee try to stifle an embarrassed laugh.

Cassie Lee plunked them in the bowl. "You are so bad, Juanita."

"You ought to try one. Or have you already—only not in this form?"

"Go get the lace tablecloth from the upstairs linen closet and stop talking foolishness," she said, fanning her friend away.

Once she heard Juanita's footsteps on the stairs, the plums called to her. Cassie Lee went over and placed one in her hand. The look was familiar, and stirred long-buried thoughts within her. She looked at its color next to hers and rubbed her thumb across the smooth, dark texture of the plum—once, twice, three times—before gently squeezing the roundness of it. She felt it give ever so slightly beneath her gentle touch.

195

She swore she heard Solomon moan.

The next morning as Cassie Lee went to check on her Market Street fruit stand, she spotted a man walking just ahead of her. He was more than six feet tall and a dark wiry beard hid his face, but the duster and broad-brimmed hat were unmistakable. His gait was familiar. She pushed past the people through the crowded street. With every step she was sure it was him, looking for her. She ran, feverishly calling his name, the sound of her voice lost in the cacophony of the city. She reached his back, grabbed his elbow, and whirled him around with a force that scared them both.

"Whoa, little lady!" He grinned down at her. "A woman as fine as you don't need to be so forceful." He watched the smile drain from her face like the last of amber whiskey from a glass bottle.

"I'm sorry," she said.

"I'm not." He turned his full body to hers.

"I thought you was someone else."

"I'll be anybody you want me to be," he said to her retreating form. "How 'bout we jaw on it over a drink?" He yelled after her, but she had gone as quickly as she had come.

Chapter XVI

Cassie Lee enjoyed taking Sierra for a morning ride when time and weather permitted. She liked riding out and looking down on the trail south to Los Angeles. Someday she'd visit there too, and San Diego. Life was as good as it got without Solomon. She accepted that there was no place for true love to hide. Solomon would always be a three-syllable word that equaled love. She quickly turned her thoughts to the Thanksgiving and Christmas that were like none she had ever known. The first days of the new year had been given up to reflecting.

San Francisco proved to be the land of milk and honey. Fortunes were made and lost overnight, but Cassie Lee kept her wits about her, safeguarding her property and investments. It had almost been a year since coming here, and already she was financially set with money to spare. She had even backed Cephas Nesbit, a runaway slave they called Blue because he was so black, and so ugly that no one called him at all. Cassie Lee didn't need any more steady help, but she gave him odd jobs and listened to Blue talk on his dreams as he ate her fried chicken, cornbread, and hash browns and onions while they sat out back on the steps. Folks around town claimed they were unsettled by his homely looks, but Cassie Lee figured it was mostly the reminder of where he came from, and what some were trying to forget, that gave them pause.

She liked him because in him she saw every man who had the gumption to run from the Whedoe plantation—every man who made it and was never brought back, strung up, and whipped within an inch of his life only to be spared enough breath to become the worst plantation-lackey ever born.

Cassie Lee helped Blue because he had bypassed the Bottoms for hard work, and she figured, everyone who has a dream ought to have a shot at it. Blue struck it rich. And when he did, they all started calling him Mr. Nesbit, remarking on how he wasn't so ugly after all. When Cassie Lee refused to accept any money beyond what she had lent him, Blue started putting money directly into her bank account. With it, Cassie Lee, in turn, made withdrawals to various civic associations and extended business loans to help the community. Last she heard, Blue was living free and easy in Indian Territory.

Cassie Lee was proud of the new gleaming-gold steeple she bought for the Community of Faith Baptist Church and the upright piano that sat in her parlor. It was not as fancy as the one at Bohemia's, but she relished sliding next to little Marcia Rance on the polished bench while Miss Lois Webb taught them their lessons. Marcia didn't have a piano, and even when Cassie Lee was too busy to stop and join the pair, she could listen to the lesson taught by the teacher and practice later.

* * * * * * * * * * * *

She fed Sierra a green apple before biting into one of her own. As she sank to the grassy ground and stretched out her long body, she thought on how well everything was going. From her "big house" vantage point where she watched white folk's dealings, coupled with the advanced schooling at the hem of Bohemia Jones, Cassie Lee had learned how to keep a level head and a tight rein on finances. It had served her well. Her house was paid in full with three years' worth of repair-money in the bank for incidentals. What had started as a fruit stand turned into a stall, and now a permanent store run by Egypt and her husband, George. At the insistence of some of San Francisco's leading citizens, Cassie Lee had entered the catering business with Egypt and George Parham. The money was as bountiful as the appetite white folks had for her food. But after just one cotillion season, Cassie Lee decided that she wasn't cooking for or serving white folks any more. Some things couldn't be bought, and her services were one of them. But, Parham Catering was thriving.

Cassie Lee even owned a bit of Travis Lee's Livery and Feed business, part of his expansion from blacksmithing. He was hiring on more help and training them to his liking.

But ever since she ran that man down on the street, she thought she was losing it when it came to Solomon. Wouldn't Mrs. Bumbry have loved to witness that? A "leading citizen" running down a man in the street. So she had decided to immerse herself, not just her money, into more civic-minded, community activities. At Juanita's prompting, Cassie Lee reluctantly joined the Community of Faith Church Choir. She was impressed at how well her friend took charge of church activities, and what a nice complement she was to Nathan.

Cassie Lee wondered if they realized what they had. The distraction of all her civic and church memberships worked for awhile, but then, one bright Sunday morning, while the choir sang *"His Eye Is on the Sparrow,"* Solomon appeared outside the church window. She was sure the familiar hymn had conjured him up. By then, she had accepted seeing his image every now and then, but she dared not approach any man and be so embarrassed again. Through the church's opened stained-glass window, when she saw him in the distance, she didn't even flinch. She accepted that he would just haunt her until she found a man to take his place, or at least distract her from him.

* * * * * * * * * * * *

She drew her legs up and tucked them beneath her as she rested her chin on her knees and Sierra grazed after finishing the green apple. A gentle breeze curled around her face, and she smiled into the sunshine. These rides were sobering and freeing, opening her mind to flit or rest as needed. She wished she could send for Nubby, buy her from the Whedoes, but she knew Nubby would never come. Her dear old friend was small-minded and didn't see that she had control over some of her life.

Cassie Lee thought of Samuel, and wondered if Lucas Davenport had found anybody to occupy that other porch rocker. She thought of

199

Bohemia, Gypsy, and Scarlet, and of Elijah Cobb in Texas, maybe. She could think of Exum without retching, as long as she didn't have to lay eyes on him. She was sure Exum was the one who had given her the extra five hundred dollars. He started this all with his mangy-dog ways of wanting a woman like his ma. He set all this in motion. He spun this universe for her. And Cassie Lee wouldn't be surprised if Tante Fatima was stirring up some brew for her in that mighty black cauldron of hers deep in those Georgia woods. Everybody left Tante Fatima alone—said she was touched, but they feared her too. Who else could live with mosquitoes as big as bees and a sting twice as poisonous? Who else could dwell where the moss hung from trees like a witch's stringy hair, with only critters to talk too? And only God and Tante Fatima had such far-reaching powers.

Sierra snorted and bent toward her, and Cassie Lee rubbed his nose before feeding her horse another apple. She didn't linger on the significance of the round green fruit too long, but pronounced to her equine companion, "This is the year I find me a husband, Sierra." Cassie Lee stood and brushed off the seat of her pants. "Pick him this year, and marry him by the next." She swung up into the saddle and said, "One thing Solomon taught me but good, was that no matter how much you love somebody, it don't mean they'll love you back. So I'm going to pick a man who already has a sweet spot for me, make it easy for the both of us. I think you'll approve of my first choice."

* * * * * * * * * * * *

"Cassie Lee," the old woman whimpered as Nubby applied a cool cloth to her fevered forehead. She chanted more jibberish from her cracked lips and repeated, "Cassie Lee."

"She gon, Tante Fatima. Cassie Lee ain't here no mo'," Nubby said.

"She crazy out her mind," Geneva said, and the others of the death watch agreed.

"She jus' sayin' goodbye is all," Bethesda, her old friend, said.

Tante Fatima could feel the presence of folks in her swamp cabin, and she knew who was missing: Atticus Whedoe. She hadn't seen him close up since the night he came by to tap into her supernatural vexing powers when Charles took off after Cassie Lee. She remembered the dark consuming his light-colored suit much the way her dark body consumed him when he visited her years ago. She was a young girl then, just up from a Louisiana plantation, trying to drown the pain of having three babies sold from her tit. During one of their night trysts they produced a daughter, Mattie, and Atticus swore Fatima could keep her forever. That beautiful baby turned into a gorgeous woman who loved a man, and they too had a child. But Mattie had helped her man escape to freedom. He was coming back for her and their child when she was old enough to travel and not give them away with her cries on the freedom trail. The Whedoes didn't care that this man had been a warrior, a prince in Africa. They just knew one of their prized bucks had escaped. With him gone, they punished the one who helped him and sold Mattie down river. Tante Fatima's mind cracked and shattered, and the quarter's root-woman and midwife took off from the plantation the only way she could—through her mind.

She was out of her head, and everybody left her alone, especially when she went to live in an abandoned cabin deep in the swamp. She was touched, but the slaves knew her to have powers that seemed further enhanced by her isolation and living with all those swamp creatures. Some years later, when she came from the swamp to tend to a slave, she saw a pretty little girl with Mattie's eyes staring back at her. In her insane state, Tante Fatima had forgotten about her granddaughter, Cassie Lee. She was two when Mattie was sold; she was about four when Tante Fatima remembered her. Not being able to love a child and have her sold off again, Tante Fatima kept her tongue, letting others believe she still did not recognize the child. Each time she came up from the swamp, Cassie Lee's eyes followed her. Despite the shabby clothing, Cassie Lee was clean, her hair in two long braids, and her hands were always laced through Nubby's except when they were separated by work. Ruth was taking good care of her grandbaby. There was no reason to claim her. No reason to wrestle her away from Ruth and Nubby just to live deep in a swamp, which could be dangerous to a curious child, with a strange old woman who talked to both God and the devil.

So everyone kept a silent tongue even when at five Cassie Lee's father had returned, as promised, disguised as a rich white man's coachman—tall and finely dressed. But his regal stature crumpled when he learned of Mattie's sale further south. In the company of his white "boss," he immediately went off in search of her, leaving Cassie Lee's curious eyes staring at the back of the coach. Bethesda, who later told Tante Fatima about his hurried visit, was sure he thought his wife and child were sold together. All tongues remained silent still when a seven-year-old Cassie Lee ventured off, looking for Tante Fatima's swamp home. The whole quarter was out searching for Cassie Lee, and when they found her, they worried that the crazed old woman would harm her. But Bethesda looked into the eyes of her old friend and knew that Tante Fatima was back from Satan's edge and only wished the best for Mattie's child. "She ain't gon hurt dis baby," Bethesda decreed. Thereafter, whenever Cassie Lee was missing, folks knew she was more than likely with Tante Fatima.

* * * * * * * * * * * * *

Tante Fatima's body jerked, startling Nubby, so Bethesda took over reaching for her friend's hand. She stroked her work-worn hands, recalling how in more than two decades had no one breathed a word about Cassie Lee's parentage: to what purpose? Everyone who knew was dead, sold off, or wedded to the secret.

The spasms returned in waves before easing out again, and Tante Fatima struggled to remain on earth, not ready to let go, waiting on a sign, and remembering that the whole time Atticus was here praying for his son, he had never mentioned his grandaughter, Cassie Lee.

Responding to the gentle strokes of her friend, Tante Fatima's eyes, seeing a vision, fluttered open, and she said, "Cassie Lee be free. She safe now." The sign had come to no one but her. Tante Fatima smiled and released the hand of her friend to board the sweet chariot that had swung low to carry her to her heavenly home.

* * * * * * * * * * * * *

"My, my, my," Juanita said, as she strolled up to the picket fence where Cassie Lee was planting new rose bushes. "We gonna have to move out of here if your suitors don't stop giving you bushes."

"They look real pretty next to the fence, though," Cassie Lee said, stretching her back.

"Who is that one from?"

"Bernard Meeks."

"Oh, he doesn't stand a chance," Juanita said, as she entered and locked the gate. "He's pudgy." They chuckled.

"Got all the whitewash for the painting party?" Cassie Lee asked, as she finished watering her newest thorny addition.

"All set. You are bringing the apple pie, pineapple upside-down cake, and some fried chicken?"

"Do I have a choice?" Cassie Lee set the watering can down and followed Juanita up the four steps.

"July Sessoms said he wouldn't come if you didn't, and he's supplying the paint." Cassie Lee collapsed into the porch rocker. "Which one of these is his?" Juanita asked.

Cassie Lee pointed while she poured two glasses of cool lemonade, as Juanita set the other rocker in motion.

"He'd make a fine husband. He already been broke in once," Juanita teased of the widower Sessoms.

"He's always suited up. Neck all choked up with a tie, and his hands are softer than mine," Cassie Lee said.

"That's a lot of laundry for the wife."

"He can keep on sending them where he's sending them now," Cassie Lee said, and they shared a chuckle.

"He's got mountains of money just waiting for the wife who can set it all to music," Juanita said, as she sipped the tart sweetness.

"I got money of my own. Besides, he's a surrey-with-the-fringe-on-top kinda guy, and I'm a open buckboard gal."

"That's Profit Foster's rose next?"

"Yep," Cassie Lee exhaled her answer after a long, thirst-quenching sip.

"You love his carpentry. You always bragging on the wardrobe in your bedroom and the dining room sideboard."

"I love the gap between his two front teeth too, but not enough to marry him. I'm mad at him for selling that dining room sideboard right out from under me. Said I already had one. But that one was a real beauty, and why are we discussing this?" Cassie Lee just realized.

"Like them a little more rugged, huh?" Juanita went right on talking. "Got one for you. Seth Santini."

"Oh, my," Cassie Lee agreed. "Well, now, he is rugged. He's a good-looking man. He knows it, and all the women in town, married and not, know it."

"Must be that mixed blood."

"Well, the Negro part wants a black woman like his mama, but I'm afraid I'm moving too slow for his daddy's Italian part. He's keeping company with Clara Keswick."

"Among others."

"That grapevine he gave me is growing all over the chicken coop and attaching itself on the fig tree," Cassie Lee said, "Spreading itself around just like Seth."

"There ain't no Forever Man in these parts, huh?"

"Not a one." She was glad the name of Travis Lee hadn't come up. "Maybe a peg or two lower."

"Maybe you and him are destined to be together."

"Well, I'm not gonna die to be with him, Juanita." Cassie Lee rolled her eyes. "I know who and what I'm looking for."

"A man who can walk on water and make you feel like you can sail a ship on dry land."

"Well, at least a man that's got something besides a hand full of 'gimmie' and a mouth full of 'thank you please.'"

"I hear you."

"Until *I* decide who, I'm not going to fill my life with cheap thrills and expensive regrets. He's got to be somebody I'm willing to give up my bear cover for."

"That's a tall order." Juanita's comment met Cassie Lee's quiet. "Suppose I told you I found someone I'd be willing to give up my bear cover for. If I had one."

Cassie Lee swung her face around to meet her friend's. "Well, I'd say, it's about time."

"It may be just one-sided. I don't want to jinx it. Forget I said anything!" Juanita sprang from her rocker like a tack was in the seat.

The thought of Juanita and Nathan made Cassie Lee's heart smile, but she honored her friend's request. She above all knew how important and private affairs of love were.

$$* \quad * \quad * \quad * \quad * \quad * \quad * \quad * \quad * \quad * \quad * \quad * \quad *$$

Cassie Lee set the pies on the window sill to cool in the night breeze. As she finished cleaning up the kitchen, Juanita entered with cups, saucers, and cake plates in hand.

"Nathan gone?"

"Yes," Juanita answered.

"He didn't even say goodbye to me," Cassie Lee teased, as she took the chinaware from her friend and slid them into the soapy water.

"I'm *in love*, Cassie Lee. I never thought I'd ever be—but I am." Her wide-eyed innocence touched Cassie Lee's soul. "It's the first time I said it out loud." She burst into laughter.

"Scary to admit, ain't it?" Cassie Lee smiled at her friend as a mother would to a sixteen-year-old who just made the same admission. "I think you two make a perfect couple."

"Like you and your Forever Man?"

"No. But close."

"I think he's gonna ask me to marry him. Maybe after the paint party tomorrow!"

"You'd be the only one in San Francisco who'd be surprised."

"Really?" Her eyes grew enormous. "He's such a good man, Cassie Lee. He's strong and decent, and he treats me so good."

"You deserve it." She ran a sudsy dishcloth across the rose pattern of the dessert plate and handed it to Juanita for rinsing and drying.

"Should I tell him?" Juanita's questioning eyes searched Cassie Lee's.

"What?"

"About Bohemia's."

Cassie Lee plunged her hands into the rinse water. As she wiped them on her apron she said, "Yes."

Juanita answered in a volley, "But I'm a respectable woman now. I go to church, I teach, I don't swear or smoke or drink, and I haven't been with a man, any man, since we left River Bend." Her eyes pleaded.

205

"You still got to tell him."

"Why? What good would it do? Who am I hurting? Nathan would be so hurt if I told him. I've changed."

"I know. I know," she soothed. "But you'd be starting out your life with a lie—"

"I don't care what Nathan did before me."

"You *know* what Nathan did before you. It must have come up in conversation. What did you already tell him about your past?"

Juanita went to the far side of the kitchen and started playing with the edge of the gingham curtain.

"I told him the truth; that my mother was black and my father was half-black and Mexican, and I left home after my mother died and—been on my own ever since."

Cassie Lee walked over to where Juanita stood. "So Nathan assumes that you taught Spanish and English all this time?"

"I didn't tell him no different."

"So you lied by not telling him." Cassie Lee looked at her distraught friend. "You know it may seem a little thing to you, but you seen what a little burr under a saddle can do to a horse?"

"What?"

"If you clear it away, nothing. But if you leave it there, it'll irritate, then fester, make a sore, get infected, and kill that big old horse."

"I can't lose him, Cassie Lee. He's the most decent man I've ever known!"

"This is how you treat decent men? What happens when you and him and your children run into, say, Elijah Cobb one day downtown?"

"That won't happen. Besides, Elijah Cobb wouldn't say nothing."

"He wouldn't have to. All Nathan has to do is ask how you know him, and the guilt would fly to your face like a heat rash in the Georgia sun." Juanita grew visibly agitated. "You don't want to live your life like that, do you? Wondering who'll be coming around the bend. Men not as nice or forgiving as Elijah Cobb. They could want money from you for keeping quiet. This is no small sleepy little town, this is San Francisco, Juanita. Folks come from all over."

"I can't worry about what might happen," she spat.

206

"All right. What about Nathan? Don't you think he deserves to know all about you? About the mother of his children?"

"That's just it. If I tell him—there won't be no children, no marriage, no nothing, and I'll end up just like you!"

Cassie Lee flinched, and her face turned as hard and brittle as frozen mountain snow.

"Oh, I'm sorry, Cassie Lee. I'm so sorry. I didn't mean—"

"I'm going on to bed now. You get some rest," Cassie Lee said, her mouth barely moving. "Big day tomorrow."

"Cassie Lee! I'm sorry."

Juanita's words hurled through the air, hit the back of Cassie Lee's bedroom door, and slid onto the floor where they evaporated, unanswered, into thin air.

Chapter XVII

The sun cut across the back of the Community of Faith Baptist Church and wrapped its warmth around the building and its congregation. From its perch you could see the ships in the harbor and smell the fresh air cut with a salt chaser. The young people, and those courting, gathered their buckets and brushes and sectioned off a piece of the church to call their own, while some directed games for the too-young-to-work. Others, like Cassie Lee, busied themselves unpacking, preparing, and arranging a cornucopia of food on the tablecloths of seven long tables.

Many hands make quick work, and the hungry parishioners descended on the tables to devour the plenty, almost before the Reverend Burris could give his blessing. He calmed the crowd and their hands as he admonished them, "Don't forget to remember who makes all this possible." He thanked the Lord for this perfect day for painting and preparing His house of worship for Palm and Easter Sundays. He concluded by asking Him to "remember those of us who remain in bondage, and to help others continue to prosper in their new lives. And a big thanks for making the Community of Faith Baptist Church the best of three Negro churches in San Francisco," to which the congregation said a loud, "Amen!!"

No one noticed the tension between Cassie Lee and Juanita as they participated in this rite of spring, gave thanks for the uneventful winter, and prayed for the coming summer. Even Hannah Weams and Rebecca Bumbry, who held court beneath the canopy of a huge oak tree, were more preoccupied with deploying their parasols imported directly from Paris, France. They similarly felt the need to chastise, from a safe distance, Cassie Lee for competing in the three-legged race with Aurrie and Marcia, and then Wilma and Vanessa, especially when the trio fell and cavorted with laughter.

"They say slaves are but children themselves," Hannah Weams, who bragged that one could not find a person of bondage in her lineage, was apt to point out.

Cassie Lee sat and ate with Dorothy Soames. They chatted awhile before Dorothy asked, "So, tell me about Juanita."

"What about her?" Cassie Lee thought her perceptive friend had noticed the tension between the two.

"The tall dark man. I've seen her with him twice."

"Who?"

"I don't know. She has failed to introduce us. She hasn't told you about him?"

"No." Cassie Lee recalled how Juanita had been smiling at her like the cat who swallowed the canary, but assumed it all had to do with Nathan.

"Oh, well, if she hasn't told you about him there must be nothing to it. Maybe she's just trying to bring another lost soul to the fold—for Nathan." Cassie Lee thought of the man she accosted in the street.

"Hello ladies," Isabel greeted the pair, and stole Cassie Lee's attention away from Dorothy's discussion of Juanita.

Cassie Lee visited awhile more before making her way home. Nathan made it clear that he expected her to fulfill her duties in the auxiliary choir on Sunday, occupying the first three pews and joining the main choir on certain selections. She'd missed many practices, but the Reverend Burris wanted *all* of his choir members—the faithful and the delinquent—robed and ready three times a year, and Easter Sunday was one of them.

Well, at least I get a seat, Cassie Lee thought as she walked past the Chapman home and thought of Dorothy's curious observation. Juanita with another man? Juanita was invested in Nathan and his church. It was clear that she only had eyes for him, and he for her. She agreed with Dorothy that Juanita was probably recruiting for new members and dismissed any further interpretations as she approached her house.

Cassie Less climbed the steps, pinching off a dead leaf from her hanging basket of petunias. She entered into the welcoming coolness of her home, changed from one skirt and blouse into another, freshened up her face, and redid the bun at the nape of her neck. As she walked into the kitchen she thought of Blue. This was about the time he would come and sit a spell with her. He would have been welcomed, but not conversationally engaged at the annual paint party picnic, so he would have moseyed on down to see Cassie Lee, who was both welcomed and engaged, but weary of the pretense by now.

She walked to the pump and, as she placed a glass pitcher at its mouth, saw the rise of a head pass her window.

"Well, afternoon, Travis Lee," she recognized and startled him at the same time.

"Afternoon to you. Thought you'd still be at the picnic," he said, slinging the two bags of feed from either shoulder of his built body.

"Don't you have boys to help you with that now?" she asked as she sauntered down the five back steps to where he was.

"Some customers I like to deliver myself." He flashed an even-tooth smile in that handsome, sun-kissed complexion of his. His eyes were the color of hay.

"Can I get you something to drink?" she asked without moving. She wanted to wipe his sweaty brow.

"That water in your hand sure looks good."

"I haven't had none of it," she said, offering it to him.

"I wouldn't mind if you did, Cassie Lee." He took it from her, and gulped it down in one swallow.

"Well," she said with a flush of heat. "Just two bags?"

"Yeah. I had to get this from Mills because Faraday sold all his feed to some black rancher up in Napa who was in a hurry, and gave him cash on the barrelhead."

"Does Faraday know what a good customer you are?"

"Now I got both Faraday and Mills bidding for my business, and my price is going lower and lower. It all works out, Cassie Lee." His honey-colored face lit up in a smile.

"You want some more water?" was all she could think to say.

"No, thanks. What I would like, if you was agreeable to it, is—" He stopped, and then said, "I've hired four new men to help me work the livery, and as soon as I get them to where I can trust them not to harm the business I built up—" He stopped again. "I'm going to have some free time on my hands, and I'd like to come calling on you sometime, if that'd be all right with you?"

"That'd be just fine," she heard the exaggerated drawl in her voice, accompanied by a smile as bright as his.

"Mister Lee? Mister Lee!" A man came running around the side of the house.

"Yes, Roscoe?"

"You better come quick, that palomino got Lester backed up into a corner! He's pretty, but he's meaner than a one-eyed dog!"

"Excuse me, Cassie Lee!"

"Surely." She watched his physique move with fierce grace away from her and said, "One day, someday, soon, Travis Lee."

Cassie Lee went over and filled the pan with chicken feed, thinking it would be awhile before he came a-calling, but she'd be ready when he did. She opened the gate of the coop he had built for her almost a year ago. The chickens surrounded her as she sprayed them with grain, and she noticed how that grapevine was taking off again this year. Even the fig tree had little figs burgeoning about. Spring. It was so different for her here than it was in Georgia.

"Cassie Lee! Cassie Lee! Reverend Burris say come quick. Some slavers trying to get runaways on Market!"

Cassie Lee closed and locked the gate, and followed William the few blocks to where the others had already gathered. There were white slavers yelling at a family of slaves who looked scared, angry, and confused. The black women cowered while the men who tried to protect them were whipped back. The assembled crowd watched the scene as if it were theater and not human lives at stake.

Cassie Lee pushed her way through the remotely amused white spectators just as Nathan was making a plea.

"Boy, you must think I'm dumb and stupid," the horseback-bound white man was shouting down at Nathan. "I can get good bounty on these nigras!"

Just then more black folks from the other two churches came down wielding sticks and clubs, and the white spectators peeled away to allow them entrance into the middle of the melee.

"I can haul all you in and make good money."

"If you live!" a bemused white man shouted from a distance.

"What makes you think we will allow you to take our people from here?" Nathan asked the mounted man.

"Let go of my horse!" he shouted at Nathan. "You educated nigras is the worst of them." He spat tobacco juice at the reverend's face and missed.

"Eustis!" Cassie Lee yelled, marching her way from the side lines to the little boy. "Boy, you didn't come to work today." She grabbed the shocked boy's hands and began leading him away.

"Where the hell you think you takin' that boy?" The mounted slaver yelled, then realized that he was alone in his quest.

"To work where he's suppose to be," Cassie Lee said as she walked around the horse. "He got chores piled up, but he always likes to come down here where the action is."

"This boy ain't no relation to you."

"He works for me."

"Where's he live?" His sarcastic pale face contorted triumphantly.

"With me," Elgin Soames spoke up before Cassie Lee could say anything.

With that, different black folks started claiming the runaway slaves, pulling them every which away, so that the mounted white man couldn't keep track.

"Come on, boy," Cassie Lee said, and pulled him with a walk that equalled a jog as they steered through slender walkway shortcuts no outsider knew about and no horse could travel.

After two circumvented miles to her house, Cassie Lee slowed the pace and asked, "So what is your name?"

213

"Eustis, just like you said."

She looked at the shabbily dressed boy, breeches hiked up to nearly his knees, shirt more torn than covering anything, and the hand she held ripped by the familiar deep cuts that only the pricks of cotton picking could wield on tender flesh. He had old hands, gnarled, cut, and bruised with raised scars.

"How old are you?"

"Thirteen."

"Well, thirteen is your lucky number. Your whole life is about to change."

Cassie Lee had Eustis haul the tub from the upstairs room down to the back porch. He needed to be as close to the pump as possible. He had months of trail dust, stale odor, and crusted dead skin to wash away. In the second wash, she poured a little of her soap into the bath water.

"Dat's not gon to make me no girl, is it?"

"No. I promise."

During his second soak, Cassie Lee threw his rags into the trash and found him a pair of pants and a shirt that they all kept in their houses for just such an occasion. Clothes were the first line of defense—the first thing to make them not appear as slaves.

He was on his third plate of food when Dorothy and Elgin Soames came to claim him.

"I was going to take him to Wiley for a haircut, but he kept eating," Cassie Lee said, as the trio plus two of the three Soames children left. "I'll see you at eight o'clock sharp tomorrow morning, Eustis. You do have chores!" she yelled after them and waved.

Cassie Lee gathered up her chicken feed and resumed her uncompleted task. She wondered when black folks were going to be born free and stay free. She loved this community that rose up and fought when they could to keep their fellow brethren from bondage. Even Hannah Weams, who wouldn't be caught dead on the streets helping folks, established Hannah House on Monroe Street for just such people and families who ran and needed temporary support to start their new life.

The benevolent help could take many forms, like the recent street scene, or in the courts where the rights of blacks were limited, or with the help of sympathetic white groups. That was the case when the Ross

Brothers, who ran a successful clothing store downtown, had their goods seized because they refused to pay a poll tax levied only on black businesses. Iva Ross called it a "flagrant injustice," as white men put their goods up for public auction. Davis Jackson, a white friend and businessman, moved among the crowd telling them why the Ross goods were being sold, and advised potential buyers not to bid. There were no bidders, and the goods were returned to the Ross Haberdashery.

Cassie Lee knew all about the 1849 constitutional convention at Monterey where delegates spent more time debating whether to exclude black migrants from the state than any other topic. They decreed that blacks could not vote or serve in the militia. Now, with two thousand free blacks in San Francisco and 17,000 Chinese, the whites turned their attention to the newest "locusts of their land," the Chinamen. But blacks were still harassed.

In Sacramento, a street brawl erupted between a master and his slave that led to a court hearing. A lawyer came to the defense and won the slave's liberty. It also happened to Frank Mason in San Francisco. He won his freedom because three lawyers argued that Frank escaped in California and had not crossed state lines, therefore not bringing into question the Fugitive Slave Law of 1850. Frank's own testimony that he was a Missouri slave was judged inadmissible because California law prohibited the testimony of black people. Frank now had a prosperous milk, butter, and cheese business.

Cassie Lee read in the white newspaper that the Negro community of gold rush California was one of the most culturally advanced and probably the richest black communities in the country. Cassie Lee delighted in the fact that, right now, the leading black citizens of San Francisco were proposing and voting on building a two-story cultural center to house eight hundred volumes in its library and reading room. The members were expected to be moral and intelligent, and regularly improve themselves by reading the newspapers and books on display.

"Times, they are a changin'," Cassie Lee told her chickens as she threw the last of the feed and closed the gate behind her.

"Hi," Juanita said weakly.

"You left early," Cassie Lee said as she wiped her hands on her apron.

"Yeah, Hyacinth and Howard officially announced their engagement. After that, wasn't no reason for me to stay. I wasn't the center of attention no more." Juanita laughed and Cassie Lee chuckled, and the tension evaporated into the California sunshine, the way it always does when friends remember what is important and find their way back to each other.

"I decided to tell Nathan." The smile froze on Cassie Lee's face. "I'm gonna tell him not because you told me to, but because it is the *right* thing to do."

* * * * * * * * * * * *

As Eustis and Cassie Lee beat dust from a parlor rug, she wondered how he was doing at the Soames household. It was a lovely home, and surely different from any one he'd ever lived in. He was not as talkative as Samuel, but Cassie Lee understood about inside scars and slavery. His fingertips were as torn and tattered as his soul. His back was smooth, but at his age the lash of the whip was sure to come, which was probably the reason he ran. Cassie Lee never pried or bothered him about where he'd come from. She understood all too well about being alone, on your own, and responsible for yourself—and tending inside scars while folks poked at you from the outside. He was a good worker, and maybe in time he'd open up to her. As they turned the rug over, Juanita tearfully entered the house without returning her hello.

"After you finish that one, you can start on the barn," Cassie Lee said to Eustis, never taking her eyes from the door Juanita had disappeared into. "I'll be back as soon as I can."

Cassie Lee knocked quietly on her friend's bedroom door. When there was no answer she began to walk away. The door whined open. Cassie Lee entered the neat room and looked into the tear-drenched face of Juanita.

"You told him," Cassie Lee said.

"I did." Juanita blew her nose hard, trying to put an end to it.

"He had a problem with it?" Cassie Lee surmised when all Juanita could do was shake her head. "Like Noah having a problem with the weather, huh?"

216

"Oh, it was awful, Cassie Lee. He said awful things to me." Juanita's resolve melted and she collapsed into her friend's arms.

"Shhh!" Cassie Lee soothed. "I know, I know it hurts." They sat on the edge of the bed. "Humph, some man of God. I am so disappointed in him. I expected more . . . did you remind him of Mary Magdalene?"

"He said I was no Mary Magdalene, and he was no Jesus."

"Well, that's the truth. Why not just be human?"

Cassie Lee continued to rock her friend, hoping to pump some of the pain from her body. "Just because you know the words to a song don't mean you can sing. I have no use for a preacher who just knows the words and not how to live them."

"What about Cassie Lee?" Her tear-stained lips questioned.

"What?"

"That's what he asked me. 'Was Cassie Lee a whore too?' I told him you were the cook—just the cook. He said 'too bad you wasn't just the cook.'"

"You did what you had to do to stay alive—to get where you are today. He can't hold you responsible for what you did before you met him." She resumed rocking her friend. "It's a small-minded man that can't give you the credit you deserve for bettering yourself. You need a man who can see that. Your man's job is to stand by you when other folk don't. If he can't do that, then what good is he?" Cassie Lee took a breath, then said, "Myron Brickman."

"What?"

"He's crazy about you. He just stares and smiles at you all the time. Much richer than Nathan will ever hope to be."

"Ugh, he's an undertaker," Juanita said with a cringe, and the pair laughed like twelve-year-olds sharing a naughty secret.

"Maybe I'll go on down to San Diego and teach—"

"What?" The smile leapt from Cassie Lee's face, and she looked directly into Juanita's brown eyes. "You are not going anywhere unless *you* want to. No man, Nathan included, is going to chase you away from the comfortable life you've built for yourself. You are not at fault here, Juanita. It's him—not you."

"But I—"

"Listen to me and hear me good." Cassie Lee grabbed her by the shoulders, "You belong here until *you* decide you want to leave. You are a good, decent woman. You are loved and respected, and looked up to and needed in this community. Why would you give all that up because a man can't deal with your past?"

Cassie Lee's eyes locked with hers, and when she saw the pain, she relaxed and said, "I'm sorry for him. He is missing the best chance at happiness he'll ever have. I'm sorry for the beautiful children you two could make. I'm just sorry, but if he can't handle it, then it's best you find out now and not marry the simpleton."

"Oh, Cassie Lee." She hugged her friend. "Thank you."

"He may come to his senses. If he does, *you* have to decide whether you want him back—whether he is good enough for you. Then again, maybe this is it." She thought of Solomon and continued, "If it is, it ain't gonna be easy, but you have to go through it to get to the other side. Kinda like dying—something everybody's gonna have to do for themselves. The road is going to be long and lonely, but if you just keep on doing what you been doing, you'll come up on a clearing—and there, waiting for you, will be at least one man worthy of you."

"You think so?"

"All you can do is keep living and hope."

Juanita chuckled through her tears as Cassie Lee went over, poured water from the pitcher over a cloth into the basin, and handed it to her. "You just remember that you are living the words of the Bible . . . not Nathan. You got nothing to be ashamed of, and if the man you love can't stand beside you—then, to hell with him."

Cassie Lee accepted the used cloth back and hoped that the dark stranger Dorothy Soames saw her with was still around. Juanita might just need him.

"Just keep doing and build your own life. He may come, he may not, but meanwhile you have a life worth living."

"Thanks." The woman, born free who had a mother and a father, hugged the woman, a former slave, who had nobody but herself.

"Now, you just rest up today. I'll handle dinner just fine." She gently forced her friend to accept the softness of her mattress. "Healing a heart is hard work," she said from the door.

As Cassie Lee bantered with her boarders at dinner, Juanita entered the room with her hymnal in tow.

"You feeling better?" Cassie Lee asked, stealing the attention of the guests.

"Yes, I do. I'm going to choir practice now." Juanita smiled at her friend. "I got a life to lead."

"Sing pretty," Cassie Lee said with a smile.

Chapter XVIII

The Community of Faith Baptist Church was all done up for Easter Service, as was the congregation. The frocks were configured from some of the finest materials Cassie Lee had ever seen worn by children and adults. Hers was hidden beneath a beautiful, purple satin choir robe with a hand-embroidered gold mantle and CF. Even Travis Lee, who had a reputation for coming late—just in time to leave a healthy donation in the basket—and leaving early, was there on time. Cassie Lee smiled back at him from the first pew.

When the auxiliary choir joined the main choir at the altar, they lifted their voices in a song of praise. As they sang, an imposing figure walked up and stood in the church's doorway, his massive frame blocking out the sun. Cassie Lee couldn't help but notice the hat and the duster. Her placement in the choir was directly in front of him. The center aisle led from him to her. He was silhouetted against the sunshine, which plunged his features into darkness. It was surreal, as if the sun's rays radiated from his very being.

Millicent Soujay nudged her. Cassie Lee looked at her, and then realized that the song was over and the choir waiting for her to lead the procession back to the pews. Through her momentary embarrassment, she did, and when she looked back—he was gone.

Cassie Lee barely heard the sermon, and didn't put much stock into what Nathan had to say as of late anyway. He was hypocrisy at its zenith. Don't do as I do, do as I say. When Juanita stepped forward, center altar from the choir, it surprised Cassie Lee. When her friend opened her mouth on some internal cue, it shocked her.

"A—ma—zing grace. How sweet the sound." Juanita's unaccompanied voice was strong, pure, and clear. The congregation was stunned at its gentle ferocity. *"I once was lost, but now I'm found. Was blind, but now I see."*

Juanita's voice wrapped around each note, caressing and stressing the words. She sang and sent her melodic praise directly to the ears of God, as the residual splendor rained over the grateful congregation.

Water sprang and fell from Cassie Lee's eyes. She was moved by the simple beauty of the song's words, and so proud of her friend. She not only understood their meaning, but saw this songful contrition as a declaration of self-affirmation and acceptance for Juanita.

As Juanita closed her eyes to render this soulful prayer, a single tear slipped from its perch down her round, brown cheek. The choir and organ joined in toward the end, raising the roof and shaking the rafters. When she finished, Juanita opened her eyes, smiled down at Cassie Lee, and unceremoniously returned to her seat. Neither Juanita nor Cassie Lee realized that she had left the entire adult congregation dissolved in tears, especially the Reverend Nathan Burris, whom she didn't give a glance to.

"Well," he finally said in a hoarse, emotional voice after dabbing his left eye free of moisture. "What can be said after such an outstanding rendition of that hymn?"

His voice broke and found itself again with some words. "Thank you, Sister Juanita. Go in peace."

No one remarked on the abrupt ending of the service. All attention and accolades were given to Juanita who was besieged with folks. But Reverend Nathan Burris had mysteriously disappeared.

"Who are you looking for?" Juanita tore away from the well wishers to ask Cassie Lee.

"I thought I saw someone I knew. Didn't you see the man at the back of the church?"

"What?" Juanita's eyebrows knitted into one.

222

Oh, God, is it happening again? Cassie Lee thought, but said, "I didn't know you could sing like that."

"I feel really close to that song."

"So will everyone else from now on. I'm going on back home to finish up dinner."

"All right," Juanita said, and started to go with Cassie Lee.

"No, you go on back over there. Folks are waiting to congratulate you."

"Oh, I won't be long."

"Take all the time you need. It's two hours to dinner."

* * * * * * * * * * * * *

Cassie Lee looked at her table all decked out with an Easter feast set for thirteen. As usual, her house was filled with eight boarders. She and Juanita were most impressed with the Comptons, the newlyweds who'd come out here to make a fresh start. She and Juanita liked watching them cuddle and coo, with amusement and a little envy. They had found each other so young, and had an entire life time ahead of them. Dexter was working at the livery with Travis, and Ruda was helping Cassie Lee around the house, cleaning and mending. She was a seamstress, and planned to open a dress shop when they got on their feet.

There was an unoccupied seat for Travis who was still finishing up at the livery, and then there were the Biases. Even though they had lived in their own home for three weeks, Mr. Bias had wangled his seat and one for his wife, Isabel, at Cassie Lee's Easter dinner table, requesting his favorite red-eye gravy. There were so many for dinner that Cassie Lee had to set up an extra table and extend it into the living room near the piano bench.

The smell of good food, the sound of good conversation, laughter, and the gentle clatter of silverware on good china wafted from the yellow house with the white gingerbread trim.

"How about dessert now, Mr. Bias?" Cassie Lee said brightly, rising from her table.

"Dessert?" Mr. Bias said, "I want some more of that red-eye gravy!"
They all laughed.

223

"I tried that recipe three times, Cassie Lee. You sure you told me everything?" Isabel teased.

"Everything I know 'bout red eye," Cassie Lee replied. "More red eye for Mr. Bias, and peach cobbler, apple pie, pecan pie, and divinity for everybody else."

Juanita and Ruda brought in the desserts while Cassie Lee filled the gravy boat.

"Isabel, tell your husband this is it. Although I don't know what you gonna put it on. The pineapple upside-down cake?"

Cassie Lee laughed along with everyone, and then—she saw him.

Standing just beyond her picket fence, his figure cut black in the sunshine. The hat, the duster almost grazing the ground, the thin brown cigar. Cassie Lee went for the coffee pot and began pouring the hot java into the waiting cups. Dare she look up again? His vision would vanish as it always had.

"As usual, Cassie Lee, you have out done yourself," Isabel was saying, and Cassie Lee used this moment to look out the window again.

Slowly she thought, if I do it slowly maybe I can hold fast to his image for just a mite longer. She allowed her eyes to ease up over the back of her sofa, onto her white painted window sill, over the back of her porch glider, past her hanging flowers to the spires of the picket fence to him . . . he was still there!

Cassie Lee stood up. Her lacy curtains billowed in the breeze, interrupting her view of him. When Juanita saw her friend staring out the window, she harnessed the fancy material and pulled it back. She was just going to stare at him until he evaporated, Carrie Lee resolved to herself.

"Well, Cassie Lee," Juanita said, stealing the conversation that was going on without her. "You just gonna let the man stand out there in the hot sun?"

Cassie Lee jerked her head toward Juanita. "You see him too?"

"A man that big is hard to miss!" Juanita said with a grin wide enough to wet her ears.

"Solomon!" The coffee pot crashed to the floor, splashing brown liquid over the starched white linen tablecloth onto the imported Abusson rug.

Cassie Lee flung open the front door and stepped into the blinding light of the porch.

"Solomon!!" she yelled and ran down the steps, banging open her gate. She stopped short of jumping into his arms.

She wasn't the naive young girl who'd seen him outside the Chinese laundry in Exum that day. She had evolved into a confident woman. In fact, she moved a little to the left so that his frame would block out the sun in her face as she silently cursed her heart that had immediately flown to him with wild abandon. Her emotions were colliding inside of her, gushing up and crashing into one another, straining desperately to sort themselves out. Her sober mind was trying hard to adjust to seeing a sight it was convinced it would never see again. Despite her inner chaos, her facade was cool and collected.

"Well, Solomon. It's good to see you. How have you been?"

She fastened her arms over themselves to stop her fidgeting and rein in the urge to run to him. At the sight of him, thunderous spasms shook her inner body, ripping open all her inside scars from which blood oozed anew, seeping from every pore. Casually, she looked down to make sure she wasn't standing in a pool of her own redness. Again, she silently damned herself when she realized that the juices flowing from her body were preparing to welcome him.

"I'm fine, Cassie Lee. I see you got your boarding house."

His voice was like a warm embrace around her soul.

"Yes, I did."

She looked back to discover that all of her guests had poured out onto the porch to watch the curious couple.

"Looks right prosperous." He switched the thin brown cigar from one side of his luscious mouth to the other.

She watched his lips, those gorgeous lips that had tasted and delighted every inch of her body. She reached to clutch Nubby's cross and, touching her bare neck, remembered leaving it for Solomon in his cabin. She scooped her hair back behind her ear.

"So you've come to get your money back?"

"That was a gift, Cassie Lee. Free and clear."

"I don't see my starburst mirror. So what'd you come back here for?"

"For you."

His words hit her hard and made her sway.

"What'd you say?" Her mind was confused, but her heart and body rejoiced.

"I didn't tell you what I should've awhile back." He looked down the street, his keen profile whittled against the stark blue sky. "I hid my heart and what was in it for long enough. So I'm gonna say it flat out." He turned back to her. "I love you, Cassie Lee."

A gust of air sprang from her lips. Tears burned her nose and stung her eyes. Her fingertips touched her lips as if she didn't trust her words, or his. Did she hear him right, or did she hear what she wanted to?

"What did you say, Solomon?" she drawled, and he smiled.

"I love you and I miss you, and I want you to marry me."

"Oh, Solomon!!"

She rushed into his waiting arms. He scooped her up and swung her around in circles. He kissed her, and she wrapped herself around him, burying her face against the smoothness of his newly shaven cheek. The people on the porch clapped.

These were the words she had longed to hear from this man but never in her entire lifetime thought she ever would. Heaven's trumpets— how sweet the sound!

"I love you and miss you and want to marry you too." She giggled tearfully into his neck, and noticed Nubby's cowrie shell cross hanging low around his neck. "Legend has it, you only give that cross to folk you never plan to see again. I never thought I'd see you or it again, Solomon."

"I told you things ain't always the way they seem." He kissed her cheek. "Sometimes people do come back, Cassie Lee, when it's right. When its destiny," he said, as he began walking slowly up the street with her in his arms.

"Who is that man?" Isabel asked Juanita on the porch.

"That's her Forever Man—turned into her Lazarus Man, just in time for Easter," Juanita said with a smile amid her teary eyes.

As everyone else filed back into the house, Juanita recalled that night she saw a bright, winking, red glow in the sullen darkness from her bedroom window. She had tiptoed outside with her gun drawn, asking who was there. The glow was gone and there was no answer, just the faint smell of burnt tobacco. When she turned to go back into the house, a man blocked her path—and before she could scream, he had grabbed her around the neck, covering her mouth with one massive hand.

"I swear I'm not here to hurt you. I'll let you go if you promise not to scream. Promise?" She had nodded, and he released her. She knew something about men, and he was big enough to snap her in two if he wanted. Her best bet was to trust him.

"I'm an old friend of Cassie Lee."

"If that's the case, you should be calling at a decent hour at the front parlor door."

"I can't rightly do that," he'd said, and pushed his hat back from his head.

"You're him, aren't you?" She advanced, and he backed away.

"Who?"

"Her Forever Man." Even in the pitch black of night she saw his face break into a wide grin at the sound of his sobriquet. "You don't look nothin' like your picture."

"Say what?"

"I was looking for a pair of earrings one day, and way back in her top drawer was this folded-up paper of you. A wanted poster."

"Hummm, the first I heard of it."

"$5,000."

"Fair price."

"I speck Cassie Lee thinks you worth much more."

Since then Juanita had relished helping Solomon get all the things Cassie Lee loved and admired. All the things that would make her friend happy—although Juanita knew, even if he didn't, that all Cassie Lee really needed to make her happy was him.

* * * * * * * * * * * *

"Be happy, Cassie Lee," Juanita said to the dust left by the loving couple when they were finally out of sight. "Be happy." She turned and walked back into the yellow boarding house.

* * * * * * * * * * * *

"Where we going?" Cassie Lee asked, although she didn't care. If he were walking her back to his mountains, she'd go.

227

"Home. We're not getting any younger, and we've got lost time to make up for."

"Solomon, I own this house and the one next to it."

"I know."

"I have a store down on Market, and I'm part owner in a blacksmithy."

"I know."

"I can't have children," she blurted out.

He stopped walking abruptly, but she couldn't look him in the eye. He picked her chin up with his hand, forcing her gaze to meet his, and said, "I don't want or need children, Cassie Lee, as long as I have you."

"Oh, Solomon." She melted into his neck and began crying. "I got a lot of money, Solomon. I keep some in the bank, some in my dresser, some in the barn, but mostly in my root cellar. I learned that from a wise old friend."

"You still talk too much."

"But you love it," she drawled, as he placed her in the open buckboard. "Don't ya?"

"Yes, I do."

He took the reins, and she snuggled close to him, kissing him on the cheek, oblivious to the fact that they had just passed Travis Lee who was putting on his jacket to come to Cassie Lee's for Easter dinner. Travis looked at the couple so in love that they did not see him, smiled, removed his jacket, and went back to work.

"Solomon! You a wanted man!" Cassie Lee just remembered. "$5,000 by them Whedoes, I'm sure of it."

"Cassie Lee, don't you fret none about them or nobody else. I only care about one person wanting me." He shot her a side glance and a smile, and she just melted under his gaze.

"Solomon Hawk, where you taking me?"

"Home."

Chapter XIX

The rock and pitch of the buckboard over the rugged terrain soothed Cassie Lee to sleep. With her head on his chest and her arm laced through his, Solomon thought of how complete his world was now with her beside him.

Solomon reflected on how he thought his life in the mountains was all he ever wanted. He had a solid cabin, a predictable living, game for food, firewood for warmth, water to drink, and a flourishing fur trade to work. He couldn't want for more until a snip of a slave girl entered his life, turned it upside down, and showed him, just by being, how empty it all was without her.

He and Exum had often joked about preferring to tangle with a wounded grizzly or a half-crazed mountain lion than a decent woman. "The scariest thing for a man to come up against is a decent woman who can go for that unprotected jugular and kill the life outta you in one swell blow."

Solomon had refused to admit that he had met his decent woman and that she had shattered his solitary life, which was both his weapon and vaccine against the ills of the world.

He had braved the first winter without Cassie Lee and felt the worse was over, that immediate missing and longing for her. He had denied his feelings and fought remembering her, but she seeped into him. Her constant chatter about nothing in particular bouncing from one side of the cabin to the other. The way her drawl stretched and purred around her words like a lazy cat preparing for a nap in the noonday sun. The smell of her freshly washed hair and body, and her incessant preoccupation with cleanliness. Her cold toes touching the back of his legs in the night. The way she scrunched up into the small of his back to sleep. The way he found himself facing her in an embrace by morning. The sight of his smoking chimney after he had cleared his traps, knowing it was she who tended the fire, while he tried to guess what that delightful smell was coming from his cabin.

Cassie Lee had no pretense. The way she wanted to learn to read so badly that she strained her eyes next to the dying night fire. The way she delighted in the simplest things—green apples and a hot bath sprinkled with the fragrant peels. The way she loved him—unashamedly, and could tell him so. The way she wasn't afraid of anything. He knew that's why he had to let her go. She was so easy to love, but he never allowed himself to *say* it. He felt more than he ever thought possible—more than a man could ever feel about a woman. If he had told her, she would have stayed. And he could have kept her up on that mountain, a prisoner to him and been happy with her forever, but he *had* to let her go; to free her again to catch harness of her dream and find out if that was what she really wanted. He would have been unable to bear the pain in her eyes, the yearning of her heart for what might have been, if she had not gone after her boarding house. Letting her go was the ultimate act of love and the hardest thing he had ever done, next to burying his own son.

He managed to hold himself together that first year, but he saw her everywhere. Her body's imprint where they had played in the snow. Their footprints where he had taken her along to lay his traps. Where they had taken a dip in the river, and made love on the bank beneath the bear coat. She was all over that cabin—in every splinter of wood, every pelt, every mud crevice. The sight of the dry, empty bucket she used to gather snow at night and let it melt for her use during the day. The way he would play possum as he lay in bed watching her use that water to cleanse her body. The way he'd grab her fresh body and soil it with his love.

Her essence was all that was left of her on that mountain, and he drank her in deeply, while telling his conscious self that he had lived without her before, and he'd live now without her again. He worked his days hard and slept fitfully at night, listening to his once content world speak around him. All he could hear was the lonely howl of the wolf against the full moon, the whistle of the wind encircling his bleak cabin, the crack and spit of the blazing fire, and the hollow scraping of his fork against a tin plate.

When he ventured out, he could see her smile stamped in the snow. Hear her laugh lilt through the tall pines. She had demonized his woods, his cabin—him. Could he live without her?

It was almost a full year before he found the cross under a cup. He'd discovered it as easily as he had discovered her. He remembered just staring at it for the longest time, laying there where she last touched it, before he picked it up, and held it dangling freely between his work-weary fingers, back and forth on that leather string. A simple cross that had meant so much to her, and she had left it for him.

She was gone and still declaring her love for him, and again he was reminded that he never told her he loved her. But he did. He loved her so much it scared him, and if he had told her, he would have expected her to stay with him on the mountain. So he kept the words to himself, hoping that his actions spoke loudly to her. The hurt in her eyes when he told her to go stabbed at his heart. He supposed he could stomach that deep-down inside pain until it went away on its own, but it wasn't until his accident that he realized the outside pain of his mangled arm was nothing compared to the heart-wrenching pain he had living without Cassie Lee. Through the heaven-sent epiphany, he realized that he didn't want to die alone. He didn't want to die without Cassie Lee.

After discovering the cowrie cross, he hid it in several places out of sight around the cabin—but no matter, it always called to him from beneath pelts, from the root cellar, from a joint in the rafters, from behind a cup or plate. So he put it in the middle of the table in clear view. The centerpiece of creamy-white shells rested on its pile of worn leather string, until he finally hung it on one of the points of her starburst mirror. That clean-corner became a shrine to her.

After his accident it was the healing test for his arm when he could cut the string in half, join her leather with his piece of leather, and then

231

tie it so that the two knots were even on either side. He hung it around his neck, where it stayed until he no longer needed a reminder of his love lost—until Cassie Lee was with him once again. Now she was.

Now, as the wagon rolled on, Solomon was glad he had told her to go. Glad she had the opportunity to fulfill her dreams. Glad that after she got it all, she still wanted him. Glad she was beside him now. Glad that she would be with him forever. A tear slid down the left side of his cheek, the same way it did when he first found the cross under the cup and realized that she *truly* loved him as much as he did her.

It took that winter for his arm to heal, and for him to cozy up to the idea of leaving the mountain behind, and face the fear that her life without him might now be complete. That she could be married with a family, and he was too late. Or that upon seeing him, it would be her turn to exact festering hate, and she would send him away. There was more fear that she would still love him, but even he could not compete with the memory of him she held fast all this time—and he would disappoint her.

Not knowing exactly what he'd find when he looked for her, he had to similarly carve out a life he could live with, for she had shown his hollow life for the empty hand it was.

He set down the mountain following her path to San Francisco, through River Bend where she had been caught an entire year. He pressed on and searched for a hunk of land he could be happy in, with or without her. He found it, bought it, and built a fine house on it. Far too big for just him, ten times the size of the cabin, with a barn, corral, and bunkhouse.

He began to stock it with cattle and hired Lupe, the Mexican, to work them while he did what he loved best, wrangle wild horses. When Solomon went after the elusive palomino on the open range, he found an Indian, Red Bird, vying for the same spirited animal. This quiet contest lasted for nearly four months as the two men, never speaking to one another, tracked this prized horse. Sometimes it seemed that Solomon would be the victor, and at others Red Bird. When Solomon finally captured the coveted stallion, Red Bird came along in the bargain, paying homage to the animal and the skillful man who won it. It was with Red Bird that he raided the surrounding country for the best horses for which his ranch was becoming known.

Madison, a black man, angled into the homestead late one night and

232

was hired by the next morning. He preferred cattle to bronco busting and, having worked in Texas, had the patience needed to handle the cows. Other men were hired and let go accordingly, but Solomon had found trusted companions and long-lasting friendships with Lupe, Red Bird, and Madison.

His ranch in Napa was building a sterling reputation and was working well, but when Solomon "visited" Cassie Lee he noticed her inner restlessness, a state only the one who loves can recognize in the object of his affections where others cannot.

He supposed it was time to see if she was ready to become Mrs. Solomon Hawk or not. He enlisted the help and advice of Juanita and finally, at her friend's insistence, decided to make his play. It was with the nervous uncertainty of a schoolboy that Solomon approached the prosperous boarding house Easter Sunday. It was an immeasurable relief that Cassie Lee loved him still. Fear was a stranger to Solomon, but she brought fear and love out in him like no other woman he had ever known. His happiness knew no bounds. The total of all his wants and needs was right by his side.

Solomon brought the wagon to a halt, and the cessation of motion awoke Cassie Lee. In a sheltered niche, Solomon and Cassie Lee traded the buckboard for two horses, saddled and waiting for them.

"He's beautiful," Cassie Lee said of the gorgeous palomino.

"He reminded me of you."

"What? We the same color?"

"No, his spirit. He's wild and beautiful."

"Where are we going?"

"To our destiny. Our ranch."

"You did it." She smiled into the stream of moonlight.

"A compromise between your world and mine."

"You are my world, Solomon."

* * * * * * * * * * * *

They rode until dawn brimmed the horizon. From a high bluff, Solomon stopped Cassie Lee and pointed.

"This is all ours, Cassie Lee. If you'll have me and it."

233

Cassie Lee looked at the lush green valley swathed in the pale gold of the rising sun. The gently rolling hills alternated in a patchwork of trees and grasslands. A stream etched a serpentine path, appearing and disappearing on the terrain. It was monumental to absorb. It was Eden, and they were Adam and Eve.

"It's breathtaking, Solomon."

"The Indians call it Napa. It means *plenty*."

Nestled in the middle of this bucolic setting was a house, circled by a fence.

"Solomon, you're the black rancher who bought up all the feed and the—"

"Yep." He winked at her. "Let's go home."

They guided their horses down the winding path to the flatland. As Cassie Lee approached the house, her house with Solomon, she thought she might awaken from this dream only to find a phantom pang of regret and shards of broken memories of what might have been, what should have been. But this was all a dream come true.

She opened the gate of her picket fence and climbed the steps of the wrap-around porch, complete with two rockers. Upon entering the house, Cassie Lee was dwarfed by a gracious center hall with a generous front parlor on the left and a dining room and kitchen on the right, flanked by the stairway to the second floor. The kitchen housed all of her favorite utensils, all manner of dishes and silverware, jars, goods, and spices. The table was big enough to seat six comfortably. She couldn't get over the scale of everything, the height from the floor to the ceilings—but then Solomon, the man of the house, had to be comfortable. She went and hugged him.

"It's perfect. It's big, but perfect. I don't know how you knew what I liked. Ahh!" she gasped as she approached the gorgeous sideboard. "Profit Foster sold this right out from under me! I loved this piece." She rubbed her fingers across his signature carving.

"I know."

"How?"

"I had help." He grinned wickedly. "Juanita."

"She knew? You're the dark stranger!

"She was the one who told me about the things you liked that I

234

could buy, and the things you'd like to get yourself. She also told me to speed it up, or you'd be Cassie Lee Lee before you'd ever be Cassie Lee Hawk."

"Cassie Lee Hawk," she giggled. "I love the sound of that."

"I'm right partial to the sound of it myself," he said.

Solomon had guided her around the house full circle, until they were in the room behind the front parlor—his office.

"Now, upstairs," he said. He pulled her hands to him as he ascended the steps backwards.

"Why would I want to go upstairs?" she teased.

"Thought you might want to check out the bedrooms."

"Do I have a separate bedroom until the nuptials?" she drawled with a smile.

"Cassie Lee, you can have whatever you want. I'll sleep in the barn if you want me too."

"Not without me, you won't."

She eased up against him as she reached the landing, and she could feel his real gift against her thigh.

He showed her five huge bedrooms, and Cassie Lee was saddened when she spotted the cradle in the corner of the second room, knowing she wouldn't be filling it or any of the other rooms with Solomon Hawk's children. She didn't feel badly for herself; she had come to accept it as fact, like the sunset in the west—but she was sorry for Solomon, who would make such a good father.

Sensing her sorrow, he said, "So when your friends come to visit they'll have a place to stay."

"Where's our room?" she asked.

"You can't miss it."

Their bedroom stretched across the entire front of the house. She looked out at the scene that would be hers every waking morning for the rest of her life, and she cried.

"I hope they're happy tears." He came up from behind her.

"Oh, Solomon. I love you so."

She closed her eyes and leaned into him as he held her, soaking up the feel of him, the warmth, the love, the protection, the security, the tenderness of this man. Finally, this little black ex-slave girl had a home. She

235

could unpack that tattered tapestry satchel and throw it away. She'd never have to worry about running to or from any place ever again.

"Oh, Solomon!" she exclaimed as she saw the huge brass tub in the corner near the upstairs pump. "If I hadn't known until now, I would have guessed Juanita had a hand in this." He smiled proudly at her.

"And my starburst mirror!" She smiled at her happy image and smoothed a tendril behind her ear before looking at the tub again. "Can we take a bath right now?" She clapped like a ten-year-old.

"Well, that takes a mighty long time to fill. I was thinking we could—catch up."

"Oh?" A slow grin claimed her face. "Let me look around then." The huge four-post bed called to them both. "Let's say we christen this bed."

"I was thinking the very same thing," he said, and began peeling off his suspenders when Cassie Lee darted from the room. "Where you going?" He followed her out into the hallway and not seeing her, headed downstairs. "We starting from the bottom up?" he asked as he descended the steps.

Then he heard her footsteps overhead. When he approached the stairs, he found her shoes, then her stockings. She shed singular articles of her clothes up the stairs, littering the hallway with her underthings. He followed the trail to its predictable end. Cassie Lee sat up in the bed with covers up to her chin.

"Looking for me, handsome?" she drawled.

"All my life."

As he undressed Cassie Lee's eyes filled with the magnificence of him. Nectars began to flow at the anticipation of him near her. Like watching a leaf fall from a big oak tree and drift down, striking certain points, Cassie Lee's eyes did the same over Solomon's glorious body. Her eyes left his, grazed his powerful shoulders, his massive chest and chocolate nipples, the color of a thousand midnights, down to his abdomen, reminiscent of the washboard she used on Saturday mornings, on down to his—plums and their solid companion in the middle. She couldn't tear her eyes away, and she cast him a naughty smile.

"Like what you see?" He stood boldly in front of her.

"I'd rather feel it. Come on in," she said, throwing the covers back, giving him his visual turn to feast on the beautiful nakedness of her body. His eyes crawled all over her body. From her parted lips waiting to taste him, to her breasts, firm, pointed and ripe with desire, over her smooth belly to her dark, curly triangle. His eyes seemed to invade the unseeable. She moved her thigh suggestively, revealing her blossoming flower, its fragrant bud summoning him to her. He wanted to just look at her, but he also wanted to feel the sap of her moist cocoon tight around him. He couldn't have it both ways.

He came to the bed and reverently removed the cowrie cross, draping it over the bedpost before he bent down to suckle her upturned lips. They kissed as if it were pitch outside, instead of the beginning of a new day. Her skin was ablaze, and everywhere he touched, a cool-hot seared her flesh. The kisses were long and hard, and he broke away from her lips to etch a scorching trail down her neck to her pert mounds. His hand held her breast like a bunch of succulent grapes, and he offered them to his mouth and gently began to toy, tickle, and taste their lusciousness, treating her ripe tip to the rough-smooth texture of his tongue. Her body quaked in response.

"Oh, Solomon," she moaned in long-dreamed-of pleasure. Her hands stroked the buried scars of the whip on his back, rendering them all smooth with her soft, velvet touch.

While his tongue busied itself becoming reacquainted with the source of his undeniable pleasure, his hands explored the body he had craved for so many torturously lonely nights. He wanted to savor her, but the urgency of it all was too much for them both to bear. His hands slid down to her triangle forest, and the heat that whirled up through her could not be restrained.

"Cassie Lee, Cassie Lee, Cassie Lee." He breathed the music of her name, and all the years of love, want, and desire, as he slid his magic wand, teeming with pleasure, into her. He released a thousands stars that cascaded through her—lifting her, propelling her toward the heavens, and they exploded together immediately.

"Cassie Lee, I love you so much!"

His river flowing into her stopped her heart, stole her breath, and shook her body, filling her with all she ever wanted from life. The sheer joy of being with him stifled her speech, a deliriously happy mute caught in the throes of ecstacy. He shifted his weight to the side of her, and she tightened her throbbing center.

"Don't," she commanded. "I don't want you to leave me yet," she panted, cherishing his pulsating maleness.

They lay there winded, as if they had just raced their horses over their land of plenty. Exhaustedly happy, they tried frantically to restore their breath.

"So when you gonna let me make a honest woman out of you?" he finally managed.

Cassie Lee's laughter filled the room, then the house, and lilted out onto the noon spring air, raining upon the ears of Lupe, Red Bird, and Madison.

"Sounds like somebody is happy," Madison said as they all casually glanced at the top front window.

"The boss deserves it," Lupe said.

"Yeah, he do," Madison concluded.

Chapter XX

Two weeks later, Cassie Lee stood at the back of the Community of Faith Baptist Church with Juanita, waiting for her cue. She didn't care that everyone wanted longer to plan a wedding that Cassie Lee had dreamed of all her life. She just wanted Solomon. This whole ceremony was just for God and her friends. She was married to Solomon already in her heart, mind, body, and soul.

Her dress was long and white, with an overcoat fashioned from the same lace as her veil. The flower girl and the ring bearer fidgeted as the congregation sat anxiously anticipating these nuptials.

The San Francisco folk had grown to accept the grouchy Solomon Hawk, who seemed to have no use for them, liking him by association due to Cassie Lee. They respected him because Cassie Lee adored him—and he her. So who were they to be persnickety?

"A man that big, strong, good-looking, and rich don't need our approval," Hannah Weams had proclaimed as she snapped open her imported Oriental fan against the imagined heat of that bright May day.

Cassie Lee was not the least bit nervous. This was the moment she had waited for all her life. She couldn't believe that a slave girl from Georgia could end up so blissfully happy without dying first and going to the glory they all prayed about in a makeshift plantation church deep in the woods.

There was nothing to prevent her from becoming the wife she wanted to be to Solomon Hawk. She had sold her boarding house to Juanita, and now Ruda helped her out. She sold Travis her part of his livery and feed business, and sold her vegetable store to Egypt and her husband, George. All Cassie Lee wanted to do was marry her Forever Man and return to their Napa ranch. Destiny.

Juanita shoved flowers into Cassie Lee's hands and kissed her on the cheek before making her way down the aisle to the beat of the music. It was Cassie Lee's turn. She proceeded slowly down the center, the joyous congregation pressing in closer for a look. At first, all she could see was a smiling Nathan—and then she saw him. The first time she had ever seen Solomon in a tie, and he looked as uncomfortable as she was sure he felt. It made her smile as she caught him tugging at his collar, and then he saw her. His motion froze. His awe at the sight of her weaned him into a smile. When she reached his side, he took her hand with no direction from Nathan. They didn't know or care what Nathan was saying as they looked into each other's eyes. Through the thin veil, they vowed that the imported French lace would be the only thing to ever come between them in life.

"Cassie Lee, you had something you wanted to say to Solomon," Nathan prompted.

"Yes." Cassie Lee turned her body to face her husband-to-be. "There are two things that have been with me all my life: God and you. I knew about God and I knew about you, but I didn't know who you were. There was a Forever Man who has always been with me. To comfort me, to tell me I'm somebody special, tell me not to fear nothing, and that he was on his way. You were him, Solomon, my Forever Man. I always had you in my heart and soul, and now I have you in the flesh. You been with me since time untold, you know the hidden part of me, you know the lies around me and the truth of me. You know everything about me, and you still love me. I need more than a lifetime to give back to you all you've given me. You the only love I've ever known. You changed my life." She smiled, losing herself in his eyes. "Before, it was the right hearts but the wrong time. Now the time is right for us

Solomon. Some things are meant to be, and one of those things is us. One love, one lifetime," she blushed and, sensing she was talking too much, she concluded, "You are now and forever always mine, and I am yours, and I am proud to become your wife."

"Solomon," Nathan directed.

He cleared his throat, and began, "I'm not much for words, in fact the fewer the better. You ain't never at a loss for them, but I can say that I love you more than any man ever loved a woman, Cassie Lee." He cleared his throat again, then all his trepidations were quieted by Cassie Lee's loving gaze.

"You are my peace in this crazy world. I love you deep and strong and pure and complete. I will love, honor, and protect you as long as I have breath in my body. All I ask in return is that you come to me with all your hopes and dreams, so I can make them mine too. Come to me with your joy and laughter. Run to me with your tears and fears. My name is yours alone to call. From now on, we will always have one another, and remember, above all, that you are *never* alone. Whatever life has planned for us, we will face together. It's you and me, Cassie Lee Hawk," he pronounced before the preacher did. "As long as we both live, we will love." He raised her hands to his lips, and kissed them gently as a tear broke from her eye beneath her veil.

They only looked at one another as Nathan said some other things before he pronounced them what they had always been destined to be— man and wife.

"I give you Mr. and Mrs. Solomon Hawk!"

The ecstatic coupled pirouetted through an elaborate reception and posed stark-still, seemingly forever, for a wedding portrait. Friends had given them a hotel room so they wouldn't have to make the long journey back to the ranch.

"I'm ready to go, Mr. Hawk," Cassie Lee drawled in her husband's ear after they had cut and fed each other a slice of cake.

"On to the Carlton Hotel," he said.

"No, I want to go home and make our first marital love in our own bed."

A wide, knowing grin bloomed on his face.

"Shall we go to Eden?" she asked coyly.

"Destiny," he corrected her with his name for the ranch.

"Oh, is this our first married argument?" she teased.

"If this is all we got to worry about, we'll be just fine."

"We gonna be that anyways," said she.

He swooped her up, kissed her hard on the lips, and made for the carriage amid a hail of rice.

* * * * * * * * * * *

Over the next few weeks, the newlyweds made love over every inch of their house, and once in the backyard garden where Cassie Lee was planting vegetables in the fertile, rocky soil.

Luckily, Solomon's three trusted ranch hands could do three times the work of ordinary men—with the exception of Madison, who could do the work of two and talk the worth of another man. Cassie Lee rewarded them all with deliciously cooked meals even though they proclaimed, as they stuffed their mouths full, that she needn't cook for them. She'd told them that this was light duty for her since she was used to cooking meals for at least ten, and she didn't have to clean up behind the three of them.

"One hand washes the other, gentlemen," she said and cast a sultry glance at her husband as she served them under the canopy of a nearby tree. "You do, so my husband can have afternoon playtime with me. The least I can do is feed you."

"Seems we're getting the best of that bargain," Madison said, as Solomon shot his wife a mock-frown for her brazen remark.

Cassie Lee Hawk loved waking at dawn's first light with her husband, tweaking the cowrie cross as it hung from the bedpost and fixing Solomon coffee, which was all he could stand at that hour. Sometimes, depending on his chores, she got a little reward of her own before he left to meet Lupe and Madison who lived in the bunkhouse on the other side of the barn. Red Bird would show up before dawn on his Appaloosa and leave for points unknown at sunset. You could set your watch by his comings and goings.

Mrs. Hawk would begin her day cooking. Cleaning was easy, as they only used a few rooms of the immense house: the bedroom, the kitchen, and its attached dining room. She would wash their clothes on the washboard, and sometimes Solomon surprised her with a kiss in the middle of the day as she hung their things to dry in the California rays.

She loved finishing up early and going to the corral to watch her husband and Red Bird break horses. Sometimes as she changed the linen of their bed she would catch a glimpse of Solomon working a horse outside, and her heart would skip a beat. She'd smile and unknowingly bite the bottom of her lip in remembrance of their last tryst and anticipation of the next, especially if it was Saturday night. Their established tradition was to bathe together in their big tub. Cassie Lee would partially fill it during the day, leaving the rest to be filled with hot water. Solomon would wash off a bit of surface dust before submerging his splendid black body into the waiting wet. Cassie Lee would wash his back with the French soap from town before she would ease in in front of him, and he would reciprocate. There, they would discuss their day, the week that passed, and the week to come until the water grew tepid. Depending on what they wanted to do at the time, they would either warm up the water or each other, usually on the kitchen table—their second favorite place in the house to make love.

In the afternoon, Cassie Lee could tell by the way her husband's footsteps fell on the porch and he entered the house, that he had more on his mind then lunch. Having a really good day with the horses made him horny as ever. He'd sidle up behind her as she stirred a pot, and that circular motion drove him crazy. She'd feel his hard maleness rise against her soft derriere, and she'd lean back into him, massaging him with her. He'd encircle his hands around her small waist then raise them upward, undoing her top button and sliding his hand into her camisole, cupping one of his favorite parts of her anatomy while nibbling on her neck. He'd thumb her engorged nipple, and she'd whimper. He'd let his other hand gather up her skirt, his dark fingers probing toward her beckoning floral center; and when he found the moist softness of it, she'd turn into him, and they'd kiss explosively.

Solomon would back up and sit on the chair, making himself available to her, and the sight of him would make Cassie Lee cave in. He loved the way she'd look around to see if any of the other hands were coming while adjusting herself atop his outward display of love for her. But once her flesh touched his, Cassie Lee Hawk could care less who was around.

Her shy smile gave way to needful desire, and all her purity was replaced with a thin sheen of sweat. With a couple of bronco-busting motions, they eclipsed into raving ecstacy that often shook the hair-knot from the nape of her neck. She'd collapse into his neck as the delicious spasms subsided for them both.

"Cassie Lee Hawk," he'd say throatily, "you a high-natured woman."

"You a wicked man, Solomon Hawk." She'd blush and try to get away, but he wouldn't let her.

"C'mon, let me go," she'd say without moving away from him but twisting her hair back into place, suddenly concerned about somebody catching them in this position.

"Who you lookin' for?" he teased.

"C'mon, Solomon." She started giggling.

"You didn't care none 'bout nobody a minute ago," he laughed.

She laughed her forehead into his. "You bring out the bad in me."

"I bring out the good in you, Cassie Lee Hawk." He kissed her, then licked her bottom lip. "You want some more, huh?"

"Yeah, tonight."

"Oh," he exclaimed as she angled up from him. "Don't hurt me now."

Every night Cassie Lee snuggled against her Forever Man, and once every other night, she slid beneath him, pleasuring him as much as he pleasured her. She was used to the cadence of his breathing and welcomed his massive leg slung over hers as they snuggled beneath the bear coat from long ago. She could ride and shoot as well as anyone, and rode range with him during spring roundup, sleeping and snuggling with him under the diamond-studded sky. They never slept apart.

The Hawks traveled to town for Easter and Thanksgiving services, but skipped Christmas because Cassie Lee wanted to celebrate at home. They did go in for the New Year service and the annual paint party marking spring, and returned for special occasions: Nathan and Juanita's wedding, Eustis' baptism, the christening of Dexter's and Ruda's first baby, the dedication of the Cultural Center, and Sarah Lester's graduation from the white San Francisco Spring Valley school. Cassie Lee went along when Solomon was forced to conduct business or order special supplies, and enjoyed catching up with old friends, but she was always happy to return to Destiny.

In November of 1855, Solomon accompanied his wife to Sacramento where black Californians were meeting on the twenty-first for their first convention. Forty-seven delegates of businessmen, lawyers, journalists, ministers, teachers, and community leaders gathered to defeat the state's black laws.

The antislavery sentiment of California was mounting. A black woman in Auburn County was seized and about to be returned to slavery when her freedom papers were produced. A black man, Stephen Hill of Gold Springs, who had lived in the state long enough to be prosperous, was seized and his freedom papers destroyed, but when he was taken to Stockton, after a daring mass effort by the black community, he was freed.

In San Francisco, the court said a black man deserved his freedom, and then returned him to his master. Again the black community reacted so angrily that the legislature considered registering all black residents and banning further black emigration to the state. Thus, the convention was called and held to address the threat to free blacks' right to liberty.

The delegates proposed the formation of a black newspaper to serve the needs of their community, and a bank for black residents. Most of the convention's effort was spent on the testimony issue. Delegates reported on how black men were driven off their land claims and assaulted in broad daylight with no recourse in the courts because blacks could not testify.

Cassie Lee did not return to the convention of 1856 where sixty-one delegates attended and produced its first black newspaper, *Mirror of the Times,* circulated through agents in thirty counties from the Mexican border to Oregon. The Hawks did not attend the third black convention assembled shortly after the Dred Scott decision of the U.S. Supreme Court. For something that occurred at Destiny that kept them both home.

* * * * * * * * * * * *

Cassie Lee lay in the shadow of her husband's sleeping body when she heard night riders leave their front. She eased out of bed to the window in time to see two horsemen riding into the stream of moonlight. She took the pistol from beneath her mattress and crept down the stairs. She

245

heard no crashing glass, saw no fire, smelled no smoke. Only the bright lunar rays poured across their furnishings. She turned the knob, and the door whined open just in time for Lupe and Madison to come running into the house.

"You heard 'em?" Madison asked, his gun gripped by his hand.

"Yeah, did you see anything?" Cassie Lee asked just above a whisper.

"We'll look around," Lupe said as he took off.

As Cassie Lee stepped out onto the porch, her foot kicked something in the darkness. She nudged it into the moon's rays, and saw it was a basket of some sort covered with a blanket. She heard a whimper.

Some animal? she wondered as she carefully peeled back the cover. A pair of round eyes set in chocolate stared up at her.

"Ah! Solomon! Solomon!!" she screamed, rousing Lupe and Madison back around front.

"What is it?" Solomon was at her side in a flash, his gun raised and poised.

"Look what the Lord brought us!" Cassie Lee held up the squirming black baby.

"Please look after my son," Madison read the note fastened to the basket. "He healthy and needs a good home."

Jared Hawk changed the lives of Cassie Lee and Solomon considerably, for the better. It took some time for Solomon to warm up to the rambunctious little lad for fear that the person who left him would be returning for him. But a year and a half passed and, after a hard day's work, Solomon went to his son before kissing Cassie Lee hello.

"Glad I'm not a jealous woman," Cassie Lee teased as Jared played about her legs when they ate dinner beneath the coolness of the grape arbor.

Jared brought a new dimension to their lives, and she got to keep her figure, Cassie Lee would tease as she showed him off at Easter Service, hoping that his natural mother would think she was doing a good job caring for their precious son.

Apparently others took note, because over the next five years, the Hawks were brought three more children. Cassie Lee and Solomon quickly bought and dedicated The Colored Foundling Home before folks got the wrong idea that Destiny was for that use. It had a staff of six and ten children almost immediately, and the Hawks made it known that the director of the home preferred working with families to keep their children instead of giving them up.

Losing the two-month-old baby girl, Louise, was hard on Cassie Lee, but the doctor said that the girl was sickly from the birth. That loss only intensified the fear that she could also lose their three sons if their parents decided they wanted them back. But none ever came forward.

* * * * * * * * * * * *

"Door, Mommy!" Jared said, and ran to open it.

"Yes?" Cassie Lee said, as she instructed Verbena, who had been hired right after Nash was left on their doorstep, to take Iva.

"Cassie Lee," her name slid from his lips like butter off a hot biscuit.

"Cassie Lee Hawk," she corrected the handsome, vaguely familiar young man.

She looked at the carriage at her gate and hoped this wasn't a sign that their quiet haven had been discovered and was going to be overrun with lost intruders. She didn't like uninvited folks at her door. Over the years Solomon had done an excellent job of allaying her feelings about the wanted poster. She never thought about it until a stranger presented himself. He didn't look like a bounty hunter.

"Will you marry me now?" the man asked.

"What? Who are you?" she asked point blank.

"You really don't know me? You broke my heart," he said, as he fished in his jacket, then dangled a pocket watch before producing a traveling Bible.

"Samuel!" Tears sprang to her eyes and she grabbed him. "Samuel. All grown up! Oh, you're beautiful!"

"Daddy, Mommy's hugging a man," Jared said as his father approached the bottom step coming into the house.

"Solomon, this is Samuel Davenport."

"Hello, sir." Samuel stiffened and swallowed hard at the sight of this big, dusty man.

"Hello, Samuel. Heard a lot about you," Solomon said, scooping up his son. "You'll stay for dinner," he commanded, as he kissed Cassie

247

Lee's cheek. "I'm gonna wash up," he said to her and then directed, "Well, come on in, Samuel. Welcome to Destiny."

Samuel sat at the dining room table with the Hawk family, and was awed at the ease with which Cassie Lee fed her husband, their three sons, and managed to stay charming.

"This life really suits you," Samuel said at the meal's end.

"I couldn't be happier." She rose and hugged Solomon around his neck from the back.

"I think Jared looks like you," Samuel said of the mischievous oldest son as Cassie Lee smiled into Solomon's neck.

"I think he looks more like his daddy," Cassie Lee offered.

She knew her three boys ranged in complexion from her caramel to Solomon's black coffee, and it would be natural for their children to fall on any color in between. And Jared, Nash, and Iva Austin Hawk did just that.

"How's your dad?" Cassie Lee took the coffee from Verbena.

Verbena did the cleaning and some of the cooking only after Cassie Lee could trust her with the seasonings. By the time Iva Austin came along, Cassie Lee·was a devoted wife and mother who spent most of her time caring for and teaching her sons skills from first-riding to reading.

"He remarried a real nice woman, Iris Cropp, and I have two more sisters and a baby brother," Samuel responded.

"Isn't that nice? What about Bohemia? I wrote her three times, but she never answered."

"River Bend went bust about two or so years after you left. They say Bohemia went down Texas way."

"Hump! Bohemia down South? Not likely." Maybe she went East and reconciled with her family, Cassie Lee·hoped.

"So what you doing in these parts?" Solomon asked as he sipped the piping-hot coffee. "I don't have any openings here, but I'm sure Cassie Lee would like for you to stay awhile. You're welcome to."

"Thank you, sir, but I have a job in San Francisco."

"Really?" Cassie Lee handed her husband some cobbler.

"At the *Mirror of the Times*."

"Doing what?" Cassie Lee asked.

"A reporter."

"Really!" A smiled radiated from her eyes to her cheeks. "So you'll be working for William H. Newby?"

"Right hand man for Mifflin W. Gibbs, the founder. You all subscribe?" Samuel asked.

"That's where we get all the news about our community," Cassie Lee said before continuing. "Thanks to you, Samuel, I can read it." She smiled. "I always knew River Bend was too small for you. I thought you'd go to college, but a reporter for a newspaper—that's almost as good," she teased.

"Well, I best be getting back," Samuel said.

"Tonight?"

"Got an early morning tomorrow. I wanted to see you before I settled in. I don't know how much time I'll have once I start."

"With Newby as a taskmaster—not much. Well, at least I'll get to see you when I come to town," Cassie Lee said, as the couple walked their guest to the door.

"I'm going to hold you to that. Next time I'd like to take you both to dinner at the hotel."

"You better save that money," Cassie Lee said.

"I could take you and your whole family to dinner till kingdom come, and I could never repay you, Cassie Lee. You gave me a vision beyond River Bend."

"She's good at giving people vision," Solomon said with a sideways smile at his wife.

"You guys gonna swell my head," she drawled, accepting a goodbye kiss on the cheek from Samuel and watching him shake Solomon's hand. "Don't be a stranger!" The Hawks waved from the doorway of their large home.

As the couple prepared for bed, Cassie Lee thought of how their lives had changed yet stayed the same over the last few years. How much she still loved Solomon and Destiny, and always would. The way the small grapevines grew into a canopy of arbors, making a covered walkway that ran the length of her garden, under which they ate their noonday meal. The way she still loved the smell of sheets dried by the Napa air, and how it still delighted her to see the wind tickle the sheets and billow them into a laugh in the fresh sunshine. She still loved nudging

249

fleshy vegetables from the warm earth, and preparing exciting meals for her family.

Actually, the most remarkable thing that had changed was her love for Solomon. She thought that she could never love him more than the day they married, but her love for him had grown deeper, wider, and taller—more physical and spiritual than she ever imagined possible. Their Saturday night baths continued, but ended too soon, thanks to the interruption of one of their three sons despite Verbena's best efforts.

The weather stayed the same: hot, dry days with no haze or dampness, and cool, mellow nights. As was their tradition before the children came, each night they still unwound in the two rockers on their front porch and read the papers chronicling the times around them. Well, what Cassie Lee had to tell him tonight was astounding, never-before-heard news, and would not be in any paper, even the *Times*.

"Solomon," Cassie Lee said quietly, as the hush fell over the house, and only the distant rustle of the familiar night wind coaxing the trees to sleep could be heard. She snuggled beneath his comforting arms.

"We going to have a baby."

"Another one?" he asked and kissed her forehead absently. "When we getting this one?"

"In about five months."

"What, someone 'planning' to give you a baby?"

"He's planning to give 'us' a baby."

"He who?"

"God."

Solomon looked down at the top of her head and when she looked up at him with those pretty doe-eyes and a strange glow, his heart started beating uncontrollably. "What are you talking about, Cassie Lee?" he asked slowly.

"You and I are going to have a baby." She placed his hand on her rising belly.

"You mean? Are you sure?"

"I waited till I was. It's a miracle."

"You just needed someone to love you for true, is all."

"That someone is you, Solomon."

"Now we got a miracle of our own coming." He laughed and rubbed her stomach. "That's what we'll call her. Miracle Hawk. Oh, Cassie Lee!"

"At least you didn't name her Destiny."

She accepted his fervent kisses splashed in wild abandon all over her face before he went down to her belly. She felt the wet there, and knew it was her strong, handsome husband's tears.

"We are truly blessed, Cassie Lee."

"I don't want to tell nobody in case something doesn't—"

"Shush!" He quieted her fears with gentle kisses.

"You don't want a boy?"

"I got three. I want a girl with your big, round eyes, your nose that sweats when you get mad, your long black hair, and your pretty face."

"I'll see what I can do," she teased.

* * * * * * * * * * * *

As was her tradition, Cassie Lee managed to give Solomon exactly what he wanted. Miracle Destiny Hawk came screaming into the world that December 13, 1861. She was a perfect baby girl, with all her toes and fingers and a shock of wild, black hair. Her three older brothers looked after her like the prize she was.

Epilogue

That January 1, 1863, as the Hawks sat on their velvet rockers in the parlor, Solomon reported to Cassie Lee that President Lincoln's Emancipation Proclamation set the slaves free in states in rebellion against the Union, except in counties in Louisiana, West Virginia, and Virginia. More than four million set free, while 150 million had already died in slavery.

"I sure am glad we didn't wait on him," Solomon said sarcastically, thinking of his three sons sleeping quietly upstairs and looking over at his daughter nursing quietly in her mother's arms.

"I pity Blacks, Indians, or Chinamen who have to wait on anything from a white man," said Cassie Lee as her eyes perused their far-as-the-eye-can-see ranch through the window.

* * * * * * * * * * * * *

With white men fighting among themselves, Cassie Lee knew no one was interested in an old 1850 wanted poster for a man named Hawk. The years between 1861 and 1865 were some of the most peaceful and productive for the Negro. In 1862, California blacks were granted the right to testify in cases where white men were defendants. Susie King Taylor, at fourteen, became the first black American army nurse, and Nathaniel Gordon of New York was found guilty and hung for slave trading. Mary Ellen Pleasant sued the San Francisco Car Company because of rude treatment given to her and other black women.

Silver from the Comstock lode financed the Union army to victory, and the vacation for people of color was over. From their rocker observation, Solomon and Cassie Lee Hawk acknowledged the end to the Civil War and the beginning of the Indian wars as whites pushed west. With the railroad's completion in 1869, settlers could get to San Francisco in six days where it used to take from four to six months to cross the country in life-threatening travel. San Francisco would no longer be isolated, and goods as well as people could be shipped in record time.

Cassie Lee's fears about the old wanted poster surfaced anew, and Solomon finally dismissed any worries by saying, "If any of them Whedoes are still alive and got $5,000, they won't be spending it on finding me. The South is dirt poor, and so are they."

Cassie Lee had read the reports and heard the eyewitness accounts of the devastated and desolate South and how it was burned and plundered, which was apt payment for a people who held themselves so high and treated another people so foul, so inhuman. Now there was only one class, poor. Blacks and whites who came over to America on different ships were now in the same boat. Now some old massas were no better off than the newly freed slaves. Now it was carpetbaggers who went in to sweep up any leftover remnants. Like Bethesda used to say, "The last shall be first; don't pay them white folk no never-mind. They gonna get theirs, and we gonna get ours." Only thing Cassie Lee never liked was that in order for black folks to get theirs, they had to die first and go to glory. Until now.

Cassie Lee wondered about Nubby. Did she leave once they were set free? Did she survive the war? And after the war, did she move on out from that Whedoe place, or stay around Georgia? Shoot, Cassie Lee thought, if she hadn't left before with Solomon, she'd sure be hightailing it out of there now, dragging Nubby kicking and screaming behind her. That land was too tainted with the blood and bodies of too many black folks to ever be any good to or for us. She heard tell that some of the whites were trying their damnedest to turn black folks back into slaves with nightriders scaring them into staying put. Other whites were telling black folks they could stay and work the land on which they were slaves for a "share of the crop." Yeah, we know who'll get the biggest share of those crops, Cassie Lee thought. White folks haven't learned anything from that war. It just didn't seem smart to stay in jail once they popped the lock and opened the cell.

Cassie Lee tried to imagine all the blacks set free at one time, with no set place to go and no set way to take care of themselves. Competition on that freedom trail must be fierce and crowded, she thought. Imagine all those folks fleeing from the South meeting up with those coming down from the North and Canada to try to find those they left in slavery. Got to be a powerful mess. But they were going to have to learn, just like she did, that the road of freedom is hard, but it's worth it. You just couldn't give up or give out. Tante Fatima used to say, "Don't look back unless that's where you wanna end up."

Cassie Lee chuckled when she thought of Tante Fatima who was match enough for any Johnny Rebs or Blue Coats if they ever came across her. Could be that Tante Fatima didn't even know there was a war on, she was so deep in that swamp. Whether there was a war waging or not, it made no never-mind to Tante Fatima. She was going to live the way she wanted to live. Cassie Lee wondered if the old woman had survived.

As she took the clothes from the line and folded them gently in her hands, Cassie Lee was surely glad she didn't wait for her freedom—glad she took the chance when she did. Her ebony eyes did a quick survey of her garden, her home, and her children laughing and playing in the noon-day sun. She smiled, always preferring to count her blessings, not her bruises. She gathered up her basket of clean clothes and headed for the house, because Solomon would be coming in soon for lunch. As Verbena took the basket from her, Cassie Lee headed for the kitchen. She didn't take anything she had for granted, and she prayed dearly for all those who were starting out and starting over as free.

As the steel knife sliced through the thick ham, she thought of Exum. She halfway expected him to appear at Destiny weighed down with gifts and telling the children to call him "Uncle Exum," expecting the fierce argument that he and Solomon had, which ended their friendship, to be erased by time. He always had a way of finding out and knowing everything about people, and maybe this was no exception. Maybe Exum knew how happy she and Solomon were, and had decided not to intrude. Maybe "the devil" in him wouldn't let him come and enjoy a stay with them, then leave. What would be the point of his visit? Solomon got the devil in him when he proposed that they make Exum Iva's middle name. Cassie Lee had reacted violently at the thought of naming their precious son after such a man. After they decided on Iva Austin, Cassie Lee had wondered out loud what ever happened to Exum.

With an appreciative grin, Solomon had said, "Probably shot through the heart by some woman's husband or some young girl's daddy. He was a character, that Exum Taylor."

If Exum showed up and Solomon accepted his visit, Cassie Lee would have treated Exum cordially out of respect for her husband. The way Solomon would have treated Nubby. Their old friends would always have a special place in their hearts. Even if you never saw them again, thinking on them made you remember and smile.

* * * * * * * * * * * *

The wizened old man smiled weakly as he staggered up to the bar to collect his pay. Despite his disheveled, drunken appearance, he was a silver-tongued storyteller who, between violent coughing episodes, swapped spellbinding tales of his gold rush days for a shot of whiskey. He spun stories of when he made and owned a town; of whores, cards, drug runs, miners, and mining. The saloon girls acknowledged that he must have been some dandy in his day, when that curly gray hair was black, when the shriveled body once stood proud, when his face was unwrinkled and his eyes, even with that faded scar, still sparkled. On a good day, Exum pathetically tried to prove with a wayward hand or gnarled finger what a ladies' man he had once been. But when he was pitifully rebuffed by the girls of the Black Dove Saloon or when he spoke of his investment in the Commstock Lode of Virginia City, his smiling eyes turned cold. "Them white boys got rich and I lost my fortune and shirt." He managed as much anger as his puny, sick body would allow.

Fast women, reckless living, dangerous dealings, and hard times had eaten away at the man whose reputation once ruled in the Sierra Nevadas and California, leaving his scavenged body racked with disease, part

256

brain fever from syphilis and part corroded insides from years of rot-gut. He didn't know which would get him first, but he wished one or the other would hurry up. In his younger days he hoped a bullet from a jealous lover would spare him the humiliation of old age and a slow, painful death. But he was living proof of one of life's ironies—of life going on when the thrill of living is gone.

When Mack slid him a half-empty bottle, he snatched it and wove a serpentine path from the saloon to its adjoining alley where he threw up blood and cursed before falling against the wooden planks and sinking his withered body onto the dirty ground. He took a swig of liquor and smiled as his demented mind chose this time to carry him back to younger days when he and Solomon ran from McArdle's, strapping young bucks tasting freedom for the first time. His brother, Solomon. If Exum could mark his own decline, it would be when he broke their lifelong code and accused his brother of doing something he knew Solomon would never do—steal by sampling wares that weren't his on the way West. Exum often wondered if he hadn't sent for that girl, where would he and Solomon be now? He wouldn't be dying alone in an alley behind the Black Dove Saloon in Texas.

Cassie Lee. That woman had unwittingly bewitched them both and neither of them knew it. She drove a wedge right between the two of them. Exum suspected he felt something for her when she cut him and he didn't kill her. He knew it for true when he found himself watching her in River Bend and saw her burying that pouch in Bohemia's backyard. When he dug up the money he had every intention of taking it. In the end, he emptied his pockets of all but seventeen dollars before putting it back in the hole. If he'd had more on him, he would have given her that too.

"Sheet!" he mumbled, and took another swig before coughing and remembering he'd had a good life. He'd had the life he wanted—free and full of women, money, and power. He'd had everything except maybe the love of one good woman. One who'd be taking care of his sorry, broke-down butt now. If he had just listened to Solomon when he brought Cassie Lee to him and said, "She's a decent woman." He could have kept his saloon and businesses and settled down with her and raised some children—youngings he'd want to claim.

He knew where they were—the Hawks. He always meant to drop in on them, but his business dealings kept him too busy, and then when he lost it all, he wouldn't go. He went South and ended up in Texas, still running from Cassie Lee and Solomon. He knew when he heard of the damnedest woman who went to San Francisco looking like a man but washed up into the prettiest black woman this side of the Sierras, it was her. He heard she'd built herself a boarding house and livery stable and such—he knew that was one woman. Then when he heard of a black rancher of his friend's description coming to fetch her and take her to his ranch in Napa—he knew it was Solomon. Exum figured that's the way nature planned it all along—Solomon and Cassie Lee. They had each other, and he had—nothing, he thought as the bile churned up in his throat and spilled out of his mouth. He coughed explosively, and between breaths he cursed. He tried to stand, but the pain cut him back to his knees. The bottle crashed to the ground, and the man toppled into the brown liquid, his face drowning in whiskey. His body convulsed and jerked as red slowly eeked into the brown, creating a mocking montage of his life. In his mind's eye he screamed, "Cassie Leee!" No one saw or heard him. In reality, his yell was just a whimper.

* * * * * * * * * * * *

Despite the neighboring chaos of Indians trying to hold on to the land promised but reneged on by the government, Destiny continued to prosper economically while remaining the Hawk homestead. Jared Hawk, an Oberlin College graduate, became a celebrated, world renowned pianist. Nash Hawk became a college professor at Howard University and civil rights activist who was elected to one term in the U.S. Congress. Iva Austin Hawk, after two years of college, bypassed formal education and became a real estate tycoon. Cassie Lee wondered if Solomon's suggesting Exum as his middle name was the reason their renegade son took a less traditional route. But his profits from his deals financed much of his civil rights work, where he championed causes for equal justice not only in California, but across the country.

By the turn of the century, with her mother's good looks and gift for gab, and her father's tenacity and clear thinking, Miracle Destiny Hawk parlayed the beef from her daddy's ranch, bought a meat packing house, and became one of the premier suppliers in the region—and the only woman to sit on the cartel. She married Dupree Yancy, a wealthy Creole businessman from New Orleans who built her a mansion on Nob Hill—the first blacks to have that regal address.

Solomon and Cassie Lee Hawk traveled to Europe when Jared was the toast of Paris, and to the Caribbean to attend his wedding when he married a native from Martinique. But once they returned to Destiny, they had no desire to ever leave again. "Everything I want and need is here," Solomon had proclaimed, and Cassie Lee agreed as the couple preferred to sit and rock on their front porch by day, and treasured listening to each other's heart beat at night as they lay in bed watching the stars fade.

On a warm autumn day in 1903, Solomon Hawk drew his last breath. He'd been thrown from a horse and never regained consciousness. Cassie Lee never left his side. He was 89.

"I once loved a man, and his name was Solomon Hawk—my Forever Man," was all she managed to say at his funeral.

Cassie Lee bent down and scooped up a handful of his gravesite dirt. She couldn't release it here, in this tight little space. She clutched it to her breast and walked off from the service.

Her grieving was as private as all the moments they had shared with a glance, a smile, a kiss, a touch.

Cassie Lee stood on the bluff where Solomon brought her and first introduced her to Destiny—her lifetime home. The wind whipped her silver-gray hair, and she caught hold of a tendril and placed it behind her ear with one hand. Her other hand, raised against her heart, clutched the dirt from Solomon's grave.

She inhaled the sweet smell of the land—Solomon's land, and all he ever meant to her. She folded her long lashes over her doe-eyes, and images of her husband paraded before her—the first time she saw him at the Whedoe plantation, the journey to Exum, outside the Wong's, their glorious days of winter paradise in his mountain cabin. She sighed aloud and saw him standing in front of her San Francisco boarding house—bold, tall and handsome. Then he brought her here. She opened her eyes again, beholding the grandeur of Destiny with its patchwork of rolling hills on which all their magnificent time together was etched. She smiled, remembering how they would send I-love-you echoes down the valley by day, and lie awake at night until they came back around again. All their precious, too-short years flooded her senses, and she cried. She was so happy . . . they were so happy.

Cassie Lee smiled through her tears and extended her hand before her. She opened her five fingers, and the wind stirred, whipped, then carried the dirt away. Scattering and sprinkling his essence all over Destiny.

"Goodbye, Solomon Hawk. You will always be my Forever Man."

Cassie Lee later told her children that when she died she wanted to be buried with her bear coat, on top of her husband, not beside him.

"Oh, Mother, that's absurd!" Miracle had laughed.

"Who will know? Your brothers will be too embarrassed to tell."

$$* \quad * \quad * \quad * \quad * \quad * \quad * \quad * \quad * \quad * \quad * \quad *$$

Cassie Lee spent the last twenty-five years of her life without Solomon, as active as ever. Her grandchildren, her community, and her civic activities kept her busy as her travel from Destiny to San Francisco became more routine. She, her family, and the Community of Faith Baptist Church congregation survived the San Francisco earthquake of April 19, 1906. Cassie Lee lived long enough to use electricity, a telephone, and own a motor car. And when it came time to bury her with her husband, her family granted her last wish to be buried with her bear coat on top of her Forever Man. Her sons and daughter enjoyed their mother's pluck as mourners asked why only one grave seemed freshly turned.

As the attendees sang "His Eye Is on the Sparrow," the Hawk children were less bereaved and more amused at their parents' grave site. It was Cassie Lee's best gift to them ever—her unconquerable spirit.

The grandchildren of Solomon and Cassie Lee Hawk reveled in the love story of the unlikely pair who enjoyed their lives as living testaments of a people whom life kicked in the teeth at every possible turn but got up again and again, and kept on trying until they got their break—each other.

As Miracle Hawk Yancy said at the dedication of the Hawk Library in San Francisco, "My parents were born into a system. A system of slavery that could not contain them—not in body, mind, soul, or spirit."

260

Miracle paused one minute, remembering the four of them as children fighting over the stereoscope, or listening to their mother play the piano as they sang and danced. She remembered how play stopped and learning began, and how important education was to her parents, neither of whom had any formal training.

In her mind's eye, Miracle revisited dinner conversations devoted only to the six of them, the Hawk family, especially their children, where they discussed their days and hopes and fears. She remembered how the after-dinner discussions on the porch dealt with national and international issues, and how they impacted their black community in general, and them specifically. As soon as a child was able to express a concrete opinion and read, it was an expectation and rite of passage to be included in these conversations. Potential girlfriends and beaus were rated on their ability to join in Hawk family discussions. Miracle remembered being prematurely privy to these treasured moments as she sat between her mother's legs while her hair was oiled and braided for the night. Despite their lack of education, her parents saw to it that every one of their children attended college, and when they finished, the Hawks sent others.

They were the most uneducated, educated people Miracle Hawk Yancy ever knew. She fingered the cowrie cross fashioned into a brooch, and thought of the tapestry slave satchel in the attic at Destiny, and the wanted poster for Hawk with the $5,000 reward, before saying aloud, "They would have loved this." She cracked the champagne against the brick building dedicated to their memory.

* * * * * * * * * * * * *

The trail west is littered with many unmarked graves of heroic people wrapped in black skin who stepped off the well-worn paths to blaze a trail. African-American she-roes and heroes who forged, tamed, and settled the frontier, leaving behind an unacknowledged legacy of adventure, vision, resiliency, and spirit.

This was the story of just two of them.

SUMMER 1997

July 1997

Love Always
Mildred E. Riley
1-885478-15-1 $10.95

Financial consultant Simone Harper is suddenly confronted by a grievous mistake from her teen years. This indiscretion threatens not only her marriage and career but her life as well. Will she finally accept her husband's love and understanding as she struggles to resolve the set of circumstances presented by Dayton Clark, the man from her past who insists that she is his wife?

August 1997

Body Rhythm
Valarie Prince
1-885478-14-3 $8.95

It was tit for tat from the very beginning. Rachel, would not be outdone by the infamous Rhythm Malcolm Cates, a former male dancer. Egos clashed and so did they as each attempted to out do the other.

But, when the sparks began to fly, passions exploded . . . passions so hot Rhythm's touch curled Rachel's toes!

August 1997

Hidden Memories
Robin Hampton Allen
PB 1-885478-16-X $10.95
HC 1-885478-18-6 $24.95

It's a natural mix. Sex, power, and politics. With it comes corruption, competition, and betrayal. Robin Allen takes the reader on a journey out of today's front pages as we see the rise and fall of black political elite in the African American mecca of Atlanta.